WARM MONTANA HOME
LARGE PRINT EDITION

CYNTHIA BRUNER

Montana Inspired Arts

CHAPTER 1

The tiny town of Moose Hollow seemed to have grown; the main street was narrower, the buildings darker. Maybe it was just the storm that made it look that way, Poppy thought. She found an empty stretch of road and stopped in front of a three-story Victorian house. Plaster statues adorned the corners of a balcony above its elaborate entry. The entire building was warped and peeling. She had thought for certain someone would restore the building to the beauty it must have been, but the one thing she'd expected to change was the only thing that seemed the same.

She shifted and stepped on the parking brake. The town's brewpub had good food. It had been a long time since she'd eaten anything—except for pumpkin seeds and a pack of tiny powdered-sugar donuts that tasted like chalk and artificial sweeteners.

Poppy pulled on her well-worn denim jacket, turned off the ignition, and slipped the car key into her breast pocket. She'd left the mail, front door, and storage keys on the kitchen countertop, still attached to her University of Arizona keychain. He'd have found it by now, and neatly slid each key off the ring, adding them to the "secret" spare key box that was attached to the underside of his Land Cruiser. Moose Hollow didn't have to be her destination, she reasoned.

Nothing in her rearview mirror looked familiar. Her own reflection was distracting—her eyes were so red that her gray irises looked artificially pale. In fact, she looked like a zombie. She didn't even bother to look at her hair. It was always straight and limp, and she hadn't done anything to improve it since getting into her car this morning. Fishing a comb out of the glove compartment, she untangled the mess the headrest had made in the back.

She opened the door to the cold rain and strode in the direction of Broadway, the only main street in Moose Hollow. Half a block later the water was soaking through her jacket. She stopped at a corner to get her bearings. To the north was the three-story brick hotel she had stayed in last summer. She turned to the south, uphill toward the mountains, which were hidden by the weather. Just a little more than a block down the road she saw the Combine.

Geoff had made a joke about the name. "A great place to get together and talk about farming." She hadn't gotten it, and he'd given her that look of patient condescension and then painstakingly explained that although it was pronounced differently, com-*bine* was spelled the same as a *com*-bine, which was a piece of harvesting equipment. He had expected her to know. And to laugh at his joke.

Poppy hurried across the street and opened the brewpub's heavy door. Warm air flowed out, smelling of yeast and spicy food and carrying the sound of an old George Strait song. She pushed her damp hair back off her face and wiped her leather soles dry on the entry rug. When she glanced up, she saw a nearly empty bar and two people staring at her. It struck her that she had absolutely no idea what time it was. Sleeping at the rest area in Colorado had messed up her internal clock. It looked as if the bar had just opened.

The first set of eyes were familiar. That woman had been the bartender when Poppy had been here last July. She was wiry and athletic, with short, spiky blond hair, and Geoff had found her attractive. Instead of eating, Poppy decided to ask for directions and leave.

"Can I get you something, honey?" the woman asked. "Something warm?"

The woman did have an infectious smile. And it would be strange to walk in without purchasing anything. "Sure," Poppy said. She glanced around at the empty tables. Was it near lunchtime? Or dinner? She didn't want to waste a four-top on just herself.

"Come over here and join us, honey. You don't want to get near those old farts." She gestured toward a table in the back.

One of the old men seated there leaned back and shot a look at the bartender. "Hey now, Missy," he said. "Ain't nobody farted. Well, not yet." They all laughed uproariously.

Poppy walked toward one end of the bar. There was a man at the other end, the owner of the other set of eyes she'd felt watching her. She wanted to sit at this end, far from him, but she didn't want to be rude. Or to have to talk to him. One stool in from the end would be good, but then if couples came in it would leave an odd chair, and that wouldn't be fair.

"I don't bite," the bartender encouraged.

Poppy sat in the middle, right where the bartender had pointed. The woman handed her a menu and Poppy scanned it. It was her kind of food, but now, for some reason, the thought of it turned her stomach.

"Get you a drink?"

Poppy remembered loving the brewpub's huckleberry beer. Maybe a couple sips would calm her nerves so she could eat. "Do you still have huckleberry ale?"

"Always. It's my favorite."

"A small glass, please."

The woman's eyes narrowed. "I do remember you. You were here with that fellow with the cool patch," she said, gesturing to the spot between her lower lip and chin, right where Geoff grew a spot of facial hair. "And the Red Wings hat. Last summer. I remember your belt—Navajo pawn, right?"

Poppy touched her waist where the turquoise and coral concho belt had sat. "Good memory."

"Distinctive name, too. Hold on, I'll remember." She pulled a pilsner glass from beneath the bar and turned to a tap behind her.

When Geoff liked someone, he used their

name often while he was talking to them, and so Poppy remembered the bartender's name. "Danny, right?"

The bartender glanced over her shoulder. "Right. Now I have to remember yours. Don't tell me." She set the glass down in front of Poppy. "So where is Red Wings boy?"

"I don't know."

Danny considered that for a moment, her hazel eyes searching Poppy's face, then she tossed a bar towel over one shoulder. "Good. He was a jerk."

Poppy grinned halfheartedly and looked down at the menu, blinking to make sure her eyes stayed clear. That was when she became more conscious of the man sitting to her right. Was he watching her? She tried to concentrate on the menu. A salad with grilled chicken. If she ate that, maybe her stomach would forgive her for the awful donuts.

Danny took her order and then disappeared through a narrow door behind the bar. The tinny sound of rap music on small speakers leaked out as she went in. That left Poppy alone with the man at the bar, and if her peripheral vision was correct, he had turned in his stool to face her. She took her phone out of the small holster on her belt and looked at the screen. No messages. She wasn't sure if the man to her right got the hint, but he didn't try to start up a conversation.

Not that he would. She was a rain-soaked, zombie-eyed girl who was never much to look at even on her good days. She was comfortable in the background. Until two days ago, at least.

The door behind the bar opened and Danny burst in, pointing her finger. "Poppy! Your name is Poppy."

Poppy slipped her phone back in the holster and nodded at Danny.

"And there's more. Something about your middle name."

Yes, Geoff had let that slip for shock value, even though he knew she didn't like to talk about it. No doubt Danny would remember in a moment or two. "Field," she offered, just to end the anticipation. "Poppy Field Marsh."

"That's it!" Danny said triumphantly, and Poppy heard the man at the other end of the bar chuckle.

She looked directly at him for the first time. He must not have liked what he saw in the zombie death stare she gave him, because he held up both hands in a gesture of surrender. His eyebrows rose. But a smile tugged at the corner of his mouth, and a deep dimple appeared on his right cheek. "Poppy Field Marsh?" he queried. "How did you get that name?"

Of course he'd ask. Often the question was phrased, "Are your parents hippies?" A simple yes in reply usually kept people entertained long enough for her to beat a retreat. She rarely gave the full answer, but this time she did, just to see if she could wipe the smirk off his face. "I was named for the place I was conceived," she said flatly. "My surname was just bad luck."

"Wow," Danny said.

The man never even blinked. His smile spread, and she braced for a snide comment.

"They must have thought you were going to be something special," he said.

As much as she searched for it, she couldn't find a hint of sarcasm in his voice or his expression. Without it, she had nothing to say. Even worse, she could feel the warm tingling that signaled a florid blush across her cheeks. She turned back to Danny.

"Danny, do you know of any places for rent?" she asked. Not that she had decided to stay here. It didn't matter where she went. All she needed was a link to the Internet and time to finish her research.

But her question did serve to change the topic of conversation. Danny put her elbows on the bar and leaned forward. She wasn't exactly busty, but that gesture combined with her tank top could keep the bar stools full of men, Poppy imagined. Some women just had an air about them. Did Danny know it? Was she just born that way? Nothing about Danny seemed affected. Whatever she possessed, it was something Poppy didn't.

"Honey, this is the worst time of year to find a place to live. The ski area won't be open for a while, but the snow ticks have already filled up the rentals. It's pretty well set by the end of August. Here, let me get the paper." Danny went to the other end of the bar and ducked under an opening, emerging on the other side. She snatched a paper off an empty table and handed it to Poppy. The *Thrifty Buyer* seemed to be nothing but classifieds. "Make sure it says Moose Hollow or just MH," Danny added before heading over to the old men's table.

Poppy scanned the advertisements. Her heart sank. There were only two Moose Hollow entries, both resort homes renting in the thousands of dollars per month. A movement made her glance to her right, and she saw the man lift the bar top to his side so that it propped against the wall, making room for Danny as she came back with empty plates. A click and a strain of rap music, along with the sound of dishes clanging together, marked her exit. Poppy reached for her phone again.

"Are you looking for a year lease? Longer?" she heard the man ask.

She glanced at him. He was wearing a threadbare plaid flannel shirt over a white T-shirt, and a black cowboy hat sat upside down on the bar beside him. His eyes were a deep green. Geoff had green eyes. She didn't want anything to do with green-eyed men. "No. I was hoping for a month-to-month." She took a sip of the beer.

He shook his head. "That's hard to find, except for some vacation rentals, but they rent by the week. And they're pricey. Regular landlords usually want a year lease. When are you planning on leaving?"

She didn't owe him an answer, but he was waiting so patiently for one. Did the man ever blink? "I don't have a particular time. I'm finishing a thesis, and I'll be defending it sometime early next semester. I guess it would be nice to have a place to stay for a couple months." She thought about that for a moment. Driving north, she'd pictured the snow and silence of a remote place she could rent alone. Judging by the prices of rental homes, a lot of people wanted that same thing. "Maybe through the holidays," she added, although her heart was already letting go of the wish. Moose Hollow was a popular resort town. Maybe she'd drive to Idaho and stop in some well-wooded old logging town. Someplace without a ski resort and resort prices. She took another sip of the beer and decided that was probably enough. She didn't need to feel any more lightheaded. After all, she was going to be on the road again soon.

The man nodded slowly, seeming to consider her words. She wondered if he knew about a place, and just as quickly as she'd given up, she began to hope again. Fickle, she told herself. But she had to ask. "Do you know someone who has a place for rent?"

His jaw shifted, and she was sure he was chewing on the inside of his lower lip. "Are you looking for a place in town?"

"No. Yes. I want to be here, but maybe not right in the thick of things." She sounded silly and spoiled. "I was hoping for someplace quiet."

His eyebrows raised. "What about cows?"

"What about cows?"

"They make a lot of noise."

She didn't follow what he was saying and wasn't in the mood to be condescended to, so she was grateful when Danny came back through the narrow door with her salad. The man stood, and she looked his way as he pulled on an oiled canvas rain slicker and donned his hat. He was tall, and the hat just made him taller. What was it about black hats? They were a world apart from the bent-brimmed, beat-up straw hats men wore in Arizona—and so was the effect they gave. He took one step and then shifted awkwardly. She looked away and concentrated on unrolling her silverware from the cloth napkin, but he stretched like a much older man.

"It's the getting up that gets you, right?" Danny said, giving him a grin.

"Aw, darling, it's always been the falling that gets me." He took a few steps.

And another step, right up to where Poppy was seated. She froze. She caught the scent of something green and grassy, and leather. And something else, like he'd been in a room with a Christmas candle. He leaned right over her shoulder, so close she could feel the heat of his body through the damp denim of her jacket and T-shirt. He placed his right elbow down on the bar, clicked the pen in his hand, and wrote numbers across the top of the *Thrifty Buyer*. The back of his hand had a smear of something black and powdery across it. "If you don't find a place, give me a call. I might have something open, but it's going up for sale January first. If you don't buy it, you might be out of a place to live."

He stood straight again, and she could feel cold seep in over her right shoulder. Before she could think of how to respond, he was heading toward the door. She resisted the urge to look his way, partly because her face had turned red again —she could feel it. She moved some lettuce around on her plate. The door opened, shut, and she waited a moment before finally looking behind her.

At that moment he turned to look through the window, grinned, and touched his hat with his fingertips. A tip of the hat? Who did he think he was, a movie star? Her cheeks, in full bloom now, were burning.

She turned back to find Danny looking out the same window. "Well then," she said. "Can't believe Colton's going to sell the place. Wonder if it's just Emmaline's house or the whole spread." She shrugged and turned to Poppy, wagging a finger at her. "You'd better take him up on that offer. You're not going to find a better spot than

Emmaline's house if you don't mind being a few miles out of town. It used to be even prettier, back when she had the energy to keep it up."

"Do you know him well?" Poppy asked. It sounded as if she was looking for a date, so she clarified. "I was just wondering if he'd be a good landlord."

Danny raised her eyebrows. "I don't know."

Poppy nodded. "Oh. So you don't know him very well."

Danny laughed and walked around the bar to check on her men again. "Honey, I've known Colton for decades. We all have. But that doesn't mean much anymore."

Poppy contemplated that as she once again pushed the lettuce around her plate. She tasted the next bite, and it was delicious—nuts, tangy cheese, and a slightly sweet dressing. A good combination with the grilled chicken. She took her time eating, not sure how it would settle in her iffy stomach.

When would she feel okay again? Everyone she knew had been through this kind of thing and survived. Then again, maybe they just got used to it. She set her phone next to her plate and scrolled through social media updates, mostly to disguise how slowly she was eating. Her sister had posted a gorgeous sunrise photo over an empty highway. "On the road," its caption read, followed by a few dancing hearts. She hoped that didn't mean Sierra was leaving Portland. Things were working out for her there, weren't they?

All the while the back of her mind was humming, vibrating between two thoughts. It was time to go, to get back in the car and find a safe place to land for a few months. But the other thought was that little bit of hope. What if Colton's place was as good as Danny said it was? It didn't have to be perfect. She'd be heading back to Tucson in a few months. Moose Hollow was just another town, not her home.

Poppy paid cash and got change back from Danny before she disappeared to place another order. Geoff had been a 15 percent man, but he'd always rounded to the nearest five cents because he thought pennies were a waste of time, a drag on the economy, and should be abolished. Poppy left a hefty tip, bills only. She didn't stick around to say good-bye.

She hunched her shoulders and braced for the weather as she pushed through the brewpub's door, but not a single drop fell on her. She walked, slowed, and then stopped. Dark gray clouds hung above her, cotton wisps drifting here and there below them. The colorful old buildings of Moose Hollow were shining brightly after their rain wash. For no good reason, she turned to face south, up the road and toward the mountains and the narrow pass that led to the national park. Dark, forested mountains dominated the view, and with their peaks hidden by the clouds, they looked impossibly tall. Just below the clouds she could see the palest dusting of snow. And as she watched, sunlight broke through on the ridge to the east, lighting the yellow leaves of the cottonwood trees and crowning the buildings in front of them.

"I'm staying," she said to no one in particular.

CHAPTER 2

*P*oppy walked straight to the Third Street Inn. She watched the corner tower, topped with turrets as any castle tower should be, emerge into view. As a kid she would have loved to stay in a tower room. She walked up the two stone steps that led to the inn's front door, slowing as she caught sight of purplish glass plugs in the sidewalk, as if there might be a secret dungeon beneath the building.

A gentle cough behind her reminded her that she was holding up traffic, and she hurried through the narrow glass doors and into the hotel.

The Third Street Inn lobby was small, oddly shaped, and decorated in dark jewel tones. The empty registration desk was immediately in front of her. Poppy reached for the call bell but pulled back her hand when she heard a woman's voice through a crack in the door behind the desk.

"I am sorry to bother you," the woman said, "but I wanted to speak to you about your reservation for this weekend." A chair creaked and Poppy heard taps on a computer keyboard. "Well, there's a bit of an issue. We've been notified that there has been a rockslide on the Beartooth Highway. Although they're working very hard on clearing it, there's a chance it won't be open before..."

The chair creaked again. Poppy busied herself by picking up a brochure from the pile on the desk.

"That's right, it's the only direct route into the national park from Moose...Yes. I understand they may be booked. Yes, that's true. Under the circumstances, I would be happy to refund your deposit. If you would like to reschedule...Of course. I'm very sorry for the inconvenience. We'll email you the receipt immediately. Good-bye."

Poppy heard a long sigh, then a series of taps on the keyboard. She coughed gently into her hand and tried to look busy as a woman emerged from the back room. "I'm sorry to have kept you waiting," the woman said.

She had large, heavy-lidded brown eyes with long lashes. Her brown hair was pulled back into a neat bun, and she was wearing black pants and a black shirt. On her shirt was a gold pin that bore the name Julia, and in tiny block letters below that was the word Clerk.

"No problem," Poppy said. "I was hoping to get a room."

"Tonight? For how long?" Julia typed something on the keyboard and looked at Poppy expectantly.

That was a good question. "At least tonight," she said, thinking out loud. She'd need time to find a place to stay, but she didn't want to pay for nights she wouldn't be using. "I guess...through the weekend?"

Julia's eyes narrowed and Poppy now saw that the woman was older than she'd first thought, probably in her forties or fifties—but Poppy was horrible at guessing ages.

"Yes, through the weekend," Poppy said firmly, even as her resolve was crumbling. The rain had ended. She could be on her way to a less expensive town.

"You've picked a good weekend. We're usually

booked in advance." She punched a few more keys and quoted a price to Poppy.

Poppy bit her lip. It was pricey. Like it or not, she would need to transfer money from her trust fund as quickly as possible. "Do you offer any discounts? I don't need a large room." Her face began to burn. What kind of person walks into the most expensive hotel in town and asks for a cheap room? The local motel had a TV and a bed; she didn't need more than that. She tried to think of a graceful way to back out. "Never mind. Your hotel is lovely. I should have checked around—"

"We do have a discount," Julia said. "Right here." She gestured vaguely toward the screen, which Poppy couldn't see. "I'm sorry, I didn't see it at first." She typed. "Yes, we've had a few cancellations, and that triggered some discounts in the remaining rooms." While Poppy waited, she could feel the older woman's eyes on her, from her lank hair down to her pointy, worn cowboy boots. "Twenty percent?" It came out sounding more like a question than a statement. "That would be ..."

Poppy had finished the equation in her mind before Julia shared the actual numbers. As she started to apologize for wasting the woman's time, Julia added, "I'm sorry, I read it wrong.

Thirty percent off, plus 50 percent off the weekend."

They stared at each other. Poppy, for one, felt terribly uncomfortable, and she was sure she was blushing enough to make that evident to Julia. "That would be lovely, thank you," she finally said. She wondered if the hotel was in financial danger. Or maybe the manager was responsible for keeping a certain occupancy rate. Or did she think Poppy was a charity case? "I can pay for tonight now."

The woman blinked. "Um. Sure, that'll do." She nodded, and the narrowed eyes returned, along with pinched eyebrows. Poppy began to wonder if Julia had just been making up numbers.

She received the keycard to room 221 and went up to inspect it, mostly because Julia asked her to, not because she thought the room needed inspecting. She passed the elevator and chose the stairs.

Her room was near the end of the hall, facing the back of the building. Poppy opened the old wooden door and found herself in a small room dominated by a queen-sized bed placed diagonally in the corner. It had an antique wooden headboard, and its oversized mattress and fluffy bedding hit Poppy hip-high.

She sighed happily. There was something about hotels she loved. Her parents never stayed in one, a quirk that had something to do with her mother's family. Or the fact that they never had any money. Or maybe they just preferred the old van that housed the four of them on long trips. Or was it the six or seven of them? The story changed with every telling.

Along with the bed, the room held a tall antique dresser with narrow drawers and a door to a very modern-looking bathroom with a small closet hidden inside. She maneuvered around the bed again. If there were two people in the room, they'd have a hard time getting past each other.

She didn't remember what the room she'd shared with Geoff had looked like. She remembered thinking it was cozy and light, just like this room. And now that she was thinking about it, she could remember his resentment at spending so much on a hotel and the way it dampened her pleasure in staying there. She hoped she hadn't left that same impression with the hotel manager.

In fact, the room was perfect. And for five days, it was hers, so long as she paid for it. She needed to get a local bank account set up. She put the room's keycard in her back pocket.

The only bank she remembered was the one

down the road a couple of blocks, a shiny new brick building with a ranching-related name she couldn't remember. After one more look, she left the room, headed outside, and walked north on Broadway until she found the bank.

The bank's interior was a nondescript modern style with expensive western touches: a wide antler chandelier, bronze cowboys and bison. There was a coffee carafe nearby, and judging by the aroma that drifted her way, the coffee was awfully good.

"May I help you?" The woman at the front desk was young and wore makeup that seemed more appropriate for a night out on the town. And in a much larger city.

Poppy filled out the account paperwork, got herself a cup of coffee, and ended up in the glass-walled office of another well-dressed woman. With similar clothes, makeup, and perfect golden hair, she could have been the receptionist's mother. And since Moose Hollow was a small town, Poppy supposed it was possible.

The woman told Poppy her name, but it went in one ear and out the other. Something about banks made Poppy feel as though she'd been called to the principal's office, making it hard for her to concentrate.

After entering Poppy's information into her computer and scanning her driver's license, the woman noted the Arizona address.

"I'm in the process of moving here," Poppy explained.

"I see. So you plan on returning to Arizona?"

The woman smiled sweetly, but her eyes were piercing. Did she think Poppy was scamming her? Just the thought of it threatened to bring the color into Poppy's cheeks again. "I have to defend my master's thesis in Arizona in December, so I'll be returning for that."

"Oh, I see." *Click, click* went the keyboard. Did they keep track of information like that in bank computers? "And how much would you like to deposit today?"

Poppy had a twenty-dollar bill and some change. "I'd like to transfer some money, electronically, if you don't mind," she said, reaching for her phone.

"Of course. There might be a three-day waiting period."

Not good. Poppy tapped her bank icon on the phone but nothing happened. "No service provider," the screen read. She supposed that was to be expected now and then in a mountain town.

"I'm sorry, I'm having trouble connecting. I

can make a phone call to my other bank if you give me the routing information."

The bank lady's smile was noticeably stiffer. "Of course," she said, rotating the desk phone. "Dial 9 first. It is toll-free, I assume?"

As Poppy searched her phone for the proper number, she saw that her hand was shaking. This was silly; she had nothing to hide. "Never mind, I'll just use my computer when I get back to the Third Street Inn." She used the hotel name in hopes that the fancy location would lend her credibility. She reached into the breast pocket of her jacket. "Will twenty dollars do in the meantime?"

"Yes, of course. Let me just change the type of account." She typed rapidly. "I can issue you a debit card now, and we can complete the application for a credit card."

"I don't use credit cards," Poppy said. "The debit card will be just fine."

If the rest of the transaction hadn't made the bank lady suspicious, that last line certainly had. But there wasn't much Poppy could do about the assumptions people made about her. There had never been.

The bank lady handed her a card and a folder full of information and disclaimers, and at that moment Poppy realized Geoff had probably just cut service to her phone. She should have known. She was on his plan. "Thank you," she said hoarsely, and she left the bank on stiff legs.

Outside everything still smelled like rain, and the mountains were beginning to peek up out of their misty shroud. She leaned against the building and thought for a moment.

She needed a new phone provider. Fast.

Poppy walked uphill toward the south, all the while simmering over how foolish she'd been and wondering what other nasty surprises might come her way. She passed multistory brick and stone buildings and then small houses that had been converted to house businesses. Ahead, the road began to turn and narrow as it entered the canyon. Just as she gave up hope, she spotted a small, pinkish house advertising both a cell-phone provider and a real estate company. She walked up the squeaky steps to the ornate front door.

Inside, the house was neatly divided into two very different worlds. To her left was a wallpa-pered Victorian haven that smelled of cinnamon and vanilla. To her right was a sleek, modern business decorated in shades of gray, with spotlights marking cases full of electronics. She headed to the right.

The long-haired young man who helped her seemed a moderately friendly nerd. Poppy didn't realize he also had excellent salesperson skills until she'd decided to trade her phone in for a pretty piece of electronic magic with a glittering tangerine-color case and a more expensive usage plan. She calculated how long it would take her to go back to her truck and get the cash she needed.

But the phone store didn't want cash. They wanted a credit card, but all she had was her new debit card, with its whopping twenty-dollar balance. Did she even have enough to pay for all five nights of the hotel if the bank transfer was delayed? She couldn't imagine the humiliation if that happened. If she wanted to be careful, she couldn't buy a new phone.

"Thank you for all your help," she told the salesman. "I can't afford this today, but I'll be back soon."

The young man's smile was a little strained. "But you haven't got a phone."

"I'll be back. Again, thank you for all your help."

She tucked her disconnected phone back into

her pocket just as a woman walked over from the sister shop next door.

"Brody, I wanted to show you...oh, hello!" She reached for Poppy's hand. "I'm Bettina Moore. I was in the back doing some filing. I didn't even realize Brody had company." She cocked her head sideways. With her narrow nose and pointed features, the motion gave her a birdlike look. "I don't remember meeting you, are you new in town? Do you need to find a place to live?"

Poppy wasn't in a position to buy a home here or anywhere. The real estate agent was out of luck. "Only a place to rent. Just for a few months."

Bettina's eyebrows rose. "That can be a little difficult in this town. But lucky for you, you've come to the right place. I own Moose Hollow's largest rental service, and I'd be happy to show you what we have available."

Poppy couldn't afford to turn the woman down. It made perfect sense to have a real estate agent working next to a cell phone shop, she realized. Between them, they practically sold new lives.

By the time the sun was setting, Poppy had seen every available rental, plus two units for sale, all of which left her feeling hopeless. Bettina, however, was a fountain of optimism. She seemed fairly convinced that with a little reflection, Poppy would consider buying a home in Moose Hollow.

By the end of the tour, Poppy was ready to retreat to the cozy hotel room, but her stomach had other ideas. Rather than going inside, she walked here and there, not finding a restaurant that piqued her interest until the cold drove her inside the Combine once again.

CHAPTER 3

The tables were full now, although there were still spots at the bar. Colton was no longer sitting at the end of the bar, of course. Poppy decided that was a good thing. But Danny was still there, and she flashed a genuine smile and called, "Poppy!" as if she were a good friend. Half a dozen faces turned toward her. It made her feel both welcome and uncomfortably conspicuous. "Have a seat," Danny said, gesturing toward an empty barstool. "The usual?"

It might have been a sales gimmick, but Danny's words made Poppy smile. *The usual.* It felt good to imagine she had a usual—and people who would care to remember it. "Sure." Whatever Danny thought it was, she'd take it.

She glanced around her. At five o'clock on a weeknight, the place was already packed. "It's busy."

Danny shook her head as she handed her a huckleberry ale in a small glass. "I probably have the rockslide on the Beartooth Highway to thank for this rush."

"So do you work every single shift here?"

Danny let out a chuckle. "Just about. I was supposed to be off at six, but I'm stuck here until things thin out. But that's okay. I'm only working as hard as I want to tonight. Besides the beer, can I get you something to eat?"

"I'm not very hungry, so something light."

"They made some soup tonight, how does that sound?"

"Sounds good, thank you."

Danny wrote something down and disappeared through the door at the end of the bar. Poppy immediately felt uncomfortable, as if everyone was staring at her. Out of habit she reached for her phone, then remembered it was useless.

"Are you new in town?" a voice beside her said. Poppy turned to see a man at least a decade older than her, athletic and trim and clothed in an ugly Hawaiian shirt. No doubt her expression wasn't welcoming, because he jerked backward and raised his hands. The gesture reminded her of Colton. "Don't worry, I'm just being friendly."

Poppy sighed. "Sorry, it's been a long day. And yes, I'm new."

"That's what I figured. I hang around here way too much, so I know just about everyone." He took a sip of his beer and then picked up the cardboard coaster it had been sitting on and flipped it over a few times, examining it. Then he stuck out a hand—suddenly, as if he'd just re-membered he hadn't introduced himself. "Cash Gunnerson."

She held out her hand, and he shook it once, firmly. "Poppy Marsh."

He nodded. "Your tan gives you away as a newbie, you know. This time of year, the sun starts vanishing pretty early in the day. No one gets tan again until ski season."

He was a good-looking man in an outdoorsy way. His face was sun-weathered, and he looked like a distance runner, partly fit and partly hag-gard. Late forties, maybe. He was still playing with the coaster, and just as he opened his mouth to say something else, a large hand came down hard on his shoulder. He looked up and smiled. "Well, hi, Randy! Haven't seen you in awhile."

She glanced up to see a portly older man, his hands worn from decades of work. He looked at her with raised eyebrows, and Cash spoke up. "Randy, this is...what was it? Poppy Marsh. She's new in town, so be polite."

Randy snorted. "You'll learn to stay away from the Gunnerson boys." He turned sideways to point his finger at Cash's nose. "And what kind of deal are you trying to pull? I got the inspection back, and the whole foundation's sideways."

"You knew that, Randy! I told you all about that. You should answer my calls."

Poppy took a sip of her beer. It tasted as if it should have been tinted purple, a berry color, but it was as pale a blond as she was. She looked around for a newspaper, and, not seeing one, she engrossed herself in the laminated appetizer menu she found nearby. She couldn't help but hear the conversation beside her as she did. Cash and Randy were discussing rental properties, sales, and renovations. Randy was doing the renovating, and Cash seemed to be the owner of several rental properties. As soon as she realized that, she waited for a break in the conversation and turned to face Cash Gunnerson again.

"I'm sorry to interrupt, but did you say you handle rental properties?" Both men gave her a curious look but didn't answer. "Do you have any vacancies? I only need a place for a few months."

"Nope, sorry Poppy," Cash said. "There are more bodies in this town than houses."

A girl with long, wavy brown hair delivered Poppy's soup and bread. "Thank you," Poppy said.

Cash leaned forward onto his elbows. "Terra! Darling, I have been trying to get your attention all night."

"And I've been avoiding you," Terra said before moving on.

Cash laughed like it was the funniest thing he'd ever heard. As Danny came back from touring the tables, he said, "Sorry I can't help you, I'm all booked."

Danny threw the towel down on the bar next to Poppy's plate. "You need to call Colton."

Cash leaned forward, around Randy, to get a better look at both women. "Colt?"

"Yeah, he's been thinking about renting out the main house," Danny said. "Didn't he tell you?"

"I thought he was going to renovate it."

"Last I heard, he had all the plumbing and most of the electrical done."

Cash shook his head and whistled. "Good for him. But rent it out while he's working on it? What a mess that would be."

Danny shrugged. "What do you think, Poppy? Are you willing to live in the middle of a construction zone?"

"I don't mind." She had done work on each and every rental she had ever lived in since her budget was rarely up to her comfort level. "I have a little bit of experience fixing places up," she added. "Just the easy stuff."

Cash slammed his palm down on the bar. "Well, see! That's exactly what he needs. Bet he'd give you one heck of a deal if you were willing to help out here and there, paint or something since he hates that. Danny, have you heard what's going on? Is he going to sell the house, or some land, or all of it, or what?"

Danny shook her head. "You know as much as I do. He won't talk to me about it. Besides, you should be asking him, not me." She gave him a sharp look.

Cash lowered his head and shook it slowly from side to side. "You know, it's just a darn shame. This was supposed to be a good thing for him. But everyone's got their troubles. And he won't ask for help." He glanced at Poppy, and his countenance changed. "Poppy, you should live there. If nothing else, you can chase the mice away."

Danny reached over with lightning speed and hit him on the arm. He flinched dramatically. "What was that for?"

"Do you have his number?" Danny asked.

Poppy shook her head. She still had the newspaper, but it was back in her hotel room.

Danny snorted at her expression. "Girlfriend," Danny said, "these opportunities don't come around every day." She pulled a phone out of the holster on her belt, touched the screen, and handed the phone to Poppy.

Poppy took the phone out of reflex, just because it was handed to her. She was startled to see that the screen read "Dialing: Colton." She tried to hand it back, but Danny leaned away from the bar and shook her head. Poppy pressed it to her ear. "Hello?"

"Hello?" His was a slow, deep voice. Poppy became very aware of all the happy, loud noise around her. "Um…Colton?"

"Who is this, and what have you done with Danny?"

Poppy flinched. "This is Poppy Marsh. You probably don't remember—"

"Hard to forget the name, Poppy F. Marsh," he said.

She felt the color rise to her face and wished her audience would find someone else to look at. "I've been having some trouble finding a place to rent, and I know it's only been one day, but there were only three places available, and they were so ..." She was rambling, she knew, so she stopped before she did any more damage.

"I'm your last resort, then," Colton said. Poppy could hear the smile in his voice.

"Yes."

"Are you at the brewpub?"

The noise around her must have been unmistakable. "How did you guess?" she said wryly.

He laughed at that. "I can meet you at the homestead tomorrow around noon. Ask Danny to draw you directions."

She said good-bye and then stared at the strange phone, unsure how to hang up. Danny took it out of her hand and slid it into her pocket without a second look. "What did he say?"

"He said I could take a look at it at noon tomorrow. He also said you could draw me a map."

Danny pulled out a clean coaster and a pen. She drew Broadway and then a county road that zigzagged off of it, trending southwest, and finally a dashed line that turned back toward the south. "The house is yellow," Danny said, "so you can't miss it. And I don't think you want to miss it."

CHAPTER 4

"Who was that?"

Colton tucked his phone into his coat pocket. "That, Aunt Julia, was Poppy Marsh. My new tenant."

Which should have made him happy. It was what he wanted, after all, although offering her the rental had been an unexpected decision. Emmaline would have said it was a "God thing," how he felt compelled to ask a complete stranger to live in the homestead. The only way to know what kind of thing it was, he supposed, was to watch it play out.

And when it played out, his home would be gone. He plastered a smile on his face.

Julia didn't look surprised by the news. She

had a pretty steady hand most of the time, and raising three boys—three and a half, if he counted himself—had made her hard to startle. But she didn't even ask who Poppy was, and that was unusual. "You've met her, haven't you?"

"She's a guest here."

"And what was your opinion?" He could tell by the look on her face she had one.

"Polite. And in trouble."

Colton leaned over onto one elbow and crossed one ankle over the other, careful to put his weight on the good knee. That was what he'd thought about Poppy too. But he didn't say so. "Nah. She seemed just fine."

"You think?"

He chewed at the inside of his lip and thought about it for a minute. "Maybe she was a little jumpy."

"She had red, swollen eyes from crying. Her voice was hoarse and her clothes wrinkled, she didn't seem to have any ID, and she paid for everything in cash. Small bills. Like she's broke and hiding from someone."

Colton tipped his hat back and gave Julia a serious look. "Have you considered a career change? Because they're looking for the next *Murder She Wrote* lady."

"I see a lot of people in a lot of different circumstances, Colton, and I notice things. And you promised to stay away from troubled girls. They're...trouble."

He tried not to let her see how her words cut him. He knew she had every right to doubt him. But he wanted to believe he'd changed, and healed, over the last few months. To see her doubting him now made him feel like a broken man. Except for the headaches, things were better now. Unless she saw something in him that he couldn't see. "I'm looking for a tenant, Julia. Not a girlfriend."

"She's cute."

"Nah." Cute? Not really. Pretty, though. Outdoorsy-hippie cute, if you like that sort of thing. Except for that second when he thought she was going to cry for no good reason. He'd been thinking about that last night, while he wondered what made him ask her to move in. He had a vacant house; she needed a place to stay. That's all. It wasn't because he was attracted to her.

But he did like the way she practically growled at him when he tried to speak to her. Good to know she wasn't looking for anything more than a place to live.

"Are you going to go say hi to Anson before you go?"

Julia asked nicely. And Colton knew she made sure not to ask too often. He acted as if the thought had never occurred to him. "Nope, sorry, I'm in a hurry," he replied, looking at his wristwatch. "Don't want to miss curfew."

"It's nowhere near curfew, and the two of you have to talk sometime."

"It's so much more fun to pass messages through you." He winked at her and hurried toward the door.

Julia was right about Anson, Colton thought. He didn't want to talk about it. Not until he knew where he was headed. If he talked to them about the ranch, they'd know he had no plan, no hope, and a stubborn streak that might ruin his family. But like a runaway train, he wasn't ready to stop. Not yet.

CHAPTER 5

The evening air had turned from cold to freezing. For all their traveling, Poppy's parents had never spent much time in colder climates, and she wasn't used to it. She buttoned even the uncomfortable top button of her jacket and started back down the street to the hotel. One block into the walk, she drew up her collar and tucked her hands into her pockets. Two blocks in, she hunched over and let her hair fall over her face to block the wind. She wondered how on earth she was going to make it through December in this frozen town.

She recognized the bright lights of the Third Street Inn shining onto the sidewalk, put her head back down, and sped up as she approached the door. She looked up just in time to see something rush at her, hit her full on, and knock her backward. Her arms wheeled as she tried to regain her balance, but she couldn't get her feet back under her. Just before she hit the ground, someone grabbed her.

He had ahold of her, but as she was being lifted, she felt him start to fall over with her. "Whoa!" he said. They were both going down, and she still couldn't find her feet.

But with reflexes faster than hers, he got his footing, and with his arm wrapped around her, he hoisted her straight up into the air. She was pretty certain who it was holding her close against his Carhartt jacket. The man was haunting her. Wasn't he supposed to be at his house outside of town right now? Instead, some part of Colton's tall frame had hit her right in the face.

He looked down at her. "Are you all right?"

She tried to blink the tears away, but they kept coming. Her face hurt, and he was holding her too tightly.

"I thought I hit you," he said.

In the middle of the chaos caused by her pounding heart, watering eyes, and the feeling she'd just gotten her bell rung, she realized it was nice to have someone's arms around her when she felt cold and miserable.

At that exact instant, the pain on her face narrowed into focus. She wrestled one hand free to reach up and touch her nose.

He gasped. "I broke your nose!"

Just hearing the word "broke" made her nose throb with pain, and with tears filling her eyes, she could hardly keep them open. She felt around a little bit along the bridge of her nose, then gently wiped. Blood traced across the back of her hand. "It's not broken," she said, but he was already talking over her.

"I'm so sorry! Poppy, I am so, so sorry." He grabbed ahold of her arms again and pulled her forward. Her eyes were watering so badly she could hardly see as he dragged her through the doorway, nearly running her into the doorframe as he did. "Julia! I need help!"

"It's fine," Poppy mumbled. "It's always been a little crooked."

"It was not crooked. And you're bleeding! Julia, I hit her in the nose. With my elbow. I was just reaching up to put my hat on."

"I know," a woman said, and Poppy recognized the voice of the brown-haired, brown-eyed hotel clerk. "I saw the collision through the window."

Poppy gave up trying to see and just closed her eyes against the onslaught of tears. Why was it that getting hit in the nose made your eyes water so much? She was a biologist. She should know these things.

"Thank God," Colton mumbled. Poppy wondered what he had to be so thankful about, and she would have shot him a stern look, but all her eyes were good for at the moment was soaking her face with tears.

Julia steered Poppy behind the front desk and into an office, seating her in a creaky chair. Poppy heard the *whoosh*, *whoosh* of tissues being drawn, and then a wad of them was pressed into her palm. "I'll be right back," Julia said. "Stay here."

Poppy focused on trying not to bleed on anything except the tissues.

"You need to hold your nose, like this," Colton said. Poppy glanced up to see him holding his nostrils shut. "Lean your head forward a little. If you lean back, all the blood will back up into your throat."

That was a revolting thought, so she did as he said. But the pain was already beginning to subside, settling into a nasty throbbing that didn't make her eyes water as badly. So she gingerly placed her forefinger and thumb over her nostrils and pressed. "How long?" she asked.

"Until it stops," he said. The dimple on his right cheek made a momentary appearance; then it was gone again, lost in a worried expression.

"For ten minutes," Julia said as she returned to the office. "Exactly ten." She took the bloody tissues out of Poppy's left hand without the slightest trace of squeamishness, then placed a small cold pack in that same hand. "See if you can get this over your nose and cheeks, but don't stop the pressure on your nostrils."

Poppy did as she was told. Something about Julia reminded her of her best friend's mother, the unflappable Mrs. Kraft back in Washington State. When that woman said jump, she could make a whole gang of juvenile delinquents fly. The icy pack on her nose made her eyes water as badly as before, but she didn't dare take it off.

"How are you feeling?" Julia asked.

"Fine."

"You might get two black eyes from this."

That was okay, Poppy thought. She already felt as if she stood out like a sore thumb in this town. A tan sore thumb. Black eyes wouldn't change much.

Julia identified a drop of blood on Poppy's jacket and fetched a cold, damp paper towel to wipe it off. That was also something Lily Kraft's mother would have done. At age eleven, Mrs. Kraft's attention had been welcome, but at twenty-four, it just felt awkward. "If you don't mind me borrowing the cold pack, I think I'd like to go back to my room."

"Certainly," Julia said, and she stepped back to give Poppy room to stand. Colton, however, hovered over her and reached for her elbow. That bumped her arm, which bumped her nose, and she winced.

"I'll take you to your room," Colton said.

"That's okay. I know where it is." She tried to sound firm, but if she succeeded, Colton didn't notice.

"Let me carry your...where's your purse? Did you drop it outside?"

"I don't have one. I'm fine, Colton." Talking through the pinched nose and cold pack, she sounded like Rudolph the Reindeer. "I'm going now."

It was Julia's hand on Colton's arm that finally got him to step out of her way. "You'll let me know if you need anything, right, Poppy?" she said.

"I will." Poppy nodded out of habit, but her hand didn't nod with her head, and it hurt. Before more tears sprang to her eyes, she made a quick exit. As she headed for the stairs, she heard Colton behind her.

"What if she presses charges?"

Press charges? For walking right into him? Poppy sighed. He was a strange one. Carefully, step by step, Poppy made it up to the third floor, into the bright room and a heater she could turn up to Arizona levels.

CHAPTER 6

*W*ho would be knocking on her door?
Poppy blinked into the light and
sat up in the bed. There it was again, a knock. "I
don't need any room service," she said, her voice
hoarse with sleep.

"I'm not room service," a voice replied. It was
unfamiliar, but clearly a man's voice. "Poppy, this
is Zane, can we talk for a sec?"

Zane who? She threw the covers back and
reached for her denim jacket to put over her tee.
The Black Watch plaid pajama bottoms would
have to do. Hadn't her sister bought them in
Scotland? More likely in the airport on the way
out. She opened the door but kept the upper latch
hooked. What she saw was a very tall and very

young man. He gave her a meek grin. "I didn't wake you up, did I?"

She closed the door, undid the latch, and then opened the door. But she stood on the threshold with her arms crossed, making it clear he was not invited in. "Yes?"

The young man's hands were jammed deep into the front pocket of his jeans. "Hi. Wow, you did break your nose. I was wondering if I could get a ride this morning."

Poppy took a moment to process everything he said. By the time she was ready to respond to his request, Zane had shifted position and shoved his hands deeper into his pockets. If he got more nervous, she thought, his jeans would slip right off his non-existent hips and land around his ankles.

"I'm Julia's son," he clarified.

The clerk at the front desk? Well, this was un-usual customer service, she thought.

"You know, Colton's cousin?"

That took a little longer to process. That would make Julia Colton's aunt. And it would go a long way to explaining the almost maternal way she acted around him.

"I'm on my way to work on the homestead, and Colton said you were coming by to see the place. My car's in the shop, and there's no way I'm getting it back now because I got home a half hour late last night. So Colton said he might come pick me up, but you know how he is."

No, she didn't, but breaking promises to one's younger cousin did say something about Colton's character.

"So what do you think?"

Poppy thought it was probably best not to answer that question. "What time is it?"

"Eight. Seven-thirty. Somewhere in there."

She took a deep breath. "I wasn't supposed to go to see Colton's place until noon."

"Oh." Realization dawned on him, and he seemed to shrink from his six-something feet height down to a more reasonable size right before her eyes. "I'm sorry. Hey, no problem. I can hitch a ride with my girlfriend." He grimaced. "Okay, maybe not her. But I'll find something. Sorry I woke you up."

Poppy felt bad for the kid. And the truth was, she didn't have anything better to do. It might be a good idea to see the house earlier; then she could have the rest of the day to pursue other living arrangements. Or leave. "Give me half an hour and I'll take you," she said.

"Really? Awesome! Thank you!" With wide

eyes and his hands dangling at his side, he looked a little like a puppy. A big skinny one, like a Great Dane. She closed the door without another word, a grin on her face. Nice kid. A bit goofy, but nice.

She didn't have much time to shower off the traces of last night's few hours of sleep. After her ten minutes of holding her nose were up and her face had gone from a sharp throbbing to a steady ache, she'd gone out into the cold to get her laptop. Then she'd set up her new online account at the Moose Hollow bank and logged into the account where her trust sat. For the first time in a long time, she regretted shredding the debit cards that bank sent every few years. But it was a temptation she didn't want in her life. Poppy thought of her sister then, and her disconnected phone, and took a moment to send off a quick email to Sierra to let her know she was okay.

She had finally managed to transfer some money to the new account, then she logged back into the Moose Hollow bank. The money hadn't shown up yet, which wasn't a surprise. Neither was it there after she'd watched two episodes of her favorite house renovation show on TV and gotten caught up on the latest pictures her friends had posted online. She'd started to get nervous.

She had tried to sleep, but her mind ground

over all the decisions she'd made this week, before the breakup and after. How could she have turned her back on all her obligations in Tucson? She'd tried not to wonder what Geoff was doing, or who he was doing it with. She missed leaning her head against his shoulder as he read in bed.

Finally, at midnight, she'd logged onto the computer again. This time, she'd drafted a check from the trust fund and had it mailed to the Third Street Inn. As decent a backup plan as she could manage, considering that the bank was in San Francisco. But with the cash she had on hand, she didn't have enough to cover the hotel, let alone the deposit for a new rental.

With barely half an hour to get ready, she started the shower to get the hot water running, then logged into her new account again. There it was, sort of. She had $120 available and $9,900 "pending hold release." Beside those words was a date—ten days from today.

Ten days? What modern bank took ten days to process an electronic transfer?

She rushed through her shower and dressed quickly—a light orange sweater over a cami. Other than a sweatshirt and one flannel shirt, it was the only warm clothing she owned. She might have to do a little shopping to make it through the winter. She put on a few drops of her favorite rose essential oil and brushed her hair, which was wet enough to look brown in the bathroom mirror. As usual, she thought of Sierra's auburn hair and wished her hair had such vibrant color. But as various people had commented, their hair matched their distinct personalities. Poppy faded into the crowd. Sierra was a standout.

It was their names that were backward. Poppy was the rock. Sierra was the beauty who should have been named for a wildflower. But Poppy would stand out today, thanks to the burgundy bruises under her eyes. Given time, they might turn into two genuine black eyes.

According to her "no service" phone, twenty-five minutes had passed, though there was no telling if the time on it was still correct since it no longer connected to the outside world. She put on a little light-brown eye makeup and tried the hair dryer, but it was so loud she worried she'd miss Zane's knock.

She put on her parka, which she had grabbed the night before, and her favorite boots—brown ones with bluebirds and orange flowers across the toe—and pulled her jeans over the bright turquoise shaft. She wondered what "work on the homestead" meant. Her mind conjured images of discovering beautiful hardwood beneath rotting carpet and the smell of fresh paint. She shook her head. More like dead mouse retrieval, if what Cash said was right. The thought chased all the romantic images away.

Finally, the knock came, and she tucked her wallet and keys into the parka pocket and opened her door. Zane was there, looking vaguely guilty again. She gave him a slight smile and closed the door behind her, heading down the hall toward the lobby.

"Hey, we should go this way," Zane said. "It's faster."

She turned the other way and went down the back stairs. He galloped down ahead of her, leaving vibrations in his wake. At the bottom, she found him already outside, waiting for her in an alley. He was looking around. He stopped to smile at her, hike up his jeans and said, "Which way is your car?"

The sky above was blue, but the air felt cold enough to freeze her damp hair. She zipped up her parka as they walked down the alley to the parking lot where her truck was parked. By the time she got there she had decided the direct approach was best. She faced Zane across the hood, leaving the doors locked. "Zane, are you skipping school?"

"No," he said, but he looked at her like a deer caught in headlights.

"You didn't know where my truck was, but you knew the back stairs would be a quicker route."

"Yeah, well, they usually—"

"I'm assuming your mom is working the front desk again, which would explain why you wanted to go out the back door. And of course, it's Friday."

"It's a PIR day."

Poppy frowned at him.

"That's a day when only the teachers go to school. They do seminars or something."

"Then why are you avoiding Julia?"

Zane deflated a little. "I'm not avoiding Mom. I just don't want her to know I'm going with you."

"You're not allowed to drive your own car and not allowed to have your girlfriend drive you, so how am I supposed to believe it's okay with your parents for me to drive you somewhere?"

"Because you're old," he said. When he recognized the expression on her face, he added, "Not *old* old. I'm not allowed to drive or ride with another teenager. I could quote you the stats on car crashes when there's more than one teenager in a car; I've heard them often enough."

"I'm not driving you anywhere until you let your mom know you're with me."

"I will, I promise, just not now."

Poppy stood her ground, but so did Zane.

He crossed his arms and looked her in the eye. "I can't call them now. They're arguing. About me. As usual."

Poppy hadn't spent time with a teenager for months. She'd almost forgotten how freely information, especially the kind that was usually kept quiet, could flow from their lips. "You have to promise me that I'm not causing you to break any rules. And that you'll let your mom know I drove you to Colton's house."

"Deal," Zane said. He put a hand on the door, and she unlocked it by turning the key twice in the lock.

"No remote?"

"Nope," she answered. "I don't even know if this model came with a remote key." And if it had, she was certain it wouldn't be worth the cost of replacing it.

"Cool. It's an antique."

She pulled a cardboard box of books off the passenger seat and put it in the back of her truck.

Her trunk was jammed in behind the seats, so Zane's knees barely cleared the dashboard. They put on their seat belts and she pulled out onto Broadway Avenue and headed south.

"What does PIR stand for?"

"I don't know. Mara says it's People Imbibing and Relaxing. She figures all the teachers fill their coffee cups with wine and complain about the students."

Poppy laughed. She figured Mara was the girl-friend, and she sounded like someone Poppy would like. She slowed down at the intersection where she thought Danny had said to turn, and just when she'd decided it wasn't the right one, Zane said, "Turn here." She barely slipped into the turn lane in time.

The road wound up and over a hillside, where a view of the mountains took her breath away. Ahead and to the left were pine-covered moun-tains, their knifelike gray ridges jutting straight into the sky.

"I'm not hiding anything from Mom, I swear," Zane said. "And I'm not grounded, it's just...it's complicated."

"I think raising a teenager sounds complicated."

"I know." He looked out the side window,

away from Poppy. "I haven't made it easy for them lately. But I'm doing my best."

Poppy felt his last words as a pressure in her chest. He'd summed up all of her memories of being a teenager with those words. It was better to be older.

At least it had been for a while, hadn't it? She'd been so sure of herself as an adult, so certain about the reasonableness of her decisions. Obviously she'd been wrong about Geoff. But it seemed like everyone went through breakups. It was just a rite of passage.

But a passage to what? She wondered briefly what the best outcome could be. Probably to be more independent. To learn not to fall in love so hard that another man held her happiness in his hands. She'd made a mess of her life. *But I'm doing my best*, she said in her mind, as if she was talking to someone who could forgive her.

They drove for a few miles, and the houses became more and more dispersed until she could see miles of rolling hills covered in golden grass spread out before her. Everywhere she looked, the grass was sparkling from the rain the night before. The land seemed to slope downward toward the mountains, and here and there she could see cattle, all of them black. "Wow," she said.

"Have you been here before?"

"Not out this way. I hiked up in the Beartooths. See that big reservoir up top? That was beautiful."

"You know the speed limit here is 65, right?"

She was doing 55, which was the speed limit back when the Nissan was built, and it was as fast as the old truck liked to go. "I know."

"I always wanted to build out here on the ranch. I guess that's out of the question now that it belongs to Colton." He gave her a sideways glance. "I think I've had enough of hotels for a while."

Poppy didn't understand most of what Zane was talking about, but she'd learned that with a little time and listening, most of the important things in life came clear soon enough.

"See that old grain augur?"

Just ahead on her left, a rusty piece of metal that looked like a cannon jutted out of the grass. It was the only thing other than grass near the road, so she supposed that was it.

"Turn left after that."

She slowed and looked to her left. An overgrown and poorly maintained dirt road went north toward the mountains, crested the hill right in front of her, and disappeared out of sight. She had decided about ten miles before that the house was too far out of town, and if Zane hadn't been in the car, she would have turned around and left by now.

Over the hill was a wide spot in the road with a parking area to one side. There were stacks of massive, round bales of hay, fencing, a ramp and chute of some kind, and a number of metal barred panels laying in the grass. Zane shook his head. "I know this drives him nuts," Zane said.

"What?"

"The bales."

She slowed the truck again and gave him a questioning look. "What's wrong with them?"

"Wait, what?" He clearly thought she was joking by asking such a silly question.

"I live in Arizona. We're not big on grass in general. They look fine to me."

"Well, the bottom row is supposed to be stacked on end, and it's not. The top is supposed to be on its side, but all facing this way so the snow runs off. These bales are just tossed over there, and that means you lose a lot more to rot. And see those panels? They're worth about a hundred each, and here they are, laying on the ground, rusting. Colton hates stuff like that."

"So why doesn't he clean it up?"

Zane turned all the way around in his seat to stare at her. "You haven't done much ranching, have you?"

"None. Why?"

"Never mind. Keep going, we haven't even gotten to the barn yet."

Ahead of her, the mountains were lifting higher as she approached. At the top of the ridge, the snow-covered trees glittered with ice and snow. She drove past a beautiful barn with a huge roof, domed with a peak at the top.

"Hang a right. The one on the left goes to the bunkhouse."

Poppy could see it now. Her heart started to beat a little faster, and at the same time her brain was listing all the reasons she should not even consider renting this house.

It had two stories, and across the top story, narrow dormer windows jutted out of the steep roof. The driveway approached the front of the house and then dissolved into a myriad of tracks on what should have been the front lawn.

A front porch spanned the entire length of the house, appearing to encircle it. To the left of center was the front door. Her mind added a porch swing, new railings, and fresh paint where there was peeling, faded yellow chips. There was a tangle of bushes to one side, which she recognized immediately as never-pruned rose bushes, and there were big windows with lots of small panes on the first floor.

It looked like a storybook home. It looked just the way homes were supposed to look, with big families and stories to tell.

Zane was already gone, out of the truck before she had turned off the ignition, and the slamming door made her jump.

She got out and slowly followed him, taking note of the sinking front steps, the slump in the porch on her right, the extra-wide planks of splintering wood. She turned around and looked at the barn again. The whole thing looked in danger of collapsing, but it was beautiful, and it matched the rolling hills beyond it. There were rows of fences in front of the barn, gray with traces of white paint. As many of the posts leaned as stood upright.

She heard a loud crash and bolted inside the house, afraid that someone was hurt. Or worse, had hurt the house.

CHAPTER 7

What she saw inside was just the sort of mess Cash and Danny had been talking about. She was in the middle of what was probably a living room, but beneath her feet lay a half-demolished subfloor over a plank floor that gaped here and there and was entirely missing in other places. A big roll of stained carpet sat in the middle, stinking of mold and mildew. It had been a long time since she'd smelled that, and it reminded her of the old house in New Orleans. She winced.

To her right was a pretty set of French doors with floral curtains hiding what was behind them, and ahead of her was a 1950s dining table, complete with tarnished chrome and a red

Formica top. There were even two matching chairs, each upholstered in torn white vinyl. She couldn't see past that, since whatever had happened to the wall beyond was hidden with plywood.

She walked forward, careful to avoid holes and other dangers. A dust-covered wood-burning stove on slate tiles sat on top of the only patch of new subflooring in the house. She walked through the dining room to the kitchen, which was completely dismantled. And off kilter on the floor was what appeared to be a new white farm sink, covered in sawdust.

She looked up. There were three perfectly matched holes in the ceiling where lights should be. She tallied it up: no lights, no floor, no kitchen, no wall or window or whatever belonged in where the plywood was. Then she stepped up to the window that faced the mountains. The view was breathtaking.

Poppy heard male voices coming from somewhere above her, then footsteps trodding down wooden stairs. She exited the kitchen. Being so wrapped up in the house, she hadn't even noticed the stairs.

There was no railing on the staircase, so she could see the jean-clad legs coming down, the first pair wearing gaudy, untied basketball shoes and the second stained leather work boots that might have been yellowish once upon a time.

"Mara's here," Zane said, rushing straight out the door. Through the open doorway, Poppy saw a shiny black Cadillac Escalade pull up in front of the house.

Before he reached the bottom step, Colton called out to her, "So what do you think?"

His hair was a mess and covered in a fine white dust, as were his arms below the sleeves of his white T-shirt. Below that was a worn tool belt over equally worn jeans. Poppy looked back out the door and saw Zane catch a girl up in his arms and twirl her around.

"I wasn't expecting you to come early," he said.

"Me either."

"Are you here to work?"

Yes, she wanted to say. All the unfinished projects made her fingers itch. But she wouldn't presume. Besides, she had more important things to do than work on a house she would never live in. "Zane said he needed a ride."

Colton nodded, then his smile fell and his eyes narrowed. He let out an expletive. His expression changed again, and although she didn't know him at all, she could tell he was embarrassed. It certainly wasn't the first time she'd heard that word. She decided he must think her a prude. It wouldn't be the first time someone thought that, and maybe she was. Or used to be.

"I'm sorry," he said, his voice low, and he tucked his thumbs into his jeans pockets. "I've been trying to cut that out, but years of practice, you know. Thanks for driving Zane. I'm just angry I forgot to pick him up."

He stepped out into the demolished living room. "So I guess you've seen the living room. My buddy Travis came by yesterday morning and we got the pipe installed, finally." He pointed to the stove pipe.

She looked up to see where the pipe angled backward and went up through the ceiling. Directly above the stove was an ornate grate to let some of the warm air up to the second floor. She was intrigued. Was that original to the house or had Colton added it? And the pipe, which appeared to go through the wall to the kitchen before going up—why make it so complicated? She wanted to see the upstairs and figure it all out.

"The kitchen cabinets are next. They're easy to install. They're those new laminates, but not the cheap kind." He chewed on his lip. "I guess you'd need a kitchen sink, right? But I won't have

Zane around to help me with that until next weekend."

"I could help." She couldn't believe the words came out of her mouth. She tried to backtrack. "I mean, I've helped rehang cabinets before. With my dad. Not that I would hang these, of course, I'm just saying ..." She locked her teeth together. I bet this is what truth serum feels like, she thought. Random but true nonsense pours out of your mouth for no good reason.

Colton looked amused. His eyes glittered green, and the lines around his eyes settled comfortably into grooves that seemed deep for his age. Not that she knew how old he was. Looking at him made her feel young and naive, and she didn't like it.

"I have a hard time picturing that, Poppy Field," he said.

She smirked and almost corrected him. Maybe he'd gotten her middle and last name mixed up. Or maybe he just enjoyed bothering her the way Geoff did. It used to be funny. But near the end of their relationship, there was something about his barbs that she couldn't put her finger on. Something bitter. She turned away. "Can I see upstairs?"

"Sure, go on up. Look out for the cords." His

boots sounded loud behind her, so loud that she thought he was entirely too close.

The upstairs was a disaster. The vaulted ceiling was covered with cheap, old paneling, as were the walls, except for the many places the panels had been ripped to shreds.

"Drywall's not in yet," he said. "I've been thinking about tongue and groove, but I'm not sure."

Upstairs, she could fully appreciate the dormer windows. The house was symmetrical—three window dormers facing the mountains to the back, three more in the front. At the end of the house were two more doors. One was open, revealing a wallpapered disaster of a room with water damage.

She headed into the bathroom. Clean, new white tiles, pale gray paint. It had a new toilet, which looked as if it was working, and a double sink, although Colton hadn't connected the plumbing to the faucets. But at the end of the room, tucked under the dormer, was a claw-foot tub. It was gorgeous. Colton caught her staring.

"Found that in a neighbor's yard," he said. "She used it as a flower garden. I found a place in Billings that put new paint on it. Not paint, what do you call it?"

"Glaze."

"Yeah, that's it. Gotta get the sink in, sorry."

It was beautiful, clean, and bright. Although sinks would help.

She walked back out without a word and opened the only closed door.

Colton had finished that bedroom. The floor was a dark-stained wood, the trim and the angles of the ceiling a bright white, and the lower walls a peaceful shade of pale blue. There was a built-in desk beneath the window, with shelves and a couple of drawers. It looked old, but everything bore a fresh coat of white paint. She looked down. That was where her laptop would sit, books tucked into the shelves below, with a view of the front range of the Beartooth Mountains glistening above her.

"Here's the closet," Colton said. He opened a small door to a long and narrow closet. It had been carved out of the space between the bathroom and bedroom, and the ceiling sloped downward into barely usable space. "It's not very big," he added.

There was more than enough space for all of her belongings, but she didn't say so. It would be insane. And to live in a house like this, with all of its shortcomings, would be far beyond her budget. But she was curious.

"How much?" she asked, her voice sounding stupidly meek.

Colton started chewing on his lip. He put his hands on his hips and walked from the closet to a window and back again. Finally, he said a number and Poppy stood in stunned silence.

"I could take some off if you help me with the cabinets."

"You're way too low."

He cocked his head sideways and frowned at her. "Low?"

"Low."

"There's no sink. Anywhere in the house. I didn't mean it to be that way, but walking through right now it's pretty obvious."

"For that money, I'd get a shared bedroom in an apartment in town," she said.

"Depending on who you share it with, that could be a good deal," he said with a grin. Then he coughed and corrected himself. "I think it's fair."

"Hey!" Zane called from below. "What do you think, Poppy?"

She needed space and time to think. She started to walk out of the room, but as she did, Colton caught her by both shoulders and turned her toward him. It was such an intimate thing for him to do that her only response was to look up into his eyes. They looked different now, a dark gray-green, as he frowned at her. "I gave you two black eyes," he said.

She blinked. His hands were hot on her arms. It couldn't be normal to put off that much body heat.

"I'm sorry," he said.

"It was an accident."

He looked relieved, she decided. It struck her as an odd response. Did he think that was the reason she was hesitant to say yes to renting the house? Because he couldn't be that desperate for tenants. If he was, why? She felt vaguely suspicious.

And she was still staring up into his eyes. She pulled away quickly and looked down, picking her way across the power tools and the cords that led to an old red compressor. This time he took his time following her on the stairs.

Tucked neatly under Zane's arm was a short, curvy, black-haired girl. The first thing Poppy noticed was an abundance of black makeup. The second was the gum chewing. "Hey," Mara said in a most disinterested way.

"Hi. I'm Poppy."

"Poppy? Really?"

"Yes."

"Were your parents high?"

"Probably."

Mara laughed and Poppy smiled—not because it was funny, but because when Mara laughed, dimples dove into her cheeks and she showed a brilliant white smile that was impossible to ignore. Just as fast as the laughter came, it disappeared. For a moment Mara looked as annoyed—or was it embarrassed?—as Poppy felt.

Zane squeezed Mara's shoulders with his arm. He stared at her with open admiration. "Ready to get at it, babe?"

"Sure. I wore my work boots." She smirked and lifted up a high wedge heel covered in buckles. It matched the black leather adornments on the outside of her jeans, ones that gave a hint of motorcycle chaps.

Footsteps on the stairs above her meant Poppy was trapped. The happy couple blocked her escape below; the landlord blocked her escape above.

"You're going to stay, right?" Zane said.

"I have an extra pair of gloves," Colton said behind her.

"My gloves are in the truck." There it was

again, the talking without thinking. It wasn't like her at all. She was far more nervous than the situation called for. And she hated being pressured into a decision, and yet here she was. Getting the gloves meant renting the house.

"Great," Zane said, and he backed himself and Mara away, leaving room for her to escape. So she did, without another word. She closed the front door behind her.

She could drive away right now, she thought. She didn't owe anybody anything. She could find another place to live. In Billings, the prices were better, Bettina the real estate agent had said. But it was just another cold city in the middle of flat land. She didn't want to be there, she wanted to be here, tucked safely against the mountains as winter closed in.

It was so cold in Montana you could throw boiling water in the air and it would turn to snow before it hit the ground. She'd seen it on the Internet. Who would choose to live this far north when the whole country was open to her?

She opened her truck and saw her work gloves tucked into the pocket of the door. Why not stay? "I want to stay," she said out loud.

She picked up the gloves and slipped them over her hands. The leather was stiff but molded to fit. She looked up at the fading yellow house. She could stay. But she couldn't fall in love with this house. It wasn't her home, and it never would be. Come December, she'd be back in Tucson where she belonged.

She took a few tools from behind her seat. It suddenly was important to look useful, even professional. If the room she would be staying in had once looked anything like the peeling, water-stained mess of the other bedroom, Colton knew what he was doing. The last thing she wanted was to have nothing to contribute to the renovation.

CHAPTER 8

$\mathcal{P}$oppy heard a crashing noise above her as she came into the house and jogged up the steps. Mara was standing just outside the door of the unfinished bedroom with her arms crossed and hips cocked to one side, and inside she could see a shower of dust falling as Zane swatted it away with a gloved paw. Once she stepped inside the room, she saw Colton. He wielded a huge black hammer over his head, apparently aimed at nothing in particular, and it crashed and ripped through layers of plaster and laths along the angled ceiling of the room. "Yee-haw!" he cried out, and the hammer fell again.

Colton took a break to rip away pieces of the

lath wall. "Hey, wiring," he said. "Maybe there was a light here once."

"Did you turn off the breakers?" Zane asked.

"Nope. Guess I should."

"I'll get it," Zane offered as he jogged out of the room.

Only the window near Colton was open, so Poppy opened the other. When she turned back, she saw Colton toss something out the window, and it hit the ground with a clank. Curious, she peeked out. There was a trailer parked below.

Colton looked at the tools in Poppy's hands. "You call that a hammer?"

Poppy's hand tightened around her purple-handled hammer and the matching adjustable screwdriver and wrench. "Yes, I do."

"Here, take this." He picked a hammer off the floor, an ancient one with a wooden handle and a bent claw that looked nearly as old as the house. Her arm dropped from the weight of it as he let go.

"I'll take yours," Mara offered, and she ventured into the room, carefully stepping over debris in her high-heeled boots. Her hands covered in black leather fingerless driving gloves, she reached toward Poppy. Poppy offered her the hammer, feeling—ridiculously, she decided—as though she was betraying it.

Without warning, Colton swung the hammer again, and Poppy had to step back and cough as more debris rained down.

"You're a jerk," Mara said to him.

Colton smiled and kept swinging.

Poppy started removing the frame from around the far window, and after watching her for a while, Mara joined in. The cold breeze through the window was blissfully clean. Poppy tried to concentrate on that rather than the deafening noise as Colton and Zane gleefully demolished the ceiling. Poppy was pretty sure they should have been wearing masks and goggles, but she wasn't going to be the one to bring it up. Besides, they were doing in minutes what would have taken her hours.

She and Mara started in on the baseboards next. Mara never asked for direction, but once Poppy did something, Mara was quick to pick it up. Curious, Poppy glanced at her. Mara's perfect black hair was covered in plaster dust, and her clothes were already a mess, but she never stopped working. Poppy had to work hard to keep ahead of her.

The men had cleared nearly all of the ceiling when Zane said, "Whoa, is that a bat?"

Mara jumped to her feet. "Is it alive?"

Poppy saw the small, shriveled form against a bare rafter above their heads. Colton poked it with his hammer, and it fell to the floor. Mara jumped and yelled an angry "Hey!"

"It's dead," Poppy said. She wanted to reassure the girl, but she hadn't done more than state the obvious.

"How did it get in there?" Zane asked.

There was a patchwork of wood near where the bat had been, covering what was probably a hole in the roof. At some point that hole might have been the entrance to a handy place to live, and she wondered if the bat's descendants still lived nearby.

"Who knows," Colton answered. "But if you're looking for corpses, wait until we get in there." He swept his hammer around, indicating the walls close to the floor. "It's like a mouse burial ground."

"Dang," Mara said. "I'm not touching that."

"Then let's eat before we dig them all up," Zane said.

Poppy's purple-handled hammer dropped to

the floor as Mara rushed for the door. "I'll help you get it ready."

She and Mara had managed to remove all the wood trim, label it, and move it out into the other room. Now what remained was to shovel more of the debris out the window, and Poppy wasn't looking forward to it. She saw a nail protruding from one of the rafters, one of many, and started to pry it free.

"You don't have to do that," Colton said. He spotted a similar nail and sank it flush with one strike. She was jealous of his perfect, casual aim.

"But what if you hit the nail head when you go to hang drywall?"

"Then I'll hammer it in somewhere else. That's better than sinking it in an old hole so that it won't hold tight for the next hundred years."

Well, that was one way to look at it. It still seemed like a sloppy shortcut to her, one that might leave extra holes in the drywall.

"Besides," Colton added, "it's a piece of history. Scars add character."

She had noticed he had a few scars of his own, white lines along his arms below his T-shirt sleeves. She realized her gaze was headed that way, and she made herself look him in the eye instead. Dazzling eyes. Lots of colors, flecks of this and that. She wondered what single word he chose to put on his driver's license. "Green" didn't seem sufficient. They weren't green, exactly. Not a real grass green or the color of leaves, at least.

"If you're wondering, I have enough food for you, too, even though you're an uninvited guest."

He didn't hide the fact that he was teasing her. The dimple on his right cheek deepened.

"I'd be happy to head out before the mouse-travaganza starts."

He laughed. "It's not as bad as I made it sound. It's just fun to watch Mara squirm. And even though he's better at hiding it, Zane isn't a fan of mice, either."

"I'd probably better stay since I'm Zane's ride home."

He frowned. "I forgot to apologize to him." He jogged out of the room and down the stairs, hammer still in hand. Poppy followed, and she heard Colton say from downstairs, "I was supposed to pick you up. I forgot!"

Zane laughed. "You remembered. Just not in time."

At the bottom of the stairs, Poppy turned the corner to see a pile of sandwiches on top of the old red table. Mara swatted Colton's hands away from the food, and Zane took that opportunity to grab a pickle. But there was nowhere to run, and she caught him three steps into the kitchen and demanded the pickle back and a hug for payment.

Poppy smiled, but inside her feelings were a jumble. She felt out of place. Things were too close, too intimate here. She didn't belong.

"Have a seat," Colton said. "All the sandwiches are the same, today's special from Marty's." Mara returned and handed Poppy a sandwich as Colton unwrapped the paper from his.

"What is it?"

"I have no idea," he said and took a huge bite.

Too many onions, Poppy decided, but delicious. It was something like a Philly cheesesteak, but with a sweetness to the sauce she couldn't identify.

"So are you selling the house or the whole ranch?" Mara asked.

Colton, who had been pretty animated, stopped all movement except a slow chewing. Across the table, she saw Zane throw Mara a pleading look.

"What?" Mara said. "Zane said that's why we're fixing the place up."

"I didn't ..." Zane started, then reconsidered his words. "I didn't say I knew." He looked at Mara, the table, and behind him to the boarded-up wall. No one spoke, and the silence drew out to an unnatural length.

"Not sure yet," Colton said. "Bettina is looking into a few things for me." He took another bite of his sandwich.

But Mara wasn't done. Either she didn't feel the awkwardness or she didn't care, Poppy thought. Or maybe the girl even enjoyed the drama, as teenage girls sometimes do. "Anson said you'd lose the whole ranch if you try to hold on to it."

"Mara." Zane's voice held disappointment. He glanced toward his cousin, not quite up to eye level, and swallowed. "He didn't say that. Not like that."

Colton set his sandwich down and leaned back in his chair. "Oh, I bet he did." He crossed his arms over his chest and looked around, eyes skimming the old wallpaper and the bare flooring before fixing on something beyond the boarded up wall. "You're dad's got good business sense, Zane."

Mara leaned forward. Just seeing her gear up to speak made Poppy want to run and hide. "Dad said it's a good thing your Grandma's ranch is run-down, or else you would have had a huge inheritance tax."

This time, Zane just put his head in his hands. "Mara."

"What? He's an investment broker. He handles estate taxes all the time. Colton, your dad, and your uncle all got a piece of the ranch when your grandma died, and if they sell it now, there won't be any capital gains taxes. I still don't get why Colton inherited a third of the ranch instead of his dad, you know, split it between the three sons? I guess that's because he took off, right?"

"Mara, please."

"What your girlfriend said is true," Colton said to his cousin. "I'm sure your dad told you. Anson, Cash, and I all have a chance to walk away with a pretty penny. And knowing Anson and Julia, they'd pass a lot of that on to you and your brothers." He looked sideways at Mara. "And Beau did get something. He got his loans forgiven. Believe me, it was more than he deserved."

Mara shrugged. "Whatever. Dad says you should sell it before the end of the year. Price it however it'll sell."

Colton gave her a slow grin. "Mara, as much as I admire your dad, and I don't, I'm not going to base my future on what he says. Although it's special to know I'm the talk of the town. Again."

"Dad's not gossiping, I swear. He's just worried about you," Zane said.

"He's worried I'm going to screw this up."

"It's not like that. He just thinks there's no way to pay for all the work that needs to be done without selling off the cattle, and if there's no cattle, there's no ranch."

Zane's last words seemed to sting Colton worse than anything Mara had said.

"Zane, I won't let this hurt your family or the hotel," Colton said.

Mara snorted and began picking at the insides of her sandwich.

"It'll work out," Colton said. He sat straight and started eating again.

Disappointment. It was as clear in Zane's expression as it had been in Mara's. But Colton didn't look up in time to see it. Did Zane want him to sell the ranch too?

Mara and Zane recovered first, and their conversation quickly changed to the new counselor at the high school. Mara had just moved from Louisiana, and besides talking funny, the students were in agreement that she'd never make it through her first Montana winter. Poppy wondered if they had the same opinion of her, the Arizona girl.

She needed some cold-weather gear, but she didn't have the cash, and that fact reminded her of the ten-day hold on her transfer from the trust fund. She wondered if banks in a small town like Moose Hollow closed early and decided she still had time to drop by and figure out what she could do about it. The whole thing made her nervous. And that five-thousand-dollar check she'd sent herself? There was nothing to guarantee that would be deposited any sooner. She should have done more research before choosing a bank, of course, but she knew she'd only be here for a couple of months, so it didn't seem worth switching now. She could survive on her cash savings if she were careful.

She knew how to be careful. She glanced at Colton and found whatever expression she was wearing had made him frown.

"What's wrong?"

"Just doing a little math in my head. You'll want first, last, and a deposit, right?"

He looked perplexed.

"She means rent," Mara supplied. She went back to her conversation with Zane.

"Oh. Sure. First and last month's rent. Although I can't see any reason for a deposit, since you've already left the place better than you found it."

"But what about prorating the utilities, electricity, Internet service?"

"Don't worry about that; we can figure it out later."

"Figure it out later" had rarely worked in Poppy's favor in the past, but she let it go. Mara added, "There's no Internet here, you'll have to order it. And the phone service is spotty too. That's why I get to ignore the last two text messages my dad sent me." She held up her phone and wrinkled her nose.

"The landline is still connected here. I'll give them a call and get it sorted out." She half expected him to stand up and start making calls, but he didn't. He finished his sandwich. When he finally stood and stretched, he said, "Time to get back at it. We spent more time eating than working."

Poppy wanted to get back to the bank, but she felt guilty at the thought of leaving the project unfinished. Another hour wouldn't hurt.

Finishing the walls stretched into installing the second bathroom sink, and while Mara and Zane went for a walk, she and Colton discussed codes and where to place the side walls in the large upstairs family room. That conversation trailed off, and for a while Colton stood with his arms crossed, eyebrows pinched, staring at her. "I'm sorry about your nose," he said gruffly. "It looks awful."

She wondered if he saw something she didn't. She'd decided this morning her nose looked much as it always did, maybe a little puffier. She wondered if the bruising was getting worse. She ducked into the bathroom for a look. The bruises seemed to have spread, streaking farther now from the inside corners of her eyes out along her upper and lower eyelids.

"Oh, I don't know," she said. "It's not that bad. Besides, I've seen professional models with makeup just like this. If I slicked my hair back and wore a lot of black clothing, I'd be avant-garde."

The dimple on his right cheek deepened but his lips stayed pressed into a thin line. "You're being nice."

"Is there a problem with that?"

He stuck his left leg out in front of him and bent and unbent it at the knee as if it was troubling him. "No. Sorry I freaked out so bad last night. I should probably tell you...well, I mean, if you're going to live here you should know ..."

Mara's stifled laugh turned their attention toward the front door, and a moment later the young couple came inside, jostling against each other and giggling. "Colton," Zane said, "it's getting late. If I don't get home in time to help with dinner, Mom's going to flip."

Before he could respond, Mara walked over and pointed at the phone. It was an old model, with a cord, hung on the wall just inside the kitchen. To the side of it, at least a dozen names and numbers had been scribbled in pencil. "Did you call the Internet company?"

"Ah! I will."

Mara glowered at him like a stern mom, not a girl who was probably a decade younger than him.

"I will right now," he amended. He glanced back at Poppy. "Testy, testy, testy," he muttered.

While Colton rummaged through a stack of mail near the phone, Mara gave Poppy a satisfied look. "You'll thank me later."

Did he really have such a bad reputation for following through on his promises? She would need to remember that. If she wasn't careful, his problems could become hers.

She turned her attention to Zane. "Need a ride home?"

"That would be great," he said.

Mara shook her head. "Your parents are so hard."

"They worry about me," Zane said. Poppy's opinion of him went up a notch.

"No, they worry about me," Mara said. Poppy could tell from the way Mara tipped up her chin that she meant to use the same sassy tone she used for most everything she said, but there was a hint of something plaintive in her voice, as if her throat caught as she was speaking. Mara cared what Zane's parents thought of her.

Poppy thought of gathering up her tools, but they were tucked away upstairs, and she couldn't imagine she'd be using them at the hotel. So she grabbed her jacket and waved at Colton. He covered the phone's receiver with his hand. "Thanks, you guys. If you're bored tomorrow afternoon ..."

"Yeah, yeah, yeah," Zane said with a smile.

Poppy went to her truck to make herself scarce while the teenagers said good-bye. She tried not to watch, but she noticed that they looked nervous and smitten, holding hands but avoiding eye contact. Soon after, Poppy heard Zane loping over to the truck. If they'd managed a kiss, it had been a brief one.

She turned the ignition, and her truck considered waking up, then went back down for a nap. "How long have you guys been dating?" she asked.

"Almost a month. I don't know if it was dating at first. We were just friends."

Mara didn't look like the "just friends" type, especially since her fondness for Zane was pretty clear. The girl spun the black Escalade's tires, and Zane waved as she pulled away.

"Maybe three weeks," he said. "I should figure that out."

"Your first kiss would be a good starting point." Poppy turned the key again, and although the motor sounded more hopeful, it didn't catch. She let it rest for a minute. No need to stress a weak battery.

Zane gave her a sideways look. "I've never kissed Mara."

That would explain the awkward good-bye. "Oh. You guys seemed closer than that."

"We are close," he said. "We just don't kiss."

Poppy nodded, trying to look as if it was perfectly normal for two good-looking and in-love young people never to kiss. "Sorry, it's none of my business."

"No biggie." In an effort to make room for his long legs, Zane pushed his seat back as far as it would go. "Colton's going to need help with hanging drywall. I wish Dad would come out. He's great at that sort of thing. He's great at fixing everything. You might want to have him look at your truck."

Poppy ignored that and gave the ignition another go. This time, the starter sounded even more sluggish. "Does your dad work at the hotel too, then?"

"Yeah. It keeps him busy since a lot of the stuff there is old. There's always something to fix—furniture, the plumbing, the boiler, everything."

"And your mom?"

"She runs everything else."

Poppy thought of how Julia looked when she first checked in, wearing a simple uniform and a name tag. "I thought she was just a clerk."

"Yeah, she does that on purpose. She says it looks bad to have the owner working the front desk all the time, like they don't have enough money to hire more staff. Which they don't."

"What happens when someone demands to see the manager?"

"They dress my dad up in a suit."

Poppy laughed. "That's clever."

"It works, too. He's tall, really tall."

That meant something, coming from Zane. She glanced over at the way the teen's knees rested against her dashboard. Whatever he looked like, Anson Gunnerson probably wouldn't fit in her truck.

"He can be intimidating. He throws a few big words around, looks down on people, and then everything gets settled. And Mom gets back to running things."

Poppy took a deep breath. She was ready to get going, and she hoped her truck was too. Sure, it was cranky sometimes, but except for a few battery issues, it had never failed to start before. "They're both busy, then," she said, ready to give the ignition another try. She only meant to affirm what Zane had been saying, not to ask for more details, but he kept talking, so she waited.

"Yeah. My brothers are older, and I'm the only one left to help." He drummed long fingers on his bony knee. "I don't know what they're gonna do when I'm gone. But I don't want to work in the hotel forever. And I can get better pay. The refinery is hiring again. It's a long drive, but it's worth it. The insurance coverage is great."

Refinery? Insurance? Wasn't he too young to think about such things? "How old are you, Zane?"

"Almost eighteen."

"It seems like all you should be worrying about is prom and college."

He laughed. "Yeah, you'd think so. It doesn't always work out that way."

Worry bubbled up in Poppy's chest. A family struggling to run a large hotel wouldn't be in a position to pay for college. He sure seemed smart and hardworking to her, but maybe he didn't have the grades to get a good scholarship. And she'd never wish the debt load of student loans on anyone.

She tried to start her truck again. She tried pumping the gas, then she tried holding the pedal down in case she'd flooded it—even though the darn thing didn't have a carburetor—and with each attempt, the battery was running down.

As she continued her futile efforts, she pictured Zane commuting to whatever refinery he was talking about, wearing a hard hat, coming home to a girlfriend he never kissed. You just never know about people, she thought. You never know what makes them tick or what secret burdens they carry.

Zane gave her a big, sympathetic smile. "You know it's not going to work," he said. "You'd better just give up."

CHAPTER 9

*I*t was four o'clock, and she was about twenty minutes from the bank. That left her with forty minutes to park, stand in line, and get the hold removed from her deposit. Watching two Gunnerson men lean over her engine compartment and make jokes about the lawnmower having more horsepower than her truck was making her head hurt. And although they seemed to be reaching a consensus about what was wrong, they weren't moving very fast.

"I'll just call a tow company," she said finally.

Colton leaned sideways to give her a funny look. "Why, you got a friend there?"

"No. I need to get to the bank before it closes."

"And I gotta get home," Zane added.

"No problem." Colton dropped the hood, and it fell with a *clang* that made her jump. She half expected the windshield to break. "I'll grab a jacket and drive you guys into town. We can fix the truck later."

The only other vehicle around was parked a few yards away. It was a pickup, a big one that was possibly newer than hers, although it was hard to tell. The sides of the bed were dented, and the hood was buckled in the front. Even the top of the cab looked dented. She had a hard time believing it had rolled without collapsing the cab, but something had happened to it. Or many somethings. She checked to make sure her wallet was in her pocket and locked the doors of her truck.

Zane was ahead of her, climbing into the cab as she walked over. There was one bench seat, and he was trying to fit into the middle, looking for a way to arrange his legs that would leave the stick shift free. "I think you'd better let me sit there," she said. He threw her a relieved look and slid back out.

She was shorter than Zane, but she wasn't short, and as she climbed into the cab, it wasn't clear to her what she was going to do with her legs. The long stick shift lever came back close to the seat. She put a leg on either side of the hump over the drive shaft, but as the driver's side door opened, she realized the driver would have to reach between her legs to shift. That wouldn't do. She crossed her legs to the right of the stick, bumping into Zane.

"You guys cozy?" Colton asked. He put his cowboy hat upside down on Poppy's lap and started the truck. It rumbled, sounding like it had no muffler, and the whole cab vibrated and hummed. He pulled out slowly and cruised down the ranch's dirt roads. All the while she was waiting for him to put his hat somewhere else, but he never did. And there wasn't a lot of space between the top of his head and the roof of the truck.

Poppy glanced at her watch.

"Colton doesn't like driving fast on these roads because it makes washboards," Zane said.

She nodded, embarrassed her impatience was obvious. The truth was, the truck jarred and bounced so much at this speed, she was happy they weren't going any faster. She didn't have anything to hold on to, and it took a lot of con-centration to make sure she didn't kick Zane in the calf every time they hit a bump. To make matters worse, the gear shift knob, stuck down in second gear, was poking into her left thigh.

When they drove past the hay bales, she glanced at Colton, and she could have sworn there was a frown on his face. So the way they were stacked *did* bother him.

"I promised you I'd tell Mom you drove me into town, Poppy," Zane said. "I didn't forget."

"Julia didn't know?" Colton asked.

"Nope, and Poppy didn't want her to be mad."

"Shoot. If I'd remembered, there wouldn't be any problem. But Julia will be okay with it; she just might be a little mad you asked a guest to drive. We'll just make it clear you're not a guest anymore, Poppy, you're a roommate."

"Roommate?" She felt the color rise in her face. Had she been so stupid? She had assumed Colton lived someplace else, but his truck was parked at the house. What had she missed? Hadn't he asked permission to come over to work on the homestead?

He was smiling at her. Instead of looking at the road. "Scared you, didn't I? Don't worry. I live in the bunkhouse about a quarter mile up the other driveway."

She heard Zane snicker.

Once they hit the paved road, all hell broke

loose. The truck engine roared, the back wheels skidded, and Poppy watched the speedometer needle rise way past a reasonable speed for a two-lane road. She was about to say something when she spotted a speed limit sign. Colton was doing exactly four miles an hour over the speed limit. It wasn't enough to start a fight over. Besides, he was doing her a favor.

She was relieved when they got closer to town and the speed limit dropped. So did Colton's speed, to exactly four miles an hour over that. She wondered about that. Maybe he just wanted to make sure when he got a ticket, it wasn't terribly expensive.

Come to think of it, she hadn't seen a police officer at all. In Tucson she'd never driven more than five minutes without passing one.

The speed limit mercifully dropped to twenty-five, and Colton turned down two alley-ways and pulled into a small parking lot near the hotel. After he got out, she held his hat out to him, and as she climbed out, she thanked him for the drive and then headed toward Main Street.

"Hey, this way," Colton said, gesturing to the same door Zane had used to leave this morning.

"I have to go to the bank."

"Come on, you've got to convince Julia you're

an okay chaperone. It'll only take a second." He yanked on the door and held it open.

Only a second, she reassured herself, reluctantly heading inside. And as she passed by him, Colton said, "You might not want to mention that they went on an hour-long walk alone together."

"They aren't allowed to take a walk? He's seventeen."

"Don't worry, it didn't break any rules. It's just not worth poking the bear."

Julia was a bear now? The nice woman who had nursed her not-quite-broken nose? That was hard to imagine.

"They're upstairs," Zane said, catching up with them. "Melissa said they're in the corner room."

"Uh oh," Colton said. He took hold of Poppy's elbow and turned her back toward the stairs. It took her by surprise. No one had ever done that to her before—physically led her somewhere. At least not as an adult. It was annoying, but by the time they reached the stairs, he'd let go.

"Do you think the roof caved in again?" Colton asked.

"Don't even joke about it, Colton," Zane said. "Whatever it is, it can't be good. I don't think either one of them has set foot in there in a year.

Or more. Maybe this isn't the time to talk with them, okay?"

The men jogged up the stairs, leaving Poppy behind them, but they slowed when they reached the landing. "Nah. It'll be all right," Colton said.

She could hear voices down the hall and see a slit of light through a door there. As they walked, the voices became clearer: a man and a woman, speaking in less-than-friendly tones.

A few words came through loud and clear. "And pay for it with what?" the woman said.

Colton stopped, and a few steps later Zane did too. "Zane, are you parents having money trouble?" Colton asked.

Zane shoved his hands deep into his jean pockets and shrugged his shoulders forward. "It's a little tight." His gaze remained fixed on the ground.

Colton strode for the corner room. "What do you think, Zane," he said loudly, "should we do beadboard or drywall on the ceiling upstairs?" He was announcing their arrival, Poppy realized, giving Julia and Anson time to gather themselves.

A beat passed before Zane said, "Um, I like the wood paneling," at equal volume.

Colton pushed the door wide. "Julia! Anson!"

Julia's eyes took in the three of them quickly,

her expression remaining neutral. Anson, however, was only looking at Colton. "Long time no see," the older man said.

"I've been meaning to drop by."

But he had dropped by, the night before, and he and Julia had seemed close enough then. Evidently, his relationship with his uncle wasn't as close. And Poppy knew none of it was her business. She had to get to the bank, so the sooner she left, the better.

Colton spoke up again. "I wanted to let you know that I forgot to pick up Zane this morning, but since Poppy was on her way, she gave Zane a ride."

"Oh, thank you," Julia said.

No bear there, Poppy thought. She was distracted by the room and wondered if a change of topic would be good. "This room is amazing," she said, taking it all in. The majority of the room was within a rounded corner of the building, the top room of the castle tower she'd admired from outside. Near the corner of the building the ceiling was open to the structure of the roof, and around it the remnants of a lovely plastered ceiling showed terrible water damage. But the bare bones were good. "The high ceilings, the architecture. And you've still got a lot of the original woodwork. It's really beautiful. It looks like the ceiling was raised in the tower part—that must have been something to see."

"How's the ranch, Colton?" Anson asked.

Startled by how thoroughly she was being dismissed, Poppy turned back to Anson and Julia. Julia was looking at the ground, her arms crossed across her chest. Anson's hands were on his hips, and he was staring at Colton. They had similar looks, the two men, and Poppy suspected that if Anson had been wearing a hat, they'd look like brothers, not uncle and nephew.

"Good. Good enough."

Everyone stood silently. The moment was so awkward that Poppy didn't dare make a move to leave.

"I'm putting the house up for sale, along with a little land," Colton said. Then, more brightly, "Poppy's my new tenant in the meantime, and it looks like she'll be pretty handy with the renovations."

Poppy could feel the color rising to her face. She wanted to be anywhere but there at that moment, watching the way Anson's gaze bored right into Colton. But she felt glued in place.

"That's a pretty big decision," Anson said. His tone was low and measured. "I would have thought you'd talk to Cash and me about something that big."

"Well, I am now." At that moment Colton's voice lost all its normal volume and he sounded almost exactly like his uncle.

The feeling that someone was about to say something awful pressed in on Poppy, until at last she said, "I'd better go. I love the chandelier. I rewired one just like it...well, not that ornate, but I've done it before, so if you're looking for any help, I know a few tricks." No response. "I'm off now. Nice to see you again, Julia, and to meet you, Mr. Gunnerson."

And she turned tail, leaving more silence behind her. Halfway down the hall, she heard footsteps behind her, and Zane met her at the stairs.

"My mom and dad are nice people, usually."

Poppy wasn't sure about that. But Mara said that Anson's mom, Colton's grandmother, had recently died. And she'd left them a big ranch and a financial mess. Death, inheritance, money issues —that didn't bring out the best in anyone. But they didn't need to be so cold to her. All she'd done was compliment them on the tower room. "It's okay. I had fun working with you and Mara today."

A smile spread across his face. "Mara's great, isn't she?"

Oh, dear. He was in love. "Yeah," Poppy said.

She gave him a quick wave good-bye and trotted down the steps. She had to get to the bank.

The sun was gone, but the sky was still bright. Days were shorter this far north. She was grateful when she ducked into the cozy warmth of the bank. Coffee. The place was filled with the scent now, and it triggered a craving in Poppy.

There was no one at the front desk, but there were two tellers behind a counter and no customers. "May I help you?" a very young woman called. The older woman to her side, a beaded necklace dangling from her glasses, didn't look up.

"I hope so," Poppy said, stepping up to the counter. "I made a transfer yesterday, and when I logged into my account today, I could see that the transfer went through but there's a hold on the account."

"I'll check into that," the girl said cheerfully. They did hire their tellers young, she thought. The tellers at her Tucson bank, which, Poppy assumed, demanded someone with a solid work record before granting her access to so much cash, were never this young.

The teller typed, paused, typed some more, then finally asked, "Your account number?"

She'd been handed a card with a six-digit number on it when she opened the account, but it was back in the hotel room. The teller asked for her name instead, and after what seemed like a lot of searching, she found Poppy's account. "I'll need to call the bank where this came from." More typing ensued, and the teller's expression grew increasingly confused. She shot a couple of furtive glances at the older woman but kept trying. Poppy shifted her feet, waited, and shifted again.

"Carla? I can't find a phone number," the girl finally said.

"Mmm?" Carla didn't look up.

"Could you help me?"

Heaving a sigh, Carla came over to help. She leaned over the girl's shoulder and pointed to the screen. "See this? Click there. Press F4."

The girl did as she was told, and smiled. "Thank you." She wrote something down on a sticky note and said, "I'll be right back."

Poppy heard the door behind her open, but Carla never looked up. If a customer had entered, he'd have to wait for Poppy's spot. She looked down at the pen holder anchored to the polished wood counter. She wished she had a working phone to play with, because it would make her feel more invisible.

The girl was dialing again, for the third time. And she was glancing over at Carla, silently pleading for help. Finally, she asked, "Press nine to dial out, right?"

"Mm-hmm."

The girl dialed again.

"Isn't there a code for dialing long distance?"

Poppy looked at Carla. Was there even such a thing as long distance anymore? "I'm not sure," Carla said.

"Could I use your code? They haven't given me one yet."

Carla slowly pushed her glasses back up her nose and turned around to face her coworker. "Is there something wrong?"

"It won't go through. I've checked the number twice, but it won't go through."

"Maybe they're not in business anymore," Carla said. She turned her gray eyes on Poppy, then went back to whatever tiny task was engrossing her. Dissecting mice for fun, perhaps, Poppy thought.

The girl returned to her computer screen and double-checked her sticky note against what she saw on the computer screen. "Did you get this electronic transfer from someone who lives out of the country?" she asked.

Poppy felt the color rising in her face. Were they suspicious of her? Really? "No. It's my account. And it's not a foreign account, it's located in California." She was considering what to say about long-distance phone codes, ten-day holds, and Carla's helpfulness when she heard the customer who had entered the bank and stood behind her move for the counter. When the customer brushed against her shoulder, she nearly jumped. Colton.

He handed a phone to the teller. "Here, Merry. Try the number again, but use my phone. I think you might be having a little trouble dialing out."

He lowered one elbow onto the counter and turned to face Poppy. Her face embarrassingly hot, she realized that Colton didn't care to maintain the same personal space around him that she preferred. In fact, with his cowboy hat in his hand at his stomach, pretty much all the space between them was used up. She stumbled for something to say and settled for "Thank you."

"No problem." He just smiled at her.

She tucked her hair behind her left ear, and her right hand went up to her throat. She had nothing to say in the face of his unrelenting smile. When he looked over her shoulder, she finally exhaled.

"How ya doing, Carla?" he asked the older teller.

"Just fine, Colton." She didn't sound fine.

The young teller spoke into the phone. "Hello, this is Merry Stenson from First Main Bank in Moose Hollow, Montana. I was just hoping to check …"

"Just like magic," Colton said to Poppy, the dimple in his cheek showing again. He lifted his chin toward Carla. "Sorry about your long distance code, Carla. You know they say memory is the first to go."

Poppy's eyes widened.

"At least I think that's what they say," he added. "I can't remember." Colton gave her such a brilliant smile the poor woman probably couldn't figure out if he were insulting her or flirting with her.

"I'll give you your privacy," Colton said to Poppy in a low voice, stepping away from the teller station.

"That's right, Poppy F. Marsh," her teller was

saying clearly and loudly into the phone, account number six, four ..."

Poppy took a deep breath. Good thing the bank was empty except for Colton. The girl might as well be using a megaphone. She wished Carla would finish what she was doing and help Colton so he could be on his way. But one glance at Carla's pinched face made it clear she'd decided she'd been insulted and had no intention of helping him.

Merry Stenson's call ended. She looked relieved. "It's already been initiated," she said as she returned to her station. "They said there are sufficient funds to cover the transfer. All I have to do now is get Jeff, our bank manager, to sign off on the transfer."

"He just left." Carla sounded almost pleased.

"What?" Merry said. "But ..."

Carla had to have known Merry would need Jeff's approval, and yet she'd done nothing to stop the manager from leaving, or even let Merry know he was about to leave.

The young teller gave Poppy a sad look. "I'm sorry," she said.

"I'm sorry for you too," Poppy said, tilting her head toward Carla. She didn't care if Carla saw her. "Don't worry about it. I'll come back in the morning."

"I'll leave him a voice mail, so he's expecting your visit. I hope it won't take long."

"Thanks for trying," Poppy said.

Merry handed Colton's phone to Poppy. He was sitting in a comfy chair near the front desk, and he unfolded himself up to his full height as Poppy approached. She handed him his phone, thanked him again, and then marched for the front door. She couldn't get out of the bank soon enough.

CHAPTER 10

olton stayed with her as she walked. "Didn't you need to...?" She gestured toward the bank.

"Nope. Not my bank. I just need to know what to do with your truck. I knew you were going to a bank, so I decided to check all the banks in town to find you."

Poppy put her hand over her mouth. "Oh, I'm sorry."

He smiled. "Don't worry. There are only two, and to be honest, this was the first one I tried."

Even though there was still daylight, the temperature was dropping fast. She zipped her parka up to her neck. "It's getting too late to have it towed."

"You still want to do that?" Colton asked. "It'll cost a hundred and fifty dollars to tow it off the ranch, plus a part worth about forty dollars, and labor. I'm guessing they'll find a way to round it up to three hundred dollars or so. You could have it towed into Billings if you want to pay more."

She didn't have three hundred dollars to spare. What was she supposed to do, leave the truck with the repair shop until the hold on her account cleared?

"Here's what I think we should do," Colton continued. "We should go buy the part before the shop closes. Then we should go out to dinner. Then tomorrow morning I'll fix your truck, drive back here, and move you and your storage area full of belongings out to the house."

She shook her head. "I can't do that."

"You think I'll break your truck."

"I do not." She tried to find the words. She didn't like owing anyone. She didn't like depending on others, either. This wasn't the right way to start out her life as Colton's tenant, a woman without cash or transportation.

"Prove it. Come on." He started heading downhill, away from the mountains. She sprinted to catch up. "Where are we going?"

"Car parts store. It's pretty small, but if they

don't have it, they'll get it from their Billings store in the morning."

"Are you always this stubborn?"

He turned to look her in the eye. "Yes. Yes, I am." And he seemed a little proud of it.

She had about fifty dollars in her wallet. If Colton were right, she would have just enough to pay for whatever car part he was planning to buy.

When they walked into the shop, a grizzled man with blackened hands greeted Colton by name. Colton told him what he was looking for, and the man promised to have it in stock by ten the next morning.

As it turned out, the part was fifty-five dollars, plus tax and a five-dollar delivery fee to have it brought in from Billings. Poppy found an extra twenty dollars stashed in a hidden pocket in her wallet, and after paying for the part, was left with a couple of bucks and some change. She calculated quickly. She had a little cash in the hotel room and what she called her "10 percent" savings, whatever small amount that added up to. If she stayed tomorrow night at the hotel as she had planned, she wouldn't have the money to pay for it all.

"So Colton," the salesman asked, "did you trade your big Ram in for an old Nissan?"

Colton shook his head. "It's hers, Joe."

Joe eyed Poppy. "Were you in a car wreck?" He gestured toward his own eyes and she realized that he meant the spreading bruises around her own. She kept forgetting about that. It didn't hurt anymore; it just felt stuffy and sore to the touch.

"No."

Joe gave her a strange look, as if he was owed an explanation and she was being deceptive by not sharing.

"I was just a klutz."

Apparently satisfied, Joe turned back to Colton. "So which do you like better, fixing trucks or fixing horses?"

"You never fix horses. You fix the rider."

"Now you sound like your buddy Travis. I'll stick to trucks. And tractors. How's that old one running for you?"

"It's not, which means I'll be back for another visit soon. Or soonish."

Poppy was quiet as they walked out of the auto-parts store and into air that seemed to get colder by the second. "Were you serious about me moving in tomorrow?" she asked finally. "Although it might be too late to cancel my reservation."

"No worries. I know people." He took out his

phone, tapped the screen, and held it to his ear. "Hey, Julia, this is Colton. Do you mind if I take Poppy off your hands after tonight? She's going to tape and mud a room for me. Let me know if you'll let her cancel her reservation. Thanks." He slid the phone into his back pocket.

"I said no such thing. I hate doing drywall seams. I hate the sanding part."

"That's perfect. I don't mind the sanding so much; it's the mudding part that makes me crazy. I think we can work something out."

Poppy considered. She still didn't have enough to pay Colton. "I transferred some money from my bank in California, but they put a ten-day hold on it."

"So I figured. Not that I was trying to listen in. Although I did write down your account information so I can steal all your money."

Poppy laughed. "So you noticed that."

"Yeah." He scrunched his face into a funny expression. "Merry's new. She got the job because she's the bank manager's niece. But she's smart, she'll figure it out. Maybe even before Carla poisons her energy drink."

"How do you know these things, Colton?"

"Poppy, in this town, the problem is trying not to know things."

She looked up Broadway. Even the stone and brick buildings had brightly painted trim. The street was lined with hanging baskets of flowers, and even in the cold air she could catch their scent. There were people everywhere along the sidewalks and hardly any cars. When a town is so small that it's one main street is about a dozen blocks long, it made sense that everyone would know everyone else.

"What I was trying to say, Colton, is that until they release that money, I can't pay you rent."

"I know you're good for it."

She wondered if that was just a line he used or if he meant it. And if he did think she was good for it, she wished she knew why.

When they reached the hotel, he opened the door for her, then followed her inside. He leaned closer to talk to her. "What had you planned to do for dinner?"

"I don't know," she said. "Last night I went to the Combine. I don't know the other places in town."

"A few are pretty pricey. The Combine...sure. Why not? It's still early. Mind if I join you?"

Poppy didn't know how to respond to that. Then Julia stepped up to the desk, and her time to graciously decline the invitation was gone. Instead, she mumbled, "I'm going to go get something from my room," waved halfheartedly to Julia, and headed up the stairs.

Her hair was filled with plaster dust and who knows what else. And her face, which had looked a little dusty in the truck's rearview mirror, was streaked and grimy in better light. She brushed her hair out over the bathtub and washed her face. She started to change clothes but reconsidered. That would be like dressing up for a date, and this was most definitely not a date. But what was it? She'd heard a reluctance in his voice. It was as if he felt he had to go to dinner with her.

Of course. She could barely pay for the part for her truck, and she had told Colton she couldn't pay for rent. He felt sorry for her and probably figured he was going to buy. It was the worst kind of attention to get. If only she'd managed to say no as soon as he'd asked. Now he was down in the lobby talking to Julia, probably about her financial situation.

Then again, he hadn't said he was buying. Maybe he was just trying to be polite to his new tenant. Poppy opened the small wooden box with her 10 percent money in it, two neat stacks of one-dollar bills. She'd once heard a money expert say that for every ten dollars you pay someone else, you should pay yourself one dollar. She called it a "tenth for the future." Poppy liked the idea, and so for every ten dollars she spent on groceries and such, she saved one. Pretty soon she was piling up the bills for a rainy day.

She never thought she'd need it so soon. There was enough cash in her bag to pay for the hotel through tonight, and to tow the truck if she needed to, but dining out was pushing her comfort zone.

But this was the rainiest day she'd had in years. She counted out enough one-dollar bills for dinner.

Poppy often thought she should exchange the ones for larger bills, but it was motivational watching the pile grow. And the same principal worked in reverse. Counting out thirty ones for dinner made her want to skip the meal altogether. She tucked the money into the pocket of her jacket and promised herself she'd pay it back as soon as she could.

But from what, her trust fund money? Talk about robbing Peter to pay Paul. The whole mess made her feel worthless and fearful. Worthless because she was taking, not making, money, and threatening her future. Would she get a good job? Would she even pass her thesis defense? If not, what then? Paying for another semester's tuition was just too much to think about. Every cent was important now. She had to cancel their dinner plans.

She was halfway down the stairs when she heard Colton's booming laugh. He was talking with Julia, but when he saw Poppy he smiled and turned her way. Julia smiled too, but it was as if her whole body stiffened. Poppy realized just how much she'd hated the awkwardness in the tower room, and how much she wanted to avoid any conversation with Zane's parents again. Just the thought of it threatened to make the color rise in her face, and instinctively her hand went to her throat, the first place the redness usually showed.

"Ready to go?" Colton said.

Talking to Julia suddenly seemed a lot worse than getting a pity dinner from her landlord, so she nodded and followed him out the door. Realizing she was being rude, she turned back to say good-bye to Julia, but she was already attending to a guest. With a sigh, Poppy went back out into the cold.

She wanted to ask Colton about what had happened with the corner room. The conflict between him and Anson seemed serious, but there was no trace of conflict with Julia. Had they worked everything out after she'd left? She doubted it. Money, inheritance, the sale of a family home—things like that ripped families apart.

They made it to the Combine without exchanging a single word, and he opened the door for her, a gesture that startled her every time he did it. The bright, warm interior of the brewpub drew her in, and she gravitated toward the bar. But the bar was full, faces turned toward her with whoops and shocked expressions, and she began to hear Colton's name called out. She ducked sideways as two men came over to slap his back and welcome him. "Long time no see!" everyone seemed to be saying. The same thing Anson had said.

The group looked like Poppy's idea of real Montana cowboys. Heeled boots, tight jeans, plaid shirts, slouchy hats, and an abundance of confidence. Surrounded by them, Colton fit in well. Maybe he was a little older, though, and she wondered again about his age.

Colton extracted himself, motioning toward her and a table, which brought more unwelcome stares her way. Her black eyes weren't helping, she realized. She made quite a sight with the dirty clothes, too. Like some sort of refugee. One from a nice townhouse in Tucson seeking an advanced degree in botany, she thought wryly. She was tired of looking and feeling like a charity case when she'd worked so hard to be self-sufficient. In the morning she'd get things straightened out with the bank and buy a good concealer.

She felt Colton's hand on her arm again, leading her toward the only open table, a two-top near the front door. As more people entered the brewpub, she felt a cold draft down her back.

Danny came over, took one look at her, and said, "What happened to you?"

It was nice to be asked outright for a change. "Last night I was walking in the hotel as Colton was walking out, and I ran straight into his elbow."

Danny made a face. "Ouch. Is it broken? It doesn't look broken."

"No. It feels fine."

"Good." Danny turned to Colton. "You have a way about you, don't you?"

He shook his head. "I don't want to talk about it."

"I don't blame you," Danny said. She turned back to Poppy. "What would you like? Soup and salad? Creamy tomato tonight."

"Sounds great."

Colton cracked open the menu on the table. "Prime rib night?"

"Yes, you celebrating?"

"Yes. You brought me a tenant with renovation skills. I'm celebrating that."

"Anything else?"

"Nope."

"Good." And with that, Danny was gone, leaving Poppy with the feeling that although she'd heard their whole conversation, she'd missed something.

A burst of laughter from the bar filled the brewpub, and she turned to see most of the cowboys smiling Colton's way. A few were shaking their heads, and one, a young man in a white hat wearing a blue and yellow shirt, lifted his pint of beer in a toast. "Your ears burning, Colton?" he called.

Colton took his hat off, placed it upside down on the table, and ran his fingers through his hair. He was grinning, but he didn't look comfortable. The plaster dust in his hair looked like streaks of gray, and she revised her estimate of his age toward the older end. He clasped the arms of his chair and looked down at the table. The silence between them dragged on.

"Are they friends of yours?" Poppy asked. It was the first thing she'd said in ages, and it was a stupid question. She never had anything good to say when she felt forced.

"We were on the circuit together."

She ran over the word "circuit" in her mind and didn't come up with any reasonable definitions. One stupid question deserved another, she decided. "What circuit?"

She wasn't ready for the surprise in his eyes. "Rodeo," he said, watching her.

It was her time to be surprised. "Rodeo? Do you do rodeo?" She had no idea if one would do rodeo, ride rodeo, or join rodeo. However she said it, it was going to come out awkwardly.

"Do I *do* rodeo?"

She bristled, but he didn't look as if he was making fun of her. He looked confused.

An older man walked up to the table. He nodded toward Poppy, set a full mug of beer on the table, and reached his hand out toward Colton.

"Mr. Gunnerson, I just wanted to come over here and shake your hand."

"Call me Colton," he said, taking the man's hand.

"Call me Tom. Tom McMurphy, Triple T

Ranch near Rifle. My wife and I"—he gestured toward another table and a woman seated there smiled their way—"we were at the finals year before last, and I gotta tell ya, I knew you and Badlands Bodie were going to hit the jackpot. I called it. You can ask the missus. You know those ponies like no one else, Mr. Gunnerson."

"Well, thank you." Colton didn't look surprised, Poppy thought. He looked comfortable. Smooth.

"That was the ride of the whole NFR, son."

"Don't tell that to the bull riders."

The man laughed. "My family's been ranching in Colorado for over a hundred years, son. Not one of us was ever stupid enough to climb up on a bull. It's the horses that show who the real cowboys are." He gestured to the beer. "That's for you. Can I get something for your girl?"

Poppy realized he meant her. "No, thank you," she said.

"Well, there you go. You have a good night, son. Sure hope we get to see you back in the saddle someday."

Colton's smile didn't falter, but it changed. And so did his eyes. They lost some of their glitter, leaving only a murky green. "Thank you, Tom. That's very kind of you."

As the man walked away, Colton turned to- ward Poppy, traces of the smile still lingering on his face. "I'm sorry. This was a bad idea."

She wasn't sure what he meant. Was it that she didn't fit in with his friends—or his fame? It was hard to imagine Colton being famous, and if she hadn't seen him slip into that smooth per- sona on hearing the man's praise, she wouldn't have believed it. He had fans, and more than a couple.

Danny arrived with a tray, set two glasses of water down, then placed a small juice glass full of beer in front of Poppy. Poppy smiled. Each time she'd visited the Combine, the glass had gotten a little smaller, and this time, Danny had brought one that Poppy might be able to finish. That left a basket of bread and one nearly empty mug on her tray.

To Poppy's surprise, Danny picked up the full mug the man had given Colton, put it on her tray, and put the almost empty mug in its place. Then she put the bread down and left without a word.

She had replaced his mug with someone else's leftovers. It was a strange mistake, but it was equally strange that Colton hadn't said a word about it. Maybe he hadn't noticed yet. Poppy thought she should warn him. What if he went to take a drink of it? Who knew what kind of bacteria was on that glass?

When she looked up, she found Colton staring at the mug. He stared at it as a minute ticked by, then looked up at her as if he'd just realized she was there. "So Tucson's a pretty big town. Ever see a rodeo there? Camp Verde? Flagstaff? Phoenix? I think the PBR has a show there."

She shook her head. "Sorry."

"Ever seen a rodeo at all?"

"Not that I can remember."

He nodded. "You're probably not missing much." He moved the mug farther away from him and put his elbows on the table. "So how did you end up in Moose Hollow, Poppy Marsh?"

She shrugged. "I'm finishing my thesis. My fieldwork is done, so I can do that anywhere. I visited here once and thought it was nice. And I guess I needed a break from Tucson."

"Do you ski?"

"No."

He nodded. "Just broke up with your boyfriend?"

Her eyes widened. "No." Had she said something to give that away? "Why?"

He smiled, and the dimple appeared again. "You are a terrible liar. I like that in a person."

"Danny said something to you, didn't she?"

"Nope. It was that black cloud hanging over your head when I first met you."

Of course. He'd been lurking at the other end of the bar, and he must have overheard Danny talking about "Red Wings boy."

"It's not the only reason I left. I had other things going on."

He reached over for her glass of ice water and handed it to her. "Better drink this. I think you might catch fire."

Sure enough, the blush she'd battled her whole life was in full bloom, heating her whole face. She took the glass and for a moment she considered tossing its contents onto him.

He put his hands up. "Please don't," he said. "Even if I deserve it."

How did he read her so well? It was disconcerting. Served her right for trying to tell a white lie about Geoff, though. She didn't like lies. Or half-truths.

"I'm sorry," Colton said. "I shouldn't have teased you. I don't know you that well."

She was pretty sure she would never know him well enough to be comfortable with him making fun of her.

"I'm the last person who should be joking

about bad breakups." There was something sincere in his voice this time, and she waited for more, but Danny arrived with their food. The plates left the tray faster and landed on the table harder than Poppy had seen before.

"No help today?" Colton asked her.

"Lila quit, and Terra would rather have her right arm cut off. I'm quoting."

He nodded. "I get that."

Danny paused to look at him. "You doing okay?"

"Yes."

"Looks like you're done with that beer."

"Yes."

Danny took the almost empty mug and left.

Poppy's head was full of questions, but she couldn't formulate a single one into something that didn't sound nosy. Colton took out his napkin and set it on his lap, then paused, gazing down at his hands. He looked depressed. Or concerned. She took a deep breath. "So...you don't drink?"

He looked up suddenly, no trace of depression on his face. "No, I like a cold beer once in awhile."

Poppy had been around a lot of different kinds of people in her life, but these Montana folks were a strange bunch.

Hearing a ruckus behind her, she turned around to see a girl coming through the door. "Terra!" the group of cowboys at the bar called. They seemed just as eager to greet her as they had Colton, but she was ignoring them completely. She hurried past them and ducked under the bar to join Danny.

She heard Colton say, "Guess she'll keep her arm after all."

Poppy was suddenly struck by how beautiful the girl was. Waves of rich, brown hair curled around her shoulders, and long eyelashes shielded big eyes. "Terra is another rodeo-er?" Poppy asked.

He grinned. "Yeah. She was a rodeo-er."

"Colton, I feel like I'm in a foreign country. The least you can do is help me learn the language."

"You're right." He started cutting the huge, fragrant steak on his plate, and Poppy buttered a piece of the Combine's rich, dark bread. "Terra is a barrel racer. Or was. She just showed up here a couple of weeks ago." He took a bite. "Maybe this is the place old rodeo-ers go to die."

There was nothing old about Terra. Or was he talking about himself? He wasn't old, either. When the rancher had said he hoped to see him ride again, did that mean he didn't do it anymore?

There was another round of loud voices and laughter coming from the bar, but she kept her eyes on her plate. She was suddenly very hungry, and the soup and salad were both wonderful. Almost as delicious as the bread. Searching for a safe topic, she asked Colton about the house.

"Grandma Emmaline put in a long table that stretched from where the table is now all the way into the living room. No matter what time of day, someone was always sitting at that table—family, ranch hands, neighbors, you name it. Then Grandpa Art died. He was only fifty-five. Everyone expected Anson to take over, being the oldest son and all, but he had just bought the Third Street Inn. It was nothing then. The top two floors were boarded up, and the bottom floor had a coffee shop of some sort. Everyone thought they were nuts."

"It's beautiful now."

Colton nodded as he took another bite. "They're a good team. She's got the eye, he's got the muscles. Well, he's got a lot more than that, but he's happy working with his hands." He skewered another piece of meat but let it sit on the plate. "He would have loved owning the ranch. I think he'd still rather have the ranch than the hotel."

"You never know," she said. "Why don't you ask him?"

And that, she thought as he stared at her, was why she should never speak without thinking.

"Maybe," he said, and went back to eating.

But she was enjoying the stories and wanted him to continue. "What did Emmaline do after your grandpa died?"

"She ran the ranch herself. And for a long time, she did well. At first, I think people felt sorry for her and tried to help her out, but it turns out she was pretty shrewd. She'd show up at an auction with a bunch of Flathead cherry pies and ask about everyone's grandmas, and the next thing you know a bunch of cattle had traded hands before the auction even started." He shook his head. "You're not supposed to do that sort of thing. She just had a way about her. And boy did she know her numbers. This one time we were down in Wyoming—"

"Excuse me," a woman said.

Poppy had seen her walking up behind Colton. She was hard to miss, even in what was becoming a standing-room-only crowd. She had the kind of short, sassy blond hair that only the prettiest girls could pull off well. She slipped a hand with perfect gold and white nails over his shoulder, and as he turned to face her, the gold bracelets on her narrow wrist slid down her arm and touched his shoulder. She leaned over. "Hey there, Colton. Remember me?"

Right before her eyes, Colton transformed again. He leaned back, smiled up into her face, and for all the world looked like the most confident man in America. And handsome too. His voice came out slow and steady and smooth as molasses. "Miss Keli Coulson. How could I ever forget someone like you? Congratulations on getting the NFR gig."

"Oh, you heard about that." She straightened and put one hand on her hip.

Poppy tucked her left hand under her thigh and stirred her soup with her right hand. She tried to give the woman a welcoming smile, but neither of them seemed to notice she was there. To her left, she was conscious of Terra rushing from one table to another, and to her right the world outside seemed bathed in blue tones that made it look colder. She caught another draft from behind her and shivered.

She didn't know what the NFR was, but it seemed to be a major rodeo event. Minutes ticked by as the two of them talked. She and Colton weren't on a date, but being so blatantly ignored by him made her feel weirdly conspicuous.

The woman said something about "your friend," and Poppy looked up to see them both looking at her.

"Miss Coulson, this is Poppy, my ..."

He looked embarrassed. When he hesitated to say just what she was to him, the awkwardness was too much for Poppy to take. "I'm helping renovate Colton's house," Poppy said.

For a moment he squinted his eyes. "We're working on the old ranch house," he said.

"Hmm, yes," Keli said, looking very interested. "I heard you had some business back at home. Does that mean we can expect you back on the circuit next year?"

"You'll be the first to know," he said. He looked sly as a fox. It made Keli giggle.

"Maybe you and I should get together for a beer and talk about this a little more. How about later tonight? I do like to know the cowboys I interview, and you and I haven't ever really gotten to know each other."

Poppy took a sip of her beer. She could feel the warm tingling that signaled her skin blooming again, and she tried to focus on the cold, semisweet taste of her drink instead.

"I look forward to that," Colton said, nodding his head to her. He watched her walk back to the bar. Before his gaze went anyplace else, Terra was suddenly beside them, looking at Poppy. "Want me to pack that up to go?" she said.

"Yes," Poppy said. She didn't even think about why the girl had asked; she was just relieved she had.

Colton leaned forward. "Terra, we just—"

Terra threw him a look that could have melted steel, and he shut his mouth.

Poppy slipped her coat on. "I have to go. I have a day's worth of e-mails and such, and I haven't done a single bit of work at all."

"Yes you did, you—"

"Work on my thesis, I mean. Besides, it looks like you have other plans tonight. Thank you so much for everything, Colton—the truck, the place to stay, all of it." She stood up, smiled brightly, and added, "I'll pay for mine at the bar. Thanks again."

But getting to the bar was no easy deal. She made her way to the bar, and at the same time, Terra was emerging from the "secret" door behind the bar with a box and a Styrofoam cup and lid. "Here you go, honey," she said. Poppy caught Danny's frown. She reached in her pocket for the cash. "How much do I owe you?"

"You should let Colton pay," Terra said.

"Oh, no. It wasn't a date or anything." She could feel her face growing hot.

Terra pulled a ticket and quoted the amount, which was a touch less than Poppy remembered, but she counted out the cost, a 20 percent tip, and then some. She handed it to Terra.

"Look at all those ones. Tips? You should let the restaurant cash them out for you."

"No, I'm not a...it's a long story." Her face was really hot now.

"Terra, I could show you how to earn some dollar bills," one of the cowboys beside her said, giving her a lewd look. Terra shot him the same look she'd given Colton. Poppy couldn't even make eye contact. She envied the way Terra held her ground.

With a last thank-you, Poppy headed for the door. She couldn't bring herself to look Colton's way, but she was certain he was with his blond date by now. Once she was outside and the sound from the Combine lowered to a dull roar, she could finally breathe. The cold air felt good. Cleansing. Her mind felt clear. She stood there, enjoying the feeling for a moment, before heading north toward the hotel. That took her right by the window where Colton's table was, but he wasn't there.

She didn't look for him, or her. She didn't understand women like her. They moved from relationship to relationship without losing pieces of themselves. Keli wouldn't have cried all the way from Arizona to Montana, or been fool enough to think the first man she ever loved would love her back forever.

Zane was at the hotel's front desk, wearing a neat black shirt and a name tag of his own. He was busy with his phone but set it down as she came in the door. He brightened when he saw her. "Hey, I was just texting Mara. She said she had a good time today."

"Me too."

"She even thinks she wants to come over Sunday afternoon. If it's okay with you. It is your house now."

Not really, Poppy thought. "Sure. Whatever works. The more hands, the faster the work, right?"

"Exactly. Did you have a good dinner?" He gestured toward her takeout boxes.

She told him that she and Colton had gone to

the Combine, and Zane's jaw dropped. "He went to the Combine?"

"Sure, why not? We had a quick dinner."

"Yeah. Sweet." His voice had returned to normal but his expression had not. "Maybe I'll give him a call. You know, to see if Sunday is a good day to work at the Homestead."

"Great. Have a good night," Poppy said. By the time she reached the bottom of the stairs she heard Zane say, "Colton? Give me a call right away, okay? You promised."

CHAPTER 11

Colton tried to make a run for it, but the boys at the bar were like an obstacle course, and Terra refused to help him, so he had to wait for Danny to pay for his meal. By the time he made it outside, Poppy was gone.

He knew where she was, of course, but Aunt Julia was probably there too. She would think it was strange if he came looking for Poppy. And it would be.

His phone rang. He checked the caller ID—Zane. It would have to wait until he got back home.

He walked slowly, boot heels knocking against the pavement, and gently moved his head side to side to stretch out his neck muscles. He felt a headache coming on. It had been coming for a while, actually, but the aspirin he'd gotten from Julia had staved it off for a little while. He deserved a full-blown headache for thinking the way he was thinking.

The moment he'd seen Keli, his mind had started spinning. He'd seen her work the crowd and sneak up behind him, seen those claws on his shoulder. She was still interested. One good interview with her and he'd be on the radar of all the major sponsors. Then the other interviewers would come. He was out of practice, but he wasn't out of shape. Just a few local gigs here and there was all he'd need. Sure, some of the big sponsors might be gun-shy, but some would bite.

And they'd write it into the contract that if he bashed his skull in again, they could walk away free and clear.

Keli's hand on his shoulder was like Santa Claus and the lottery all in one. He could make more money in a couple of months on the circuit than the ranch would make all year. He could fix the barn, fix the tractor, fix the air conditioning in the diesel, fix his whole life with money like that. Suddenly it felt like walking away from Keli was a stupid thing to do.

But it wasn't what Emmaline wanted. The

woman who had given him the ranch. It troubled his dreams every night, a backward blessing of some sort he couldn't escape and couldn't earn. She wouldn't have been proud of the way he'd acted around Poppy, either. She used to call his interviews "smarmy," and she wasn't fond of Keli Coulson. She'd dropped the insult of all insults on her once: "That girl needs Jesus." All because she'd said on air that Colton had lost his touch.

He had, of course. And he'd nearly lost more than that.

Poppy didn't know anything about the rodeo, or Keli, or corporate sponsors, or all the bad things he should have told her about. All she knew—Colton was sure of it—was that he'd treated her as if she didn't matter when a sparkly skirt like Keli had showed up. He'd acted like his dad. The thought made him stop in his tracks, head throbbing.

All the memories of Mom crying alone at night blurred into just a few clear moments; the rest was thankfully lost to him. No amount of money was worth acting like his dad.

CHAPTER 12

Poppy's eyes opened into the darkness of the room, but the doorway to the lighted hallway was nowhere to be seen. Somehow she was facing the wrong way. What her mind expected to see slowly gave way to what was actually there. She wasn't in the Washington house, the home from so long ago. Not the hotel, either. She was in the homestead.

She heard the loud noise again, four times. It must have been what had awakened her. She crawled out of her sleeping bag and grabbed a jacket. Who would knock at her door in the middle of the night? She stepped out of her room and crept to the top of the stairs. *Bang, bang.* It sounded like an emergency. Or a trap. For the first time, she felt the isolation of the homestead as a dangerous thing.

Then she heard a familiar voice call her name. She hurried down the stairs and pulled the door open. Colton stood there with his hair a mess, his eyes dark, and an angry expression on his face. For a moment the fear returned.

"I'm sorry," he said.

Poppy took a shaky breath and stepped aside so he could come in.

"I just got a call from Julia. Zane's in the hospital. I need to get to Billings. But I can't drive."

Poppy didn't understand, but Zane was hurt, and from the look on Colton's face, now wasn't the time to ask questions. "I only need a minute," she said, and she went back up the steps two at a time. She grabbed the nearest clean clothes and then came back down as she put a hair band in her hair. Colton was adding wood to the stove. He retrieved her keys from the kitchen counter as she put on her parka. As they hurried outside, she realized it was snowing again. She'd never seen so much snow, and it wasn't even October yet. The moment her boots hit the first step off the porch, she slipped.

Colton must have seen it coming because he

grabbed her elbow and held her steady. "It's icy. Really icy. Zane and Mara were in a car crash."

"How are they?"

"I don't know. I just know Zane's at the hospital, and he was in her car. I don't even know how Mara is doing. Julia was in the car on her way to Billings, and she wasn't making much sense."

Poppy got in the driver's side and made certain all the snow was off her boots before she touched the pedals. The truck started right up. At that moment she almost wished Colton hadn't been able to fix it.

"Would you do me a favor and pray with me?"

Poppy froze. No one had ever asked something like that of her. Never in the churches, meditation clinics, covens, drum circles, or any of the other "spiritual" places her family had visited, never at school or work or any other in the world —never had someone asked to pray with her. It was too presumptuous. Too intimate. And she felt her opinion of Colton shift a bit. He was one of those men who relied on religion rather than his own strength, and to Poppy, that made him someone she needed to keep her distance from.

A man without the strength of his own resolve wasn't a person she could trust.

He reached over and took her hand, then

closed his eyes. She kept hers open, watching him, not sure if she should snatch her hand back. It would be rude, and he was clearly troubled. It couldn't hurt to hold on if he didn't take too long.

"Jesus, we need your help. Please hold Zane and Mara in your arms. We know you are the Great Physician. Please guide the hands of those who are helping them. Keep Anson and Julia safe on their way to the hospital, and calm their hearts with the peace that surpasses understanding. Something bad has happened, Jesus, and we pray that you give us strength and wisdom and turn everything into Your glory. Amen."

"Amen," she said, thinking she sounded about as stupid and out of place saying that as when she'd asked Colton if he did rodeo. She wanted to change the topic. "I don't know how to drive on ice and snow," she said.

Colton put on his seat belt and turned to face her. "I can't drive. It's after eleven at night."

She had no idea what that meant, but she assumed he had a restriction on his license. She had heard of curfews, but those were for people who were on parole. She looked down at the steering wheel. Maybe he was on parole. She didn't really know him at all.

"Just put it in four-wheel drive and go slow."

She did as he asked, starting down the long driveway toward the paved road.

"Do you know what to do in a skid?"

"Steer the other way."

"Good. Just don't steer the other way very much, it's easy to overdo it."

She gripped the wheel harder. The truck felt as solid as ever, but she didn't trust it. As she was thinking about curfews and what they meant, she said, "Why were they out so late?"

Colton only shook his head. She drove out onto the empty road, which Colton always called the highway, and remembered reading that she should test the roads when possible. So at about ten miles per hour, she pressed on the brakes. For a moment nothing happened. "Pump your brakes," Colton said.

She did so, and the tires caught hold again. "Oh boy." She sped up slowly, watching the speedometer and doing calculations in her head. The road here was on mostly flat land; they wouldn't be hurt if she ran off the road. But she dreaded the turns ahead. She drove down the middle of the empty road and settled on thirty miles per hour for no good reason other than the thought of going faster terrified her.

Colton's fidgeting betrayed his impatience, but all he said was, "You're doing fine."

She slowed at a sharp turn, feeling the light back end of her truck slide sideways. She dreaded the steep switchbacks into the river valley where Moose Hollow was nestled. But when she got there, it looked as if sand had been laid on the road. Once she was past Moose Hollow Highway 212, the road that led to the interstate, the pavement glistened under the headlights of oncoming cars like polished obsidian. She wanted to go faster, and sometimes did, but when cars approached from the other direction, she slowed down again. Her fingers ached from holding so tightly to the steering wheel.

She could see lights flashing in the distance, just visible through the snow. As they approached, she saw two police cars on the side of the road, and between them, a vehicle being pulled up onto a large wrecker. It was black and big, like Mara's Escalade, but Poppy had to concentrate on the icy road so she couldn't be certain. As they passed, she saw the roof was caved in as if the vehicle had rolled. "Oh God," Colton said. "Please let them be okay."

But Zane's not allowed to be in her car, Poppy thought. Why was he? He was solid as a rock, no matter what. Never even said a bad word about his parents' strict rules. It couldn't have been Mara's car. How could he have been in that vehicle, especially this time of night on a school night? Where would they have been heading? It didn't make sense. Tears started pooling in her eyes, and she blinked them away. There had to be some sort of mistake.

The drive to the interstate and then to Billings left her shaking. All she could think of was the fact that 212 was the only way to get to the hospital. That meant Julia and Anson had driven by that wrecked car, and maybe Mara's father, too. Poppy hoped the car had been out of sight when they had, because as long and awful as the drive was for Colton and her, it would be a whole other world for Zane and Mara's parents. They drove on in silence.

After many miles, she saw the familiar *H* on a blue road sign. "Do I turn here?" she asked.

Colton glanced up and said, "No. This is too far away from downtown."

"I think we passed downtown."

He frowned, then said, "I'm sorry. This is the right exit. I thought this was Denver."

She couldn't smell alcohol on his breath, but her first thought was he must have been drinking.

He held one hand to his mouth, his face stern in the faint light of the dashboard, and closed his eyes. She wondered if he was all right. But soon they approached the two Billings hospitals, and he directed her to the right one without trouble. She dropped him off at the emergency exit. "I'll catch up," she said, and he nodded a thank-you. A couple steps away from her truck, he stopped. He stood there, staring at the doors. Then he startled as if coming awake and turned to glance at her. She could have sworn he looked embarrassed to see her watching. Colton strode through the glass doors, and she drove away.

She hoped he was okay. She hoped everyone was.

There was no snow on the ground in Billings, which was situated low in a wide river valley. She trudged through the sleet, shivering but not feeling cold. She wasn't sure what she was supposed to do. She would find a place in the waiting room to sit quietly, out of their way. If Colton needed a ride home, she'd give him one. If not, she'd go back, although she wasn't anxious to drive on those icy roads again.

She entered the hospital through the Emergency door. Straight ahead of her was the main desk, and beyond it was a hallway with well-lit rooms. To her right was a large waiting room. Standing in the middle of it were Julia and Anson, Anson's arm tightly around his wife, nodding slightly as the doctor in front of him was speaking. Colton was standing just behind them. As Poppy took a step toward the waiting room, Colton's eyes met hers, and he motioned for her to enter.

As she did, the conversation broke up, and all eyes turned another way, toward the bright hallway. A man in light blue scrubs was rolling Zane toward them in a wheelchair. Zane looked pale, and his arm was in a plastic splint, but he was upright and alert. The man pushing Zane turned into the closest room, but the Gunnersons intercepted him in the hallway. Julia got there first, and she leaned over to give Zane a soft kiss on the forehead.

"Poppy," Colton said, motioning again. She couldn't understand why he wanted her with him, but she inched his way. She had no intention of going into Zane's room. Anson and Julia passed her as they hurried back to the doctor, and if they recognized her, they didn't show it.

"I haven't heard anything other than she's here and she's stable," the doctor was saying.

Mara was stable. The term was probably

meant to comfort, but to Poppy, it conjured images of tubes and wires. She couldn't imagine it. She could imagine Mara complaining about wearing a hospital gown, though, and that was how she wanted to picture the girl right now.

"Your mom and dad will find out when he talks to the doctor," Colton said.

Poppy stepped out of the way of another blue-scrubbed man hurrying through the hall, and she tucked herself in behind the wheelchair, against the wall, trying not to get in the way.

"We should get you in your room, Mr. Gunnerson," the man helping Zane said.

"You."

The single word was spoken quietly, but the tone of it thundered down the hallway behind Poppy. She turned with a start. She saw a man headed toward them, shoulders hunched, his lips twisted into a snarl. He was wearing a suit jacket and a mauve shirt, dark jeans and dress shoes. She'd never seen him before, but it only took a second to register from the angle of his gaze that he was headed straight for Zane.

She stepped into the hallway to block the man, her heart racing and her blood pounding in her ears. She didn't hear everything going on behind her, but she got the impression that the wheelchair man and Colton were having trouble convincing Zane to stay seated.

She saw the angry man's gaze rise, and she knew Zane was standing up behind her. She put herself squarely between them. She was at least as tall as him, but he gave her one look from top to bottom that dismissed her in an instant. "Get out of my way."

A hand grabbed hold of her elbow. "Hold on there," Colton said, his voice smooth and slow. "Zane's not in a position to chat right now."

But the man's eyes were still fixed on a spot behind Colton.

"You did this to her!" he hissed.

Colton tucked Poppy behind him. She tried to wriggle away, but she found herself in a forest of tall men—Colton, the wheelchair man, who was keeping a hand on Zane, and Zane. Through a gap, she saw Anson and Julia rushing over. "Back off," Anson said.

"Mr. Maxwell, is Mara okay?" Zane asked. She could hear the pleading in his voice.

"Okay? She's pregnant, you hypocrite lowlife—"

Zane rushed forward, nearly out of the grasp of the wheelchair man, and Poppy heard Anson call, "No!"

Instead of stepping between them, Colton stepped out of Zane's way, pushing her farther back as he did. "Not the first punch, Zane."

Zane's eyes flickered toward Colton. It was something about the way Colton said it. Everyone around them went still. Every eye was on them. The angry man already had one fist pulled back and ready to strike, and Zane had one fist up in front of his own face. His other hand was locked in the plastic brace he wore.

Neither fist moved. Everyone was watching, everyone would see who threw the first punch, and as angry as Zane looked, he wouldn't be the one.

There was another voice from farther away, toward the door, but she couldn't see who it belonged to. "Sorry I'm late to the party," he said. Whoever it was, his voice sounded like that of a TV host, deep, rich, and slow.

Everyone took a step back, and that was when Poppy caught a glimpse of a black police uniform.

In an instant, two nurses were between Maxwell and the Gunnersons, and Anson and Julia pushed Zane into his room.

"You're shaking," Colton said. She looked up into his eyes.

"I don't like confrontations."

"Come here, let's get out of the hallway until Mike gets Maxwell calmed down." He took her by the hand and pulled her into Zane's hospital room.

Julia turned to look at them. Poppy caught the way Julia's gaze settled on their interlaced hands, and the frown lines that creased her forehead when she saw them. Poppy pulled her hand away, but she knew it was too late to change the woman's misconception.

"What was that? What is going on?" Zane was saying.

"That man's anger is that man's problem," the wheelchair man said. He settled Zane into bed and covered him with a blanket, lifting up the head of the bed like a recliner and using one big hand to push Zane firmly down against it. "You just take care of you and yours, brother," he said before exiting the room. They were wise words and they calmed Zane.

So had Colton's words. In the heat of the moment, she'd had nothing useful to say, as usual.

Zane's eyes fixed on Colton. "You drove."

"She did," Colton said, tilting his head toward Poppy.

"Is your truck working okay?" he asked her. Poppy got the feeling he was delaying the moment he had to explain all of this to his parents, and she didn't blame him.

"Yes." Her voice sounded small in the big white room.

"Good. Now he owes you gas money." Zane winced as he adjusted himself. His left arm was clearly bothering him.

"I'm so thankful," Colton began. But he didn't say more, and Zane looked down, nodding just a little.

In the silence that followed, Anson finally asked the question they were all thinking. "What happened?"

"She had a big blowout with her dad. She needed to get away. I told her not to go anywhere alone."

Anson seemed to be thinking hard about his next statement, and Colton stepped in. "They checked you for a concussion?"

"Yes."

"You know they can miss it. I saw the truck, I can't believe you don't have a concussion. You need to take it real easy, you know that, right? I mean, you better know that."

"I know, Colton."

"If you do anything to aggravate it—"

Poppy stepped back as the police officer entered the room. He was an average-looking guy with artificially black hair, a mustache, and an average build. But that TV host voice was something. "Mind if I interrupt, folks? Anson, Julia ..." He turned to look at Colton. "Colton Gunnerson."

"Officer Mike."

There was something different about the way he addressed Colton, but Poppy couldn't put her finger on it. Then the officer turned back to Zane's parents. He leaned a little to one side to look at Poppy. "And you must be the young woman living at Emmaline's house. Your black eyes seem to have healed up."

She was startled. "How did you know about that?"

"Hazard of the job, I suppose. I hear about all sorts of things. Construction accident?"

"No, I was going into the Third Street Inn." She realized he'd looped her into talking about it —not that it was police business—so she cut to the chase. "I was going in, Colton was coming out, and I ran my face straight into his elbow."

"Ouch," Officer Mike said sympathetically. He glanced at Colton, then turned back to Zane.

"I set Mr. Maxwell up with a long form to fill out. He was a little worked up, so that'll give him time to calm down. Now I'm here to find out if I need to do the same thing with you."

"No, sir," Zane answered. "I can tell you what happened. We were going down 212, and a deer crossed the road."

"I need to start at the beginning, son. And I don't mind having all your family here, in fact, I think it's a good thing, but I just want to be clear I'm interviewing you, not them." Zane frowned, and Anson fidgeted beside him. She saw the way his hands were clenched and guessed that Anson was having a hard time not stepping in.

"First of all, have you had anything to drink tonight?"

"No," Zane said.

"Did Mara?"

Zane paused. A telltale pause. "She didn't drink anything around me."

Mike nodded slowly. "I just want you to know that you've both had blood drawn, and the hospital will be testing it for alcohol and other intoxicants. Now don't get upset, Zane. I think you're telling the truth, and it'll work in your favor to have the test done. But the doctors do believe that Mara had been drinking."

Zane sighed but said nothing. The surly expression hadn't left his face.

"Which one of you was driving when you hit the deer?"

Poppy saw a flash of something different in Zane's expression. The troubled look worsened, then it vanished entirely. The young man before her suddenly looked calm.

"I was," Zane said.

And Poppy knew he was lying. She looked around the room. No one seemed to move. Didn't anyone else see it?

"I see." Slow words, followed by a long silence while Officer Mike crossed his arms over his chest. "So you were driving Mara's SUV at the time of the accident?"

"I was."

Officer Mike pulled out a tablet of paper and scribbled something down. "You hit the deer?"

"I didn't hit it. I swerved to miss it, and the roads were too slick. As soon as I hit the shoulder, things went crazy and it rolled."

Julia covered her mouth with her hand, and Poppy could see her eyes sparkle with tears.

"Yes, it did." The police officer wrote something else. "That could indicate excessive speed for the conditions, Zane."

Zane nodded. "It might have been. Or maybe just the bad roads. I don't know for sure."

Officer Mike wrote again, and Poppy wondered if he was actually writing words at all or just trying to psych out his interviewee. He knew Zane was lying. He had to know.

"When the witness found you, neither of you were in your seats."

Julia let out a tiny sound, something like a sob, and Officer Mike dropped the tablet to his side. "I know this is rough, Julia. If you'd like, I can go over this with you first, and then interview—"

"Let's do this now," Zane said.

The officer nodded once. "Were you wearing a seat belt?"

"I don't know." He sounded gruff, irritated.

"Was Mara?"

"I don't know."

Officer Mike's shoulders rose and fell with a long breath. "There was a witness who saw the deer and the wreck, Zane. They said it seemed like you two were going pretty fast, but they were going the opposite direction. That can make estimating speed pretty hard to do. We're investigating, and we'll take the road conditions into account. That being said, there are a few things you need to understand, son."

Officer Mike tucked the tablet into a pocket before continuing. "Mara was pretty banged up and the vehicle is totaled. Now, I figure you've already worked out that if Mara is caught drunk, underage, and driving, she's in some pretty big trouble." He shifted his weight to the other side, seeming to weigh his words. "You've been through a lot tonight. I know you've gotten knocked around, and I wouldn't be surprised if you don't remember what happened a little better tomorrow."

"I remember it just fine now."

The police officer held up his hand to stop Zane there. "Maybe so, son. But Mr. Maxwell is pretty worked up over his daughter, and he thinks you're responsible for all her ills."

She was pregnant! Poppy's numbed mind finally registered the significance of what the angry Maxwell had been saying. And immediately she felt disappointed. Angry, even. So much for the gentleman who had never kissed Mara. What, was it some less-than-symbolic nod to the movie *Pretty Woman*? Sex was okay, but kissing was not? Or maybe he'd just lied to Poppy's face, thinking what a stupid, naive grownup she was. She pushed the thoughts aside for now. Zane was hurt. This wasn't the time.

"He's going to push hard for us to press charges," the officer said, "and if that doesn't go his way, there's no telling what will happen. So, Zane, I need you to understand what I'm about to say."

He let his words hang in the silence.

"You need to be dead-on sure, son. You need to hang your hat on the truth, because if you're lying, you'll get found out. And the longer you wait, the worse it could be. So I just want to ask you again, are you sure you were driving when the vehicle went off the road?"

"That's how I remember it," Zane said. He looked tired beyond belief.

Mercifully, the officer said his good-byes and left, securing Zane's promise to sign a statement within the next couple days.

The moment he was gone, the drama faded, and Poppy felt the weight of what she was, a terribly unwelcome guest in the middle of a very intimate family problem. "Excuse me," she mumbled as she ducked out of the room.

It didn't take long for Colton to follow. "They need a little time alone," he said. "But Zane's going to be okay. They're not letting anyone visit Mara right now."

"I'm glad you asked about her."

"Cash is on his way in to help. I think we should just go—if you're ready." He looked back toward Zane's room. "This isn't my favorite place to visit."

She was ready to go, but she dreaded driving back. "I'm ready."

"I can drive," he said.

She must have looked at him as if he was insane.

"It's after three. I'm good to go." He acted as if this was a sufficient explanation.

She couldn't make sense of it. Nevertheless, she handed the keys to him. "I think you drive too fast," she said.

"For you, I'll go slower," he said.

CHAPTER 13

The flatbed diesel truck started up at 5:30 a.m. as it did every day, and the low rumble it made was the best alarm Poppy had ever heard. It wasn't shrill or insistent, and it never woke her up with the feeling that something horrible had just happened. In fact, she could sleep through it if she wanted, but she liked watching the sunrise with a warm fire, coffee in her hands, no place to go, and nothing to do just yet.

But this morning her thoughts were with Mara and Zane. Zane would be okay, except for the legal fallout from the accident. She just couldn't understand why he would bring more down on his head by saying he was driving.

Poppy stirred the coals in the stove and added wood. While it smoldered, she went into the kitchen, turned on the new light over the sink, and loaded ground coffee into the tiny black coffeemaker sitting on the kitchen counter. She ran her hand over the faux stone countertop. It was looking like a real kitchen.

All except for the saturated, overwhelming yellow on the walls where the upper cabinets still needed to be rehung. Poppy was ready for those cabinets to go back up. She wanted Colton to replace the doors on a few with paned glass. Either Colton was still considering it or he just didn't want to hang the cabinets. Leveling, double-checking, moving things fractions of an inch—these were not Colton's strong points, and he could get testy.

And throw a screwdriver out the open window. "Good thing you don't have a dog out there," she'd said, unimpressed by the display. And he'd laughed. In the middle of his tantrum, she'd made him laugh. She couldn't figure him out.

Poppy took one of the metal and vinyl chairs from the old kitchen table and put it in the living room where the view was best, near the warmth of the stove. On the thin coating of snow on Colton's land, she saw the sweep of headlights passing by. He was on his way out to the north-west pasture in the diesel. In another hour or so, he'd be here in his Ford to start work on the house. And above it all, the stars were shining.

The beauty and stillness of it all moved her. A deep sense of gratitude washed over her. Without thinking, she said out loud, "Thank you."

To no one. Which meant, luckily, no one was here to see her be so silly. She thought of Colton, the expression on his face when he had prayed by the light of her dashboard. She didn't have a name for it, that feeling it gave her. Maybe he knew something she didn't. But she doubted it. She'd been dragged to more spiritual leaders than she could count. They all promised the same things, and in the end, they demanded the same things. And her parents swallowed the bait every single time.

Light on the driveway surprised her. The flatbed diesel was heading up to the house. She put her cup down and poured a cup of black coffee for Colton, then met him at the door. He looked chilled, and she handed it to him as he came in. "It's colder than it looks!" he said, flipping the switch to turn on the overhead light. Just like that, the peaceful, starlit darkness was gone. "Thanks, Poppy. But I won't have time to finish this. I just came to say I'll be working in the pasture all day."

She felt disappointed, although logically, she had no reason to be. "Sure. More time for me to work on my thesis."

"They released Zane from the hospital. Not much news on Mara, other than they moved her to a regular hospital room."

"I guess that's good," she said.

Colton took a drink of coffee. "Well, I just saw the ten-day forecast, and they're expecting a change in the weather. I'm going check the winter pasture fence line, and from what I've seen, there's a ton of work to do. I want to make sure I get any strays in before we get a serious snowfall."

"It's only September."

He smiled at her. "Yes, it is, Arizona girl." He handed her the cup. "Thanks. And I have to pick up a few things while I'm here."

While she put his cup back into the kitchen, she heard him walk into Emmaline's bedroom. She gave him his privacy since he'd said the room was off-limits. But when he called good-bye, she came around the corner and caught just a glimpse of him leaving with a large box in his arms.

Then it was quiet again. But when Poppy tried

to go back to her seat to watch the sky turn red on the eastern horizon, she felt fidgety. She watched Colton's headlights sweep across the yard and drive away. She knew she should get to work on her thesis, just as she'd said. To do the work she'd been planning since the moment she'd been accepted to grad school. No, since the day in middle school when she'd realized that no one was going to get her to school if she didn't get there herself, because if she dropped out, she'd never have a chance to go to college, be something, have a home, have a family.

She'd made it this far. She was so close to a graduate degree, but no closer to the rest of her dreams.

It was her fault, of course, for bringing up the subject of marriage. The first time she and Geoff had discussed it, he'd asked her to move in with him. Months later, she'd worked up the courage to bring it up again. He'd looked thoughtful and considerate, and the next afternoon he'd asked her to go on a hike with him. He'd said he wanted to take her to a new place, a place someone had told him had beautiful wildflowers.

She'd put on a new shirt, dark blue because Geoff liked it, but when they'd arrived, she'd found that what might have been a shady pool in springtime was now just a stomped-down cattle tank. If wildflowers had been growing near the murky water, they had been eaten or covered in droppings. And there were flies. The tiny kind with sharp bites.

But she had been undaunted. She'd thought Geoff was taking her there to propose.

As they'd walked around the pond, he'd brought up his bright new Irish intern again. He'd said the girl was bringing a fresh perspective to his work with the land co-op. He had told her it was important to surround yourself with people who challenge you and teach you. She could still see his eyes, pale green in the harsh sunlight. It was important to surround yourself with people who contribute to your life, he'd said.

"What do I contribute to your life?" she'd asked like a little girl spinning around for her daddy in a new dress asks, "Do I look pretty?"

She was Geoff's rock, his cheerleader, and his patient listener, even when his friends got frustrated with his volatile moods and know-it-all attitude. She was his reminder to take a break and watch the sunset. He was her first, her only, her last. Poppy was sure she had been smiling as he'd talked, expecting a speech of some sort about everything she meant to him.

"That's just it," he had answered. "I'm not sure you contribute very much to my life."

Poppy sat down at the homestead's kitchen table and took a sip of coffee. Geoff had kept talking after that. She hadn't heard the words, but she'd understood his meaning. What she offered wasn't enough.

She'd given him her heart and her body. No one knew her better. And it wasn't enough.

They had gone straight from the hike to dinner in some local diner. When Geoff had gotten up to use the restroom, she'd been terrified he was going to get in his car and drive away, leaving her stranded. Why not? Nothing in her life was certain anymore.

He hadn't, though. He'd come back to the table, drunk his beer, and asked the waitress to change the TV channel so he could watch soccer. He didn't like soccer but had an opinion about it. They had even stayed late to catch the end of the game. She'd slept beside him that night, a dreamless night. In the morning he'd given her a kiss good-bye on his way to work, and she had packed up the things that still mattered to her and driven to the university to make plans. She had been on the highway by noon, headed north.

She put her head in her hands and cried. Every day it surprised her how much she didn't miss him, the man she'd wanted to marry. So where was the pain coming from? And why wouldn't it go away?

CHAPTER 14

She was in town when her new phone rang. She could count on one hand the people who had her new number, and this caller wasn't familiar. But it was a Montana number, so she answered.

"Is this Poppy?" a familiar voice said.

"Hello, Zane. How are you feeling?"

"I'm good. Pretty good. Listen, I need to ask a favor."

She didn't make any promises.

"I need a ride into Billings. Tonight. Like now."

He sounded more anxious than she'd ever heard him, even when he was in the hospital. "Why?"

"I need to see Mara."

Poppy looked around the grocery store. The aisle was empty. "Your mom and dad can't take you?"

"They're working." There was something in his tone of voice. Zane was a terrible liar, just like Colton said she was.

"What about Colton?"

"I can't get ahold of Colton."

He was probably asleep, from what she'd seen of how hard he was working. And Zane wasn't supposed to get in the car with a teenage driver, so that precluded asking a friend for a ride.

"Besides," Zane added, "I think it would go better if I went with you."

That piqued her suspicion. "I'm actually in town, at the grocery."

"Great!"

"But if you want a ride, you're going to have to tell me the truth."

Silence. After a moment, Zane said, "I'll be there in a few." The call disconnected.

Poppy picked up some milk and paid for her groceries, and by the time she'd passed through the automatic door, Zane was jogging up to the entrance. He took the tote bags from her with the hand that wasn't in a sling. He looked good, with no visible signs of trauma other than a few cuts and scrapes.

Zane kept his gaze on the grocery bags. "When I call Mara, the hospital says she's not taking any calls. Mom tried to stop by to visit her in the hospital, but her dad said a bunch of nasty things and the nurses asked her to leave. Her cell phone is dead, and I don't even know if anyone got it out of the Escalade."

"Sounds like she doesn't want to talk to you." Poppy led him over to her truck and unlocked the doors.

"More like her dad doesn't want me to talk to her."

"That may be true, Zane, but he has all the power right now. You just might have to wait." No matter who Zane blamed, she didn't think it was unusual for a girl in Mara's position to want to avoid her boyfriend.

For the first time, Zane looked her in the eye. "She's alone," he said. "You don't understand. Her mom won't come, her dad's a jerk, the adults in her life have turned their back on her. She's hardly got any friends anymore, either. She's going through this alone. I just don't think that's right."

Poppy sighed. She knew she would give in, as

much as she wanted to reason it away. "How are you going to handle it when we arrive and Mr. Maxwell tries to start another fight?"

"He won't be there now."

"How do you know?"

"Because he spends every night with the Internet and a bottle of gin."

Poppy closed her eyes and shook her head. It could be true. But teenagers could also be dramatic exaggerators. And Zane was pretty passionate about Mara.

He had put the groceries in her car, but he remained standing, waiting. She exhaled. "Get in." She noticed that the first thing he did when he got in the car was to click the seat belt shut. Same as when she'd driven him out to Colton's the first time she saw the homestead.

Thankfully, the roads were dry all the way to Billings. She could see the orange glow of the city lights in the distance, and they got brighter and brighter as they approached. Zane didn't have much to say, but he did occasionally glower at her tape player, which was playing an old mixed tape. Finally, he said, "You listen to stoner music?"

"This is not stoner music. It's classic, old-school rock."

"Yeah, right."

"I grew up on this stuff."

"Were your parents stoners?"

Now both he and Mara had asked about her parents' habits. "What, is there something about me? Maybe I inhaled too much as a kid?"

"Seriously, they were? I was just joking. Weird. Really? What was that like?"

What was it like? "I had a friend once who had an alcoholic mom. It was pretty much the same thing. They were easy, let us do what we wanted." Never showed up for parent-teacher meetings. Never came to the science fair. Never let other kids sleep over for fear of getting turned in. Moody. And always more worried about their next fix than their kids.

But the worst of it were the people who had come along with the drugs. Her parents had only hung out with people who got high, and anyone who got high was welcome. After all, they'd said, who were they to judge?

"I never would have guessed you grew up like that."

Poppy shook her head. "Good. I spent a lot of time trying to avoid a contact high. To this day my parents think I'm claustrophobic and that's why I need to have my windows open all the time." She meant to tell it as a funny story, but Zane didn't seem all that amused. When was the last time she'd told anyone that? Why would she do it now, to a teenager without verbal boundaries?

"Wow. I would've guessed you had super up-tight parents."

She did, of course. When she'd decided to be her own parent, that was the kind of parent she'd turned out to be.

Poppy was ready for a change of topic, and she asked Zane for directions and queried him about a couple of landmarks. Soon they were at the hospital, and Poppy parked in the visitors' lot. Her heart sped up at the thought of seeing Maxwell again. She hoped he wasn't there.

They reached the first roadblock at Mara's floor. "Mara Maxwell isn't ready for guests," a nurse told them cheerfully. "I'm so sorry you didn't know."

"She's expecting her, though," Zane said, pointing at Poppy. "Just let her know Poppy Marsh is here to see her."

The nurse looked suspicious. "It says here no visitors. Mr. Maxwell is very concerned about disturbing his daughter and asked that we turn away her friends for a little while."

"She's not a friend," Zane said. "She's
—she's a—"

"I work with Mara," Poppy said. She could tell
by the woman's expression that wasn't good
enough. She put her hand to her throat. "I'm her
mentor." Where on earth did that come from? If
Mr. Maxwell came in right now, she'd die. Would
the nurse call the police on her? "If she's awake,
do you mind asking her? It's no problem if she
says no. I'd be happy to come back later."

"Well, I guess I could check."

As the nurse walked away, Zane looked at
Poppy with a grateful smile, and she kicked him
hard in the shin with her boot. "Me? I'm here to
see her?"

"I figured Maxwell would have special instructions not to let me in," he said, leaning over
to rub his leg.

"So you planned this?" Poppy was just about
ready to kick him again.

"No. I did think Mara might want to see you,
though."

"I can't imagine why."

Zane gave her a frustrated look. "She likes
you."

That was a startling thought. She'd only
worked with the girl a handful of days. Of course,

she didn't believe much of anything Zane said anymore. "If she wants to see me, what am I supposed to say to her?"

"Tell her she's not alone. Here she comes!"

Poppy looked over her shoulder to see the nurse coming. "Go on in, Miss Marsh," the nurse said. "She's ready to see you, room 314. You, young man, just take a seat in the waiting room."

Poppy tried to act like she was happy to head down the hall, but she wasn't. She dreaded seeing Mara's injuries. And what should a person say to a pregnant teen, I'm sorry or congratulations?

She knocked on the door of room 314 and then slowly opened it.

Mara was sitting up in bed. There were no tubes or wires, which was a relief. Both of her wrists were in a brace. Her face was bruised and injured, including a few small cuts and two impressive black eyes, and there was a bandage over her nose. It was hard to believe that Zane had been in the same vehicle as her.

"I know, I look like crap," Mara said. "What do you want?"

"I want to know how you're doing," Poppy said. "But I don't want to run into your dad."

"I figured that was you yesterday night," Mara said. "Don't worry. He's at home."

Poppy stood in the doorway, uninvited and unsure what to do. Mara looked so much smaller than she remembered. More vulnerable. Maybe she'd been fooled by the high-heeled boots and big attitude.

"What?" Mara asked, clipping the word.

"You look tiny."

"You suck at hospitals."

Poppy smiled. That was true enough. She came closer and sat gently on the edge of the bed. "When are they going to let you out?"

"Tomorrow. Maybe. They want to make sure baby and me are both okay."

"Yeah. Congratulations." Poppy changed her mind about saying it halfway through the word and it fell flat.

Mara's eyes narrowed. "That's all you've got? Thank God I'm not in hospice, you'd probably bring me balloons."

"I don't do balloons. I hate when they pop."

"Well, that's one thing we have in common."

They eyed each other in an uneasy truce. Poppy tried again. "I'm sorry you got hurt, Mara, but I'm glad you're alive, and you're going to re-cover. It was a pretty bad wreck."

"That's what I heard. I don't remember a thing."

"Maybe that's for the best," Poppy said. "Your black eyes are better than mine were."

A trace of a grin passed over Mara's face. "You got that right."

Poppy took a deep breath and spat it out. "I'm here with Zane. He wanted to get a message to you. He said you're not alone."

"What is that supposed to mean?"

"I don't know. I don't know how to translate teenage Romeo. But this is what he told me, that your dad's a jerk. Well, he implied all the adults in your life were jerks, and that the kids weren't much better, and that you need to know that you're not in this alone."

Tears glistened in Mara's eyes, but her voice stayed sharp. "You're not alone. That's crap. Of course I'm alone. I'm the one here in the hospital bed, right?"

"You've got the baby," Zane said. Startled, Poppy turned around. He had managed to open the door without her hearing. "And you've got me."

"Zane, what are you doing?" Poppy said. "Does the nurse know you're here?"

"She left the desk, and I don't think the other nurse knows any better."

Poppy turned back to Mara. "If you want us to

go, we'll both leave right now." Mara's eyes were on Zane, and her tears were flowing. Poppy tried again in a softer voice. "Or do you two need some time alone?"

The girl nodded slightly, and Poppy let herself out of the room as Zane took her place on the edge of the bed. "I'll be downstairs. Don't get caught," she warned Zane.

It was almost an hour before he met her there. He just looked at her with a serious face and headed for the door, and she followed. Once they made it into the parking lot, he said, "I'm sorry you had to wait so long." It didn't look like he was going to say anything more.

They had made it out of Billings, down the interstate, and down the long stretch of river valley that led to Moose Hollow before he spoke up. "Have you ever seen one of those movies where all the bad guys get away with it, and you can't do anything about it?"

"That's not my kind of movie."

"Mine either."

He was like a dead weight in her car, unmoving, unblinking, just sitting with his right fist pressed to his lips. When they came to the intersection with the county road that led to the homestead, he asked to be dropped off and flatly thanked her again for driving him.

She didn't want to let him walk away. She wanted to stay with him until she was sure he was going to be okay. She didn't know what had transpired, but if it had been a breakup, it had been a bad one. She couldn't find a valid reason to lure him back into the car, though, at least anything that didn't sound creepy. She hoped Julia would catch him on the way home. She seemed like the kind of mom who would figure out something was wrong and do something about it. Poppy watched him walk toward the Third Street Inn until a couple of cars pulled up behind her, kindly not honking, and then she turned right and headed for home.

CHAPTER 15

October fourth crept in so darkly and quietly she didn't even know it was morning until the howling winds started. She could feel the house around her creak and brace against the winds that rushed down the mountain, gathered speed, and crashed down upon it.

When she pulled back the flap of her sleeping bag, the cold bit into her skin. She'd resisted using the small baseboard heaters in the upstairs room, but she might have to reconsider it today. One thing was for sure: she needed to get the stove going.

She padded down the bare wooden steps, focused on the small pile of wood beside the stove until waves of movement outside caught her eye.

The world had disappeared, even her truck, which was parked just outside. It couldn't be more than twenty feet away. But all that existed beyond the porch was a swirling mass of gray. "So this is a blizzard," she said to the house. As usual, it didn't answer. There wasn't much the house hadn't seen before, after all.

There were still embers in the stove, but fewer than usual. She emptied the ashes, piled on strips of newspaper, and added fresh wood. Through the glass she watched flames rise. It wouldn't be long before she could close the damper, and then the real heat would start. She made coffee under the freshly hung upper cabinets, going mostly by feel and the light of the refrigerator when she opened its door.

A flash outside made her heart jump. Colton's truck? What time was it? She ran up the steps two at a time. By the time she heard a knock, she had pulled on a pair of jeans. "Come in!" she called. He knocked again. There was no way he would hear her calling over the sound of the storm. She pulled a flannel shirt on over a tank top and jogged back down the steps to open the door.

Colton looked like a snowman. "Welcome to Montana!" The relative silence of the house disintegrated, as it did most weekday mornings.

"We've got about a foot so far. I put chains on so I don't get stuck."

He stomped his feet and then noticed the rug there, a small mat she'd bought for three dollars at Walmart. "Nice. You do know there's no floor to protect," he said, gesturing to the wooden sub-flooring.

"It felt uncivilized," she said, and he laughed loudly. He laughed at most of her jokes, even the ones she didn't mean to make.

"You don't have any shoes on. Did you just wake up?"

She humphed and turned her back on him.

"You did! Hah! Miss Morning Sunshine just woke up. Now you know how the rest of us feel."

"You wake up early, too." She kept her back to him so he wouldn't see her smile.

"I have to. But normal people aren't happy about getting up at five-thirty."

She poured two cups and handed one to him. "I just like—"

"Sunrises," he finished for her. He took the cup from her hand and raised one eyebrow. "The sun is rising a lot later than 5:30 these days, Poppy. Besides, with this weather, you'll hardly know the sun is up." He slurped the coffee and walked into the kitchen, flipping on the light switch. "We did a good job hanging the upper cabinets."

"After all the sound and fury."

"I just don't see how you can level cabinets against an unlevel wall." He leaned back against the countertop. "It looks good in here, doesn't it?"

"It looks perfect."

"Too bad someone's just going to rip the whole thing out again."

Poppy's jaw dropped. "What?"

"This house and the little bit of land that will go with it will sell for more money than you'd think."

"Oh, I can think a lot," she said. "I've spent most of my life in California. But why rip it out?"

"Because around here, people who can afford the land want custom homes."

"So why are we fixing it up?" She felt as if she was being nosy.

"Two reasons. One is that Bettina thinks every penny we put in will get us five pennies back. She said it's about letting people imagine how beautiful the house could be, not to mention fixing old problems like the wiring. And it's also about income, because she said there's a good chance someone will buy the land planning to put a mansion here someday and use this house as a rental in the meantime. She said a rental like this could pay for itself in less time than you'd think."

Bettina was the real estate agent who had tried to help Poppy find a rental—or at least she assumed it was the same woman. "So why can't you be the one to rent it out?" She realized how silly that sounded. She was his renter. "I mean, when it's finished, at the market rate."

Colton sighed, his gaze drifting over the freshly painted cabinets. "I haven't got that kind of time to raise money."

Poppy was beginning to understand what he meant. She knew there were a lot of expenses to running a ranch and only one payday, when the cattle sold in the fall. And he had to consider his co-inheritors, his uncles Cash and Anson. The tension she'd seen around that topic made her avoid asking him about them. But there was one thing she was willing to ask. "Is selling the house your only option?"

He turned back to her. "No. And it may not be the best option. It'll cut a piece out of the middle of the ranch. And you have to have road access, so we'd share the driveway. And Bettina is concerned about the barn being so close to the house. I could sell cattle."

His good mood faded away as he continued to

speak. "The ranch would lose money, and then what? No cattle, no ranch. The other option is to sell off pasture land. Before I was born, my Grandpa Art sold land to the Russet Ranch to the north. Emmaline said it nearly killed him. In fact, she thought it did. He drove himself to be able to buy it back, but he never could. I have no doubt they'd like to get their hands on more of the land adjacent to them. It has two creeks, one that is reliable all year round, and a couple of springs. I bet I'd have cash in hand in a month."

He folded his arms and crossed one ankle over the other. His leather and rubber boots looked more than well-worn now, and they still had the water from melting snow all over the top of them. His chin dropped nearly to his chest. "Anson would be able to pay off what he owes and have money left over to fix the hotel up the way they always dreamed. Cash...well, Cash would do more of what he's already doing, turning money into more money. And Zane would get some of it, and he needs it, now that he's planning on marrying Mara. Only God knows how they'll survive. Everyone would be better off if I just sold the whole thing."

Marry Mara? She thought he must be wrong. When she'd taken Zane to the hospital a little more than a week before, she was certain they'd broken up. But she wouldn't let herself get distracted. For the first time Colton was opening up about his situation, and she could see that it pained him. She wished there was something she could do. "You don't want to sell the land."

"No. The land is what's kept this ranch going. Without it we'd have to run even fewer cattle than we have now, and that isn't enough to make a living. If I sell off part of the land, I'll have to sell it all eventually. And I will have failed her." Then with a bitter smirk, he added, "Again."

"Failed who?"

His eyes met hers again, looking stormy and dark, without any of the spark she usually found there. "Emmaline. Why didn't she leave it all to Anson? He's the responsible one. He would have handled it all and taken care of the rest of us in a fair way. And Cash—if he had a chance to develop this place, all the Gunnersons would be rich. But she didn't leave it to either of them. She left it to me."

His expression was earnest now, his voice low. "I let every penny I ever had slip through my fingers. And Emmaline knew that. But she gave me exactly 51 percent so I could control it all. I'm not even her son, I'm her grandson. So is Andrew, and he's solid as a rock, and Liam, who knows money like no one else, but she gave it to me." The pain and frustration she read on his face made her heart hurt. She wanted to reach out, even to lean into him and wrap her arms around him, to let him know how she felt.

But she could imagine how he would react, how awkward it would make him feel. All she had were words. Poppy spoke carefully. "Why do you think she did leave it to you?"

"Because she knew I'd keep it a ranch." He let out a bitter laugh. "So here I am, selling off the house Papa Art and his dad built for her." He raked both hands through his hair. "I don't know if I can get this ranch running again, but I have to try. It's just that I can't let Anson and Cash carry the burden in the meantime. It's not fair to them."

Poppy imagined that Emmaline thought she was giving her grandson a great gift, but it sounded like a curse instead. She listened to the wind howl and the sound of icy snow striking the kitchen window and the glass panes of the French doors that had replaced the plywood-covered opening behind her. They were holding tight. Colton did good work, even when he didn't expect any of it to last.

"I didn't mean to dump all this on you."

"I'm glad you told me. It sounds rough."

"Yeah, well that just shows you what an idiot I am. I inherit the better part of a ranch worth a couple of million dollars and here I am whining about it."

It was a lot of money. But he didn't see it as money; he saw it as a responsibility. She understood that more than she was willing to admit.

CHAPTER 16

It was just about time to end the renovations for the morning when the kitchen phone rang, the one on the old landline. Poppy jogged down the stairs and answered it.

"Emmaline?" The voice sounded unsure. It wasn't the first call for Mrs. Gunnerson that Poppy had received. More than one person calling had mistaken her for the woman who had lived here so many years. Behind her, she heard Colton's footsteps thumping down the stairs.

"This is Poppy Marsh. I'm renting the Gunnerson house."

"Oh." A mixture of disappointment and relief. The woman sounded older; perhaps she'd been a friend of Emmaline's. "I'm trying to find Colton. Is he there?"

Poppy handed the phone to Colton.

He said hello, listened for a minute, then he said, "Yes, Mrs. Ekstrom, I know the spot. I'll head out there now. Please tell Everett I said thank you. And I promise to give him my cell phone number, okay? Yes. Cell phone number. Have a good day, Mrs. Ekstrom."

He handed the phone back to Poppy. "The problem girls are trying to take down my fence."

"What?"

"The wind is blowing out of the north. Evidently, they just started heading south, hit the Ekstrom fence line, and they're bending it pretty badly. I have to go chase them off before they rip it down."

He walked past her and pulled on his knit hat, and before she could stop herself she'd said, "Can I go with you?"

He looked at her with such shock that the color started to rise in her face. "Well, sure. But you need to get clothes on that'll keep you warm. I have a couple of extra sets of bibs in the bunkhouse."

She didn't know what "bibs" had to do with anything, and she didn't want to find out. "I have a few things." She jogged upstairs before he changed his mind, and before she turned any redder. She put a pair of running tights on under her jeans and put a pair of packable rain pants on over that. Then she put her fleece sweater over the flannel shirt and put her parka on over that. That should do it, she thought.

When she came down the stairs, he eyed her hiking shoes. "Those won't work."

"They're waterproof."

"Hmm." He gave the rest of her a once-over, which made her face heat up again. "Is that all the gear you have?"

He was holding a huge pair of gloves. Poppy ran back up the stairs, grabbed her work gloves, and came down again. He noted the pair, chewed at the inside of his bottom lip, then cheerfully said, "Let's do this!"

Do what? she wanted to ask. She didn't know what to do about cattle trying to dismantle a fence. Or why they would do that in the first place.

The first breath she took after leaving the house made her lungs close up in protest. Two steps off the porch, the first blast of icy snow shards stung her face and she could barely see well enough to grab the door handle of Colton's truck. By the time she got in the truck, her ears were stinging from not only the ice but also the rush of the wind. She reached up to brush her hair out of her face and discovered that it was soaked, all of it as if she had just gotten out of the shower.

Colton was rummaging under the seat. He pulled out a big knit hat with bits of dried grass stuck all over it and handed it to her. She gratefully put it on and pulled it over her cold ears.

"It's pretty miserable out, you sure you want to come?"

She nodded, even though she was certain by now that he considered her a liability. It didn't help that she was already beginning to shiver.

The calf-deep snow made for a slippery drive, and just as soon as warm air started coming out of the vents, he turned the truck off again. "The girls know the diesel means food, so we'll drive that," Colton said. Poppy slipped her hood over the knit hat and stepped out into the wind again.

The barn was huge. It was one thing to look down on it from the homestead, and another to stand beneath it. If it were an apartment building, it would have to be three stories tall. Maybe four at the pointed peak. Up close she could see that the creamy color she'd imagined it to be was a combination of peeling and faded yellow paint and the weathered gray wood beneath it. Colton pushed one of the doors to the side, just enough to slip through. She followed him inside and he closed the door again.

The interior ceiling was lower than she expected, just about ten feet, and it was cozy inside. There were stalls along one side, pens along the other, and dingy old windows on the outside walls. It smelled of alfalfa and fur and manure —wonderful.

One of the stalls had an occupant. A brown horse with large, dark eyes watched her over the door, and Poppy stepped closer to it. A friend had once told her that horses' noses were as soft as velvet. But Poppy had never had the chance to find out.

Colton was getting ahead of her. At the other end of the barn, both doors were open. In the shadows, she could see a tractor in the corner, partially covered by a tarp and some cardboard boxes. It was colored in equal parts rust and green paint. Parked just outside the doorway was the diesel, already loaded with two hay bales. One was shoved up against a rack behind the back window and the other suspended above the end of the truck by two arms that seemed to pinch the huge round bale from either end. She'd seen the truck with and without bales loaded on it, but she hoped to see how the whole contraption worked today.

Colton stepped inside to start up the truck, then came back out to undo a plug. "You have to plug it in?" she asked.

"Yup. Only way to keep it running when it gets this cold out. Climb in the driver's seat. You can help me get the chains on and save me a ton of time."

She did as he asked. Not surprisingly, she had to scoot the seat forward to reach the pedals. She looked around at the torn vinyl and stained floors and the thick coat of dust on the dashboard. The key was in the ignition.

Colton appeared beside her, and he rolled down the window before shutting the door. "Ever start an old diesel before?" he asked. When she shook her head, he said, "Only turn it part way. Count to fifteen, then turn it the rest of the way."

She didn't ask why, she just did as he asked, and the diesel roared to life. A cloud of black smoke curled forward from the back of the truck, but Colton didn't seem to notice. "Okay, don't go anywhere yet. I've got to get the chains ready."

He pulled two small but heavy-looking boxes

from the same corner where the tractor sat and dragged something that looked like a small ladder made of chain out in front of the truck. Once he'd situated all four, he pushed through the open window and leaned over her. There wasn't much room between the steering wheel and her, so Poppy pressed herself backward. All she could think of was that he smelled good, grassy and fresh like a dash of summer in the middle of the blizzard. He flipped a few dials and a rush of cold air, along with more dust, came out of the vents.

"Okay, pull forward a couple of feet."

She looked at the stick shift, which had a tennis ball over the knob.

"Reverse is down and left, low is up and right, first is down. You can figure out the rest."

Low sounded about right. She put it in gear, and when she let up on the clutch, the truck crept forward. Colton leaned backward and looked down at the ground. "A little more."

His hands were bare. She wondered how on earth he could stand the cold.

"Stop. Okay, hold on a minute."

He disappeared again, and she sat still, the window still down, as the heat slowly began to thaw out the cab of the truck. It smelled like fuel inside. As much time as he spent in it, Colton never smelled that way. He smelled like fresh hay and clean sweat. The kind of sweat her fellow students got after a day of fieldwork in the sunshine, not the kind they got during exam week. She supposed it was stupid to think that sweat could smell good, but it did. On the right guy. At the right time.

Funny, she'd never really noticed how Geoff smelled. Mostly he smelled like the expensive cologne his sister always bought him. It was the kind of smell that didn't leave much room for other scents. She didn't miss it at all.

She thought about Geoff's delicate sauce pan, his whiskey bottle collection, the way he sneezed, the way his eyebrows knit together like twitching caterpillars when he was angry, the way he bared his teeth when he tried to smile but didn't feel amused. There were a lot of things about Geoff she didn't miss. Stupid things, sure. They meant little compared to being with an intelligent man who led a stable life.

But there were big things, too, like his moods. She wouldn't miss the silent, brooding moods that lasted for days at a time.

Maybe Geoff wasn't as stable as she had imagined.

"Roll forward," Colton called from in front of

the truck, and after she had done so, he held up a hand for her to stop again and then disappeared once more below the big, curved hood of the truck. She felt the truck rock a little. Then without warning the passenger door opened, and he jumped in. "All right, let's go."

"You can drive now," she said.

"That's right, I can," he said with a smile. "So can you. Just follow the tracks."

Ahead of her she could faintly see two lines where the snowdrifts weren't as high. She put the truck in first gear and started forward. Farther from the barn the snow swirled so much that she had a harder time making out the tracks. Colton told her to veer left or right, explaining that she needed to avoid the drifts. But to her everything looked flat.

"See them up ahead?" he asked. "They like this truck. We should be able to get them to follow. Just get close and let's see what they do."

The dark blur up ahead resolved itself into a group of big black cows huddled together. "What are they doing?"

"The problem girls don't know what snow is, so this is scary for them. And since the wind is coming out of the northwest, they decided to head the other way. But this fence is as far as they can go unless they decide to push it down. I share this fence with the Ekstroms. They should be back by the barn and out of the wind, but they aren't that bright yet. For some reason, Ekstrom was out this way and saw them huddled up. I can't say as I blame him for calling. The fence here needs work." He pulled his hat down over his ears. "Then again, so does the whole ranch."

Two by two, big, sad eyes turned her way, and the cows started to come over to the truck. One walked by so close that she could have reached out to touch it if the window had been open, and in the rearview mirror she saw it reach up to pull some hay off the bale in the back of the truck. "They're hungry."

"Yup. Hungry is what cows do. Pull it around and face back toward the barn."

"But I'll hit one of them if I do."

He chuckled. "They'll get out of the way. Just go slow."

She crept the truck around in a tight circle, and as she did, Colton kept his eyes on the corner of the pasture. He asked her to back up toward the fence. "But I can't see the cows!"

"If you hit one you'll know it," he said.

She glowered and backed up slowly.

Colton got out and flipped the seat forward to

rummage around behind it, coming out with a stiff, coiled rope. "Hold on, looks like someone's stuck."

She opened her window to lean out and look behind her. One of the cows, a small one, was still against the fence. Poppy couldn't see her legs at all.

Colton was thigh-deep in the snow by the time he got to her. He tromped around for a minute, and she realized he was trying to break a path for her. Then he placed a loop of the rope around her neck, flipped another loop through and over the cow's nose, and ended up with a makeshift halter. Then he started pulling.

But the cow wanted nothing to do with it. Poppy opened her door to get out and see if she could help, but another cow walked right up to her. It was huge. And greenish spit was dripping from its mouth. She shut the door again.

"Back it up some more," Colton called, and she saw him motioning her closer. She did as he asked, and she felt the truck crunch into the snow bank. Then his hand went up. "That's good."

He wrapped the rope through the bumper and held on to the free end. "Pull forward. Slowly, and get ready to stop," he called.

Poppy wasn't sure if she should. But she didn't

like how the cow looked. Her head drooped so low her nose was in the snow. She put the truck in low and crept forward. Colton dove into the snow beside her, to push, Poppy guessed. The cow's neck seemed to stretch out, and just when Poppy thought she'd better stop, a chest followed it out of the snow. It looked as if the cow couldn't get her footing. "A little more," he called, and Poppy did as he asked, although she was afraid of killing the poor thing. The cow broke free, and she teetered on her back hooves and front knees, but then she stood wide-legged, puffing steam into the cold air.

Colton went over to the cow and rubbed his gloved hand on her forehead. It looked as if he was talking to her, but Poppy couldn't hear anything over the wind. He took the rope off and stepped back, and the cow took a few careful steps forward. Then he and all the snow that had gathered on him climbed into the truck. "Back to the barn. We'll see if she can keep up." He rolled down his window, since the snow and steam made it nearly impossible to see.

Just when Poppy thought they must be getting close, Colton opened the door and popped out while the truck was moving, then quickly closed the door and jumped up on the running board.

He gave her a few instructions and then he and the rope disappeared into the blizzard.

They were simple requests. Get back to the barn, turn right, go through the gate to the end of the pen and turn around. How hard could it be?

She inched forward, straining to see tracks on the formless white snow. Open the gate. She could do that. Except the cows were outside the truck, between her and the gate. The huge, low-ing, irate-sounding cows. She opened the door, stepped out, and at least a dozen cows turned to face her. The mooing stopped. To Poppy, it didn't seem like a good sign. She left the door open, just in case.

She took one step and felt something thicker and wetter than snow seep over the top of her an-kle-high hiking boots. It was too late to stop it, and she didn't want to think about what exactly she was stepping in, so she walked forward, staying close to the truck. She reached one hand out toward the gate. The movement made one of the cows jump sideways, which made Poppy jump, which made the whole herd go collectively insane. Poppy struggled to keep her balance while the cows tried to get away from not only her but everything else, including each other. Was Colton trying to get her killed? She stood still and waited, and eventually they settled back into staring at her, their ears twitching, steam puffing out of their nostrils.

Poppy managed to swing the gate open and creep back to the truck. The girls let her know exactly when she was moving too fast, so she kept it slow.

Driving the diesel was fun, especially with chains on. She felt invincible. She loved her comfortable and warm little truck, of course, but there was something about this she could get used to. She drove to the end of the pen and started to turn around. But she was surrounded by fences and cows. She and the invincible truck were trapped.

She inched forward ever so slowly. They wouldn't give her room to move. She listened for any sign of distress from the unseen cows behind her as she put it in reverse. When she heard Colton's loud "Hey!" her heart jumped.

"Just push those girls out of the way," he said, emerging from the swirling snow.

"I don't want to hurt them."

"Hurt them?" He looked amused. She assumed that meant the other cow was out of danger, which was a relief. "I read somewhere a cow's hide is as tough as leather."

It took her just a moment to get it. "Very funny," she said.

"You've got about six more feet behind you."

She backed up slowly until she had enough room to finally face the right way around. Colton stepped up onto the running board again. "Now grab that remote control. You've got to drop the hay."

"What?"

"Well, you wanted to help." The man looked entirely too happy.

"You're enjoying watching me make a fool of myself."

"I think you're doing pretty good. For someone who doesn't know snow. Or cows. Or gates."

"Fine." She took the remote, and he talked her through dropping the rear bale onto the ground. Then she pulled forward, and in her rearview mirror she saw a lumpy carpet of hay spread out as it unrolled. She drove out of the pen, and he closed the gate. Thirty seconds later, while she was still relishing her accomplishment, he informed her that she needed to grab another bale if they intended to feed the other cows.

Under Colton's guidance she drove down to the stack of huge round bales, backed into one and grabbed it with the baler, flipped it on its side, and then loaded it onto the flatbed. When the weight of the bale thumped against the truck, the whole thing lurched forward, and she was certain the bale was going to come through the back window and onto her head. She screamed. Of course Colton thought that was funny too.

But the rest of the job was fun in a strange way. They drove out into what Colton called the north pasture, and the older cows treated her like a rock star, jogging their unwieldy selves right up to the truck. Colton patiently talked her through loading two more bales. But that *wham* when the second bale shoved the first into the rack nearly got her again. The swirling snow had calmed just a bit by the time she drove back up to the barn, and she even remembered to back in the truck. Not that she got it straight, but Colton didn't complain.

When she got out of the truck, the cold pierced her again, and she hurried into the shelter of the barn. Colton plugged in the truck and closed all the doors, and they walked through the near dark to where his usual truck was parked. "Pretty good for a greenhorn."

"And you were a pretty good teacher. When you weren't laughing at me."

He laughed at that and slid the far door open. But she stopped where she was, pointing to the ceiling above her. "What's up there?"

"Some square bales. Old grain. Seed."

"Can I see it?"

He hesitated for some reason. "Yeah. I'd be happy to show you, but not now, it's getting dark. I want you to see it when the sun is out." There was something about the way he said it that startled her, and made her smile. The barn mattered to him, and what she thought of it mattered to him.

"Thanks," she said.

"For what?"

"For letting me come out with you today. I'm sure I slowed you down, since all I know about ranching I learned from watching Western TV shows. Wait." She thought for a second. "I'm not sure I've ever seen a Western."

"You what?"

The disapproval on Colton's face took her by surprise. "*Lonesome Dove? High Noon?*"

She shook her head and slipped through the door, sneaking a look at the high arch of the barn's roofline. "Nope."

"What do you watch?"

She climbed in the passenger side of his truck and thought about it. "Documentaries."

He gave her a look that reminded her she was a hopeless geek in school. "Seriously, Poppy."

"I like them. And I watch other movies, too."

"Like what?"

She wished he hadn't asked. "I like, well, chick flicks. Not the sobbing kind, though. The happy kind. I like happy endings."

"Well, I can see why, after watching all those documentaries."

She laughed. "They aren't usually cheerful, are they?"

"No. But what could be more cheerful than Clint Eastwood taking out all of the bad guys?"

She shook her head.

"You missed lunch," he said, sounding guilty. "How about you let me get dinner? I have two frozen pizzas in my freezer. You're bound to like one of them."

"I don't like green pepper."

"I don't either. So it's settled." He flashed her a smile.

There it was again. Most of the time she was perfectly comfortable with goofy, loud Colton. She was even okay with the moodier side that sometimes showed up at the end of the day. But once in awhile, she was reminded that he was an incredibly good-looking man. Then she'd remember their dinner out at the Combine, his smooth-talking ways and the way he responded to that pixie-cut Keli Coulson. No matter how nice he seemed, no matter how naturally he flirted, he was still that guy. And she'd always be the girl he was embarrassed to be with when Keli showed up. She didn't have to worry about him mistaking her friendship for something else.

Which was good. Friendship was good. One day of feeding cows didn't make her fit into Colton's life, and it didn't make him fit into hers.

CHAPTER 17

She looked out over the green pasture and thought the place had no right to look this beautiful just a couple of days after a snowstorm. Over a foot had fallen, but only patches of the white stuff remained. She turned her attention back to the bundle of hay in her hand to make sure none of the cow's sticky green spit landed on her.

Her ear tag read 222, which was easy enough to remember. That's how she knew that the cow was the same one who'd gotten stuck in the snowdrift. She looked healthy enough now. And although she was small compared to the others, she was still almost a thousand pounds of hoof, muscle, and baby. And here she was happily munching on a bunch of dried grass when there was green grass sprouting up all around her. Poppy reached out to scratch the tiny patch of white hairs that speckled her forehead. She seemed to like that. But Poppy's hand came away coated in hair and an unidentified black gunk. "You need a bath, girlfriend," she said.

The sun soaked through her fleece sweater. It was as if the day was autumn and spring all mashed together, with the wet, green smell of new grass and the golden smell of fall from the rest of the plants as they gave up and turned gold. Add that to the blue sky, the smell of hay and fur, and the sound of the small trickles of melting snow here and there and Poppy was pretty sure that this is what heaven would be like if it existed.

She heard a motor and saw Colton's truck approaching. He had said he was going into town, so she hadn't expected him to return so soon. And it was too late to make a break for it. She hoped she wasn't doing anything wrong by being here. At the very least she'd be in the way. She stepped down off the lower rung of the fence rail.

He drove right up behind her. The back of the truck was loaded with something big and covered with a tarp, and she wondered what, since it seemed as if all the big purchases for the house had been made. It had to be ranch supplies.

He got out and walked over beside her. He'd left the door open, and behind her she heard the soft *ding ding ding* of the door alarm and the strains of some country music.

"I think she likes me, don't you?" Poppy said. The hay was gone, but 222 remained. Although she was eyeing Colton warily.

He chuckled. "What I think is that she was a bottle baby."

"Don't you listen to him," Poppy told the cow. "He doesn't understand the bond between us." The cow backed up a few steps, staring at Colton all the while, then she bolted and headed back to the crowd. "See? You hurt her feelings."

Colton put his arms on the top rail of the fence and looked out over the pasture. "You think she'd be more grateful since I saved her life."

"Does she have a name?"

"Nope. She has a number."

"Why?"

"She hasn't been around long enough to make a name for herself, and I doubt she will be. Although I suppose I could call her Stuck, or maybe Cowsicle, or Frozen Beef, or—"

"That's terrible. I think you should call her Determination."

He tapped each of the fingers on one hand on the rail. "Five syllables. You want to saddle that poor little heifer with a five-syllable name? Now that's terrible."

"Okay. How about ..." Poppy pictured the cow's face and thought of the flecks of white fur. "Sparkle?"

"You want me to name one of my cattle Sparkle?"

"She has these white bits of fur coming right out of the swirl in the middle of her forehead, like fireworks in a night sky. She does." Poppy put a hand up to cover the red she knew was rising on her neck.

He was staring at her with a funny little smile on his face. She wished he would say something, even if he were going to tease her. After far too long, he said, "Okay. Sparkle it is. And speaking of sparkle, I got you a present." He went back to the truck, undid a strap, and pulled back the tarp to uncover a sofa.

It was no ordinary couch. It had a Victorian look, with carved wooden accents and velvety purple upholstery in a quilted pattern. Poppy jumped up on the bumper. "Where did you find this?"

"It was at the inn. Three of the four legs are broken, the top has a big gouge out of it, and the upholstery has stains. I guess it's a reproduction, and Julia said it isn't a very good one, so it's not worth the cost of repairing it."

Poppy drew back the tarp the rest of the way. "It's beautiful!"

"I knew you'd like it." Colton looked pleased with himself.

"How did you know?"

"It reminded me of those boots you usually wear. Western, but a lot more, um, colorful."

She laughed and went back to petting the soft fabric. The stains were evident in the sunlight, but she doubted they'd show in the house.

"Have a seat. Don't worry about the legs, I took them all off. I have one more thing to show you." She sat down in the middle, leaned back, closed her eyes, and let the sunlight wash over her. To her surprise, he started the truck and drove toward the barn. The wind felt warm and fresh, and she bounced happily along on the beautiful un-Victorian sofa.

Curiosity pulled her off the sofa and out of the truck when Colton parked. He gave her a grin and then disappeared inside, and she followed cautiously, climbing the stairs she'd wanted to climb before.

She wasn't certain what she'd expected to see, but she hadn't expected one immense room without supports or additional floors. Curved beams arched up high above her, rising to a slight peak at the very top. Over that sat dark, weathered beams, and over that were the worn-out wooden shingles she had seen from below. The whole immense room was open from end to end. Narrow shafts of light peeked through where a few shingles were missing, and she could see more light from the edges of the large barn doors at either end of the building. One large door was at floor level, and the one on the other end was well above it. Inside was a pile of square bales of hay and some odds and ends, all dwarfed by the size of the room.

She wandered in, letting her eyes adjust to the darkness. "Amazing," she whispered. She turned around slowly. She'd only felt like this once before, when a friend had taken her along for a service in an old Catholic church. She'd spent the entire service looking up, her eyes tracing the intersecting arches, wondering how the building had been designed and built. She loved the very idea of it, a forest of stone within a building, a sky that nearly rivaled the real sky in beauty.

But this was even better. The aged wood, the long curves, and the unbelievable space. It was like being inside and outside all at once.

"So you like the hayloft?"

"This is all for hay?"

"Loose hay. Back in the day, before plastic-wrapped round bales. Imagine it stacked up to the doors over there. See the contraption above us? It's a trolley with pulleys to lift the hay and move it across the hayloft. That's as old as the barn, about a hundred years old."

She wandered in a slow circle. "This is incredible. It looks as fragile as an eggshell, but it's been here a hundred years."

"Yeah, but don't count on another hundred. It needs a foundation fix, and to have some of the old dairy structures jackhammered out. It also needs to be straightened, which is a nightmare. And after all that, it'll need a new roof."

"You're going to fix it, aren't you?" she said.

"I would if I could," he said.

When she heard the regret in his voice, she turned to face him.

He gave her an apologetic look. "It would be

cheaper to tear it down and build a new pole barn."

"That would be awful." The words just slipped out, and she could have kicked herself. He already felt bad.

"Yes, it would. There's a lot of history here. There was a time when this was the hot spot for barn dances and fundraisers. Between seasons, when the old hay was dragged out and before the new hay was cut, my grandparents would clean it out, and the whole town would come."

"And why not? Just add lights and some tables. What a beautiful place this would be for a wedding." Now she was talking about weddings. She needed to stop talking without thinking.

"There have been a couple of those here," he said. He walked across the floor and climbed the ladder that led to the high barn doors, and then turned and looked at the structure. "It's just got to last a little longer. If I can get this place turned around, I'll fix it. I just can't do it now."

She sighed. She wanted to tell Colton it would be all right, but the more she learned about the ranch, the more dismal his situation seemed. She wondered if anyone else in his family loved the barn the way he did. Or the ranch. And she wondered why they couldn't just all get together to make it work. But she knew the truth, of course. They were all adults with their own lives, careers, and obligations.

"It's stood this long, I don't see why not another year," Poppy said, trying to keep her tone cheerful.

"See that?" he said, pointing above her head. She looked up and saw a patch of blue sky. "That's from the storm a couple of days ago. It's just the latest hole, and winter is still ahead of us. Once the water gets in, the structure is compromised. And that'll be the end of it." He climbed down and walked over to her. "I didn't bring you in here to make you feel bad. I just figured that since you like old buildings, you'd like this place."

"I do," she said. She thought it was magical. But she wouldn't say something as silly as that, at least not out loud. If she'd grown up here, she would have spent a lot of time in this barn, hiding, maybe studying, definitely dreaming. "Did you spend a lot of time here as a kid?"

"More hours than I could count."

"What did you dream about when you were little?" There it was again, words just slipping out of her mouth. She didn't know Colton well enough to ask a question like that.

He didn't hesitate. "Rodeo, mostly. I wanted to

go on the circuit with my dad. I guess it never occurred to me that they don't let ten-year-olds ride."

"Did you do the same events as your dad?"

He snorted. "Yeah. All the same events. Women, beer, and other ways to burn money."

She would have had a hard time imagining that if she hadn't seen how he'd acted that night at the Combine. He was ridiculously handsome, really, with his ocean-green eyes and the devious smile he'd worn, and the single, deep dimple. He looked like a celebrity, though she had a hard time imagining the man she knew as someone who wanted to be a celebrity.

"Your wheels are turning," he said, and she realized that he'd been watching her as intently as she was him. "What have you decided about me?"

That set her blush ablaze almost instantly. She was glad it was cool and dark in the hayloft. She tried a diversion. "I don't know anything about rodeo."

"Well, you're in luck. There's a good one at the Metra in November. You should check it out."

"Oh, I won't go. I wouldn't know what to do."

He smirked. "I think you could handle it, Poppy. You find your seat, you sit down, and you watch a bunch of grown men try to get killed by animals that weigh ten times what they weigh."

"I know that much already. But I don't know the rules. It would be like the time I went to a hockey game. Nothing made any sense. People were cheering and booing, and the whole thing looked like a free-skate at the roller rink." She thought about what he'd said. "And I'm not interested in the women and beer events, but money burning sounds exciting."

He laughed, and that made him look a lot more like the Colton she knew rather than a celebrity. "I can give you a primer about the real events."

"Or you could go with me," she said. Did it sound like she'd just asked him on a date? Had the dust in the hayloft clogged her brain? "I'm just joking. I'm sure you're going with a bunch of your rodeo friends."

"No," he said, "I wasn't going to go."

"I don't think I want to go," she said. She wanted to let him off the hook, but now she sounded stuck up. She tried a different tack. "How annoying that would be for you, having to explain it all. Not to mention the poor people sitting around us trying to watch while you do."

"I haven't been to a rodeo for more than a year."

She didn't know what to say. Something had made Colton leave the rodeo, and it wasn't clear if he was ever going back. If he'd done any "money burning," that must mean he'd made a lot of money. Could he go back and make enough money to save the ranch? Was it the kind of thing he could do on the weekends? She had no idea.

He took a deep breath. "Sure. Let's go. It'll be fun."

He spoke as if fun was the very last thing it would be.

CHAPTER 18

When Colton got the couch loaded into the living room, he left again, but instead of going home, he went back to the barn and up into the hayloft. His mind was crowded with images, but one kept coming back. Poppy in his truck's rearview mirror, sitting on a purple couch, her face turned toward the sun as her gold hair blew all around her head, a big smile on her face. So perfectly her. The same girl that learned to load a baler in one day loved purple velvet. Of course she did.

And of course she would name one of the heifers Sparkle and never once think about how embarrassing that would be if someone else knew it. She was the most tangled-up mix of girly and ungirly things he'd ever seen.

She didn't have any of that high-maintenance attitude that he'd known, especially in the rodeo, where every girl thought she was a princess even if she didn't win the crown. No, Poppy knew the value of hard work, and besides, she was way smarter than any of them. Scary smart. She'd started talking about hybrids and genetic engineering once, and he'd just nodded his head once in a while and hoped she didn't notice that he didn't understand a word of it.

Even so, she looked more comfortable on the ranch than he sometimes felt. And not quite like the rancher's daughters he'd grown up with. He'd known his share of no-nonsense ranch girls before, ones who could throw a punch and would never name a cow Sparkle. There was something different about Poppy. Sweet, without trying to be. He couldn't remember the last time he thought a girl was sweet. Sixth grade, maybe.

And then he remembered Poppy staring at the roof of the hayloft like it was the Jefferson Monument. It reminded him how he used to feel in there when he was young, and he saw more than just what needed to be repaired. Watching her felt as good as a kick in the gut could feel.

And just when he was getting his footing again, she asked him to go to the rodeo. It was the one place he knew he shouldn't go. Emmaline asked him to walk away, and when he did, she gave him the ranch. There were risks. He didn't like to dwell on that part, but he wasn't an idiot. But to go as a spectator? That was cruel and unusual. He'd spent his whole life dreaming about rodeo, just like he'd told Poppy. And he'd been good. Really good. There was no telling what could have been.

Could he just sit in the stands for once? Poppy would sit beside him and ask questions. She'd listen, hang on every word, and then she'd make funny observations and tease him, but never say something just because she thought it was what he wanted to hear. She'd do everything right and maybe even not think less of him for riding a chair instead of a horse.

The rodeo was everything he'd ever wanted, even if it had almost killed him. But Poppy turning circles under the Gothic arch of the old barn was his world too, if he could just find a way to make it work.

He shook his head and stood up straight. He had a barn that was on the edge of collapse, and a girl who was leaving for Arizona as soon as her work here was done. There was so much she didn't know about him. He couldn't pin his future on her. He'd been a fool, more than a few times, but even he wasn't stupid enough to take that ride.

CHAPTER 19

*P*oppy was almost certain it was rayon. She sat with her face inches away from the purple fabric, her laptop and phone beside her. The screen was open to an upholstery cleaning guide. She had a plan in place, and there was a patch of fabric underneath the sofa that could serve as a test spot. Based on the construction, it had been made in the 1980s, despite its Victorian look. "I think it's rayon."

"Is that good or bad?" Sierra asked. Her voice sounded thin over the tiny speaker on the phone.

"Both. It depends on what the stains are. Coffee, maybe? I guess I'll find out."

"You should toss the broken feet and put more modern ones on it."

"I was thinking the same thing, but wouldn't that ruin the look of it?"

"Poppy, it's purple. Purple velvet. There are no rules for purple couches. It broke them all just by existing. Are you planning to bring this thing back to Arizona with you?"

Poppy could picture the tilt to Sierra's head, the way she tossed her red hair back over one shoulder and raised one eyebrow as a challenge. She'd seen it often enough.

"It's not mine to move," Poppy said. "He's staging the house, that's all. I just want to leave it better than I found it since I get to use it."

"He said it was a present, Poppy. That's what you said."

"I'm sure he didn't mean it that way."

"He gave you a couch. Not a bunch of roses that die in two days, but *furniture*, Poppy. And you said he's coming over for your second movie night tonight."

"It's not like that. Colton just likes Westerns."

"And you don't, but you're still watching them with him. So I think it's pretty clear what he means and how you feel about it."

Poppy looked out the window. She didn't expect Colton yet, but she wanted to make sure he wasn't overhearing this conversation. "Sierra, I called you to talk about you, not to talk about my landlord."

"Not much going on here, sis. I'm in Austin."

"Where are you staying?"

"Emmett's. I told you about him. I met him in Santa Clara and he said to visit sometime. So I did."

Poppy could imagine Emmett, the place where her sister was staying, and more that she didn't want to imagine. "Do you need anything?" She couldn't ask to give her money. That made her sister angry.

"No." Sierra's answer was flat and left no room for argument.

"Where are you going next?"

"Who says I'm leaving? I got a job at a local bagel place. It pays pretty well. Maybe I'll find a place of my own. It's a cool town, great music scene."

"I don't like musicians."

"You probably thought you didn't like rodeo stars, either."

"Colton isn't a rodeo—" Poppy stopped. She had no idea what Colton's standing was. They sure had treated him like a star that night in the Combine.

"Have you Googled him yet?" Sierra goaded.

"No! That would be stalking."

"Right, the queen of Internet searches hasn't looked him up. That's not suspicious at all. Maybe you just don't want to know."

She didn't. Women and beer. None of it had anything to do with her, none of it was her business. Frustrated that the conversation had switched again, Poppy snapped at Sierra. "Why did you leave?"

Sierra was so quiet Poppy wondered if she'd hung up. Poppy stared at her phone where it sat on the purple couch, aware of how fragile the connection was between her and her sister, the homestead in Montana and Austin.

"It got complicated. I don't like complicated."

You fell for someone in Coeur d'Alene, Poppy thought. Someone broke through her sister's shell, and she ran, just like she always did. "You had a good thing going there. I wish you hadn't run."

"You ran from Geoff."

Poppy couldn't say anything to that. But she was lucky enough to have landed in Montana. Sierra was never lucky, except for Coeur d'Alene. And now that was gone. "I hope you find a place like Moose Hollow."

"Boring. Even you want to move back to Tucson. Emmett just pulled up, and I have to go. He's my ride to the bagel shop. Bye!"

"Bye. I love you." The call ended so quickly that she doubted Sierra had heard her last words.

Poppy looked at her laptop. She stared at the screen for a moment, thinking, then she shut it. Colton was none of her business.

After some fruitless attempts at making changes to the propagation model in her thesis, she made a sandwich for dinner and ate it on the front porch, enjoying the warmth and wondering what the house would look like with some landscaping. It wasn't too late to plant some bulbs. They could be a surprise gift for whoever bought the house.

It was a bittersweet thought. The sun set behind the mountains, behind the house, and painted the sky to the east in soft hues of mauve and blue. She heard Colton coming up the drive then. No doubt with a Western.

He parked wherever the truck stopped, as usual, and came out holding two DVDs. "I couldn't find what I wanted. I think I loaned it to someone. But these will do."

"I bought a router," she said. "And my laptop has a bigger screen than that TV you brought last time."

"So you want to download it?"

"Welcome to the next century, Colton," she said, and she carried her chair back to the kitchen table. It had been fun last Friday, sitting on the kitchen chairs, staring at the little box TV and DVD player on the kitchen table, their feet propped up on either side of it. But after an hour of that, her rear had gone completely numb. The legless couch was going to feel like heaven.

Colton loaded the little TV and player back into his truck and grumbled about how John Wayne would never have downloaded movies.

He made the popcorn while she propped the laptop on a chair and found the movie he wanted online. According to the image on her computer screen, it did indeed have John Wayne in it, along with one of those old crooner guys and a younger man who looked hopelessly out of place in a Western.

When Colton joined her, he plopped right down beside her and set the bowl of popcorn down on her leg. "Is it loaded yet? You're going to love this." The heat from his shoulder touching hers seeped into her skin. He adjusted himself and nearly tipped the popcorn bowl over. When she caught it, he gave her a bright smile, and she realized he was far too close. She could see all the flecks of brown and gold in his green eyes, his long lashes, and that deep dimple on his right cheek.

The opening credits started, and she turned her attention away. It wasn't as if she was sitting in his lap, she reasoned. They were just friends. It would be much stranger to sit on opposite ends of the couch, far away from the small laptop screen.

And it didn't matter that it felt good. It felt good to be next to other people sometimes, and that didn't mean anything. She used to snuggle up and read to her sister. And once Poppy had a friend who liked scary movies, and they would always squeal and grab each other's arms at the scary parts. Poppy searched for other examples. Her adult friends—if she could call her fellow students that—were more distant than that. Like Geoff.

She couldn't remember ever sitting, just sitting, close to Geoff. He liked his elbow room. But that was Geoff, and Colton was different. Poppy's mostly solitary life had just made her hypersensitive to closeness. She needed to get out more. And she would once she got back to Tucson.

Colton pointed at the screen, bumping into her again. "Ricky Nelson, do you know him?"

"I thought he was a singer. Dean Martin too." She frowned. "There isn't going to be singing in this, is there? I don't like musicals."

Colton chuckled but didn't answer her. Poppy dropped her boots on the floor, tucked her feet up to one side, and tried not to read too much into having a friend who liked to sit next to her.

The sun set and the movie ended with a scene that must have been risqué in its time. It was enough to make Poppy blush, but that didn't take much. Colton suggested another movie and Poppy agreed, even though it was getting late. But ten minutes into the second movie, Colton slumped to the side, fast asleep, his breathing slow and loud. She tried to be interested in the movie, but she wasn't. She was more interested in Colton.

Finally she got a good look at the scars on his arms and hands. Some still bore suture marks. His nose might have been broken at one time; she couldn't be sure. The skin on his face was tan, and fine lines fanned out from his eyes. His hair was longer than when she'd first met him. It bore the marks of a cowboy hat all around his head, as if he'd been wearing a crown.

Everything about him was long and wiry, from his hair and maybe-broken nose to his arms, which were bent at weird angles, as if he'd been in a wreck rather than having just leaned over and fallen asleep. One leg reached all the way past hers on the floor, the other bent and tilted strangely under him. She couldn't imagine he was comfortable, but he slept soundly. Sleeping in a position like that was enough to explain his on-again, off-again limping.

For a moment she considered feigning sleep herself, even leaning over into the narrow space between Colton and the back of the couch. She could imagine how sweet, and how safe, that would feel.

But as he often was, Geoff was right there beside her. He had been the one to lie next to her. There were times he'd fallen asleep with his arm underneath her neck or his leg over hers, and she'd felt wrapped up, safe and warm. And that had been a ridiculous lie.

For some reason she'd assumed that if Geoff had sex with her, he must love her. Everything in the world, except for a few fairy tales, told her those two things had nothing to do with each other. But Colton was no different, with his "women and beer." She was the one who was out of step with the world. The one who thought her first love would be her last.

Then why couldn't she get over him? Why this black, sickening feeling in her stomach? She didn't miss Geoff. Sometimes she felt grateful he'd ended it. So why did it still matter that he didn't love her?

She felt emptied. Something had been lost, but she couldn't figure out what it was or how to get it back again. And she was pretty sure she never would.

She reached over and jostled Colton. "You need to wake up."

He barely moved.

She stopped the movie and shoved at his leg. "Hey, Colton, you need to get up."

He opened his eyes but still stared straight ahead. Then he sat up, mostly, but with one hand he was gesturing to the middle of the living room as if he was trying to stop someone. "I'm not ready."

"It's late, Colton. You've got to go."

When he turned to her, her heart jumped. His eyes looked as if they were nothing but black holes, and the blue light from the laptop lit his face strangely. It was as if he was looking at her and looking through her at her at the same time. It was Colton, she reminded herself. Nothing to be afraid of. "It's late," she said firmly.

"What time is it?"

"Almost eleven."

"Emmaline's going to kill me."

Another small jolt went through her. "You've got to go home."

"I was just ..." his words trailed off and he opened his hands, staring at his own palms. "This isn't right."

She'd had enough. "You need to go," she said. "Now." She grabbed his coat from the staircase and threw it in his lap, and he absently put it on. "I can't find your keys." He'd probably left them in the ignition.

"I don't need keys," he said, turning those wide, black eyes on her again. "I can't leave again."

That's right, she remembered, he had that weird don't-drive-at-night rule. Although for some reason he could drive again at 3:00 a.m. Suddenly there seemed to be too much weirdness surrounding Colton.

"I'll drive you," she said. When he didn't move, she stepped forward and took hold of the sleeve of his coat. He stood up and jerked his hand away, glaring at her. He was so tall. She wasn't used to anyone being that much taller than her. With that dark look in his eyes, his every movement seemed menacing. What if she needed to defend herself from him? "You have to go now," she said firmly, and this time, he followed her out the door and onto the drive. The temperature had plummeted since her evening dinner on the porch, and it had even begun to snow.

But he stopped behind her, pointing at his truck. "I can't leave it. He'll steal it. Then what am I going to do?"

Drugs. She hadn't thought Colton was the type. And she didn't know how on earth he'd managed to take them tonight without her knowing, but it was the only explanation. Unless he was psychotic. "I'll drive your truck." Then what, walk back? And leave him with the keys when he was in this state? No way. "Then I'll put it someplace safe."

He got in the passenger side and stared at the dashboard lights. Two minutes of driving and he'll be gone, she reassured herself.

She drove down the driveway to the Y in the road and then turned the truck onto his road. She'd never been up this way, so when he said, "Where are you going?" in an accusing tone, she wondered what she'd done wrong.

"To the bunkhouse, where you live," she said.

He shook his head. "This isn't right." No knowing what to do, she kept driving up the hill.

The bunkhouse was completely dark, except for the light cast by the headlights. It was a long, low 1960s ranch, and it hid well in the mixed pines. "You're home," she said.

Colton was shaking his head. "I don't want to see him."

She closed her eyes for a moment. Okay. Either there was someone else in the house or Colton was psychotic. "No one's there," she stated firmly. He didn't respond. "I'll go check, okay?"

She got out of the truck, leaving the door open. Her own shadow went ahead of her to the front door. She knocked loudly, waited, and then tried the knob. It was open, of course. Colton wasn't one for locked doors.

The headlights were the only light, casting a narrow path across an empty floor to a big whiteboard on the far wall. She felt around for a light switch, trying to control the fear that crawled up her spine. Finally, she found one and flicked it. A single overhead light turned on.

She was in what had to be the living room. There was furniture in it, but it all looked like repurposed patio furniture. There were two doors to her left, and through one she could see the edge of a bed. To her right, behind an island, was the kitchen.

The floor was a patterned brown linoleum that had seen better days. And instead of wooden trim, the doorways and walls were edged with industrial cove molding. Overhead was a popcorn-sprayed ceiling. But it was the whiteboard that really caught her eye. There were two grids and several lists on it. One of the grids was titled "Fence," but the other had no name.

Along the side were written "Bath," "Coffee," "Breakfast," "Teeth," and more. Minutiae. The kind of things normal people didn't have to write down and put check marks beside.

A sound behind her made her jump, and she turned to find Colton. His eyes looked completely dilated as he squinted against the light of the single fixture. "He's going to take the truck."

She had to get him to stay and to let her go. She played along. "No, he's not. I'm going to take it someplace safe."

"Beau broke the tractor. And stole Grandma's money. I've got to stop him."

"You need to go to sleep, Colton," she said.

He nodded and walked toward the bedroom.

She hurried out the door and darted to the truck. It was still running, and she shifted into reverse, watching the front door. She imagined him coming out with a shotgun, thinking she was the man who was stealing his truck. But the door never opened.

She drove the truck down to the Y, backed up and went forward again to make the turn, and then stopped. She couldn't live here, she thought. Colton's flaky memory was a daily battle. She'd just grown used to reminding him of the few things she'd needed him to know, but now he'd forgotten who she was and that Emmaline was dead. Then there was the fact that he wasn't allowed to drive at night but for some reason could after 3:00 a.m. And the boxes he secreted out of Emmaline's room one by one obviously weren't in the empty bunkhouse now. What would she find in that off-limits room? What flavor of drugs? What journaled ramblings?

And why did Officer Mike know Colton so well? Poppy thought over the exchange between them in Zane's hospital room. There was a history there. And the police officer had seemed so interested in her and her black eyes. Maybe he'd suspected her of being a troublemaker, just like Colton.

Or worse. Maybe he'd thought Colton had hurt her on purpose. Maybe that's the kind of man he was.

There was nothing to do about it now. She

would get some sleep and have a talk with Colton in the morning; she owed him that much. The disappointment she felt was so thick she had trouble breathing. She didn't want to go. But this never had been her home, and as little as she knew about Colton, she couldn't even claim he was her friend.

She started driving again, and the sight of the homestead made her heart hurt. She wanted to see it with Christmas lights on, covered in snow, the way she'd imagined the first time she'd seen it.

She saw something move and gasped. Someone was inside the house.

CHAPTER 20

*P*oppy calculated how long it would take Colton to walk from the bunkhouse to the homestead. He'd had more than enough time. But then the figure walked by the window again—a woman's figure—and she took a deep breath to calm herself. Was it Mara? She wasn't in danger, at least not at the moment.

There was no sign of another vehicle, and she hadn't seen another car on the drive. She had an idea where Mara lived, but it had to be at least a few miles away. By the time Poppy walked in the front door, Mara had settled in on the new couch and propped her feet on the chair. "Hi," she said, barely glancing up from whatever she was reading.

Poppy took the laptop off the chair and set it down in the kitchen. Then she added wood to the fire and came back into the living room to push Mara's feet off the chair. The heels were lower than usual, she noticed, a mere two inches or so. Good choice for a long hike. Poppy sat on the chair and faced her. "What are you doing here?"

"I'm looking at pictures," she said.

"Breaking and entering," Poppy said. "And a curfew violation, if there is such a thing in Moose Hollow. Not to mention that I seriously doubt your dad knows you're here."

"Why would he care where I am? I'm already a lost cause."

Poppy leaned back and crossed her arms. Her mind wandered to the front door, and she wished she'd locked it behind her. Not that Colton wouldn't have a key to the homestead.

"You had a fight with your dad."

"And you are freaking brilliant."

Poppy thought some more. Mara's cheeks looked red from the cold, but her color was good. Her hair fell in perfect curly waves, but most of her makeup was gone, leaving a few streaks down the sides of her face. And both of her wrists were still wrapped, but the bandages no longer covered the cuts on her forehead. "You look good. Cold, but good."

"I'm getting fat."

"I've heard that happens to pregnant women." Woman or girl, Poppy thought. Mara was somewhere in between.

Mara plopped the book down beside her. Or was it a photo album? "You are hilarious."

"Have you had any water?"

"Yeah, I drank some when I got in. Your water here tastes weird."

"Well water. You're just used to the taste of chlorine in the city water."

Mara made a face. "Chlorine? Like a pool? That can't be good for the baby."

"Neither is walking alone at night. For either of you. Or did you get a ride here?"

"From who?" Mara blew air through her teeth. "It's too late to call Zane. He would have come to get me, then he and dad would have had it out, and Zane's mom and dad would hate me more than they already do. And my friends? Let's just say that no one wants what's wrong with me to infect their daughters."

"So you came to see me."

She shrugged. "You live closest."

"You need a place to spend the night?"

Mara's eyes flickered toward Poppy. For the first time she looked her in the eyes, and Poppy saw the fear there. "Whatever," Mara said as if she didn't care.

"That's fine with me. But you have to call your dad and let him know where you are."

"I told you—"

"You have to call your dad."

"I'm not calling him. I can't even stand the sound of his voice. If you want him to know I'm here, you call him."

A call like that probably wouldn't go well, Poppy thought, considering the first and only time she'd met Mr. Maxwell was when he was trying to attack Zane in the hospital. But she wasn't interested in getting into a battle with Mara, and despite the careless tone of the girl's voice, she knew Mara felt desperate. "Fine," she said, standing up. "Give me the number."

Poppy dialed the phone, feeling her blood pressure rise for the millionth time that night. But talking to Maxwell couldn't be worse than dealing with psychotic Colton, could it?

"Hello?"

"Mr. Maxwell, this is Poppy Marsh."

"My ID says you're Emmaline Gunnerson."

"I'm renting her house."

He snorted as if that was funny, or pathetic. "Whaddya want?"

Poppy recognized the imprecise speech, the unusual patterns, as if his tongue couldn't quite catch up to the words his mouth was trying to say. She'd bet anything he was drunk.

"Mara stopped by this evening, and we wanted to know if it was okay for her to spend the night."

He said nothing; he just breathed heavily into the receiver.

"It's just the two of us. We thought we might ..." She was terrible at lying. She could never make up something on the fly. "Watch a movie," she finished. Right, at eleven or so at night. "I could drive her home in the morning."

"Whatever." He said it just like Mara did. "Tell her to get her butt home by six tomorrow for dinner with the Kel—Kolbys, or there's gonna be hell to pay."

"I'll tell her," Poppy said. She wished she knew what to say, and had the courage to say it, but all she did was hang up the phone. "You're good to go," she called into the other room. Poppy felt exhausted. All she wanted to do was go to bed. She walked out of the kitchen. "I can get a bed set up for you, but I need to—"

She noticed the French doors to Emmaline's room were open and the light was on inside. "You can't go in there."

"I already did," Mara said. "Where do you think I got this?" Mara lifted up the photo album and then set it back down in her lap.

"Mara, Colton said that room was off-limits. It was part of the terms of staying here."

"Whatever."

Poppy decided she would never say that word again. It was annoying.

"Give me that," she said, coming up beside the girl. "It's his business, not—"

The album was open to a front page banner and photo from a newspaper, cut out and covering one entire page. The headline read, "Season Ender for Gunnerson." Poppy caught a glimpse of the photo beneath it and sat down hard on the couch.

There were stands and a chute or cage of some kind. The gate was open as if the horse was supposed to run out onto the dirt floor of what she guessed was an arena. But instead of coming out, the horse looked as if it had fallen over backward in its small stall, legs flailing, head twisted. And behind him was a man. She could make out what looked like a leg folded beneath the horse, and one arm out to the side. Where the man's head should be, in the spot between the horse's back and a metal barrier, there was nothing. His skull must have been crushed. He must have died. Poppy tried to wrap her mind around it.

"Gunnerson?"

"Yup," Mara said. "Nasty. Has to be Colton. His dad Beau had stopped riding by then. Yeah, it says here Colton Gunnerson. Must have been this spring, right before he went crazy."

Crazy?

"Well, that explains it," Mara said, casually flipping to the next page. "He's brain damaged."

Poppy sat still for a while and wondered about everything. When she didn't reach any conclusions, she stood and walked into Emmaline's room.

Behind her, Mara gave her a play-by-play of the rest of the album. "He was in a medical coma, whatever that is," she said. "It says a severe concussion."

The wallpaper was the first thing she noticed, a tiny pattern of stripes and yellow roses on a creamy background. On the bed was a quilt sewn in patches of yellow gingham and blue denim. There were two pillows at the top, and on them, two round crocheted pillows in a sparkly yellow yarn. The floor was wood, but there were a couple of high-loop rugs on it, the kind with rubber backings, like bathroom mats. In front of the window, which looked out onto the front porch, there were two fancy chairs in pastel florals, a small table between them. The curtains were drawn.

"That's the end of the album, but there are some papers in the back that haven't been put into the pages yet. Wow, he was riding again two weeks later. He didn't even make the buzzer, though. You know, the horses just aren't that bad at those local rodeos. He must have still been messed up."

Between the bed and the table the floor was covered with open boxes. Inside them were trophies, cups, plaques, books, and papers. And lots of horse items. Bridles that looked brand new, with tooled leather and silver conchos. Saddles— at least two of them. A stereo, a video game console, wires here and there.

"He ended up back in the hospital a couple of days later. Whoever put this album together got the PRCA injury report online."

Against the wall, behind one of the doors, were flat, unused boxes and rolls of bubble wrap. She walked over to one of the saddles, which had the words "Bareback Champion" embossed on the leather beneath the seat. It was a work of art, with hand-tooled flowers—they looked like poppies—on the shiny new leather. It sat on top of two other saddles that also looked new. Untouched.

"If you can believe it, he rode again in Cody a week after that. The rodeo report says he looked really bad."

Poppy looked toward the other end of the room. Against the wall was a dresser topped with a few colored glass vials. The closet door was closed. Everything was dusty, but it was a picture of neatness and peace, especially compared to the boxes and chaos between the bed and table.

"Wow. He got a DUI in Cody."

Poppy strode into the room and took the album from Mara's hands. "Hey, I'm still—"

"You're done," Poppy said. "We're done." She headed back into the room, but there was no obvious home for the album. She put it on the corner of the neatly made bed, turned out the light, and shut the doors.

Poppy sat down beside Mara. "If you have questions about Colton's life, you should probably ask him yourself."

"It's all in the public record," Mara said.

"Fine. Look it up on the Internet on your own time. Right now I just want to know what happened with your dad."

"Oh, sure, someone getting arrested a few times isn't your business, but an argument with my dad is?"

"You're in my living room. If you want to stay here, you'd better start talking."

Mara was quiet for a while. "He's just a jerk," she finally said. Then after another long pause she added, "He's never going to forgive me for ruining his perfect little world." She was quiet for a long time then, and tears glistened at the corners of her eyes. She blinked them away.

Then the words came in a rush, so many that Poppy had trouble following. Mara's father wanted her to have an abortion. He was going to cut her off financially if she married Zane. And although it was difficult to piece together, she gathered that the only other option he offered her was that she go live in Costa Rica with her mother until she had the baby. If she didn't get too out of shape, he reasoned, she could still graduate with her class.

"And just move on with my life," Mara said, "as if I didn't love this baby or Zane."

Love at seventeen. Poppy thought about that

for a while. What a huge decision, with lifelong consequences. As was abortion. She didn't know how a teenager at odds with her parents could be expected to make it.

As Mara went on, her anger seemed to give way to sadness. She talked a little bit about her father, what a great dad he was before her mother left. It sounded as if Mara had been very young then. She talked about money, her totaled Escalade, and how far behind she was in school because of the accident. And when she mentioned that she could barely remember the accident and that what she remembered didn't make sense, Poppy remembered Officer Mike's interview with Zane. She was sure Zane had been lying about driving the car.

"What do you remember?"

"I remember drinking. I remember calling Zane and meeting him at the gas station. I remember we were fighting." She closed her eyes. "Don't you see? That makes me just like my dad. And I didn't know, but I had a feeling I might be pregnant, and I drank anyway. I don't know what Zane sees in me."

Poppy knew what he saw in her, besides her looks. And those looks were pretty impressive without all the distracting makeup. But it was the traces of the sweet and smart girl that leaked through here and there that meant the most. She was pretty sure Mara had a good heart—and she'd seen marriages based on less.

"When are you planning to get married?" Poppy hoped the answer would be after the baby was born when some of the drama was gone and they could make a reasonable decision.

"November. We'll both be eighteen then. But we can't get married and then go home to our parents, you know? We're trying to find a place to live. Don't tell Julia, okay?"

"You're going to have to tell her eventually, Mara. Imagine being his mom, living with him all those years, and suddenly he takes off."

Mara's thin eyebrows closed in over her eyes. "That would suck."

"Yeah." Then again, when Poppy had gotten accepted to college, and Sierra had said she was leaving at age sixteen, her parents had thrown a party. One filled with strangers, of course.

The conversation drifted to school again. Mara was worried about graduating, and at the same time, she was dealing with the fallout from her pregnancy. Many of her friends had abandoned her, and Poppy assured her that they were probably confused about what to say and how to act. "All I am is that pregnant girl now," she said. Then, softly, "I wanted to be something more."

Poppy wondered how she would have handled Mara's situation. Running away to Costa Rica sounded good. But she'd never been a teenager in love. "I can help you with the schoolwork," she said. She hadn't decided to say it out loud, since that sort of decision required thought and at the very least a good night's sleep, but the shocked look in Mara's eyes made it clear she couldn't get out of it now.

"Really?"

"Sure."

"I can come by every day."

"Every weekday. Maybe."

"Yeah. Really? You know this stuff? Even the science and math?"

She'd better, by now. "I'm pretty sure I do."

As the late hour finally caught up with her, she realized there was no extra sleeping bag for the girl. She went into the downstairs bathroom, the one she never used, and searched the shelves. Not surprisingly there was a neat set of yellow sheets and a white blanket—even an extra pillow. From her belongings, she found a T-shirt and a pair of leggings Mara could use as pajamas. Poppy made up the couch as best she could, got the stove loaded for the night, and as the girl sat down on her makeshift bed and stared at the clothes in her hand, Poppy got the strangest urge to give her a kiss on the forehead.

She didn't, of course. Instead, she went upstairs to think and, hopefully, sleep.

CHAPTER 21

*P*oppy jolted awake. She thought first of the arched ceiling of the barn, then Colton, then Colton's dead black eyes, and then she was certain a sound had awakened her. It was nearly dawn; she'd slept in. She got dressed, listening to the usual sounds of the quiet house, and then she heard something different. A door closing.

She slipped on her boots and started down the stairs. It had to be Mara, nothing more. When she ducked low enough to catch a peek, she saw nothing in the living room.

Then she saw that one of Emmaline's doors was open, and at just that moment Colton stepped out of her room. Poppy jumped and gasped, and she nearly tripped on the stairs. Colton gave her a stern look, put a finger to his lips, and then pointed at the sleeping girl on the couch.

He was giving *her* lessons on being quiet?

He crept across the floor, looking as awkward as the coyote on the *Road Runner* show, and motioned for her to come down. He mouthed something, but she couldn't make it out. So he took her by the shoulder and whispered in her ear, "I can't find the keys to my truck."

"How did you get in here?"

"The door was open. Sorry."

She hadn't remembered to lock the front door. Some caretaker she was, leaving Mara down here without even checking the locks. And the keys were in her coat pocket, which she'd taken upstairs. She turned to go back up, and he followed her. She wanted to shoo him back down the stairs, but she didn't want to make a scene in front of the girl.

He followed her like a puppy all the way to her room, where he stood staring at her camp pad and sleeping bag. "Why don't you get a bed?"

"It's fine." She was trying to figure out what to say to him, but the words weren't coming. She pulled his keys out of her coat pocket and handed them to him.

"I don't even remember leaving last night," he said. "I must have fallen asleep. At least I didn't drive back. I can get weird when I'm tired."

She had no idea what to say to that. Before anything came to her, Colton was on to the next topic.

"So what's Mara doing here?"

"She had a fight with her dad."

He made a face. "I wish they'd quit that."

He seemed so normal, so...Colton. She hardly knew what to think, and she had no idea what to say. She tried to conjure up the fear she'd felt the night before but couldn't. There were facts to deal with, though, like the DUI. And not driving at night. "Why don't you drive at night?"

"Because I promised Emmaline I wouldn't," he said. He didn't seem bothered by the question. "And actually, it's between ten thirty and two thirty that I can't drive." He stated it as if it was perfectly normal to have your dead grandmother choose random times for you to avoid driving.

"Why ten thirty and two thirty?"

His smile looked a little stiff. Finally there was a chink in his cheerful armor. "Well, that's a long story. I suppose I should tell you someday.

But all you need to know is that she was a wise woman with a direct line to Jesus, and I always did better when I lived by her rules than when I didn't."

And with that, the creepy feeling returned. Her mind was instantly filled with the image of an old woman who claimed to hear the voice of God and Colton with his dead, black eyes, summoning her ghost.

"Besides," Colton said, "I'm on parole, and Officer Mike let Emmaline set my terms."

So much for the séance. She wasn't sure if the truth was any better than her imagination. She wanted him to tell her that his parole was a joke, but he didn't. He didn't say anything. He could express his innocence, or shame, or explain or make excuses, but he just stood there and watched her. "Okay," she said.

"Is it okay?" he asked.

"I don't know."

"Fair enough."

From downstairs, she heard Mara's waking moan. "Coffee!"

Poppy walked past him and down the stairs. She needed to figure out the best way to handle him and any new information bombs he wanted to drop on her.

Mara was sitting on the couch with her head in her hands. "The service in this place sucks."

"Oh, isn't she cute in the morning?" Colton said.

Mara glared at him. "How long have you been here?"

"About five minutes. Long enough to hear you snoring."

"I don't snore!"

Poppy started getting the coffee ready. "You don't snore, Mara, he's teasing you." She was glad Colton still had his coat on; she didn't want Mara to think something else was going on.

"Jerk," Mara said. "I need coffee." She wandered into the kitchen. Both the T-shirt and leggings were too long for her. Without heels on, she looked tiny. "Black with a lot of sugar."

Poppy got out a small container of sugar and set it beside Mara. She was conscious of Colton standing behind her. She couldn't stay in a house with a crazy criminal landlord, especially one who felt comfortable breaking in while she was asleep.

And why was he so normal this morning? Not that he ever was all that normal. He had memory problems, and he got lost in his own world sometimes. He had frequent headaches that seemed to bother him. Most important, he was a criminal. She didn't dare forget that.

"I need a shower," Mara mumbled. "And I hope you have some real makeup around, Poppy. I'm not going out in public without it."

"I have mascara and eyeliner. And probably some lip gloss somewhere."

Mara leaned her head back and groaned. "Ugh. Curse of the hippies strikes again."

Colton laughed, then he said, "I don't know why you want to put makeup on, Mara, you look beautiful the way you are. And I bet Zane feels the same way."

He was so sincere sounding that Poppy shot him a look. So did Mara, who was frowning. "What's wrong with you? What do you want?" she said.

"Nothing," he said with a smile, then his eyebrows shot up. "No, I do want something. Poppy seems to think that rain pants, a rain jacket, and a pair of hiking boots are all she needs to get through this winter without dying of hypothermia."

"It was warm enough," Poppy said. And although she wanted to tell him that she wouldn't be staying for the winter, she didn't. Autumn in

Montana was already worse than any winter she could remember.

Mara shifted her disgusted look from Colton to Poppy. "That won't work. How much money do you have?"

The girl had no way of knowing that she'd asked Poppy's least favorite question. "Enough," she answered.

"Walmart-and-a-thrift-store-enough   or Bolton-Ranch-Outfitters enough?"

Poppy didn't know what the latter store was like, but given the fancy look of all of Mara's clothes, she could imagine. "Somewhere-in-between enough."

Mara turned back to Colton. "Poppy said she's going to help me get caught up at school."

"That's great." He gave Poppy the kind of look that made her feel worse about having to back out of her promise. She was moving back early. Once she told Mara what had happened on movie night, the girl would understand.

"What?" Mara said.

Poppy's brow wrinkled. "Nothing."

"You sighed. You look upset. You don't want to tutor me now, right?"

Although she couldn't explain it, Poppy knew from the look she was getting that a lot of people had backed out of their promises to Mara. "Of course, I do," she said.

"But?"

"But nothing." Poppy poured a cup of coffee and handed it to her. "We start on Monday after school."

She saw the grin on Colton's face. He looked as if he was proud of her. Both of them, maybe. She could tough it out at the homestead for a few more weeks. And have the locks changed.

Colton went on his way. After taking turns in the shower, Poppy was given a makeup lesson from the half-cowgirl, half-Goth teenager. It turned out better than Poppy expected, but Mara's taste was a little too heavy for an afternoon shopping for outdoor gear. After a lot of groaning and lecturing, Mara let her tone it down. Everything about the morning reminded Poppy of spending time with her sister before they'd both left home. Even then Sierra had acted like the bossy older sister, not someone younger by two years. Poppy missed that. She would have never guessed they would live apart all this time.

In town, Poppy chauffeured from shop to shop, Mara told her what to buy as if she was the official Moose Hollow guide, and Poppy spent more money on clothing than she had in a year.

And all the while Poppy couldn't stop thinking that the chances of her staying in Montana for more than a couple weeks were slim. But, she reasoned, she hadn't committed to any jobs yet, and there was no guarantee she wouldn't end up living someplace else with a cold winter. Even Arizona's Huachuca Mountains got cold in the winter.

She'd liked Arizona. But there was something about that October blizzard in Moose Hollow that made her feel, of all things, cozy. Just her and the wood-burning stove while the winds raged. Of course, driving in it was another thing entirely.

After dropping almost two hundred dollars on waterproof boots insulated to -40 degrees, she asked Mara if it ever really got that cold. Mara laughed. She took that as a yes.

When lunchtime came, they headed to a local bagel shop, where Poppy ordered cream cheese and smoked salmon—an order that made Mara crinkle her face in disgust. Mara ordered a cinnamon and sugar bagel. Poppy reminded Mara that her father was expecting her for dinner with the Kroegers. Or was it the Kugels? Forgetting the name made her think about Colton, and thinking about Colton made her try to reconcile his dead eyes with the sweet smile he'd given her this morning. It was impossible.

In the meantime, Mara had grown quiet.

"What's the matter?" Poppy asked.

"I can't go to dinner with Dad tonight. I need to go somewhere else."

"He's going to be mad."

"Well, that'd be new." Mara's attempt at snarky humor fell flat. Poppy waited for more while Mara stirred the ice in her empty pop glass. "I need to go tonight, but I'm scared."

That increased the mystery, but Poppy waited. She could tell it was a hard subject for Mara to talk about.

"I need you to go with me," Mara said, looking up.

Poppy knew she shouldn't answer until she knew what Mara meant. But she felt herself being nudged. *Go with her.* Maybe it was just the pleading look in her eyes. Maybe it was the shopping high—she'd be paying for that later, in more than one way. But there it was again. *Go with her.* "Okay," she said.

Mara's face filled with such relief it almost brought tears to Poppy's eyes. The girl looked down at her bagel. "You didn't even ask me where I want you to go," she said quietly.

She said it as if Poppy was a hero. But the more they talked, the more certain Poppy was that she didn't want to go. Still, there was no going back now. "It would be nice to know where we're going."

Mara glanced behind her. It was a small shop with half a dozen tiny tables. "Later, okay?"

Poppy nodded, but Mara's response didn't make her feel any better.

"I need to go home and change. Can you take me? And pick me up again, of course."

"Sure." Sure? This isn't like me at all, Poppy thought.

Mara left the rest of her bagel uneaten and headed out the door with Poppy. They passed an older woman on the way back to Poppy's truck, and she and Mara waved and smiled at each other. As they left her behind, Mara said, "She hates me."

"What?"

"She was my social studies teacher."

"She didn't look like she hates you. Why would she hate you?"

"Because I was a jerk in her class."

Poppy almost stopped dead in her tracks. It was such simple thing to say, but how many adults spoke that way? She herself had been a jerk more than a few times. Had she ever admitted it out loud?

Had her parents? Had Sierra? Poppy felt as if the world was shifting. In her experience, apologies were met with an "It's cool" and a few days of passive-aggressive behavior as payback. "Have you ever said that to her?"

"Nope. I probably should."

Just the thought of it made Poppy's heart beat faster. She stopped herself from telling the girl not to do that.

But why not? Why not admit when you're wrong?

Because then they'll know.

"You okay, Poppy?"

"Yeah. I think the lack of sleep is catching up to me."

"It didn't help, having Colton show up so early."

"I had his keys, though."

"Why did you have his keys?" Mara asked.

Poppy wished she hadn't said that. She tried to come up with the simplest answer. "We watched a movie last night, and it was kind of late when he went home."

"Yeah, I know all about that." The girl waved

her hand through the air as if she was a conductor. "Emmaline's rules."

"Emmaline's rules." Poppy bit her lip. She didn't have the right to ask what they were. But she did anyway, in an oblique way. "I don't know them all."

"Me either, I think. No chewing tobacco, no driving during peak bar hours, no drinking in a bar. Zane didn't tell me all of them."

Peak bar hours. That explained a lot. And no drinking in a bar? She remembered Danny taking his beer away, a bit at a time. Was everyone in on Emmaline's rules but her? Did Emmaline have a rule against acting like an ax murderer in the middle of the night? "Colton didn't tell me all of them, either."

"He will."

Although Poppy knew she should let that comment go, she couldn't. "What makes you say that?"

"You guys are perfect for each other."

Poppy laughed out loud. "Yeah. No. Absolutely no." She remembered Keli Coulson. "And Colton would say the same thing."

"Oh, yeah, sure. Whatever. But you make him laugh. Colton wasn't laughing a lot before you came along."

For a brief moment, Poppy's heart hurt. She covered it up by digging in her pocket for her keys. She couldn't explain the way her breath caught, but she was pretty sure the extra cup of coffee and lack of sleep had made her irrational and emotional.

She was given a small tour of the landscape as she drove Mara home. The girl seemed to know the provenance of all the land in the area. And as they moved into the subdivision where she lived, she learned that more than a few of the residents were her father's clients. "What does he do exactly?"

"He plays with other people's money. Wealth management, investment opportunities, that kind of stuff."

Poppy had no idea what that meant, but she didn't really want to know. "So you didn't tell me about where we're—"

"Turn here! Great. Dad's home. Pick me up at seven, okay? Thanks."

And with that Mara was gone.

Poppy took a deep breath. It was like watching a train wreck—while sitting on the rails. She pulled out of the driveway and drove to the homestead. Chaos aside, she still had a thesis to complete.

CHAPTER 22

*P*oppy had made the mistake of checking e-mail. There were no more responses from the three friends at school who had written her. It seemed to her that all they wanted was the story behind her quick departure and dead phone line, and having gotten it, they were satisfied. She'd written back to keep the lines of communication open, but that had been the end of it. For almost a month.

Then there were two e-mails from her advisor. The strategy they had chosen together to analyze her data was in question yet again. One of her committee members was pushing for two completely different computer models, and she had little experience with the second kind.

She rose and paced around the room. She could fire back an e-mail pointing out that the additional model would make her thesis much bigger than the standard fare for a master's degree, but her advisor was leaving the decision up to her. After it had been suggested, and without him protecting her with an outright no, she wasn't likely to leave the second model out. She felt manipulated.

Returning to her laptop, she clicked on one last e-mail. It was from Geoff. She expected to discover that some forgotten bill had come through and he wanted payment, but she was wrong.

Geoff began by telling her about the "super bloom" in the saguaro forest. He also said his contract had been extended. He didn't mention his lovely Irish intern, of course. In closing, he said he hoped she would call when she got a new phone and phone number. She had one, of course, but he didn't know that.

And he said he missed her, that he had made so many mistakes, and he was sorry. He didn't say what he thought those mistakes were, though. Dating her in the first place, perhaps.

It occurred to her that maybe he wasn't interested in his intern anymore. Maybe the Irish girl had acted like the eighteen-year-old girl she was. Poppy stomped down the stairs. Geoff hadn't actually broken up with her when he'd told her how little she contributed to his life. He'd made the suggestion and left the rest to her. It reminded her of the way her advisor hadn't quite told her to make a second model. Was she so easily manipulated?

It was time to get ready for whatever mess Mara had planned for her. She tried to reason herself out of her bad mood. How bad could it be if Mara was willing to ask an adult to come with her? She reminded herself that Mara was just a month away from being an adult herself. And a few more months after that she'd be a mom.

Poppy drove in the dark to Mara's house, dreading her walk to the front door and a possible encounter with Mara's father. He'd scared her. She'd been insane to stand up to a worried father. But Mara must have been looking for her; she came out the front door before Poppy had even stopped the truck. The girl climbed inside the cab without a word.

"You have to tell me at some point," Poppy said.

"It's a sexual victims and addictions support group," Mara replied, latching her seat belt.

Okay, Poppy thought, that was pretty bad. Worse than anything she'd imagined. "And I'm supposed to do what?"

"Stand by me."

She wasn't sure what that meant.

"And don't judge me."

Poppy thought about that for a minute. "I can do that."

They didn't exchange another word for miles. As they came into town, Mara directed her to the parking lot of a modest old church. As they walked to a side door, she caught Mara looking over her shoulder more than once, as if she didn't want to be seen. As much as she didn't want to go inside, Poppy reasoned, it wouldn't kill her to help Mara. And when the meeting was over, she'd be sure to be busy every single Saturday night until she left Montana.

They headed down the steps to the basement and were instantly greeted by a woman. She shook Mara's hand first. It was more like a two-handed hold than a shake, so when she got to Poppy, Poppy was prepared for it. "Welcome. My name is Katherine. I'm your facilitator tonight. And your name is?"

"Poppy." She wanted to say something about how she was only there to support Mara, but doing so didn't feel very supportive. She followed Mara over to a small circle of chairs—an arrangement she hated because everyone could stare at you at the same time. There was no break from the scrutiny. She hung her coat neatly over the back of a chair, then changed her mind and slipped it on again because it felt comforting.

She noticed Mara had hers on too—a classic pea coat in navy blue. "I like your coat," Poppy whispered.

"When you like something I wear, it scares me."

Mara's sassiness was back. Poppy supposed that was a good sign.

The group was an odd assortment of women. Katherine, the facilitator, looked to be in her fifties. Another woman looked about a decade older. There was also a tough-looking woman in her thirties who was complaining that the coffee was decaf, an athletic-looking woman in brand-new running shoes and matching Lycra, and a woman who looked to be in her early twenties. She was curvy and had a soft voice and sweet smile.

Katherine called them over to the chairs. "Okay, everyone, bow your heads. And as always, it doesn't matter where you stand when it comes to God. He's standing next to you. Abba, Daddy, we ask for Your strength, Your protection, and Your healing tonight. Bless these women to see themselves as You see them, and to trust You to make all things new. Amen.

"Okay, ladies, Tess wanted me to let you know she decided to visit her mom, so I know you'll want to remember her in your prayers. Especially tomorrow morning, which is when she's going to the hospital. And since we have some new faces, I'd like to go around the circle once. Just say your name and your favorite food. I'm Katherine, and my favorite food is brisket with a couple of gallons of barbecue sauce on it."

Everyone giggled. Next to her was the tough-looking woman. She crossed one motorcycle-booted foot over her knee. "My name is Julie, and I like chocolate cake."

The Lycra runner was next, and she liked sushi, but Poppy forgot her name because she was too busy trying to figure out what to say. Times like this made her feel as if everyone knew themselves better than she knew herself. And it was even worse because she was in a church, and there was no way of knowing what she might say wrong. What did people in church eat? She remembered the church picnic her friend from

Washington had taken her to, back when they lived in a real neighborhood and had real friends. Lily was her friend's name. Lily's mother had brought deviled eggs with some kind of magical concoction in the yolk. She could have eaten them all.

Everyone was looking at her. "My name is Poppy, and my favorite food is deviled eggs." For a second she was pleased she remembered the food, then it occurred to her that "deviled" eggs was probably the wrong thing to say in a church. She put a hand to her throat, but the blush was going to crawl all the way up onto her face, she just knew it.

"My name is Mara, and my favorite food is chocolate-covered espresso beans."

Poppy tried to pay attention. The curvy girl with the smile was Danetta, and she liked carrot cake. Poppy liked carrot cake too. What kind of person likes deviled eggs best, anyway? How about popcorn? Or apple pie? The thought distracted her again and she missed the other names.

Katherine explained that once someone began speaking, the others were not to say anything until the speaker yielded the floor. Then she asked if anyone had something to share.

Julie with the motorcycle boots leaned back in

her folding chair. "Yeah. I got something to say," she said, crossing her arms over her stomach. "I screwed up again."

Katherine tilted her head sideways. "Try to speak of yourself in kinder terms. The terms you'd use to describe me, for instance."

"Oh, Kath, I'd have no problem telling you if you screwed up."

Katherine grinned and turned a little in her seat to face Julie. "That's fair. Go ahead."

"So I met this new guy a couple weeks ago. I didn't tell y'all because I wasn't sure it was going to last. We stayed up all night talking, you know? Just talking. So he asked me out and we went for a ride up the Beartooth the last day it was open. Then we went to the Transfer Station in Billings, had a few, danced a lot, spent some time in his car making out, and I went home. And I'm thinking, I'm getting the hang of this dating thing.

"Then two days later he asks me over to his place for a pizza and a movie. And I know what he's expecting and I'm thinking, no way, bud. And when things get hot and heavy, I say I'm going. And he gets kind of mad, and he wants to know what's wrong. So I say—get this—I'm not easy. Me. I said that. If he knew me better, he would have laughed."

She paused and took a breath before going on. "So he doesn't call for three days. *Three*. Then he calls and asks me out to a nice steakhouse for dinner. Then the pool hall. He asks me if I want to have a drink at his place. And you know what? He paid for everything. Everything. It was a real date. So we get to his place, and he tells me he knows I need to be treated like a lady. So what do I do? I jump in bed with him. Once a tramp, always a tramp."

"I'm going to have to draw the line there, Julie," Katherine said softly.

"Whatever. There's no pretty way to say it. And guess what happens the next day? I get up to the sound of him going for a ride. So I go home and wait. And wait. And now it's been a week. He's gone."

Poppy was startled to see tears welling in the woman's eyes.

"It's always the same with me. I pick these guys, they act like they love me, and in a few weeks they've forgotten my name, and I'm just... I'm just ..."

She didn't have to say it. Poppy recognized the pain in the woman's eyes. She felt it whenever she thought of Geoff. She felt her own eyes filling with tears and blinked them away. This wasn't the time for self-pity.

"I'm just *broken*," Julie said softly. "It's like they take something from me every single time and I can't ever get it back. I thought I was freakin' Cinderella. But I'm not some eighteen-year-old with a hot body anymore. My prince never rode up on his Harley. I thought he did, once, then twice, then more times than I can count. And now I'm forty-two. Guys used to stick around for a while for the sex, and now they don't even do that."

Julie locked her eyes on Katherine, speaking only to her. "You watch women on TV, they talk like every single guy they sleep with makes them more sophisticated, or sexy, or whatever, but I never felt that way. I felt like every single guy I slept with took something from me. I wasn't the same after the first time. But I did it again. And that guy left. And I just felt smaller. Emptier. I don't know how to say it. And the real kicker is that this guy? I thought he was...I thought ..."

"And you don't even know if you love him." Poppy said, interrupting. She'd broken the rule.

Julie leaned forward, her hands on her elbows, and glowered at her. "Are you saying I don't even know what love is?"

She saw Katherine leaning in to stop the exchange, but Poppy spoke up again. "No, I'm saying ..." She dug deep. There were no words that were sufficient. "I'm saying we might be in love, maybe it could end up being love, but we don't even have time to find out. Because we're so busy making sure the guy loves us. I don't think love is supposed to feel so ..." What was it, that clenching feeling in her gut? "Scared."

Julie lifted one hand and jabbed a finger toward Poppy. "Exactly. We don't even get to find out. We don't even get to be in love."

Poppy nodded.

"And if even the jerks don't love me, who's going to, you know?"

Poppy knew. That was exactly how she felt about Geoff and the crass and cowardly way he'd dumped her. If he didn't want her, who would? She held herself as still as she could, wishing the tears would stop, and that she'd never come to this place. But there was another feeling. She wasn't the only woman in the world who felt this way. Hookups, or living together, or whatever serial monogamy that men thought was the best they had to offer, hurt.

She tried to get herself under control. She was

here to support Mara, not to turn into the queen of self-pity.

"This is a good time to take a break," Katherine said. "I'd like to say a couple things to you, Julie, but I think we could all use a cookie or two, or a dozen. So get what you need and meet back here in three minutes."

"This sucks," Mara said, and she walked toward a table that had an assortment of store-bought cookies and a big coffee dispenser. Poppy stared at her hands for a moment, then spotted a Restroom sign and followed it out of the room. She rinsed her face, which got rid of the last traces of Mara's attempted makeover.

She couldn't help but stare in the mirror. She remembered wanting to be a princess, back when she was old enough to think it was possible. So did Julie. Did every woman, at some time, want to be the special one? How did the world bear all that disappointment?

She mentally shook herself. It wasn't about that. It was about doing good work, living a good life, moving on. And as long as this evening felt, it wasn't going to last forever. She would move on.

CHAPTER 23

*P*oppy joined Mara in the circle again. Mara handed her a cookie in a napkin. "Oatmeal raisin," she said.

"I love oatmeal raisin."

"I figured." Mara said it as if it was an insult, but a grin twitched at the corner of her mouth.

"If I can have your attention," Katherine said, calling the rest of them to the circle, "I want to say a few things. The first is that we don't sugar-coat it here. Sex, when it isn't safe, consensual, and loving, leaves a mark on a person. It's true physically, emotionally, relationally, and spiritually. Sex outside of a loving, committed relationship is a sin."

Here it comes, Poppy thought, the judgment.

"Sins are those things that a person wants to do that God thinks is a bad idea. You can get deeper into it, but I've found that to be a pretty good working model. If God wants the best for you, and He does, He wants you to do the things that bring beauty and honor into your life. Sometimes you get a choice in the matter, and sometimes you don't. But you can make the decision to give it over to God. You don't have to carry it by yourself. And it's an endless deposit box, ladies. There's no limit on how much you dump on God."

Katherine focused on Julia. "I want you to let go of the feeling that you've failed. What I want from you, dear, is to stop looking for your salvation in the wrong places."

Julia sighed. "I know that."

Katherine smiled. "I know you do. And I know you set up some rules for yourself, and you're feeling bad you broke them. But the whole point of the rules isn't to get a perfect score. It's to remind yourself who you are. How you are created, and what you are created to do."

Created to do? *You don't contribute anything to my life*, Geoff had said. Poppy knew what rule she should create in her life, and that was to avoid men. Some women could handle them, some couldn't, and she was clearly in the latter category. As she thought about it, she became aware that the conversation had moved on without her. She glanced at Katherine, who was looking right at her. So was Mara. She was doing a terrible job of supporting the girl.

"Poppy, did you have anything to share?"

No, absolutely no. "No," she said, and her words sounded sharper than she meant them to. "But I think my friend Mara has something to say, and if she's willing, I'd like to hear it."

All eyes turned to Mara, but Mara kept looking at Poppy. Poppy got the feeling that Mara was looking for reassurance. She didn't know how to give it. All she could think to do was to turn around in her chair to face her, just like Katherine had with Julia, and wait.

Mara broke one of the cookies she had into a dozen tiny pieces before she began. "I like attention. I get a lot of it. When guys like a girl, they hardly talk to her. But if they think you're a slut, they talk to you all the time. I know things about guys that they would never tell their girlfriends. It's stupid how easy it is to get attention. But there's this one guy. He started spreading it all around school that I'm just a tease."

Mara pressed the crumbled bits of cookie into

a ball. Poppy held out her hand, and Mara dumped the napkin and crumbs into her palm and then wiped her hands on her jeans. "So the girls already hate me. And now the guys are acting all stuck up with me, and so I figure I'll mosh with this guy for a little while and he'll shut up, you know? So I stole the key to the custodian's room. Because then everyone would know we made out, so he'd have to stop saying things about me. It was at school. He scared me, a little. I thought it was safe there."

Poppy felt ill. She didn't want to hear anymore. But she wouldn't look away.

"At first, it was okay. But he was so fast. And strong. Things went farther than I wanted them to. I didn't think it would go so far. We hadn't even talked about birth control. I was trying to—I don't know what I was trying to do. Then it was done. He just left."

"Did you report him to the police?" Katherine asked.

"No. The whole thing was my idea."

"But you said to stop."

"I don't even know what I said. I know I wanted him to stop, but I could hardly breathe. And I didn't want anyone else to hear me, or they'd think...I don't know. Besides, what am I supposed to say to the cops? I'm me. Like Julie said, once a tramp, always a tramp. Who's gonna believe me? He's a star student. People like him."

"I think you need to tell the police," Katherine said. "I went through something similar, and I know how frightening—"

"It's too late now," Mara said, her eyes fixing on Katherine for the first time. "I'm pregnant. And I'm gonna have this baby. And she's gonna be loved and protected, and not just by me, but by my friend Zane." Her voice wavered and she coughed. "And he's gonna be the best daddy any girl ever had. Everyone thinks he's the one that got me pregnant, and he's okay with that. He's proud of this baby." Mara's tears started to fall. "He's proud of me."

Mara drew a few ragged breaths. "None of you can tell me that it would be good for this baby to know what happened. Her creator is God, not some piss-ant who pushes girls around, and that's all she needs to know about the day she was conceived. God gave her to me, and now he's given me Zane too. It's going to be good. It is."

"Not telling the police is your choice," Katherine said. "But don't be surprised if I bring it up again."

"But you won't go to the cops," Mara said

firmly. "You promised what we said in here was a secret."

"Yes," Katherine said, "which makes this a good time to bring these out." She pulled a handful of something from her bag and stood up, sorting them out as she walked over to Mara. "These are bracelets. Please pick one."

Mara looked them over and chose a sparkling bracelet made of red, purple, and black glass beads.

"You too," Katherine said, stepping in front of Poppy.

Poppy looked them over, wondering if she was supposed to take one since she was only here to support Mara. And she wasn't a Christian either, like everyone else here seemed to be. She hesitated over a simple leather band with ribbons woven through it.

"You are a thinker, aren't you?" Katherine said, raising an eyebrow. "When in doubt, sometimes it's best to choose the one that caught your eye first."

So Poppy picked the band made from braided horsehair and ribbons, although she was sure it was expensive and she shouldn't have taken it. It had caught her eye from across the room. The horsehair looked palomino, and the tiny ribbons were pink, peach, and red.

As Katherine walked back to her seat, she said, "Each of us has one of these. They're all different. Some of them I've picked up at craft stores, some I made, and most were made by a friend of mine. But they all have something in common, and that's the red ribbon."

"Like the scarlet letter?" Mara said bitterly.

"No. Like Rahab."

Poppy pictured an old man in a boat hunting down a whale. But Mara's expression changed, and she said, "Oh, yeah. Rahab. The prostitute."

Poppy didn't like where this was going.

"She was a lot more than that," Katherine said. "But for today's purpose, all you need to know is that she was the kind of woman people underestimated but God didn't. She hung a red ribbon on her home as a sign of her faithfulness, and in return, she and her family were saved. There's more to it, but I don't want to ruin the ending. We have these red ribbons to remember that we're here to keep each other safe. The secrets you hear stay here. Each of the other women in this room has made the same promise. Don't worry, Mara. This group has been around for almost two dozen years. You're safe here."

Poppy looked down at the bracelet in her hand. She couldn't tell the police about Mara. She couldn't tell Colton, or Zane's parents, or anyone who should know about what had happened to her. Not if she was going to keep her promise. But Mara was underage, if only for one more month. Where were Mara's parents in all of this? Were they keeping this secret too?

Whoever this Rahab was, she was a world of trouble.

CHAPTER 24

"So how is Mara doing?"

Poppy used her arm to push a few stray hairs from her face since one hand was holding the roller and she had paint on the fingertips of her other hand. "Better this week. But it's still hard."

Colton looked sideways at her. He was nailing the trim around the dormer window. It was a race to see if she could get the paint done on this wall before he was ready to do the other window. "You knew it would be hard, I hope."

She snorted. "It's hard because she doesn't think she can learn. It's like someone told her a long time ago she was bad at math and science, and whenever anyone criticizes her work, she takes it as proof that she can't do it. She's been making good progress. But this week I think *she* can see she's making progress. She said the principal even commented on all the work she's turned in."

"Did she give you credit?"

Poppy grinned to herself. "Nope. I told her not to if she could get away with not lying. We've had a few good laughs about the possible scenarios the rumor mill will generate. She told someone she'd been possessed by the spirit of Albert Einstein."

"Just so long as the teachers know she is actually doing the work."

"No problem with that—she takes tests at school during advisory. She was nervous about that, but she got a B-plus and an A-minus on the first two. It freaked her out that she did that well."

"It would have freaked me out if I'd done that well," Colton said. "Wish I'd had someone like you around when I was in high school. Then again, it probably would have worked out about as well as it did with the other pretty teachers." He stopped and looked over his shoulder. "Don't you give me stink eye, Poppy Field Marsh. It's just an honest observation."

She looked back at the wall and its "Weathered Fence" paint. He didn't need to see her blushing. An honest observation? Doubtful. She'd been the quintessential wallflower in high school, and some things never changed.

She wished again she'd taken off the bracelet, but by the time she'd remembered it was still on her wrist, her hands were too messy to touch it. She didn't want to get paint on it. She'd read that Rahab was supposed to be a legendary beauty, but then again, most historical figures got a makeover of one kind or another. And Rahab was a prostitute who'd offered protection for two Israelite spies. The spies were in the city in advance of an Israelite attack. She'd said she would hide them if they promised not to harm her or her family.

From what Poppy had read, Rahab was responsible for taking care of her brothers, sisters, their kids, and her parents. Money-making opportunities were limited for women in those days. A situation like that made the whole prostitute thing come into focus.

The spies had told Rahab they'd save her and her family, and they'd asked her to hang a red ribbon from her home, which was built into the exterior wall of the city. And they had kept their promise.

"So Rahab is admirable because she sold out her own people?" she said aloud.

Poppy was in the habit of talking to herself because it often helped her clarify things. But the work and the noise that Colton put off had gotten so familiar that she just blurted things out once in a while as if she was alone. She squinted her eyes shut and tried to think of a reasonable excuse for why she would have said such a thing.

"What?" Colton said. She didn't turn around. She could imagine the shock on his face.

"Oh, just something Mara told me about." A lie, kind of, but she'd pulled it off, hadn't she? She made the roller continue its path across the slanted ceiling. "Some woman named Rahab."

"Yeah, I've heard of her," he said. Of course he had, he went to church with Anson and Julia every single Sunday. Poppy hoped there weren't some Christian rules about talking about Rahab, like avoiding her name or maybe making the sign of the cross, or some other way that made it easy to identify unbelievers. Although Colton already knew she wasn't a Christian, and he hadn't acted any differently around her.

Except for that second movie night. And when he got headaches. And when he asked her the same question twice in a row because he forgot he'd just asked it.

"Well, I guess she wasn't very fond of her people," Colton added, "and they certainly weren't good to her. But it wasn't really about them. It was about their gods. You know she was a prostitute, right?"

"I heard that." And read it, last night.

"Did they mention she was probably a temple prostitute?"

"A what?" she turned around to stare at him.

"She was supposed to represent a goddess so men could think they'd had sex with a goddess. Virtual reality at its best."

Poppy set the roller in the tray. "That's sick."

"Yup. A lot of prostitutes were slaves. But some had protection—they could inherit and own real estate, unlike most women. That might explain why the house was hers. No matter what her life was like, I'm guessing she didn't buy into the whole goddess/god/sex thing since she saw the darker side of it. But she believed in God. She said so to the Israelite spies. She knew they were going to wipe her city off the map because God said they would."

Poppy shook her head. Rahab was still a weird

and confusing mascot for a group of troubled women.

"But that's not all she was, of course. Mara told you the rest, right?"

She and Mara had never spoken of it, actually, but she remembered Katherine saying something about "ruining the rest of the story" that first night. Poppy wanted to say no, she hadn't, but she didn't want to feel any more stupid than she already did. Colton hammered in a few finish nails with Poppy's pink hammer.

"She's Jesus' great, great, however-many-times-great, grandma."

That was news. Was it in the Bible? Did they include that part? Did most Christians know? She knew it might make her look ridiculous, but she had to ask. "It says that in the Bible?"

"Yup. She's singled out when they talk about Jesus' genealogy. Mostly they just name the dads, but they take special care to name a few moms, and she's one of them."

Poppy considered it. She'd have to see it for herself. But if what Colton was saying was true, how strange was that? Naming Rahab, someone else's religious sex slave, as a point of pride.

She'd check it out. But for now, there was painting to do.

She beat out Colton, but the paint wasn't dry enough to put the woodwork on yet. It was getting close to eleven thirty, time to get back to her thesis. She needed to check her e-mail to find out what her advisor thought of the regeneration models. All along she hoped she'd stand out since she had the sense to start her test plots in the summer before her first year, but as it turned out, it had just doubled her committee's expectations of her work.

She was cleaning up the paint when Colton said, "Well, I have one more job to do before I go." He didn't sound happy about it. "Emmaline used to have trouble with the water lines freezing when it got cold, so I need to put in a new light bulb and add some heat tape and insulation to the pipes in the cellar."

"Is that the crawl space under that corner of the house?" she asked, gesturing toward the southeast. There were old steps there, either concrete or stone, that led down to a short wooden door. It looked like the entry to a crypt, and she'd given it a wide berth.

"Want to go down there with me?"

"Nope," she said.

"Come on. It'll be fun."

"Holes in the ground aren't generally fun, Colton."

"You're scared, aren't you?" His eyes looked bright green today, with gold flecks. That wasn't necessarily a good sign.

"I am not."

"You *are* scared."

"I'm not. But if you need someone to hold your hand, I'll happily escort you down there." She said it flippantly, hoping he'd be offended and tell her not to go, but instead he looked triumphant. She wasn't good at these sorts of games.

"Great. Let's go." He bounded down the stairs, making even more noise than usual and causing the floor around her to vibrate.

I can do this, Poppy thought. It's just a cellar, not a cave or a mine. She grabbed her jean jacket on the way and followed him outside. It was a beautiful autumn day with a bit of bite to the wind, hinting at a coming change in the weather. Colton got a plastic bag out of his truck and pulled out some heat tape, an extension cord, and a pack of light bulbs. He tore off all the packaging and grabbed a couple of lengths of pipe insulation as he did.

"Ready?" he asked. He smiled without any

trace of cheerfulness and marched toward the northeast corner of the house.

Just around that corner were the steps leading down to the cellar. They were overgrown with grass and branches from a stray rosebush angled over the doorway in a thorny arch. It looked foreboding and completely out of character with the rest of the house.

He stood on the top step for a second, marched down two steps, then jumped straight into the air and landed back up on ground level. "That's huge," he said.

Poppy stepped forward and expected to see a snake. It would be a great place for snakes, especially ones that wanted to sun themselves on this beautiful day. But all she saw was grass. "Are you trying to fool me?"

"There's a huge spider down there."

"Well, you know the big ones aren't usually the problem," she said. "Around here there's something called the aggressive house spider, and they love the foundations of houses. Tiny little things, and mean. They'll come right after you."

"Okay. I get it. Do you see it yet? Just stomp on it."

Poppy bit her lip. She'd seen him catch and release moths and flies. He had amazing speed.

And he'd dealt with a few mice in her presence, but she'd never heard this clipped tone of voice. She took a few steps down and noticed a daddy longlegs—an unusually large one, but still, a daddy longlegs. She parted the grass for a better view. "This one?" she asked, teasing him. She knew it couldn't be the spider she was pointing at, it had to be something big and hairy and impressive.

"Just stomp on it."

She looked down to hide the grin on her face. Instead of stomping, she ushered the spider onto the palm of her hand and climbed the steps. She only intended to find a safer home for the poor thing, but Colton backed up like she had a machete and was swinging it around.

"Get that thing away from me," he said in a firm tone. She had the hardest time not laughing. The spider was making a run for it, and as she was passing it from one hand to the other, it ran straight up the sleeve of her jacket, and Colton let out something like a moan. "That's disgusting," he said. "I'm never sharing a bowl of popcorn with you again."

She carried the spider far enough away that she was sure he'd be safe from Colton, then returned to the cellar entrance. When Colton backed away from her, she made a show of wiping her hands off on her jeans. Then she went down the steps, kicked around in the grass, and said, "Spider free. The big cowboy is safe now."

That earned her a scowl and, underneath it, a real smile. "Very funny."

She turned to survey the cellar door. The top of it was just below eye level. Just the thought of ducking down to go into it made her skin crawl. She was relieved to find a padlock on the door.

"I got this," Colton said, and he stepped down beside her. He pulled a small screwdriver out of his pocket and easily turned the lock on the bottom of the padlock. It popped open.

"Wow," she said. "This is no Fort Knox."

"Any key will do, but no one even tries. They'd be more likely to use bolt cutters to take the lock off. And all that work would be for ..." He pushed the door inward. She leaned down to look inside. There was one more step down to a dirt floor, and to the left she could see the stone and concrete foundation of the house. It looked to be almost two feet wide. In front of her were mostly empty shelves, to the right of that were the water pump and pressure tank, and directly to her right was a wooden door. She didn't even want to know where that led. All that mattered to her were the beams of wood overhead, and above that, the weight of two stories of a house and everything in it.

"What are you looking at?" he asked.

"I'm checking for spiders. I wouldn't want any to drop on you."

"They'd better not." He stepped, hesitated, then walked right in. The first thing he did was take out the low-hanging light bulb. He pulled another out of the bag, and as soon as he screwed it in, the space was transformed by light. He dug around in the bag, moving faster than usual.

"No spiders," she said. "Yet."

"You are not as nice of a person as I thought you were," he growled. Then he pulled out the blue heat tape and started wrapping a pipe that emerged from the ground to her left, went through the shelves, and then into the machinery. She took a deep breath and walked into the cellar, concentrating on the fact that the door was only a few steps behind her. The first sound of creaking wood overhead and she'd be out of there.

She helped him thread the tape through the shelves, and then he was on his own. As she backed away, she noticed the jars on the upper shelf. "Those are beautiful," she said. "Are they the real thing?"

Colton glanced up for only a moment. "I think so. Go ahead and take a few, they aren't doing anyone any good down here."

Poppy could hardly make herself step forward again, but it was even harder to think of a good excuse for not doing so. She pulled a jar off the shelf. It was the old kind, with a glass lid and a wire bale. The one next to it was a different color, so she pulled it down as well. Then there were two blue jars with metal lids, so she pulled them down to take a look.

Then the ceiling above her creaked. Poppy knew she shouldn't walk away with all four jars, but she couldn't stop herself from leaving—fast. "I want to take a look at these in the sunlight," she said.

"So much for checking for spiders," Colton replied, and so she stopped at the doorway and tried to calm herself. It was fine. She was fine. She just had to convince her foolish heart.

"No spiders," she said, scanning the ceiling above him.

He ripped the insulation open with his thumb and placed the foam tubes around the few white pipes in the room, then plugged the extension cord into a socket built into the light fixture. There were nails hung here and there, and he used a couple to hang the cord on its way to the electrical tape. Poppy imagined the nails were once used to hang herbs or flowers. Imagining a little old lady down here doing that, presumably without freaking out, just added to her esteem for Emmaline.

"Done," Colton said. He rushed past her, almost knocking her over. He was up in two steps and jogged a few more feet for safe measure. Poppy closed the door, but Colton still had the lock.

She found him brushing at the sleeves of his plaid shirt, then at his neck. "I feel like they're all over me." He slapped at the leg of his jeans. "Do I have one on my back?"

She walked around behind him. "I don't see anything," she said.

"It feels like...underneath." In a flash, he pulled off his shirt and tank top, threw them on the ground, leaned over, and brushed at his hair so hard he must have pulled some of it out. It was so weirdly out of character for Colton that she couldn't help but laugh. He tried to reach around and slap at his back. "Have I got one on my back? I think there's one there."

Poppy clenched her jaw, determined not to

laugh again. "I'll check." She put the glass jars down and walked over to him.

She surveyed his back. It was broader than she expected, and it looked a lot like his strong arms, except the skin was noticeably paler. She tried to suppress other, less appropriate thoughts, such as wondering what it would be like to trace the lines of those muscles with her fingertips. She was so busy trying not to think that way that another thought crept into her mind. She pulled out the hair band that held her hair back, removed a strand of her hair, and using it like a paint brush, reached up. "I don't see anything. Wait, maybe—" At that moment she brushed the end of the strand across his shoulder blade.

She barely ducked in time to avoid the hand that came over the top of his shoulder and landed with a smack right where she'd been tickling him. Before she could recover he'd spun around and caught her standing there, hair in hand.

"Oh! Traitor!" He jabbed a finger at her.

She backed away, and all the pent-up laughter and nervousness combined into a goofy sounding giggle. "I'm sorry," she said, dropping the hair and putting her hands up. But he just kept coming, and she kept giggling.

"You think this is funny, do you? How about another trip down into the cellar?"

"Sure," she squeaked, backing away faster. He followed just as fast.

"You think I didn't notice how you were acting. You were scared."

"I was not!"

"Then you won't mind ..."

She glanced behind her to make sure she didn't step on the jars, and at that moment he lunged. His shoulder pressed into her hips, both arms closed around her legs, and he lifted. Poppy flew up and over his shoulder, her head dangling down his back. She smacked at his bare skin. "Put me down!"

"Not scared, huh?" He marched toward the cellar, and her giggling turned into a full-on scream. "No! Stop! Stop, I'm sorry!" But the last words came out giggling again despite her best efforts.

He paused. "Admit you're scared."

"I'm not. No! Stop!" She smacked his back with both hands.

He stopped a second time. "Last chance. Suck it up, buttercup."

"Okay, okay. I don't like it."

"Don't *like* it?" He took one more menacing step toward the hole in the ground.

"I hate it! It's scary, okay? I'm sorry, I shouldn't have teased you."

He pulled on her legs, and she slid down the front of him. She landed on her toes with both hands on his chest, and still he didn't let go of her. All the thoughts she'd been trying not to have rushed in at once, and she felt as if she could hardly breathe. She watched his green eyes watching her, then watched his gaze slide down to her lips, and her whole mind exploded into short-circuited fireworks.

"Colton?" It wasn't his voice, or hers.

Poppy's heels hit the ground, and she backed away, unsteady.

"Aunt Julia," he said, but he kept his eyes on Poppy for a moment more. He shook his head slightly, breathed out, then turned around. "I didn't hear you drive up."

Poppy figured that was because she'd been screaming like an idiot. Blushing didn't begin to describe the heat that that enflamed her face.

Colton walked casually to his shirt, shook it off, and turned the whole thing right-side out. He pulled it on without undoing the buttons. "I'm glad you're here. I can't wait to show you what we've done to the homestead."

Julia shook her head. "Sorry, Colton. I was just over helping Mrs. Ekstrom get her new computer set up. She wanted to see her new great-grand-baby on a video call. But I'm late getting home. I just stopped by to tell you we got the shipment in, so we're switching out the mattresses today."

"Great!" Colton looked back over his shoulder at Poppy, then back to Julia. "Should I just follow you back?"

"That would help, because I'm not sure where we'd put them in the meantime."

"I'll get my truck." He waved good-bye to Poppy and then jogged away. She knew he'd walked from the bunkhouse this morning, so his truck was parked there.

Julia watched him go, then stepped forward, toward Poppy. Surprised, Poppy said, "It'll take him a minute if you'd like to take a look inside."

"No. Thank you." Julia's tone was firm. Once again she reminded Poppy of Mrs. Kraft, Lily's mom, back in Washington. She remembered her clean house, her hospitality, and the polite way she had of laying down the rules—while leaving no room for disobedience. Like all the kids in the neighborhood, Poppy had called her Mom. It had felt good to call someone that. Poppy's mom preferred Roz since she said being called Mom made her feel old.

"Zane tells me he's helping with the renovations."

"He's been a big help," Poppy said, glad to finally find a topic that didn't feel awkward. "He's here at least once a week."

"And is Colton always around when he is?"

Poppy's guard came back up as fast as it had come down. Zane had come over after school twice, but as soon as she saw what a distraction he was to Mara, she'd put an end to that. "Almost always."

Julia looked at the cellar door, up at the house, and around the yard. Suddenly Poppy felt as if the whole place looked shabby. "Then you know he's a pretty conscientious kid."

"Very. Your son is something special."

Julia nodded slowly, but her eyes were piercing. "When he was about five, a kid at the park handed him a used popsicle stick and told him to hold it until he came back. But the kid's parents took him home, and there was Zane, holding on to the stick. He carried it for weeks, every single time we went outside, whether it was to go to the park or not."

"I can believe it," Poppy said. "I guess he's always been dependable."

"Yes, even when he shouldn't be," Julia said. She looked away, then back, and paused when she caught sight of Poppy's bracelet. It seemed to distract her, but the expression passed. "So you might understand why we chose not to take him to see Mara in the hospital so soon after learning she was pregnant. That and the fact that she was not returning his calls and her father had left strict instructions that he not be allowed to see his daughter."

Poppy stood very still, waiting, knowing that whatever was coming wouldn't be good.

"You may or may not understand my feelings about a young woman I know very little about driving my minor son across county lines and then finding a way to sneak him into a place he was expressly forbidden to go. Not to mention dropping him off somewhere, I don't know where, in the middle of the night rather than making sure he got safely home."

Poppy took a deep breath. All true. She knew better than to try to defend her decisions. Zane was Julia's son. Poppy understood wanting to protect him. It's what she would want for her son, if she had one.

"You are what age?"

"Twenty-four."

"Just a few years older than Zane, then."

Six, Poppy thought. And what was that supposed to mean, anyway?

"I think that you are very new to this town and this family, Poppy, and that you might have pushed right into the middle of things, but that doesn't mean you understand what's going on. And you say you have no intention of staying here. So if you have no past and no future, you might want to consider just how much right you have to involve yourself in our family."

Julia turned to walk away but spun around again. "One more thing. I don't know what you're after, but I will tell you that you're just the latest in a long line of women after Colton. And if you think you're going to get the cowboy, and the ranch, and a bucket full of money, you have another thing coming."

Julia walked away. It was a good walk, graceful and sassy and sure. Poppy had confronted a few people in her life, and each time her voice had dissolved into a quivering mess and her hands had shaken so badly she looked ridiculous when she gestured. Julia looked calm as can be, and she had never even raised her voice.

But Poppy felt as if she'd been in a car wreck. She watched the white van Julia was driving pull down the driveway, where Colton's pickup pulled in behind it. The dust they kicked up was whipped away by the icy wind. She could hardly move. When she looked down, she saw the cellar lock in the grass. She went back to the cellar, put it on the door, and gathered up the beautiful old canning jars to place in the sink and wash later. She didn't have the heart to do it now. They weren't hers. None of this was hers. They would be here long after she was gone.

And so would Colton.

CHAPTER 25

*M*ara was five minutes early, which meant she'd driven too fast, and she ran straight up to the door, which meant she had news. She didn't even bother to knock before rushing in. "Look at this!" she said, holding a paper up in front of Poppy's face. "It's a test. I got an A. In calculus. Me, calculus, A." She did a little happy dance that involved some terrible boxing moves, and Poppy laughed.

"You knew you were good at math."

"I was, in middle school. Not anymore."

Poppy went into the kitchen to get the plate of snacks she'd prepared. There would be no concentrating if she didn't feed the girl first. "People don't suddenly get bad at math, Mara. You were just out of practice, that's all."

"And my teachers suck."

Poppy frowned at her before setting the plate down at the table. "Different people have different learning styles."

"I know, I know, everyone hated your favorite teacher, but she's why you chose biology. I remember from the first dozen times you told me." She shoved a piece of chicken in her mouth with her fingers. "This is so good."

"How did you do on the chemistry test?"

"Got a B. I don't like memorizing all those names."

"Yeah, I didn't either." Poppy thought about this morning's e-mails. She'd gotten a good grade as well, sort of. Her professor liked the edits she'd done to the first chapters and approved the outline of the next two. It was good to have some success after this morning's confrontation with Julia.

Geoff had written too. He wrote nearly every day now. She'd thought that responding to a couple of his e-mails would satisfy him, but it hadn't. He wanted to know when she was coming back to Arizona. He wanted her to move back in.

"So the principal told me we can't go to high school if Zane and I get married."

"He said that?"

"He said they don't recommend it."

"That's not the same thing," Poppy said. But then again, maybe it was.

"Stupid," Mara said. "Being pregnant is okay, but being married isn't? Anyway, if I'm not around, they probably won't say anything to Zane. So I think I'm going to quit as soon as we get married."

Poppy's jaw dropped. "Don't do that."

"Why not? I'm learning more from you than I am from school."

"If you put me in that position, I'll have to stop tutoring you, Mara."

Mara's eyes narrowed. "You're moving back to Arizona."

Poppy had to come at this another way. "Here's the thing. You need to go to college, and—"

"I never said I was going to college."

"Yes, you did," Poppy said, crossing her arms over her stomach. "You just don't know you did. You have a talent for electrical engineering."

"I what?"

"Electronics. Understanding them, fixing or

designing them, whatever you choose to do, you have a talent for it. You're the one teaching me about your computer science class. You need to go to college to learn more. And you'll love it. But to get into college, you have to show you finish what you start."

"I think having a baby and getting married counts for finishing what I start, Poppy."

"I agree. And especially so if you finish school and graduate with your class, even though you have extra responsibilities. I think any admissions officer with a brain would see that's something special. But if you quit, you look like every other kid who thought they had a better thing going somewhere else. I don't want to see you get lost in the crowd, Mara."

"Even if I wanted to, I won't have the money."

"All the more reason. There are scholarships out there just waiting for you to win them. But you have to do your part."

"I don't think so. Zane was always the good student, not me."

Poppy wondered about the dead end she kept hitting with this girl. Then she thought about what school must be like for Mara now. Why wouldn't she want to leave those days behind her? "Mara, sometimes college is just like high school. The same people, the same drama, just more inebriated. But there's also different people with different lives, including young moms. And there's married student housing, including campus childcare while you're in class—everything all on campus. Why couldn't you both go to college?"

Mara hesitated. "Zane's brother Liam did work with a Christian campus group. Maybe the group is still there."

"Think about it. And let me do a little research, okay? Because we're late. You're going to have to get moving if you want to be admitted."

"Whatever. But only close by, okay? I don't want to go too far away. Not that it matters all that much. My dad hates me, and Zane's parents aren't too far behind."

"I like you. Most of the time."

Mara made a face. "You're leaving anyway."

"I have to finish what I started, too."

"Then who's going to tutor me next semester?"

"You won't need me by then."

Mara shrugged. Poppy knew they had more to talk about, but for now, they had work to do. "I want to see your social studies research." Mara groaned, as expected, and they got to work.

At five thirty, Mara's usual time to go home, Mara leaned back and said, "Oh, look, here's your date now."

"Date?" She turned to see Colton's truck pulling up. "No."

"It's your date night."

As she walked over to the window, Poppy explained that they watched a movie on Fridays and that it had nothing to do with dating. It had started to rain, and Colton appeared to have two mattresses in the back of his truck. He hurried up the steps, and she opened the door before he got there. "I could use some help," he said. She grabbed her jacket and followed him out to the truck.

"What do you need?" The rain had come with more wind, and with the sun down behind the mountains, it was much colder than she expected.

"Grab that end. Look out, the wind is going to try to knock it over." He jumped into the truck and pushed the mattress out toward her.

"But where is it going?"

"Inside, of course," he said, and the mattress tipped. It was the deep, heavy kind, not the sort that was easy to move. They wrestled it onto the porch, and Colton jogged back to get the second one. She helped without asking, though she wondered what on earth they were going to do with them.

Mara held the door open as they brought them inside. One had taken the brunt of the weather, and she helped Colton prop it up against the wall. "Okay, time to move the other one upstairs."

The first thing they learned is that the mattress wouldn't bend, and the second was that the only way to get it onto the stairs was to lift it over the railing. After they'd accomplished that, they got stuck at the top, where the stairs met the angled ceiling of the second floor. With a combination of Mara pulling from the top, Poppy shoving from the middle, and Colton using every inch of his height to push from the steps below, they got it up and over.

Colton came up to survey it. "I think we can wait to do the other one just now, right?"

"Where did this come from?"

"The hotel. Sometimes Anson and Julia have to replace things. One of these has a squeaky spring that a guest complained about. The other one is supposed to be uneven. They don't have any box springs to change right now, so all you'll have is a mattress on the floor. But it's better than your camp mattress, right?"

Poppy hadn't even considered that the mattress was for her.

"I figured you could stack them up," he said. "Then if Miss Mara or your sister stay the night, you could slide one into the other bedroom. You said you wanted her to come visit, right?" Colton looked pretty pleased with himself. Then, second by second, he began to look more unsure. "That's okay, isn't it? I mean, I understand if you don't want to sleep on someone else's mattress."

"I loved it at the inn, so I'm sure I'll love it here," she said, and the smile came back to his face. Mara had walked over to Poppy's bedroom door and was looking down at her bed. "This is pretty pathetic," she said. "You might want to consider using actual sheets, too."

"Got that taken care of," Colton said. "I got the stained stuff that Julia was going to recycle."

"Ew," Mara said.

"Not like that. Like, blue nail polish on the corner of one sheet, the other had a burn from something like a curling iron—"

"People are pigs."

"I agree, Miss Maxwell," Colton said. "And I got a pillow someone had cut with a knife. I'm sure there's a story behind that. Duct tape should fix it up."

Duct tape? Hardly. "I can fix it," Poppy smiled. "And thank you. It's great." And thoughtful. She decided not to tell Sierra about it.

"No blankets this time," Colton said.

"I have my sleeping bag."

"Yeah, right. Good. Ready to get the next mattress?"

She and Mara looked at each other. Neither one jumped at the chance. Colton didn't seem to notice as he slid the mattress across the new carpet toward her room. "Hey, Mara, want to stay for movie night? I bet we could get Zane to come over."

Mara gave Poppy a sideways glance. "I wouldn't want to interrupt anything."

"You wouldn't," Poppy said, a little too sharply. But after this morning's conversation with Julia, the last thing she wanted was Zane at her house. "But I can't stay up too late tonight. I got my marching orders today, and I owe my committee another chapter by next Friday."

"I can take a hint," Mara said. "Besides, if I don't get Dad's car back in twenty minutes, he'll kill me."

It never ceased to amaze Poppy that Mara wanted to spend time with her. It probably said more about the state of things in her home than how she felt about Poppy, she thought, and she immediately felt guilty for pushing the girl away. "It's not that. It's ..." And there she was, with no subtle way to speak to Colton alone. "I got the feeling from Julia that she's not happy having Zane spend so much time here."

"That's silly," Colton said. "Besides, he just agreed to rent one of Cash's apartments starting November first. He'll be a free man."

"Woo-hoo!" Mara said. "He got it? I've got to call him!" She bolted down the stairs.

The news didn't make Poppy feel any better. "How did Julia take that?"

"Hard to tell. She plays her cards pretty close to the vest sometimes." He leaned the mattress against the doorway. "She expected him to leave in May. It's not that big of a difference."

"Yes, it is."

He seemed surprised by her words.

"And it should be," Poppy continued. "A mom shouldn't be happy to see her kid go. At least I don't think so."

"No, I guess not." Colton bit at the inside of his lower lip. "Maybe I should give her a call, see if she and Zane had plans for tonight."

Mara called up the stairs. "He'll be over as

soon as he's done. He said to call the pizza order in to Dottie's."

Poppy sighed. Then she headed downstairs. Mara was ending her call. "You need to call your dad," she said. She was pretty sure Mr. Maxwell would put a stop to their plans.

"Right." She dialed the phone, and Poppy took the plate and glasses of water over to the sink.

"Where are you?" Mr. Maxwell's voice was clear as a bell to Poppy, even though Mara's phone was close to her ear.

"I'm at Poppy's. We just finished up, and I wanted to stay and watch a movie."

Poppy didn't hear a response, and she assumed that the volume had been turned down, but she was wrong.

"What is it with this woman? Don't you think it's strange how much time you're spending with her?"

Poppy rinsed the plate, hoping the sound of water would drown out his voice.

"I can bring the car back now if you want, Dad. I'm pretty sure she could give me a ride back here, and I could just spend the night."

"Fine. Spend the night. With your thirty-year-old girlfriend. That's perfectly normal. No wonder you're so messed up. Look at the people you're spending your time with."

Poppy wasn't sure why her age was suddenly such an issue with all the parents in her life. Was twenty-four so old? Or was it too young? It was giving her a headache. Which would be a good reason to send them all away, she could just say she wasn't feeling well.

"Whatever you want, Dad."

"As if you do what I say. I don't give a crap."

"Bye," Mara said, but Poppy was pretty sure the call had already disconnected.

Colton came galloping down the stairs. "I just put the order in to Dottie's and texted Zane. It's all good. So what do we watch?"

"Something funny," Mara said.

Colton wandered into the kitchen and grabbed an apple. "Why would we do that?"

"Really? You're as bad as Poppy, with your stupid Westerns. You two are a perfect match."

Poppy made the mistake of looking over her shoulder, and she caught Colton's look and the way he wiggled his eyebrows at her. Was he joking or flirting with her? Joking, of course. She'd be an idiot to take it for more.

Mara invited Colton into a card game, one that involved some fast moves and smacking the table loudly, which seemed to be just his style. They talked smack, too, so much so that Poppy found herself laughing along. Then Zane arrived with no less than four large pizzas. He'd remembered her favorite, and evidently the others' favorites as well. She slipped him money for the pizza and then some.

Colton popped open a beer and poured about a quarter of it into a glass for her. Then he arranged the mattress on the floor in front of the couch and fetched her laptop while she made popcorn. He picked a movie starring Tom Selleck because he said that although it wasn't great, everyone liked it. A few minutes later the lights were turned down and Zane and Mara were seated on the mattress and doing a poor job of watching the movie instead of each other. She shared a bowl with Colton until she remembered.

With wide eyes, she stared at him. He looked confused. She pulled her hand out of the popcorn and held it up in front of his face. "Spider hand," she whispered.

He laughed silently. Then he reached over with his hand, laced his fingers through hers, and gave her hand a squeeze.

Colton let go and turned his attention to the movie. Poppy felt the world swirling around her.

What a strange mix of people in her life. Two young people on what seemed like a disastrous course and at least two parents who wanted her out of their lives. Plus there was the conundrum that was her friendship with Colton. She hadn't forgotten the night he'd frightened her. She hadn't forgotten his flippant admission that he was on parole.

She also remembered the way his skin felt under the palms of her hands. Like a plane headed straight for earth, she had to pull up, and fast. Everything was going the wrong way. But the odd people surrounding her, all lit by the same blue light, made her feel good. It was just one night, she thought. She could let all the worry go for one night.

CHAPTER 26

She had just cracked some eggs into a large cast-iron frying pan when Colton showed up. "You'd think he lives here," Mara muttered, even though she'd been the one to spend the night.

Poppy opened the door for him. "Smells wonderful," he said. He kept his coat on and walked inside.

"Did Zane end up spending the night at your place?" Poppy asked him.

"Nah. He had to get Julia's car back home. Good morning, Mara."

"That movie sucked last night," she said.

"I saw you crying."

"I did not cry."

"Your mascara told a different story." As he sat down at the table, Poppy handed him a cup of coffee. "I can't stay," he said, then he leaned back and got comfortable.

She cracked three more eggs into the pan and started making toast for three.

"I just came by to tell you I'm going to make good on that promise I made you."

Poppy gave him a suspicious look.

"To take you to a rodeo and explain what's going on."

"You're going tonight?" Mara said. "Oh my gosh. Frost Elliot is riding. He is so...so ..."

"Dreamy," Colton said flatly. "So I've heard. Give it up, Mara, you're getting married. There will be no more dreamy for you, ever."

"Zane is dreamy."

He rolled his eyes. "Anyway, Poppy, I bet you thought I forgot."

"No, I didn't think that. I thought you didn't want to go." With me, she added silently. She imagined he would love to go since he'd been a part of rodeo for years, but he'd seemed reluctant to drag her along.

"She can't go," Mara said. "She looks way too crunchy for a rodeo."

"Crunchy? What does that mean?" Poppy asked.

"Never mind," Mara said, dismissing her with a wave of her hand. "We just have to go shopping. And besides, you need an outfit for my wedding. You can't go in Levis and hiking boots."

"I don't know," Colton said. "She does have those fancy Arizona cowboy boots."

"True. And she has a couple of cute T-shirts. But her jeans are too big."

Colton looked at her with a broad smile and said, "Did you hear that, Poppy? Your jeans are too big."

She ignored them both.

"She just needs a shirt with a little more shine to it. But for the wedding, she needs to wear a skirt."

Poppy had to correct that. "I don't wear skirts."

"That's because you haven't gone skirt shopping with me. Seriously, anyone who has a purple velvet sofa in their house needs to go shopping with me."

Poppy filled two plates and brought the food over to her guests. They both looked ravenous and happy, which made her feel good. They didn't have to know that breakfast and soup were the beginning and end of her culinary skills.

She filled her own plate, refilled her coffee, and sat down between them. Colton teased Mara about her makeup. Mara teased Colton about his "old" age. Poppy reveled in it all. There was something about this, something she couldn't put her finger on, that just soothed her heart.

After breakfast, Mara announced that she had a plan.

She and Poppy shopped until lunchtime, and when they came back to the homestead, Mara insisted on doing Poppy's hair and makeup. As soon as she'd finished, it was time for Mara to go, and Poppy's mood shifted. Since she was going to the rodeo, Mara would be going to her meeting alone. Poppy wasn't sure she would follow through with it, or if her father would allow her to borrow the car again.

Poppy had once hinted that Mara should tell her dad. That idea was shut down as fast as expected. Poppy wished Mara's father would see through all the trouble and try to get to the root of what was going on. Then again, if he suspected something bad had happened to Mara, he would probably find a way to put the blame on Zane. It was such a tangled mess she couldn't imagine it ever getting sorted out.

And it felt strange to shop for something to wear to a wedding that had no date or venue. Not to mention the fact that Poppy still had mixed feelings about it. She felt the need to do something helpful for Mara, so she spent some time searching admission information at the University of Montana, Montana State, and a number of other colleges near Billings.

In the meantime, she received two more e-mails from Geoff. He sent her a photo of the two of them at a party she could hardly remember. In it, she looked tan and fit. She wore shorts and a cami, and had a short, practical hairstyle. She had her arm around Geoff and looked happy. She hardly recognized herself.

After struggling through some of the editing that her committee had sent and eating leftovers for dinner, she had wasted all the time she could. It was time to change for the rodeo.

The jeans she'd bought weren't smaller, exactly, but they certainly were tighter in some places than she was used to. And the shirt wasn't a loose knit like she liked to wear. It was a tailored, woven shirt. She did like the cornflower blue color very much, but it smelled new. Poppy put a couple of drops of rose essential oil on her skin to cover up the smell. Her concho belt had met with dubious approval, so she wore that, along with the boots Colton liked to mock. And because she had promised, she reapplied the lip gloss Mara had given her.

The result was a little strange. Like the photo Geoff had sent, it didn't quite look like her, especially with her longer hair and the ridiculously wide curls that Mara had ironed into the ends. But in some ways, it seemed more like her than the photo. And it didn't matter how she looked. All she was hoping to accomplish was to blend in enough not to embarrass Colton. He had seemed like something of a minor celebrity that night at the Combine. Would people recognize him at the rodeo? But Moose Hollow was a small town, after all, and he'd told her this rodeo attracted national, even international, stars.

She heard a honk outside and headed down the stairs. When she looked through the window and saw Colton illuminated in the front porch light, her heart sped up. He looked handsome. He looked better than any of the leading men in the Westerns he'd shown her. Tall, smiling, black-hatted, and wearing a black, hip-length wool coat she'd never seen before. He was wearing new jeans, too, and riding boots with angled heels.

She felt ridiculous. This wasn't a date. She shouldn't have tried to dress up; he was going to think she mistook his intentions. And a shirt and a new pair of jeans didn't make her a cowgirl, it made her a silly-looking wannabe. But she still had to open the door.

He took one look at her and said, "Wow."

It didn't sound like a happy wow. It was more like a startled or confused wow. She felt her face warming up.

"Mara went a little overboard," she said. It was the best excuse she had.

"It's different. I think I need a moment to get used to this."

She turned her back on him and tried to look busy. She could have crawled into a hole. When she thought about the whole miserable, embarrassing evening spread out in front of her, tears stung her eyes. She took a drink of water, grabbed her coat, and formulated her next words. "Are you sure about this? I wouldn't mind getting some work done instead."

"No, no, you got all dressed up," he said absently. "Besides, you don't know anything about rodeo. And I guess that makes me your guy."

Hardly, she thought. And she couldn't find a way out of it that wouldn't involve a lot more talking, which she didn't want to do. She walked right past him and out the door and got into his car.

When he got in, she tried to make small talk. She asked him what events there would be tonight, and he broke it down for her. There would be steer wrestling, which sounded like a man jumping from a horse onto a steer that weighed three times as much as him and attempting to wrestle it to the ground. There were two roping events, team roping and tie-down roping. There was barrel racing, which Poppy had seen on TV, and then bull riding, which sounded like eight seconds of sheer insanity.

She asked him which he did. "None of those," he said. "I did my work on the horses. Bareback was my main event."

"How do you do that?"

"Stay on the horse."

That was all he said, and she didn't press.

She'd never been to the Metra before, and the first thing she noticed after spotting the huge building that contained the arena was what looked like miles of parking lot. The place was enormous. People with lighted batons were ushering everyone up to the higher lots, but Colton drove the other way, to a gate where he leaned out the window and said, "Colton Gunnerson. Need my creds?"

"Glad to see you, Colton," the man said, and waved them through.

The man could be a Moose Hollow local, she thought. But she doubted it.

"Bareback's the first event, so I thought we'd stop by here real quick and psych out a few of the guys I don't like."

He parked in a sea of pickup trucks, almost all of which looked nicer than his. Then he surprised her by rushing around to open her door for her. "Are you ready for this?" he asked. He didn't sound ready. She nodded and silently vowed to stay out of the way as much as possible.

She was surprised when he took her all the way to a wide entry to the basement of the arena. A man there demanded to see their badges, and someone from behind them said, "They're with me."

She turned around to see a cowboy with a grin on his face.

"You don't mind, do you, Fred?"

The guard shook his head, and Colton turned and held out his hand. The other cowboy ignored it and gave him a hug instead, along with several thumps on his back. "Been missing you on Tuesday nights."

"Yeah, me too," Colton said. He gestured to Poppy. "This is Poppy Marsh. Poppy, this is my friend Travis."

"Ah, I've heard a little about you," Travis said to her. "And you look just exactly the way I knew you would." Whatever that was supposed to mean, she couldn't take offense because of the kind way he said it, the firm handshake, and the sparkle in his blue eyes. "Colton's my best friend. You wouldn't know it the way he's been avoiding me lately."

Colton stepped forward. "I didn't realize you were riding tonight. Guess I should've known."

"What event are you in?" Poppy asked.

Travis shook his head. "I'm just the pickup man. No trophies, no prizes, but not as much chance of getting hurt."

"If you do it right, that is," Colton said. "And Travis is one of the best." They walked into the arena. From what Poppy could see, they were in a basement of sorts, and the seats were all above them. They walked through a crowd and an area with pens on either side. There were mostly horses in this area, some saddled, some not. Colton reached out his hand as he passed, and once a horse pushed its nose out into his palm. She still didn't know if they felt like velvet. And trapped between them all, she didn't feel safe enough to find out.

To her right a horse jumped and twisted in the small enclosure as if it was scared or angry. Poppy tensed but tried not to show it.

"I'm surprised to see you here," Travis said. They were walking ahead of her, and he kept his voice low.

"Eh, no big deal."

Travis said nothing in return. He stopped for a moment outside a doorway. "Well, seeing you should be enough to get a few of the young guys to drop out."

They walked into a room to the right, and because of the uproar, Poppy stayed outside.

There was a lot swearing and a flurry of questions, all one of two basic kinds. They wanted to know if Colton was riding. And they wanted to know why he wasn't.

Colton was encircled by young men trying to shake his hand, slap his back, or puff up their chests and look unconcerned. Travis threw her an encouraging grin from inside the room, but she knew Colton had forgotten all about her. She turned to the side and leaned against the wall, listening. For a moment she'd forgotten that she looked like Rodeo Barbie. But she remembered now.

And she realized that the only other females she'd seen looked skinny, beautiful, and tough as nails, and walked like they had someplace important to be. Barrel racers. Businesswomen. All people she wasn't and couldn't be. This was Colton's world, and she was hopelessly out of place.

The next round of questions came, and they were all about how Colton was feeling. One asked nicely, one told him he was a coward, and another asked how on earth he could tell if he was brain damaged since he was born crazy. The jokes went downhill from there.

After a short pause, she heard the question, "When are you coming back?"

Travis stepped out then. He took a look at her, leaned against the wall on the other side of the door, then looked back inside the doorway. He wanted to hear the answer too.

"I guess that depends on upon how crappy you guys ride tonight," Colton said. Everyone laughed, but not Travis. Poppy realized that

Colton wasn't going to answer one way or the other.

Travis was watching her. "Colton's a good man," he said.

"Are you sure?" The question leaked out, but he didn't seem surprised that she had asked.

"I am," he said. He smiled and walked away.

Poppy didn't want Colton to find her waiting out here for him, so she wandered past the pens, then past the women's bathroom, and that's when she saw someone familiar emerge. She was wearing a red satin shirt, tight jeans, and high-heeled boots, along with a white hat encircled by a crystal band. Short blond hair spiked out from beneath the hat. The only thing different about Keli Coulson was that there was no trace of the devious smile she'd given Colton that night at the Combine. Just a serious look and a fast walk. She didn't even glance at Poppy.

Still in the wake of Keli's perfume, Poppy saw a horse turn her way, dark eyes thoughtful in a pale face. He was golden—a palomino—the same color as her bracelet. She stepped forward, and he stood still, looking as hesitant as she felt. Then she reached through the gate and held out her hand. He leaned forward, took one step, and then dropped his nose down onto her hand, blowing warm air over it. She paused and then reached up slightly and ran the tips of her fingers over his nose. It was soft and velvety. Then he tossed his head a little, but Poppy managed to keep her hand still.

The horse stepped forward and lowered his head further, and she rubbed the spot he presented to her, the middle of his forehead. The fur was soft, but it felt strange to feel the bony skull just beneath her touch. He leaned into her scratching a little, moved his head up and down, and she smiled. He was a good teacher.

"Poppy!" Colton shouted. She jumped and the horse backed up, head high in the air. "I've been looking for you everywhere."

She knew that was a lie, and she chose not to respond to it. She turned to face him, waiting.

"That's one of the horses Travis wants," he said, gesturing to the palomino. He looked around. "Where did Travis go?"

"I don't know."

"We need to get moving. The show's about to start." He turned and walked away, leaving her to follow him. She chafed at it, but she followed. They trotted up a wide concrete stairway to the concourse, he paused to wait for her, and then he took her by the elbow and kept walking. She would have pulled her arm away if it wouldn't have slowed them down.

He walked past one entrance to the arena and then turned into the next. He pulled two tickets out of his coat pocket and showed them to an usher, who smiled and directed him inside. They climbed down and down the concrete steps. The only open seats were two seats on the aisle, as close to the chutes as she could imagine. She looked down at the other end of the arena, up to the second tier of seats full to the ceiling, and figured her seat was one in a million. Or nearly so. She didn't ask how Colton had gotten the tickets because she was beginning to understand. He was *Colton Gunnerson.*

He let her go in first, then sat on the aisle. Before she could get her coat off, someone was at his side. "Mr. Gunnerson, courtesy of the gentleman over there." Poppy looked up to see a young woman with a tray full of beer hand two glasses to Colton. He tipped his hat, and across the aisle she saw an older man do the same in return. He took the beers and handed them both to her. The girl was about to leave, but he reached for his wallet. "A program, please," he asked, and she handed him one from a bag draped over her shoulder. He gave her a twenty and a ten. "Keep the change," he smiled.

Poppy stared at the beers. No, a rodeo arena wasn't a bar, so it would be stretching it to think he was breaking one of Emmaline's rules. And it was none of her business. Colton took one beer away from her and took a sip.

The arena went dark, and "America the Beautiful" played over the loudspeaker. A woman in a white outfit on a white horse rode through the arena at a gallop as the music swelled. By the time the spotlights were on a row of military servicemen standing in the arena, Poppy was getting teary. It was strange. She thought it was unbearably cheesy, but her eyes thought it was worth crying over. Then again, her eyes were unusually active today.

She applauded and stood with the others, and when the national anthem played, she put her hand over her heart and sang because it was so loud there was no chance someone else would hear her. Then she sat down with everyone else and wondered how long it had been since she'd been part of something like that, something purely sentimental and grateful.

CHAPTER 27

*C*olton took another long drink and leaned forward, elbows on knees, as the arena lit up bright as daylight and rock and roll boomed over the loudspeakers. The announcer welcomed everyone to the rodeo as Colton found the list of riders, ran his finger over it, then discarded the program into Poppy's lap.

One of his feet was tapping fast. His fingers were lacing and relacing themselves, and his expression was fierce as he looked ahead and to their left, where the horses were.

Poppy tried to make sense of it. Horses were lined up behind the small chutes, and once they were in their spot, there was a flurry of activity. A cowboy climbed onto the horse. Instead of a saddle, there was a leather-wrapped block of some kind with a big handle built into it. Nothing more.

The cowboy was wearing a hat low over his forehead, a white collar behind his neck that looked like a neck brace, and a padded vest over his shirt that had a shape of its own.

"That's Stone Fly," Colton said absently. "This kid is looking at an easy seventy-five if he doesn't blow it."

Over on the other end of the arena, Poppy saw that two men had ridden horses onto the dirt floor. She squinted. The one on the brown horse with the elaborately braided mane looked like Travis. Back inside the chute she saw the cowboy lie back against the horse's back and bring his knees up over the horse's shoulders. With his chin tucked to his chest, he nodded.

When the gate to the arena opened, the crowd roared. The horse flew out of the chute and reared so high he rose straight on his back legs. He spun and leaped upward. As he did, the cowboy smacked backward against the horse's bare back again, his legs flying up into the air. The horse bucked again, spinning as he did, but the cowboy stayed on, one arm up in the air, the fringe on his chaps flying. Leap, spin, kick. The horse kicked his entire rear end and back into the cowboy's back, and the cowboy looked like a rag doll. But he stayed centered on the horse. A buzzer sounded, and the cowboy sat up a little. As if he knew his job was done, the horse broke from the bucking and ran for the other end of the arena.

That was when the other horsemen came into play. Travis put himself and his horse between the cowboy and the railing, and as they galloped at full speed, Travis grabbed the cowboy by the vest and pulled him off, slowing enough to drop the rider neatly onto his feet.

The cowboy lifted his hat into the air, and the cheering erupted again. Poppy looked at Colton. Intense, she thought. He looked ready to do battle, not just ride a wild horse.

The next chute opened at that moment, and that horse leaped straight out, covering a lot of ground on each buck. The buzzer rang again, but this time, the cheers weren't as energetic. Travis and the other horseman came up alongside the horse and pulled the rider off, and as he walked back toward the chutes, Colton muttered, "Better be a reride."

Would he ride the horse again? It sounded like a punishment of some kind, but she couldn't tell what had gone wrong. Attention turned back to the rider with the protesting horse, and the gate opened. Poppy wished things would slow down for a moment. The rides continued. Some seemed to be better than others, but Poppy had no idea why.

The music shifted, and so did the tone of the announcer's voice, signaling a break in the action. She turned to Colton, and he turned to her, and she could tell by the look in his eyes he wasn't just looking at her. This time, he actually saw her.

"Well, hello there," she said flatly.

He stared at her. "I've been awful company."

"I get it," she said to him. "You have a lot of catching up to do."

He looked down at his hands where they gripped his knees. "Something like that."

New horses had been let through to the chutes, and the announcer drew everyone's attention to the next rider. His horse jumped up and landed awkwardly on all fours, never actually leaving the chute until the second leap. Colton made a funny sound and said, "He didn't mark out."

She wasn't going to ask, but after a moment, he explained himself. In bareback riding, he said, the cowboy's heels have to be touching the horse above its shoulders until the first time the horse's front hooves hit the ground. The cowboy finished what looked like an excellent ride, but then Poppy heard the announcer say he hadn't "marked the horse out." Poppy glanced at Colton. He winced as if the news had knocked *him* out of the competition.

"That horse is known for his crazy first moves," Colton said. "But sometimes knowing something is coming isn't enough to keep it from ruining your ride."

He explained the gear the cowboys were wearing, including the vest, which he said was a flak jacket designed to "keep your ribs from puncturing your lungs." Just the thought of it turned her stomach.

He knew all of the horses by name, and all of the cowboys but one. He knew all the saddle bronc riders, too. Poppy wondered at the small world—one with a stadium full of fans. This was just one circuit of many, Colton explained. There were professional, bull-riding-only circuits as well. Remembering the rancher in the Combine talking about Colton being in the finals, she finally asked a question. "Does each circuit have its own finals?"

"Many do, but not like The Finals. That's the

PRCA National Finals in Las Vegas."

"How do you get invited to ride?"

"You don't. You earn it." He took a long drink of his beer. Poppy hated the taste of hers, which was both bland and bitter, but he didn't seem bothered by it. "It's about money. If you ride a lot and win a lot, you earn a lot of money. And if you make it into the top fifteen money makers by the end of the year, you get invited to the finals. It's fairer than most sports. The ones who make it work hard, ride like crazy, and don't get hurt."

"But you got hurt," she said.

"I did. Then I managed to make it worse, and then worse again, and after that, it's a bit of a blur." He took another drink, keeping his eyes on the action in the arena. "By the time things started to come around, Emmaline was dying, the ranch was in terrible shape, and I'd missed more than half a year of riding. There's no way to make that up."

"Are you going back?"

"I don't think so." He didn't look her in the eye when he said it.

If he wanted to say anything more, the announcer made sure he didn't. When the bronc riding competitions were over, Colton's mood lightened. He had a lot of insight into all the events and more than a few funny stories he'd heard of or seen himself. She even heard the words "Beau told me about ..." a couple of times. She'd never heard Colton's father mentioned so freely before.

The night stretched on to the finale, the bull riding competition. The crowd went wild, but she didn't enjoy it much. Besides the fact that it was ridiculously dangerous, she missed watching the horses. She liked the smart roping horses and the way they teamed up with their humans. There was even an interplay between the broncs and their riders, and she knew it from how the horse's demeanor changed when the buzzer went off.

After the last bull rider, the prizes were given, and most people made a break for the parking lot. Colton sat transfixed, and not particularly happy, as the winners were given money and prizes. She gathered that this was the last night of a week of events, and the grand prize was impressive. It was a big red pickup to the "all-around cowboy." She couldn't tell if he won a lease or the truck itself. Either way, it was nothing to sneeze at.

"Nice truck," she said.

"I don't like it," he said. "The one I won was blue."

CHAPTER 28

Colton stood up and pulled on his coat. "Ready to go?"

Poppy nodded. It was uncomfortably late, and they were almost two hours away from home. He waited for her and walked side by side with the slow-moving crowd, up the stairs and onto the concourse. She saw him glancing over his shoulder. She wasn't surprised when he asked, "Mind if I just say a couple of quick good-byes?"

She did mind. But she didn't say it. She just noted that for future events, not that there would be any between now and when she left, she'd better bring her own vehicle. She followed him as they moved against the crowd and toward the stairs. There was a cowboy he knew at the top, and Colton slipped into conversation with him. No one stopped him as they walked down the stairs. She felt lucky to have not been singled out to stay up top. Colton might never have noticed.

But she didn't feel lucky when she got below. The mood had changed. It was partly bustling business as the animals were moved around and partly a celebration that seemed to be strongly fueled by beer. And they were walking past the livestock and toward the beer group. Colton congratulated the right cowboys and teased the others.

"Hoping for a better show?"

She turned to see a cowboy giving her a grin.

"No," she said, "I had a great time."

"Let me guess. You're in charge of a sponsorship."

"Nope."

He held out his hand. "Frost Elliot."

The name registered. She shook his hand. "Can I get your autograph?" She handed him the program Colton had purchased.

He pulled a marker out of his pocket and expertly opened the program to a certain page, one she realized was a full-page ad for jeans. Featuring him. And looking at him now, in person, she could understand what the fuss was about. "Who do I make it out to?"

"Mara. M-A-R-A."

He did as she asked and handed it back to her. "And what's your name?"

She was taken aback, which made him chuckle. "I knew it wasn't for you. You have no idea who I am, and you don't exactly have the buckle bunny vibe."

Buckle bunny? She was pretty sure that wasn't a good thing. She gave him a sheepish smile. "Sorry. No offense intended. I don't know any rock stars by name."

"Oh, I'm a rock star now." He had a great grin, she thought. It was impossible not to smile along.

"Well, there was music. And a light show. And fireworks."

"You have me there," he said. Frost scanned the crowd around them. "So are you here to look at livestock or are you here with someone?"

She spotted Colton in the throng. He and a couple of others were talking to Keli Coulson, who was wearing her brilliant smile again.

"Colton Gunnerson's a friend of mine," she said.

Frost looked at her, at Colton, then back to her again. "Just a friend, eh? Colton always was an idiot." Before she could react, he quickly changed the topic to Billings and Montana in general, and then she found out that he made his home in Cody, Wyoming. Although from what he said he was rarely there. She put that together with what Colton had said about the finals. Rodeo at this level was a full-time job on the road.

He asked about her, Arizona, and even her thesis. When she told him she was studying the lemon lily, he did a good job of looking impressed. She talked about the Huachuca Mountains, where she studied the plant and kept her description as short as she could. It was difficult. She loved the place.

He'd spent a lot of time in Arizona and asked all the right questions. Then he frowned and said, "I just don't get it. You're a smart, gorgeous woman. What are you doing here with someone like Colton?"

"He's a good guy." As soon as she said it, she realized she was echoing Travis's words. But she couldn't let Frost think she was dating him when Colton clearly wanted something else. "And we're just friends."

"I'm just surprised. He hasn't got a great track record for how he treats women. But you've probably heard about all that." He rubbed the back of his neck. "Do you need a ride home?"

"Thank you, but I think I'll wait a little longer."

"Okay." He took the program from her hand, found another page, and wrote a number across it. "My cell. I'll probably hang around for a little while, so if you get tired of waiting, just call me. I'm going your way. Besides, I've enjoyed talking with you." He left, shooting her another grin, and she watched him walk past the beer group and head for the pens.

She waited for Colton, but it was getting harder to wait patiently. It was well past ten thirty, so she knew he needed her to drive. She was tired. But Colton was nowhere to be found. Frustrated, she wandered around the outskirts of the thinning crowd and finally back toward the room where Colton had first met up with everyone. She thought she heard Keli Coulson's voice and was about to steer clear of the room when she heard Colton respond. "Well, I know you're right. It does get in your blood. I guess I can't say for sure I won't be coming back. There are some things I'd need to take care of first, but I don't see why I—"

Poppy walked in. It was just the two of them,

standing face to face, and close. Colton had found a bottle of beer somewhere, and he was wearing that big smile, the one that accompanied the overly smooth voice. Keli was the first to notice her. "Well, hi," she said. "Do I know you?"

"Hey, Poppy, I was just coming to look for you," Colton said.

Poppy could hardly keep from rolling her eyes.

"Oh, yes. You're Colton's tenant. Lucky girl," Keli added, placing her hand on Colton's arm.

"I need to go," Poppy said.

Colton looked taken aback. "Sure. Let me just finish up here with Keli."

Poppy turned and walked out the door. She hadn't made it more than ten steps before she saw Frost walking toward her. He gave her a quizzical look. "You okay?"

"Yes, just tired."

"Does that mean you're ready to go?" His eyes drifted past her, and she turned around to see Colton and Keli headed their way. She felt the color rising on her neck. How stupid did she look, waiting for a man who was flirting with someone else? Of course, she had no claim on Colton, but she looked like an idiot. And she didn't like it.

She straightened and turned back to Frost. "I'm done waiting."

He grinned and leaned closer. "Glad you've come to your senses." Then he looked at Colton. "Colton." Then he tipped his hat. "Keli."

"Frost Elliot, what a pleasure to see you," Keli said. "Do you have time for a few questions?"

"Sure wish I did, but I just heard my horse is acting up, and I need to get him loaded. We're staying at that stable Travis uses just outside of Moose Hollow." He looked back to Poppy. "Have a safe trip. If you need anything, you know how to find me." He walked past them, but before she had turned away, he turned around and walked backward so he could face her, saying, "We have lilies in Wyoming too, Poppy." He tipped his hat to her and was gone.

Keli gave Colton a quick hug, which he barely returned, and took off in a hurry in Frost's direction. That left her with Colton, who was glowering at either Frost or Keli or both. He turned to Poppy with a sour expression. "I don't suppose you want to, but a couple of the guys were going to this place. It's a dance hall, not really a bar. We wouldn't be there long. It would just be good to catch up. And since you're already having a fine time meeting all the cowboys ..."

She wasn't in the mood for teasing, if that was what he was doing. "No thanks." He frowned and his lips parted. It looked as if he hadn't even considered that she wouldn't want to go. She considered saying something about drinking beer in bars, one of Emmaline's no-nos, but instead walked briskly toward the stairs.

"We can't go that way. It's closed off by now." He walked out the big garage doors, and she followed him down a back road and out into the multiacre parking lot. Colton's truck was one of only a few dozen still out there. They walked fast, in silence, through the cold night. The air had a sharp, damp feeling, and she had a feeling that snow was on the way again.

He pulled just ahead of her and went to the driver's side. Opening the door for her was a nice gesture, for a start.

But he wasn't opening the door for her. He got in the driver's seat. He didn't even notice her as she spun and walked around the back, heading for the passenger side. She searched her memory. He'd had two beers that she knew of, over a period of many hours. But she couldn't be sure. The truth was, she couldn't see any sign that he'd been drinking at all. But the first time his driving seemed less than sharp, she was going to have him stop the truck and call a cab.

Did cabs go to Moose Hollow?

The seat, the air, even the seat belt felt ridiculously cold. She pulled her hood over her head, set the program on the dashboard, and shoved her hands in her pockets. Colton started up the truck and drove across the parking lot. "You know, if I said I was getting back in the game tomorrow, I'd have a few key sponsors lined up in no time. I'm pretty sure of it. It wouldn't take me long. I've lost flexibility, but watching those boys …" He shook his head. "I can feel it, every twitch and turn. It's like I know what the horse is going to do just a split second before he does it. I can still feel it, even sitting in the stands."

Poppy didn't answer.

"I could get someone to help with the ranch on weekends. Just three or four days a week, and the money I bring in could cover their salary. Not to mention bring some attention to the ranch. Maybe I've just been going about this all wrong."

He got onto the highway and drove down a long, straight bridge, and just as he hit the other end of it, he let out a string of curse words she'd never heard from his mouth before. He slammed on the brakes and pulled over onto the shoulder, skidding as he did. "I'm not supposed to be driving! Why didn't you say something?"

She scowled at him. "Right. Because telling you I didn't want to go to a bar was met with such a polite response, why stop there? I know, maybe I should have also mentioned that drinking and driving is a stupid thing to do, especially when you're on parole for a DUI."

"DUI? What?"

She got out and slammed the door. She walked around the front of the truck, nearly running into Colton. She stomped past him and hopped up to the driver's seat. She didn't even wait for him to get situated before she started driving.

"I didn't have a DUI. The charges were dropped. What I had was about my fourth concussion. Or fortieth, depending on which doctor you ask. I could hardly walk straight. And where did you hear about that?"

"Then what are you on parole for?"

"Something else."

Neither of them spoke for at least twenty miles. Finally, Colton said, "How do you know Frost?"

She rolled her eyes. The man was exasperating. "I just now met him."

"Seemed like you knew him better than that," he said.

She ignored him. They hadn't even made it off the interstate yet, and it was going to be a long drive. The only good news was that she was so annoyed she didn't feel tired anymore. Out of the corner of her eye, she noticed Colton pressing his fingertips to his temples. She was pretty sure one of his headaches was coming on, and she didn't feel sorry for him at all.

"You know," Colton said, "he's only flirting with you to get at me."

Her annoyance ratcheted up to anger. He was probably right, of course, although Frost had been pretty convincingly surprised when he realized she was waiting for Colton. "Why would he think I was with you? Except for when we were seated, I hardly even saw you."

"I don't know, did you tell him?" He was leaning into his fingertips now.

She rummaged around in her coat pocket with one hand and pulled out a small silver case about the size of lip balm and handed it to him. "I got this for you. It's supposed to help. Roll some onto your temples." She wasn't in the mood to help him, but neither did she want to hear him complain.

"What is this stuff?" He took off the lid. "It stinks."

"It's peppermint oil, not skunk spray."

"I don't need perfume."

She ignored him as she took the exit off the highway, but once they reached the red light, she snatched the tube from his hands and turned his face toward her. She rolled the essential oil onto each temple, and when he flinched and complained about the smell, she rubbed it into his temples with her fingers less gently than she should have. The light turned green and she put the tube back in her pocket and headed out on Highway 212. She rubbed the excess oil on her own temples. He was giving her a headache.

Colton grumpily crossed his arms over his chest. "What is peppermint supposed to do, except drive me crazy?" He reached for the program and flipped through it. "What the—? You got his autograph?"

"Yup."

"You go to a rodeo with me and ask for Frost Elliot's autograph?"

She let him simmer for a while, until finally he saw Mara's name. "Oh. You got it for Mara."

He started flipping through the pages, and she waited for the other shoe to drop. "You got his phone number? Don't you realize what a competitive little twerp—"

"Has it even occurred to you that Frost might have flirted with me for some reason, any reason, other than you?"

"Like what?" he snapped back. A minute went by in silence before at last Colton said, "Oh."

She drove up and over the railroad tracks on the overpass.

"I wasn't saying you aren't cute, Poppy. I was just saying that Frost notices all the cute girls, so you're—"

"Nothing special," she finished for him. Then she turned on the radio and spun the dial until she found something she liked and suspected he hated.

"I didn't mean that." It was the first thing he'd said that didn't sound angry, but she didn't believe him at all. "What was all that stuff about lilies?"

"My thesis topic is the Arizona population of the lemon lily."

"He asked about that?"

"Yes, he did." She knew she sounded sharp, but she didn't care.

"I knew it was a flower." Miles went by before he added, "My headache feels a little better."

She was going to say "Good," but in truth she didn't want his headache to go away.

The highway was mostly quiet, the scenery familiar again, and it soothed her.

"Well, turns out you're cute when you're mad," Colton said.

She was quiet until they reached the red light in Moose Hollow and she took the turn west toward the homestead. "You had one thing right," she said.

"What's that?"

"Frost Elliot is dreamy."

He crossed his arms and looked out the window, and for the first time on the drive she had something to smile about. But as she reviewed the night in her head, her smile faded. It was a confusing, frustrating mess, her heart was sore, and they weren't even dating. She needed to rethink her friendship with Colton. Again.

CHAPTER 29

Colton craved it. The rush that came beforehand. The sound of a crowd, the heightened sensations, the feeling that time slowed down and he was faster than lightning, every muscle taut, every nerve firing. And when it was over, there was the crowd. So many voices pouring out praise. Things like that just didn't happen in normal life.

And the money, too. It was enough to make a man think he was doing work that mattered. But just as fast as it poured in, it could pour back out. Rounds for everyone. Presents for the girls. Dinners, clothes, souvenirs he'd just leave in the hotel room. It was amazing how fast it could flow through his life.

It was too much to think of what that money would've meant to him now if he'd just held on to it. Just some of it. But he hadn't, and he'd gotten hurt. It happened to cowboys all the time.

But not him. He was strong and fast and flexible, right? He was Colton Gunnerson. Even better than Beau Gunnerson, people said. Those words built him up and stung him at the same time. Maybe he believed it too much.

The doctors said it was probable he'd had dozens of minor concussions before the crash. Tiny blood vessels in his brain were already stretched and torn. If you wanted to avoid concussions, bareback wasn't the way to go. Every stride was whiplash. He wore the collar and other gear, but that didn't change the sport. One doctor said that every buck slammed his brain into the back of his skull. When the big one came along, it hit a brain that was already injured.

He didn't remember the big one. He also didn't remember any premonitions or distractions; it was just him at his best. He'd been told the horse flipped over backward, and he ended up underneath. One knee bent the way it wasn't meant to go. The horse had landed on his skull, and they had both landed on the metal rail of the chute. He'd seen photos of it. If he hadn't known it was him, he would've said that guy died. Or ended up with a brain so damaged that he'd never be the same again.

The horse had never gone back to the rodeo. He'd heard that somewhere, but he couldn't be sure it was true.

Colton hadn't been the same after that. He didn't remember things the right way. He couldn't be sure the accident hadn't made him stupider than he already was. But it was better now than soon after the accident, and he was grateful for that. Without Emmaline, he would have been in jail or dead by now.

One more concussion, the doctor had said. One more rough landing, and he could lose his ability to talk, or walk, or think. He couldn't imagine having headaches worse than the one he had now.

But everything about the ranch made him feel like he was destined for failure. With Keli schmoozing him just like old times, he could see it. What if he was the hero, instead? Colton Gunnerson returns for one more brilliant season and saves the family ranch. He couldn't just say no to her. News went from her mouth to the ears of the sponsors. If she said he was out of the game, they'd forget his name. But by the end of the rodeo, with the guys patting him on the back and Keli's million-dollar smile shining on him, he had just about convinced himself he could do it.

He'd forgotten Emmaline's rules even existed. But Poppy hadn't.

If Poppy didn't already think he was a loser, and a fickle, lying, flirting, fame-chasing weasel, she did now.

But she made it worse, didn't she? If she hadn't dressed that way, none of this would've happened. That silky shirt, tight jeans, curly hair —and what was with the makeup? She barely looked like his friend. Sure, his friend always had long legs and clear blue eyes and smelled like a rose in late spring, but she didn't usually wear stuff that screamed, "Look at me!" And everyone did. Every male with eyeballs, at least. Frost Elliot would never have looked at her twice without that getup.

He threw his gloves across the barn, where they landed in the pile of things he hadn't taken care of yet, including the broken tractor. He knew she studied something in some remote place. Of course it had to be a lily, some beautiful wildflower in the middle of the desert. Or mountains. Wherever it was. That would be just like her. And any man worth his salt would talk to her, get to know her, and realize she was just like that. It had only taken Frost a few minutes to figure out what Colton hadn't taken the time to learn.

No, Frost Elliot had never been a skirt chaser. And he wasn't a fool, either. He realized Poppy was the kind of girl who found beauty in the middle of barren places.

We have lilies in Wyoming, too, Poppy. Colton would have loved to wipe that dreamy grin right off Frost's face. He retrieved his gloves and shook off the dust. Poppy deserved someone like Frost —someone successful, reliable. And smart. Not broken like him.

CHAPTER 30

*P*oppy sat in the chair she'd made from an old metal milk crate and the door from a long-lost cabinet and opened the Bible app she'd downloaded to her phone. She decided to use the paraphrased edition again today, because the last translation she'd read had left her confused and annoyed. And she was annoyed enough already.

"Keyword Search," the screen prompted.

"Parole," she typed. No results. She smirked and typed "butthead." Nothing. Then "criminal."

She was surprised to see eight results. She started with the one that was from Luke 23:98. Jesus was crucified alongside two criminals. Did she already know that? It tugged at her memories.

It did seem as if she'd often seen three crosses grouped together in paintings. One of the criminals had ridiculed Jesus. The other had converted right there, hanging from a cross. She read it again just to make sure she had it right. The first response seemed, although nasty, reasonable. The second seemed bizarre. That criminal had looked at the man who claimed to be the Son of God and yet wouldn't prevent his own painful and humiliating death and chose to see him as the Son of God.

As a story, it was moving. It resonated in her heart. But it was the stuff of legends and fairy tales. *He died for your sins.* No, in the real world people dragged each other down to their own despicable level. That was why her parents were so popular, right? No one had to get a job, clean the house, go to bed, wake up. Everyone was welcome as long as they brought weed, money, or fast food. All her mother's dreams of owning a flower shop had vanished. All her father's plans to tour the world had fallen away. They had asked their girls not to call them Mom and Dad anymore—maybe not just because it made them feel old but because it made them feel responsible.

The only self-sacrifice was between her and her sister. And between them and the rest of the world, because they'd had to make excuses for why friends couldn't come over, why her parents never made it to teacher conferences, and why they didn't have computer access for their home-work. They sometimes hadn't even had electricity or hot water, but they'd never told. They had lied because Mom and Dad liked to feel good, and by the time Poppy had reached high school, it seemed that nothing other than smoking felt good to her parents.

It was like watching two people embalm their own bodies.

Didn't they have real friends, once? She even remembered them dancing in the kitchen. Mom had taught a painting class in Washington. Dad had a quick sense of humor and did card tricks. Then grandma died, and the checks started com-ing, and they'd moved to Arizona to start a "farm."

They had received three thousand dollars a month as long as they were custodial parents. As far as she knew, her parents had convinced the fund manager that they were still supporting their girls. And Grandma had also created the trust fund each girl received, to which her par-ents could never quite gain access. As far as she knew, Sierra's was gone. Maybe she'd given some of it to them. And now Poppy was using hers to live in this frigid world and read about a God she couldn't begin to understand.

She looked up at the wooden beams above her; each bowed in a graceful arch to where it raised its head at the peak of the roof. How did the craftsmen who built the barn do that? Did they steam solid, straight wood and wrestle it into a mold of some kind? So much work and so much struggle. Even now, as tiny beams of light shone through places where the wooden shingles had curled back or blown away, the roof was strong, and the backbone of its peak was straight.

"I see you have your own service going on up here this morning."

She jumped to her feet so fast her phone clattered to the floor. Colton was near the top of the stairs, one hand resting on the wooden rail meant to keep people from falling into the stairwell.

"I thought you were at church."

"I overslept, and by the time I got the feeding done, I knew I'd be late. I hate showing up late."

She reached for the phone, slipped it into her pocket, and tucked her hands into pockets as well. "This isn't a *service* or anything. I was just reading."

"Reading what?" He took the last step up onto

the wooden floor of the hayloft. It creaked beneath him.

"A book."

He gave her a halfhearted grin. "I heard that's a good one." He looked around. "I figured you'd been spending some time up here. I couldn't figure out who else would have swept up."

She kicked at a trace of snow that had filtered through the roof. "Yeah. Sorry." She shoved her hands deeper into her pockets. The cold finally seemed to be seeping through her clothing.

"No, I'm glad. I'm glad you like it here."

"Well, I need to get back to the house."

"Mind if I show you something first?" he said.

She didn't answer. She didn't want to figure out what to say to Colton or how to act. She noticed that the loud confidence he'd worn like a crown last night was gone, but that didn't matter much.

"Come on." He strode toward the north end of the hayloft. Then he climbed the ladder that led to the high barn doors. "It's worth it, I swear." He pulled his glove off with his teeth and let it drop to the floor of the hayloft and then reached a hand out for her. She climbed the ladder partway. He motioned her to go even farther. Then with his free hand, he undid a rope, and the door slid down like a guillotine.

The wind was cold and took her breath away, but she stepped up and put both feet on the boards, clinging to the ladder for dear life. She had no idea how many feet she was standing above the ground, only that she was near the very peak of the barn roof. Colton had the back of her coat bunched up into a firm grasp that didn't waver. Once she knew her footing was secure on the door opening, she looked up and out.

The whole world was coated with glittering white. She could see the dusting of it down the valley toward Billings, out across the plains, and along every needle of every pine tree on the mountains. In its shining new clothes, everything in the world looked perfect.

Colton gave her time to take it all in before he spoke. "See that line out there? You can just see the fence to the right of the cottonwoods. That's the northeast corner of the property. Everything from here to there and up to the mountains is part of the ranch. And we own the grazing leases above it, too."

"It's beautiful."

"There used to be more."

Something in his voice made her look at him.

His eyes squinted against the light, and gold flecks sparkled all around the green of his irises. After a time, he reached for the rope. She took that as her cue to step onto the ladder and descend again. Colton pulled on the rope, and the guillotine door slid upward once more. "I have one more thing to show you," he said.

When he climbed down, he led her to the opposite end of the barn. At that end was a set of double doors at the level of the hayloft floor. He undid three bolts and swung them open, then sat down with his feet dangling out of the barn. He patted the spot next to him and gave her a questioning look. She sat down, but not too close. Putting her feet out the door was another thing. Below her was the diesel with its hay bales already loaded. She supposed it wouldn't be a fatal fall if she landed there, about six feet below.

Colton pointed. "You can just make out part of the south pasture fence line there. There used to be another eighty acres that direction, give or take. The Ekstroms have it now, and none of their kids want to ranch. Chances are it'll be bought and subdivided." He seemed to think about that for a while until he pointed again.

"You can even see the smoke from chimneys in Moose Hollow. When I was a kid I used to sit up here and look out there, trying to see the town. I would have done anything to live there. I couldn't understand why I lived out here in the middle of nowhere, and rode a bus forever, twice a day, while my friends walked home and played at each other's houses. When I was old enough to drive I was gone every minute I was allowed to be gone. And then some. I couldn't wait to get out of here, and rodeo was my ticket."

Colton took a deep breath. "Things here weren't great when I was growing up. Emmaline loved me. So did my mom. Beau was on the circuit. But Mom didn't want to be here any more than I did, and so she spent a lot of time away before she got sick. And when she and Beau were both here at the same time, it was awful. I think they only stayed married out of spite." He shook his head. "Sometimes I think I'm just like him. Always wanting something bigger and better." He turned to Poppy, his eyes dark and narrow. "But I never cheated anyone. And I'd rather die than cheat my family."

He chewed on the inside of his lower lip. "When I got into rodeo, I got all the fun I ever wanted. And I won, not all the time of course, but often enough. And it's a brotherhood. They'll stab you in the back, sure, but they also pick you back up. And even better, they wanted me there. I felt like I couldn't do anything right here. There, out on the road, I couldn't do anything wrong."

Poppy thought about that. "I think I get that."

"Yeah?" he asked.

She was surprised to realize he was waiting for her to say more. "School was that for me. My parents didn't care, but the teachers did, and when I did well at school, they noticed. So I made sure I did well. I remember the first time I got a B in high school. I could hardly stand it."

"Poppy Field Marsh, I have a hard time imagining getting upset over a B," he said with a lop-sided grin. "I think it's amazing that a smart girl like you even talks to a guy like me."

Her eyes narrowed. "Right. The famous rodeo cowboy? I think you have that backward."

Colton shook his head. "None of that's me."

She wasn't sure about that. "Are you going to join the circuit next year?"

"Nope."

"You said—"

"I said a lot of things. Usually, I say whatever I think people want to hear. Then I do whatever I think people want me to do." He said it with so much disgust it startled her.

"But you said you always wanted to get off this ranch."

He shook his head. "I thought I wanted that, but it wasn't right. Maybe I just wanted my family to get along." He cut a quick glance at her. "And have a few good friends."

"Then why sell the house?"

"I'm not going sell the house." He said it with a long sigh. "I'm selling the whole ranch. That's always been the plan. I just didn't want to admit it."

Poppy's breath caught. It felt like a kick in the gut.

"Both Anson and Cash want to sell the ranch. And if I try to hold on, it can end up costing them."

"How?"

"It's the wonderful world of taxes. I've had a few visits with a very patient accountant named Susan, and she tries to explain it all to me, but I still don't get it. All I know is if I sell it now, they get their quarter of the ranch in cash, free and clear. If I don't, there's taxes to pay, my salary, losses, capital gains. I just bring them trouble."

"But if you turned this place around, couldn't you make them money?"

"That's what I thought. But I haven't got a track record for that, Poppy. And besides, I know

Anson has money trouble now. They've never been rich. And they've worked a lot harder than I ever have. Why shouldn't they have money from Emmaline's ranch now? Besides, I can't do it without him."

"Without Anson?"

Colton nodded. "He knows more about this ranch than anyone. Everyone thought he'd be the one to run it, but then he went and married Julia, and she's from some fancy hotel family, and his dreams changed." He breathed. "So mine can too."

"I still don't understand why you won't go back to the rodeo if you loved it."

"It didn't love me. Remember Travis? Stand-up guy, all the time. It doesn't matter what he's doing, who he's with, he's the same guy. A Christian man. He's been in rodeo in one way or another most of his life." He shook his head slowly. "I'm not like that. It matters who I'm with, and what I'm doing. It affects who I am. I've spent my whole life acting like that's not true, but it is. It's my weakness. If I hang out with people who do bad stuff, I do it too. I love rodeo, but it's not good for me." He took another deep breath and stretched his neck. "Then there's the fact that a doctor told me I'd be dead in a couple of years if I keep riding."

"What?"

"Repetitive concussion syndrome. For me, it was mainly memory, impulse control, nausea, balance issues. Oh, and dementia."

"Dementia? What?"

"Yup. But all I cared about was my balance. If you lose your balance, you get bucked off, and when you get bucked off—"

"You hit your head."

"Nice, huh?"

"Memory issues," she said softly. And sleep issues. She wondered about that weird movie night. Or had that been a sign of dementia? Did that mean it would happen again?

"Yeah, I guess you've noticed that, and probably other equally awful things about me. I'm less foggy these days, but I have my moments, especially when I don't get enough sleep."

"I might have noticed a couple of things."

He laughed at her. "You try very hard to be nice, Poppy. I appreciate that." He looked down at the diesel below. "I wish I'd tried harder to be nice to you last night. It's not an excuse. But it feels like everything I do on this ranch is just swirling down the drain. It's hard not to get sucked in when people tell you how awesome you are. I know better. I just didn't *want* to know better."

"Why are you on parole?"

He clasped his hands together. "I had a big wreck. As soon as they let me out of the hospital, I rode again, three nights in a row in Cody. The kind of stuff I could usually do in my sleep. But I got bucked off each time and fell hard. Travis tried to get me to check into a hospital again, but this girl I knew talked me into coming home with her."

Poppy didn't know where this was going, but she began to think she was going to regret asking.

"I don't remember much about that time," Colton went on. "I remember Anson coming to bring me home, but I threw him out. I think that was the last time we said more than ten words to one another. The girl I was with had problems of her own. She liked to get drunk and beat on things. And I was so wrapped up in my self-pity I didn't mind getting drunk and getting beat on. Then one day I shoved her back, she fell and got a bad bruise on her arm, and she called the cops. And I went to jail for domestic violence.

Domestic violence. The words made her feel sick.

"It was my fault. I bit every hand that tried to

help me. She was trying to help too, as best she could."

"What happened then?"

"I'm not sure. As far as I can tell, Julia and Officer Mike got wind of what was going on. The next thing I know I'm in the courtroom, Officer Mike is there, and he's saying he's willing to supervise my parole if I move home and take care of Emmaline. I didn't know what he was even talking about. I didn't realize that she'd decided to stop treatment." He took a shaky breath. "Emmaline wrote out rules for me, and Mike read them in the courtroom. The judge said it was the most sensible thing he'd heard all week, and he released me to Mike's custody. Mike drove me to the homestead, ripped me up one side and down the other. And when he caught his breath, he did it all over again. And that wasn't even the Come to Jesus talk I got afterward about living in sin and hitting girls." He snorted. "He seems like such a nice guy until you get on the wrong side of him."

"Hopefully he won't hear about last night, then."

"He already did. I called him this morning and told him." He looked at her. "I'm sorry I was a jerk, Poppy. And I'm sorry I said those things about Frost. He's arrogant, but so am I. I knew he was interested in you, he'd have to be blind not to be. Not that I'm blind, but I'm not saying I'm interested. But I could be. If things were different."

She watched in wonder as his face turned red. It was good to be on the other side of a blush for a change.

"I'm just saying if you want to date Frost, it's okay with me. Not that you need my permission. I know you don't need—"

Poppy burst into laughter. "You'd better shut up while you can," she said.

He nodded earnestly and stood up. "Ready for the wedding?"

It took her an uncomfortable moment before she realized he was asking about Zane and Mara's wedding. "No. I guess I keep thinking it won't really happen."

"Oh, it will. You should never underestimate the tenacity of a Gunnerson man."

"$\mathcal{H}$e told them. Kind of."

Poppy slumped. "What does 'kind of' mean, Mara?"

"He told them that there was a chance he wasn't the father of my baby and asked them to pray about how they would treat our child if that turned out to be true."

Poppy couldn't take her eyes off her fingers because the task at hand was absurdly complicated. Which way did she twist it? Why weren't the bobby pins working? "And what did they say?"

"They said that he should wait to get married until he got a paternity test." She mumbled the response.

"That's a reasonable thing to ask, Mara."

"Love isn't about being reasonable," the girl said, looking every bit the eighteen-year-old she was. "They just don't understand." She huffed. "You need to cross the pins, Poppy, one over the other to make an X."

"Now you tell me." She did it, and the strand held firm.

"Just do it underneath the top part, so the pins don't show, like in the video."

Poppy would just as soon stomp Mara's phone into dust as watch that video again. They used words she'd never heard before in her life and showed a series of five-second clips that seemed to defy the rules of physics, not to mention that she was dealing with hair, which didn't stay in neat, ribbon-like curls in the real world. It tangled and frizzed and stuck out.

Poppy wished again that Mara's mother had shown up, and for more reasons than Mara's hair. She took out the pins and tried again.

"Mara, I think after so many years of marriage and raising three kids, Julia and Anson probably do know a thing or two about love."

"I don't think they like you, either."

Poppy knew it wouldn't be right to say that was because they thought she had meddled in

Mara and Zane's lives. Besides, it didn't matter. She'd never been the most popular girl in the world. In about a month she'd be gone, and the only opinions that would matter belonged to her thesis committee. But Mara's relationship with Julia and Anson mattered, because marriage would be hard enough without their support. "I think they are trying very hard to get Zane to do the right thing. I don't think it's about liking you or not. I think they need time."

"Time? Zane says he's loved me since third grade."

"And how long have you loved him?"

"We've been friends for two years."

"Not what I asked, Mara."

"Okay, three months. Almost. I loved him before, but I just didn't know it."

Poppy considered that. It sounded silly, like something her sister would say to justify her next move. Something like "I've always wanted to live there, I just didn't know it." Poppy formulated her next words carefully. "Mara, you know you love him. And you know he loves you. So just be patient with them. As the months go by, and then years, they'll understand, and then everything will be okay. All you need to focus on now is Zane, and your future together."

"I hope so." She sighed and then squinted at Poppy. "I wish you'd let me put more curl in your hair."

"I'm not a curly person, Mara. And we've spent entirely too much time on how I look." It was bad enough the girl had talked her into wearing a long skirt and a lacy top. Not to mention the outrageously expensive boots, which she secretly loved. They were a pretty version of motorcycle boots with two-inch heels, which put Poppy just shy of six feet tall. She loved that, too.

"You need to look good," Mara added. "Lots of people find the man they marry at weddings."

"Not looking for one, Mara."

"I hear Liam is pretty hot. And he's all business; you guys could be geeky forever after."

"I'm not interested in Zane's older brother, Mara. I'm not interested in anyone."

"That's because you and Colton are already perfect for each other."

Poppy rolled her eyes. "Mara, Colton and I are barely friends." And there hadn't been a movie night since the rodeo two weeks ago.

"If he's dragging his feet, it's because he doesn't want to be unequally yoked."

Poppy had no idea what she was talking about,

and she didn't want to ask, but Mara just kept talking. "That means that believers are supposed to marry other believers. That way the marriage is a three-strand braid—you, him, and Him," she said, pointing at the ceiling. "But that's okay. I've been praying a lot, and I know Jesus is working on you."

Poppy didn't want to get irritated, especially right before Mara's wedding, but she couldn't help but mutter, "He is *not* working on me."

"You're reading the Bible."

"That's because going to those meetings with you is like showing up at a final exam for a class you've never attended. You all talk in code and nod knowingly, and I have no idea what you're talking about. It's just another textbook, that's all. It's what I do."

"You are the geekiest girl I know," Mara said.

"I have to excel at something."

"Speaking of geeks, Zane sent in his college application. I helped him with it. It surprised his parents that we were both hoping to go to college."

"See? Just keep pushing forward, Mara. It'll sort itself out."

"Of course, I'll never get into college."

"Stop with that talk or I'll put your hair in pigtails. Besides, look how great you did on the tests. Eighty-ninth percentile. Booyah."

Mara made a face, but her smile shone through.

Poppy stepped back from Mara's chair and squinted at her handiwork, trying to see the ways it differed from the dreaded online video. Mara grabbed a hand mirror and ran for the big mirror in the bathroom. "Oh! My! Gosh!"

"Where did I mess up?"

Mara popped into view again, her mouth agape. "It's perfect. You did it." She ran into Poppy's arms and gave her an awkward hug as she leaned her head—and hair—safely out of touching distance. "Not the makeup, not the makeup."

"I won't mess it up. I like your makeup."

Mara made a face again, as if she couldn't bear everyone else's perpetual lameness. "This is how Zane likes it," she said as she disappeared into the bathroom.

Her makeup had less black and drama. Although it had plenty of sparkle. Mara was still wearing a bathrobe, and there was no telling what her dress would be like. All Poppy knew was that Mara had ordered it online, it was blue, and it was "so steampunk." She had seen the boots. They were a marvel—black leather and burgundy velvet creations, with a tall version of Victorian heels all laced up with black ribbon. The bouquet was a burgundy-red ball of roses with blue and black ribbons. If they were any indication, the wedding dress could be epic.

But when Mara came out of the bathroom, her dress was nothing like Poppy had expected. It was an empire-waisted, vintage-looking dress of handmade lace over the palest blue satin lining. The neckline was high and modest, and short lace sleeves fluttered over her shoulders. Western, Gothic, whatever she wanted to call it, the dress was timeless. "You are so beautiful," Poppy said. "I wish you knew that. And not just today." Tears stung her eyes.

"Don't you dare," Mara said, fanning her own eyes. "I have three layers of mascara on here. Stop it."

The girl disappeared into the bathroom again, and Poppy felt a twinge. She might have chosen the same dress. She wouldn't have had curves like Mara, of course, but she would have been drawn to it. If things had turned out the way she'd expected, she would have been the one buying a wedding dress. And marrying Geoff. Now she doubted she would ever get married.

It was ridiculous to be jealous of Mara. There was nothing about her life that she would trade with the girl. But she couldn't shake the feeling that she was missing out and always would be. So many thoughts threatened to cloud her mind— about Geoff, about what she'd learned at the women's group meetings, even about Frost Elliot. Not that she would ever date him. She didn't have room for dating in her life.

Had she ever? Was she the reason her relationship had failed? Or maybe it hadn't failed. Geoff wanted her to move back in when she returned to Arizona. What if she did?

"Ten minutes! I'm going to be married in ten minutes!"

Poppy's heart jumped. She heard a knock at the door and answered. Julia stood there, looking more than a little uncomfortable. "Is she ready?" she asked.

Mara exited the bathroom, and Poppy watched as several expressions crossed Julia's face, one after another, until she settled on a smile with just a trace of tears at the corners of her eyes. Poppy didn't understand Julia enough even to guess what the tears were about. But the smile seemed enough for Mara.

"I was wondering if you had your something old, something new," Julia asked.

Mara's eyes widened. "Oh no. Poppy, give me something to borrow. Oh no! Everything I'm wearing is new. How old does it have to be?"

"I have something for you," Julia said. "You can borrow them, and they're old enough." She reached into her bag and pulled out a jewelry box. Even the box looked old to Poppy. Mara reached out, opened it, and shook her head. "These are amazing."

She tugged her earrings out with one hand and quickly put on Julia's. They hung in tiers, sparkling in the light. Poppy would never have guessed that Julia would own something so showy. She glanced at the name in the box, looked again at the earrings, and decided that they were most likely real diamonds, and if she was right, there were a few sapphires as well. Mara probably had no idea they were far more than costume jewelry.

Julia looked pretty with her hair down and heels on, but Poppy was almost positive she wasn't wearing a new dress. She thought about the carefully stitched repairs she'd seen in Julia's pants, the polished but worn shoes, and the corner room that, as far as she knew, still remained unrenovated. The earrings were an extravagant thing for such a modest woman to own. Curiosity got the best of her. "They're lovely," she said to Julia. "Is there a story behind them?"

"They were my grandmother's. She had eccentric tastes."

Mara laughed. "Cool. Me too." With the earrings dangling at her neck, Mara looked perfectly Mara. Just the way she should look, Poppy thought.

Julia led them down the hallway to the back stairwell, and there they took a detour. The stairs went all the way down past the first floor and into what appeared to be a basement. There, Julia unlocked a door marked No Admittance and led them down a short hallway and into a plain-looking and rather shabby living room.

Julia took them swiftly across the room and down yet another hall. Poppy noticed the low ceiling and, beyond, the small well windows, a kitchen almost four decades out of date, and a table that matched the one at the homestead. They passed by a tiny bedroom, its walls decorated with posters featuring brightly colored, menacing robots and laser beams, and then they climbed a steep, narrow staircase. Julia peeked through the door at the top of the stairs, turned to face them, and said, "The coast is clear."

This was where Julia lived? All that beauty and elegance above them, and this was where she'd raised three sons? It wasn't what Poppy had expected. It was more like someplace Poppy's family would have lived. No matter where we go, we live in a Marsh, her sister always joked.

Poppy followed Julia out the door and found herself in the small office where she had tended to her not-quite-broken nose. Through the open door in front of her, she could see she was directly behind the front desk of the Third Street Inn. And she could hear voices in the lobby. "Stay here," Julia said. "I have to move everyone back into the parlor. Poppy, you're with me."

"No!" The urgency in Mara's voice took them all by surprise. "Poppy, you have to walk in with me. My dad...my mom ..."

She didn't have to say anything more. Both her parents had chosen not to attend. Their absence was the elephant in the room Mara had avoided addressing until then. There was no one to walk her down the aisle. "I'd be honored," Poppy said.

She saw pain cross Julia's face, but Julia put on a practiced smile and left.

"No dad, no mom, no big brother. That leaves my big sis, right?" Mara said quietly.

Poppy nodded. And blinked rapidly. "Not the makeup."

Mara laughed.

They got the signal from Julia, counted to twenty as asked, and then Mara took Poppy's hand and they walked through the lobby, past two older women who looked delighted to see a bride, and through the doors of the "parlor," which was a narrow reading room filled with comfortable furniture and large windows that looked out over the street. Sheer curtains had been drawn across the windows, most of the furniture had been pushed to one side or the other, and everywhere were dark red roses. From the center of the room cascaded a canopy of impossibly small lights on thin copper wires.

"Wow," Mara breathed.

Zane was standing in the middle of the room beside a thin young man with an unruly beard. Poppy realized he must be the youth pastor who had been counseling them. He wasn't at all what she'd expected and was at least three decades younger than she'd imagined. He motioned to Mara to stand on his other side. Poppy squeezed Mara's hand and then let her go.

If she was the praying kind, Poppy thought, she would have prayed that this marriage would be blessed. She wanted the best for them so much that it made her heart hurt.

Suddenly she had no idea where to go. She was standing in the middle of the room, surrounded by unfamiliar faces, except for Julia and Anson, who looked like they were about to get tandem root canals. She swung around, and her gaze landed on Colton. He was smiling at her. She walked forward gratefully and stood beside him. He bumped her shoulder with his arm. "Nice job," he whispered. Like most of Colton's whispers, it was loud enough for everyone in the room to hear. She could feel her face go red, but she smiled. It was good to have a friend here. At least he felt like a friend.

The pastor said was that everyone present had a responsibility to uphold this marriage, and that was why they were arranged in a circle around the couple. Poppy thought it might also have something to do with the small turnout. She saw a young family with two kids. That would be Drew, Julia and Anson's oldest son, his wife, and their two kids. Cash was there too. Poppy recognized him from her first day in Moose Hollow, the cheerful landlord who was on good terms with Danny. Also in attendance was a serious young man in a sharp suit—that would be Liam, she guessed, Julia's middle child. And two young women who were probably Mara's friends, three young men who were probably Zane's friends, and another woman about Poppy's age, standing alone.

If they had the job of holding this marriage together, they had their hands full.

The pastor spoke about Zane and Mara, about the work they'd done with him, learning about finances and about love and respect in marriage, and he told everyone they'd been to their first childbirth class. Poppy wondered if he felt it necessary to justify marrying two eighteen-year-olds or if he was simply trying to win over Zane's parents. The words drifted through her scattered mind. Then he talked about the role of women and the role of men in marriage, neither role being what Poppy expected, and about how a man was supposed to lay down his life for his family. She wasn't certain how any of it applied to Zane.

Then again, he was about to become a father to someone else's child.

There was some talk about the man being the

head of the household. It just seemed to be part of the laundry list the pastor had for Zane.

Zane, in the meantime, was looking at Mara like she'd hung the moon, and Mara looked the same way at him. Poppy wasn't sure she knew how to recognize love, but they made a convincing case for it.

When the pastor announced it was time for the vows, he asked everyone to hold hands. Colton reached for her hand and held it tight. On her other side, one of the teenage girls inched a little closer and held out one limp hand. But all Poppy could think about was the way her hand felt enclosed in Colton's hand. He'd held her hand over popcorn, once, and now this, and she got to hold him right back. She was so lost in the way it felt that the wedding went on without her.

"We will," Colton said, and so did everyone else.

"We will," Poppy said softly. Whatever it was that had been asked of her, she would do what she could to support this marriage. That's what big sisters were supposed to do.

And that meant Sierra, too.

The limp hand on her left side fell away, and she saw other people's hands letting go, but Colton held on. Didn't he realize the vows were over? No, he was no longer holding the hand of the woman next to him. She felt heat rise in her face. Don't read too much into this, she thought. And she resisted the urge to hold tighter.

The pastor was saying something about a three-strand braid, just as Mara had, then he said, "You may kiss your bride."

This is their first kiss, she thought. And she might be the only person in the room who knew it. Zane stepped forward and gave her one slow, sweet, gentle kiss. Then he pulled her closer and Mara's arms went around him, and the kiss turned into something more movie-worthy.

"Wow," Colton chuckled beside her. "Kid's got moves."

Poppy rolled her eyes. Everyone applauded, and reluctantly she drew her hand away to clap. That was when Colton's hand slipped onto the small of her back. She hoped she wouldn't blush again, but she knew she would. What was happening? It's just the togetherness of the wedding spilling over, she thought. The heat from his hand seeped all the way to her spine. It felt too good.

Everyone congratulated the couple, and the two high school girls squealed, apologized for not having a gift, then left. If Mara noticed, and she probably did, she didn't care. She could hardly take her eyes off Zane. The young men left looking relieved, as if whatever Zane had could be contagious if they stayed too long. Then the pastor exited, along with the woman standing alone, who turned out to be his wife. That left Poppy as the only person in the room whose surname wasn't Gunnerson.

"I'd better go," she said.

"You're staying for dinner," Colton said. "Mara's expecting you to stay."

He was right. The problem was, she was pretty sure Julia wasn't expecting her to stay.

CHAPTER 32

When the photos were taken and they walked into the empty dining room and saw the long table decorated with white lace and dark red roses, Poppy was surprised to find there was a placard with her name on it. Even better, she was seated between Colton and Mara.

The young couple found their places across from her, and Colton introduced Drew and his son Max, resting contentedly in his father's arms, and then gestured to Drew's wife and introduced her as Lindy. Lindy reached out a hand. "Hi, Poppy, nice to meet you." With her other hand, she balanced a young girl on her hip. "This is Sam."

"Samantha Ann Gunnerson," the girl corrected.

"Pleased to make your acquaintance, Samantha Ann Gunnerson," Poppy said, holding out her hand. The girl took it and shook it once, firmly. A better grip than that limp-handed teenage girl, Poppy thought.

"You can call me Sam," the girl said.

Lindy sighed, and Poppy kept the smile from her face. "Thank you, Sam."

Beside her, Colton was pulling out a chair for her. That had never happened before. Suddenly very self-conscious, she said, "I'm going to go see if Julia needs any help," and she hurried to the doors through which Julia had disappeared.

Behind the doors was a spotless, large kitchen filled with tantalizing aromas. In front of her, a stainless-steel table was covered in food. Julia was there, along with another woman Poppy didn't recognize. "I'll help you get these out," the woman said.

"I can help too," Poppy said.

Julia glanced at her, her face inscrutable. Had she intruded by coming in the kitchen?

"Thank you, Poppy. Val, I think we have it from here, so—"

"I've got the hotel covered."

"And if you have any trouble at all—"

"I'll handle it myself and tell you about it later. Have fun, Julia. It's not every day your son gets married."

Julia gave a faint smile. "Yes. Okay." As Val left, she looked at Poppy. "All right, then. This all has to go out on the table. One platter of turkey at each end, then the rest of it we can pass around."

Poppy was distracted by something on the table. "Deviled eggs."

"Yes. Mara requested that. I guess they're a favorite of hers."

Poppy picked up two of the closest serving dishes and waited for Julia. Then she tried to copy what Julia did. But by the third trip to the kitchen, her end of the table was a packed jumble, while Julia's end looked like perfectly arranged puzzle pieces. By the time she had found room for her dishes, Julia had returned for the final items and sat down. Poppy hurried to do the same.

Immediately everyone held hands again. Mara's hands were cool and a little shaky. But Colton's touch was all Colton—steady, a little rough, very warm. It made her whole arm tingle. Just her mind playing tricks, of course. She knew better.

Anson said grace, and as they passed the food around, everyone complimented Julia on the Thanksgiving feast. "Val did most of it," Julia said, deflecting the praise.

"Not true," Anson said. "Julia's been working on this for days."

One of the two plates of deviled eggs came her way, and Poppy tapped on Mara's shoulder. "You like deviled eggs?"

"Gross," Mara whispered. "So disgusting. They get stuck in the back of my throat and make me gag."

Poppy smiled. "Thank you for asking for them."

Mara shrugged. "Whatever." Then once more, her sweet smile broke through. Poppy took two halves and passed the plate to Zane.

Anson popped a cork and poured what looked like champagne into Zane and Mara's glasses, but when he set the bottle down between them, Poppy saw that it was sparkling juice. Not old enough to drink at your own wedding and too pregnant. What a weird time, Poppy thought. Mara leaned over the table to pour some into Sam's empty sippy cup. Then Anson popped open another bottle, and another, and filled everyone else's with champagne. The moment he was done, Colton stood up. "A toast," he said.

Of course. The teenagers were gone and Colton was as close to a best man as Zane had. "Zane, Zane, Zane," he grinned, and he gave the young man a devilish smile. "This is your life."

Colton told a story about six-year-old Zane deciding he wanted to ride Grandpa Art's stud horse, Firestorm. He'd reasoned that the horse was short so he'd be perfect for a kid. The only problem was that Firestorm had never been ridden, and he wasn't very fond of people. When Anson realized Zane was missing, they'd searched everywhere. Finally Zane, who had been watching everyone run to and fro, called out, "Whatcha doing?" At that point, Colton and Anson saw him in the middle of the pen, sitting on top of Firestorm.

"And when I say sitting, I mean sitting. He had his bony little rear on the top of the horse's rear end, and his bony little heels dug into its back, and he was rocking back and forth. Keep in mind, he weighed about fifty pounds soaking wet, but that couldn't have felt good to the horse. But that horse liked him. He was the only human being Firestorm ever liked."

Colton went on to talk about how Zane talked

the mail carrier into taking him along on rounds when he was eight, and about the popsicle stick Zane had safeguarded for a kid he saw at the playground—the same incident Julia had described to Poppy.

"Now, it's been fun embarrassing you, Zane, but it's a lot more fun to see you grow into the young man I figured you'd turn out to be. You've always had a way about you. There's a reason people trust you. You're a good man. And your parents are good role models. In fact, they seem to have this marriage and parenting thing down."

Poppy glanced at Julia. She and Anson exchanged what seemed to Poppy a bittersweet look.

"But you do like to do things your way, in your own time, don't you?" They all laughed. "It's all good. You've got God, and He's got you covered. Mara, welcome to the family. Cheers."

As soon as the glass touched her lips, she saw all eyes turn toward her. Oh, please no, she thought. Her face burned. Next to her, Mara leaned over and whispered, "You don't have to say anything. I know you suck at this stuff."

Poppy nodded. But there was no one here to speak for Mara as Colton had spoken for Zane. She stood and took a deep breath. She was aware of the awkward silence, but she knew herself well enough not to rush it. That would only lead to a disaster.

Colton's speech was the perfect model. Tell a funny story, say something kind, end on a good note. But the only Mara stories she could think of were about her absentee mother, her drunk father, and the horrible date-rape incident at school. Not exactly wedding-toast material.

"I don't have a good, funny story about Mara," she said. Her voice sounded thin, but it seemed to echo in the empty room. What a perfectly dreadful way to start, she thought.

"What I do have is about a hundred little stories where Mara has made me smile." Of course, she couldn't think of one right now. But it was true; Mara made her smile a lot. "Sometimes it's something funny or snarky or, more likely, something true that no one else has the guts to say."

Zane nudged Mara, and she smiled and looked back up at Poppy. Cheers, she wanted to say, ending the toast, but she knew she hadn't said enough. She was the beginning and end of Team Mara. She had to do better than this. So she turned and faced Mara and spoke only to her. "That's pretty fun, but that's not really what I think about when I think about you. I think about the fact that you carry a lot. A lot of things that other people don't even know about. And you know it, but you don't...live in it. You don't swim around in the bad stuff. And it's not just because you don't want to bring other people down. I guess ..."

Words were failing her. *Please,* she thought, *please let me get this right for her.*

"What I admire about you is your faith." She stopped. She saw the words in her mind, capitalized. *Her Faith.* It wasn't what she'd intended to say, but there it was. "Your faith that ..."

Her faith. What Poppy admired most about her was her faith. She'd never admired anyone for that before, had she? In a flash, she saw the parade of gurus and mentors and glorified dealers her parents had clung to, granting their faith to each one—and usually a fair amount of money with it. To her, faith was a sign of weakness and lack of reason. Somehow with Mara, it was more like confidence. Or rebellion, even. A good sort of rebellion.

"Faith that things happen for a reason," Poppy continued. Faith that someone up there will make everything all right somehow, she thought. "And that you can make something beautiful out of your life." That there's a plan. *I have a plan for you.*

How the women in Mara's group clung to that line. "And that's admirable, Mara." It was more than that. "It's inspiring. And I can't wait to see the wonderful life you and Zane can build together." She raised her glass, which was shaking. "Cheers."

Miraculously, everyone clapped. Mara's eyes were teary, and they didn't look to be tears of embarrassment. Poppy sat down and took another sip from her shaking glass.

"Nice job. But you were only magenta," Colton whispered.

"What?"

"Your face. You fell short of maroon. I was hoping for maroon."

She cut him a nasty glance, but his green eyes were sparkling, the lines around his eyes were crinkled, and his dimple was showing. She couldn't help but smile back. He reached for a bottle of champagne and topped off her glass.

Anson stood and gave the last toast, a slow and heartfelt speech about the young couple's future that sounded like a prayer as much as anything else. When he finished and the last applause faded away, the eating began in earnest. And so did the teasing. Cash lead the charge with several awful suggestions for baby names and asking how Julia liked the thought of being a grandma of three kids. She said she was relieved not to have to dye her gray hairs anymore. Lindy asked about Mara's pregnancy symptoms, and Liam told a funny story about the first time he saw Drew change a diaper—an exercise that involved a face mask and four separate diapers.

Poppy felt all the stories surround her like a warm blanket. So many people, all in one family, all with a history together. She surveyed the food on her plate and reached for another deviled egg. It melted in her mouth and brought with it a flood of memories. Sunshine, grass, paper plates, lots of laughter. So many smiling faces. That was what was so wonderful. Deviled eggs were made for happy get-togethers, not lonely dinners at home. Not even restaurants dared serve them. They were handmade, meant to be shared.

No, this wasn't a summer potluck, but it felt the same. So many smiling faces. And she thought...I wish this was mine.

All of it. The family, the town, everything. And most of all she wanted Colton's hand around her own. Envy hit her harder than it had earlier, when she saw Mara in her wedding gown. She didn't often feel envious, and when she did, she didn't like it. It felt too much like being frightened. She tried never to dwell on the things she couldn't have.

All she could do was be happy for Mara. And enjoy the moment. She wished that she had Mara's faith that there was a God who had already planned wonderful things for her life. Although she did have something wonderful waiting for her, the master's degree she'd planned on so many years ago. And she had deviled eggs. Poppy ate another and enjoyed it just as much. That was one more thing she could do to chase away some of these feelings—learn how to make them. Preferably this exact recipe.

She felt as if someone was watching her and turned warily to her left. Colton was staring at her with an amused expression. "What?" she said before realizing her mouth was still full.

"Nothing," he said, and went back to his meal.

About a minute later he asked Drew to pass the deviled eggs. He took four, one after another, and put them on his plate, then added one to hers. Then he passed the plate over to Mara, who was about to pass the plate on when Julia asked if she liked the recipe. "Love it," Mara said, and put two on her plate. Then the plate was gone, looking as if it wouldn't make it around the table again, and all Poppy had on her plate was one last deviled egg. She picked at the other food. A remarkably moist turkey. Cranberries, not too sweet. Yams with a buttery brown sugar glaze. Mashed potatoes that tasted as if they contained a hint of sour cream. Yeasty rolls—and she slathered the butter on.

She listened and laughed as stories were exchanged until even Anson looked relaxed and happy. She noticed Colton and Anson had little to say to each other, but things were civil. Kind, even.

She'd waited long enough. She ate the last egg and savored it, then washed it down with a sip of champagne, which didn't taste nearly as bad as it could have tasted. Zane asked her a question about college prerequisites, she answered as best she could, and then she looked down to find another egg on her plate. She looked to her right. Both of Mara's eggs were still there. She looked to her left. There were three on Colton's plate. He was busy talking to Liam at the other end of the table.

She ate it without hesitation. Then sat back happily and listened and laughed.

And somewhere in the middle of it all, two more eggs appeared on her plate. Colton was down to two. Mara was down to one. She couldn't keep the smile from her face. "My good-ness. The Easter Bunny must have been through here."

Colton chuckled. To her right Mara said, "You are strange." Which by now Poppy recognized was her way of saying *I like you.*

She felt Colton's hand close over hers, out of sight, under the table. He leaned closer and spoke quietly. "When dinner is over, Julia and Anson will need to get the restaurant ready to open. I'd like to stay and help clean up."

"They have to work?"

"Thanksgiving is a present they give their employees. All the regulars, except for one or two who want to stay, get the day off. They even run the restaurant with a skeleton crew, which is okay, because they only serve Thanksgiving din-ner, and they get it all ready to go ahead of time."

"That's very generous." But why was he holding her hand?

"I was hoping you'd stay too and then go to the stroll with me."

"What's a stroll?"

He pulled his hand away and pointed down the table toward the windows. "See? They're closing down the street. There's a parade and all the shops stay open, lots of food and...you're still hungry?"

She wrinkled her nose at him.

"And everyone turns on their Christmas lights." When he saw her confused look, he said, "Well, it is a Christmas Stroll."

"It's Thanksgiving."

"Yes, but most of the other towns have their stroll on Saturday. Why compete? Besides, Moose Hollow figures that once the turkey's gone, it's time for the next big thing."

Sam, who had been watching Colton point toward the window, said, "It's snowing!"

In the cool light of the early evening, she could just see big flakes falling through the sheer curtains. The flurries from yesterday were nothing compared to these.

Poppy turned back to Colton, who was looking at her expectantly. "I said I'd drive you home, and I will do that right after dinner, but if you'd like—"

"Sure," she said. And he just stared at her, eye to eye, as a slow smile spread across his face. Is this a date? she wondered. No, not a date. Just friends. Just like movie night. It was a good thing. But the intensity of his eyes was too much, so she looked away.

Right into Mara's smirk. "See what I told you about weddings?"

"Whatever," Poppy said, throwing one of Mara's favorite words back at her.

Mara just laughed.

CHAPTER 33

G iant flakes fell out of the twilight-blue sky. Poppy was wearing her new coat, hood on, but wearing a skirt, she expected to feel the bitter cold. Surprised, she said, "It's warmer than I thought."

"It's colder than you think, Poppy," Colton said. "You're just getting used to the wind blowing eight throttle. Your blood is finally getting thicker, Arizona girl."

"It's that and the warm layer of fat I put on at dinner tonight. I don't think I've ever eaten that much. Plus dessert. And I got your joke about egg custard, by the way, I just didn't want to encourage you."

He chuckled and put a hand on her back. She wished the coat wasn't in the way; she liked the way his hand had felt earlier. Like he was saying, "I've got your back."

Which he wasn't, of course, and she didn't need to read more into this. The sidewalks were crowded, that was all.

She heard honking in the distance, and people began to press forward to the edge of the sidewalk. Colton led her down the street to where an intersection gave them an unobstructed view. She watched the honking trucks approach. They were huge, covered in Christmas lights, and they were...snowplows?

It was quite a show. The snowplows were followed by flag bearers and veterans, a few decorated vehicles bearing the logos of local organizations like the Yellowstone Association, the Yellowstone Wildlife Sanctuary, and the local Boy Scouts troop. Then it got stranger. There were what Colton called "The Olsens," which was nothing more than a family's minivan with kids waving glow sticks out the windows, and a group of friends dressed in a combination of winter gear and island wear, carrying greenish drinks and a poorly made sign that read Margaritaville Neighborhood Watch.

Riders on horseback towed skiers down the street. Then she saw the Polar Bear Club in their furry winter hats, boots, and bathing suits. A huge moose made from bare branches wore Christmas finery as it rode in the back of a pickup. The parade was fast and furious, and Poppy laughed and cheered with the rest of the crowd until Santa came down the road in a horse-drawn wagon and the stroll was over. The street filled with people, fire pits, a couple of bands, one orchestra, and a lot of impromptu dancing.

Poppy was caught up in the spirit of it all. Colton bought them each apple cider, and she bought a set of Christmas cards from a Montana artist and purchased a Moose Hollow T-shirt for her sister. She admired some of the Christmas ornaments, and Colton asked if she was going to get one.

"No, I never have a Christmas tree."

"Bah humbug," he said.

"It just makes me sad. I'd love to live someplace with a pine tree on the property and decorate it instead."

"You might have a little trouble finding a place like that back in Tucson." He lifted up a glass moose ornament.

She nodded. "I guess I don't know where I'll be. There's a lot of work in Arizona. But I know a lot about the Southwest in general, too."

He glanced at her and hung the ornament back up. "Not anyplace else?"

"There are a couple of people on my thesis committee who have good job contacts, and I know they've already put out some feelers for me. I think they're mostly local, though."

"Oh."

She didn't like the feeling of distance that came over her or the way his expression went cold. She didn't understand it and decided that he was just thinking about how little time he had left before putting the ranch up for sale.

She picked out a Christmas card with a sexy, shirtless cowboy wearing a Santa hat. "Colton. I didn't know you modeled," she said, holding it up.

He gave her a wry smile. "I had to have my chest waxed for that photo."

"Ew." She put the card back. "Too much information."

He held up a Christmas card featuring a grizzly bear. "This was before I waxed."

"That explains the smell," she said evenly. He playfully threatened to chuck the grizzly card at her but folded it into an envelope instead. "I'll send you this at Christmas, so you have something to remember me by."

As if she would have trouble remembering him.

He handed a couple of dollars to the clerk and she bagged it for him, and they were on their way again. But after canvassing one side of the street and heading back down the other, he stopped in front of a bar. "Good music," he said.

It was country, and surprisingly, it was a song she knew. Her parents had gone through a Willie Nelson phase for a few months, and a couple of his songs were burned into her brain, like it or not. "Whiskey River," she said.

His jaw dropped. "What did you just say?"

"Nothing," she said, knowing that teasing was on the way.

"You've been holding out on me. This isn't hippie music."

"I like a handful, a small handful, of country stars."

"I don't believe you. Name three." He crossed his arms across his chest. "Other than Willie Nelson."

"Alison Krauss."

"Depressing."

"Josh Turner."

"Weird choice, but valid," Colton said.

She had to think hard to find another. "Buddy Holly."

"Not country."

"Is too. More country than what you hear on country radio now."

He bit his lip. "All right. Well, then, you'll enjoy this." Before she could react, he took her by the elbow and pulled her through the door and into the bar. She tried to hang back. "Colton," she said, but she couldn't get his attention. The door opened into the bar area, and people were three deep at the bar, leaving almost no room to maneuver. And it was hot. She pushed back her hood and unzipped her coat as he pulled her along.

She saw the looks first, and then one, two, and a dozen people converged on Colton. "Colton Gunnerson! Long time no see!" one young man called, thumping him on the back and nearly spilling his own beer as he did it. Colton lost his grasp on her sleeve, and she stepped back, right into someone. She turned to apologize, but the woman didn't even seem to have noticed her since her eyes were only for Colton. Even the bartender was calling Colton's name.

Poppy glanced around. There was no place to escape. She started to move for the door but felt someone grab her hand. She turned right into Colton, who bowed his head to meet her eye to eye. "Not so fast, Arizona girl." He pushed through the crowd ahead of her, smiling, saying hi, and ending one conversation after another until they made it through the tables and to the opposite wall. There was a table with three young women sitting at it. One of them, a striking brunette, was glaring at them as they approached. And she looked familiar.

"Hey, Terra, mind if we leave our coats here?"

Terra. The other bartender at the Combine. She remembered Terra boxing up her food and helping her out of the awkward dinner she'd had with Colton.

"Yes, I mind." She turned her scowl on Poppy. "Why are you still with him?"

"I'm not with him," she said. "We're friends." And then she realized how stupid that sounded as she stood there holding Colton's hand. She snatched her hand away.

"Okay, Terra, tell me what I did," Colton said.

"You know what you did. And I believed you, the first time, but not this time. Do you always go for strippers, Colton? Do you figure they're so desperate that they won't mind you beating on them? You are the lowest kind of dog."

Poppy wondered what on earth she'd missed, and then the pieces snapped together in her mind. "Oh!" She made a circle over her face with her finger. "You mean the black eyes!"

All three girls gave her a pitying stare.

Poppy shook her head. "No, Colton didn't— well, he did, but not …"

Colton gave her an exasperated look.

"He did not hit me," Poppy said. "I hit his elbow. With my face." That sounded so stupid she had to stifle a laugh.

"Oh, this is funny?" Colton said.

"No. No, it's not." She remembered his parole, and she felt awful for teasing him. She planted a serious expression on her face. "He was coming out of the hotel, and I was going in, and we ran right into each other. He took me right in, and Julia got an ice pack, and he had me hold my nose for exactly ten minutes." She was rambling, but doubt was beginning to show on Terra's face. "Terra, I didn't even know Colton then. He's my landlord now. I was just looking for a place to stay."

"In his house?" Terra said doubtfully.

"Yes." Again Poppy was missing something.

"Alone," Colton offered. "I live in the bunkhouse."

"Oh," Terra said. She thought about it for a second, and then her mood shifted instantly, and she reached a hand out to Poppy. "Hi, Poppy, nice to meet you."

Colton turned to Poppy. "You were a stripper in Arizona?"

"No! I was a T.A.!"

"Seriously? T and A?"

"No," she said and swatted his arm. "T.A. Teaching assistant. At the university."

"Oh," he said with a chuckle, and he pulled back to avoid another swat. "It's not so funny when you're on the other end of it, is it?"

She had to agree with that. She turned to Terra. "Where did you hear I was a stripper?"

"I don't remember. Everyone said you had some money troubles, and all the cash you had was in ones. Then you moved in with Colton, and the last girl he moved in with used to be—" She stopped there, looking contrite for having said too much. "Sorry, Colton."

"Welcome to life in a small town," Colton said.

All Poppy could think was that she was glad word hadn't leaked out about the women's group she'd attended with Mara. That tidbit of gossip certainly would have fanned the flames of the stripper gossip.

"Hey, you guys just leave your coats here," Terra said. "Are you going to dance? We'll watch your stuff. We're not going anywhere."

Poppy put her coat and her purchases on an empty chair. "No, we're not dancing."

"Yes, we are," Colton said, putting his coat over hers but leaving his black hat on. He reached for her hand again and started pulling her toward the back of the bar where the dance floor was.

She dug in her heels. "Colton, I don't dance."

"No problem, I'll teach you." He pulled her forward and put his hand on her back again. That distracted her enough that he got her to the edge of the nearly empty dance floor. "I promise. Just give me five minutes. It's the least you can do for ruining my reputation."

She leaned her head back, closed her eyes, and sighed heavily. "Okay. Five minutes."

First, he told her how to hold her arms, and he was very picky about it. "Tension," he said, "Not resistance, just tension." She struggled to understand what he meant. Then with half of his time over, he pulled her out onto the dance floor. "Here we go. It's called a two-step. You're going to take two quick steps and two slow steps. That's it. Quick-quick, slow, slow."

"My right foot first?"

"Honey, we're in Montana. The woman is always right."

She rolled her eyes. But after a couple of minutes had gone by, she hadn't done two steps in a row correctly, and she couldn't help but notice all the eyes turned her way. She could feel her face turning red. "I give up," she said, stopping.

He eyed her. "You're embarrassed."

"Well, yeah. I'm embarrassing you. I'm the only woman in this bar who doesn't know how to two-step, and everyone here is wondering what on earth you're doing out here with me."

"First of all, you know me well enough to know I'm perfectly capable of embarrassing myself. Second, since when do you care what other people think?"

That startled her. She cared a lot about what people thought. Though not as much as she used to. It made her feel good that he thought of her as being independent that way. "You'd think a stripper would have better dancing skills," she said.

He laughed out loud. "Okay, try again. You know, this is supposed to be fun." She concentrated on the steps, and as he picked up the pace, things clicked for her. "It's easier when you go faster," he said.

"It is," she said, just as she tripped over her own feet. But he had her, one strong hand holding her right hand, one pressed against her back. They circled the dance floor until the song was over. "Great. Thanks for the lesson," she said as she let go of his hand.

"Oh no," he grinned. "You're not getting off that easy."

"But Terra is watching our things, and I—"

He spun her around so they were both facing the brunette. Terra waved happily and went back to talking to her friends. "If Terra wants to leave that table, she has no problem letting me know. Terra doesn't have much trouble expressing herself, at least about things like that."

"So I noticed," Poppy said with a smile. She liked that the girl had stepped up to defend her and wished she had time to get to know her better.

Another song started, a slightly faster one, and

Colton led her into the dance again. It took all her concentration to keep up. Then he made her stop looking at her own feet, and it was like having to learn the steps all over again. Poppy was aware of some movement on the tiny stage behind her, but she was startled when the song was cut to silence and the boom of a bass drum started. She turned to see a four-man band crammed together on the stage. The lights lowered, and then the song started.

Colton pulled her closer, speaking directly in her ear. "You've done well, grasshopper. Now it's time to try some combat dancing."

The floor flooded with people. It was almost as crowded as the front part of the bar, but worse because everyone was moving. As the crowd closed in, Colton drew her closer, and that made her more nervous. But as the music played, she felt her feet begin to take over. No matter which way he turned her, the steps were the same, even when she wasn't looking.

But there was a new problem. Their bodies overlapped. She could feel the inside of his right knee touching the inside of hers, sliding with each step. It wasn't the kind of thing she'd call casual contact. Then again, the floor was filled with dancers, and no one else seemed to be blushing.

Sometimes when he turned her, he held her so close that her body was pressed to his so that his belt buckle rubbed against her belly. She couldn't look at her feet if she tried. And she refused to look him in the face. If she did, he might read her thoughts.

After another song, she began to loosen up, and she couldn't help but smile and laugh. It was fun, the way he wove through the crowds, the way he sang along to every word and danced to fit the lyrics. Songs passed by, one after another, until finally the singer announced they were going to take a ten-minute break after the next song.

Colton backed away half a step. "We should think about going. If we stay too late, I won't be able to drive you home, and I promised I would."

She smiled to cover up her disappointment and started to walk toward Terra's table, but he caught her around the waist and spun her around. "There's one more song." The music had started again, noticeably slower this time. He drew her into his arms. The two-step was gone, and in its place, they just swayed from side to side near the middle of the dance floor. These were steps even Poppy didn't have to think about. As the sweet song and loud conversations warred with one another, Colton pressed his cheek to her temple, and she closed her eyes.

Sweet. The way they danced, the way he held her. That was the only word that could describe it. But she couldn't ignore the way her body responded to him. This slow dance was crossing the line, if she hadn't already crossed it before. But she stayed where she was, letting the warmth of him soak through her. One dance, she thought. *Just this one.*

It was over too soon. She stood straight, put something like a smile on her face, and avoided looking Colton in the eye as they left the dance floor. Luckily he didn't try to talk because she didn't have anything to say. They each thanked Terra for watching their things and donned their coats again. Somehow she ended up in front as they pushed out toward the street, and then suddenly the volume dropped, the lights vanished, and snow whipped at her face. She put her hands in her pockets and started to head toward the Third Street Inn parking lot.

"Here," Colton said, and handed her something purple that had been hidden in his pocket. It was soft to the touch. "You need a hat. Don't worry, she cut the tag off already."

She recognized it as one she had admired earlier, hand knit by a Moose Hollow resident of the softest yarn. It had been worth the price marked, but she'd decided it was too expensive for her budget. As was just about everything, since she wasn't making any money. And he'd bought it for her.

It moved her so much she couldn't speak. It wasn't that it was an extravagant gift, it was that he had noticed and given her something beautiful and useful. She knew she was reading too much into it. But how long had it been since someone had given her a gift, just because?

"You liked that one, right? If not we can probably exchange it."

"I love it," she said. And at the same time her heart said, *I love you*. And just the thought of that terrified her. She couldn't even take her eyes off the hat. She felt as if she moved even a tiny bit, she would shatter into pieces. She couldn't do this. Her breakup with Geoff had left her broken.

Even before the breakup, just being with Geoff had broken her. She was just beginning to piece it together from the stories she'd heard in the women's group. Something was missing, something she didn't have left to give anymore. Rahab had hung a red ribbon on her home as a sign of her faithfulness, and in return, she and her family had been saved. Poppy wasn't saved. She couldn't imagine what being saved felt like. She was just lost, wearing the red ribbon around her wrist, and no one even knew what it meant. No one knew she needed saving. No one could return to her what had been lost.

"Try it on," Colton said.

She did as he asked. It was airy and soft against her skin, but she could feel the warmth of it immediately. She loved the way it slouched, loved the interplay of colors in sunset hues. *I love him*. How did it happen? I loved him before, but I just didn't know it, Mara had said. Colton put his hands on her shoulders and came around in front of her to get a better look. There was a fire pit behind her, and the light played across his face. She watched his expression change.

Pleasure. Satisfaction. Then something deeper and a little darker. Then he took one step closer, no closer than they had been on the dance floor, and he bowed his head toward hers. She should have backed away, but she didn't. She lifted her face and felt his lips touch hers.

It was all she felt. It was everything in the world. She pressed against him and reached her hands up. Part of her registered the sound of paper bags landing in the snow, but the kiss was everything. Warm, slow, growing deeper. His hands diving into her hair, tangling underneath her new hat. The sweet, spicy taste of apple cider on his tongue. The other scent, the one he always wore, the green of alfalfa and the brown of leather, and that something else. Just Colton.

She forgot to breathe. She inhaled against him, stealing his breath. She wished she could crawl inside him. She couldn't imagine letting go of him. But he put his forehead against hers and stood still for a moment, pulling his hands from her hair, reaching down to take her hands in his. "I'm sorry," he said.

His words hurt her. She wasn't sorry at all. She pressed her eyes shut. What was she doing? Colton knew so much more than her, about sex, about love. Living with someone hadn't crushed him.

Or had it?

She didn't know what to think. But she had no reason to think love was haunting his thoughts. He was famous, a rock star, welcome wherever he went, and she was something else entirely. Her future wasn't here. It was in the desert mountains, wondering at the beauty of the last traces of a golden wildflower. Her thesis was scheduled for the first Monday in January. She was to come home and meet with her advisor over the Christmas break. She was leaving.

"I need to go home," she breathed. She meant Arizona. But Colton nodded against her and took her hand as if she meant the homestead.

CHAPTER 34

They walked in silence back to the truck, but Colton never let go of her hand. She shook the snowflakes off her coat and hat and climbed into his truck. It felt colder than the air outside.

"I'm sorry about missing our last two movie nights," he said.

"That's okay," she said. "I figured you were busy."

"I was." He didn't say anything for a few minutes, and her mind feverishly concocted images of other dates and other women. "I was meeting with Travis."

"Oh." She tried to keep her voice light.

"Yeah." Colton drove through the deep snow

much more slowly than usual. She knew that after the warm day, there would be a layer of ice on the pavement below the snow. "He's good with numbers." He was silent for so long she figured he was done talking, but he added, "Travis thinks there's a way I can keep the ranch."

"Really? Are you kidding? Colton, that would be amazing."

"I don't know if it could happen. Everyone would have to be on board, and a lot of things would have to go right instead of going wrong. Especially with the problem girls. And the rest of the herd would have to do well, too, and it's such an old bunch." He sighed. "I don't even want to tell them about it. I imagine they'll shut me down before I even get to explain."

She knew "them" meant his uncles, Cash and Anson, the co-owners of the ranch. She thought about it. "Why don't you write up a proposal? Lay out all the numbers and let them decide?"

He glanced at her. "That's not how we usually do things."

"How do you usually do things?"

"Anson tells me what to do, and I either do it or don't."

She smiled. "Maybe not the best way to approach business partners."

Colton took a breath. "Travis wants to meet with a lawyer and accountant to go over our ideas. Maybe after I get some answers, I'll try that. But I don't know anything about writing a proposal."

"I could help you," she said. "I've had to write three." And here she was butting in again. Anything that involved lawyers and accountants was too intimate to share with just anyone.

"I'd like that," he said, surprising her. "So you want to know what his plan is?"

"I do."

"Travis wants to start training full time, and he wants his own facility. He wants it close to town, but remote. Part of it near a road, part of it in the woods. It has to do with rehabilitating horses. He's good at it. And the first thing he usually does is turn the horse loose in a place where they can be away from people, to wipe the slate clean."

Colton took a deep breath. "But a place like that is way more than he can afford. So he wants to lease my land. He'd build a stable and corrals on the north end near the road and use my winter pasture when he needs to. If he goes out of business, I get a free stable. But if I go out of business—

well, we can put some stuff in writing, but as he said, there's no telling how another landlord would work with him. So he wants my word that Cash, Anson, Julia, and I are all in it for the long haul."

"So you'd get lease money," Poppy said, "but lose some of your pasture. But you'd still own the land."

"Yeah. You see, over the next two years, I need to fix what's broken and bring on another hand, and I'm running out of things to sell. At this point, the problem girls look like my best bet. Once they've all calved, I can run them through the ring. They should bring in good money as pairs."

"You'd sell them?" She realized how sentimental she sounded. She wondered how they would adjust to new ranches, away from each other. New ranches that weren't as beautiful. "I thought you needed young heifers."

"I do. The same number of older cows wouldn't sell for that much money. I have to hope they have enough healthy calves left in them to build the herd back up." He sighed. "It's a bad game. You have to guess what the future will hold and make all your decisions off that. And if you guess wrong, you lose everything. I just wish I had someone who could help me decide. Someone who knows ranching."

"Like Anson."

"He already said he doesn't want to put his money on me, and I don't blame him. I'm the one who decided to leave the ranch. I made a small fortune and lost it all. And ended up in jail."

"That's not who you are," she said. She didn't know when she'd decided that, but she had.

He looked her in the eye. "No, it's not. But I can't take any credit for that. God put me through the wringer until I was willing to give up. And within twenty-four hours of me doing that, He put all the pieces back together to make a new life for me." He snorted. "Of course, He was probably just working off of Emmaline's suggestions."

Poppy laughed. "I wish I'd met her."

"She would have liked you."

She took that as high praise, but it was a little difficult to believe. She was certain his grand-mother and she had nothing in common. "I'm not sure about that."

"Oh yeah. She never liked a lot of sound and fury in a person. That's the way she put it. She would have liked you. But there's no explaining why she liked me so much." He slowed and the truck slid. The snow was so much deeper here than it was in town, at least eight inches on the ground, she guessed. The turn onto the driveway was a controlled skid at best. "Poppy, all this talk about the girls has me worried. Mind if I stop in real fast and take a look?"

"Not at all."

He parked near the barn, grabbed a floodlight from near her feet, and left the truck. She lost sight of him in the heavy flakes right away, but she could see the sweep of the light as he went through the gate and into their pasture.

Finally, after a long time, she could see the light moving, jerking along the ground. It didn't seem right to her. She got out of the truck and walked to the gate, and that's when she could hear the stream of mild profanity, broken up here and there by "Back off!"

"Colton?" she called.

She heard him say something about the gate, and she swung it open just as she heard him call, "No, don't open it!" Just as she stepped through to get ahold of the gate again, she saw the flashlight bobbing and heard Colton yell, "Get back to the truck!"

And then she heard the pounding hoofbeats. She turned and ran. The hoofbeats were coming fast and loud, and she heard what sounded like an

angry wail from a cow, and so she leaped, cata-
pulting into the bed of the truck. When she
turned, a cow was inches away from the truck,
tossing her head and making awful sounds.

"Are you okay?" Colton was right behind the
cow, and the cow turned on him, pawing and
making an angry, loud moo. That was when
Poppy saw that his hands were more than full.
"The tailgate," he said, sidestepping the cow cautiously. Poppy reached over and pulled the handle, letting the tailgate drop.

There was a newborn calf in Colton's arms,
covered in wet fur and snow, its head hanging. "Is
it alive?"

"I don't know. Hypothermia." He edged his
way closer.

"Give him to me."

"Poppy, you'll ruin your dress. Climb down
the other side and sneak into—"

"You're a better driver."

He hesitated, and she used that moment to
grab the calf from his arms. She slipped a little in
the snowy bed of the truck, half falling and half
sitting down.

"Poppy, he's covered in muck and blood
and—"

"I've got him," she said as she crossed her legs

and bundled the calf over her lap. He headed back to close the gate, and she bent down over it, focusing all her warmth, even her breath, on the poor thing. He didn't smell like muck and blood. He smelled like earth and wet dogs, things she loved. But he wasn't moving. She found his belly with her hand and held it there.

Was that a tiny breath? She couldn't be sure it wasn't just the truck as they lurched forward.

Behind them, the cow was coming, wailing again, the sound a mixture of anger and fear. She tried to keep up in the snow, but the dirt road beneath was icy, and she slipped again. Colton slowed down. Was he waiting for her? She couldn't imagine running was good for a momma who had just given birth. Poppy put her head back down to cover the calf. She felt Colton gun the motor on the turn as they pulled in front of the bunkhouse, and it had barely stopped moving when he got out and ran to the back, reaching for the calf. She helped hand him over.

"Run inside," he ordered.

She made it to the door ahead of him, and he made it before the cow got to the front deck. She closed the door, and he motioned with his head to the bathroom door. "Pour a bath, fast."

He carried the calf into the kitchen, and she did as he asked. "How warm?"

"Bath warm. Almost hot tub."

"Got it," she answered, and did her best to gauge what that would be. When she got it going, Colton came in and laid the calf down in the tub. "You've got to hold her head up out of the water," he said, and she took over.

"Her?"

"Yup. Hold on, gotta get the colostrum ready."

She marveled at the calf's sweet face but worried over its lack of movement. Outside the front door, she could hear the sound of the cow over the running water. "Your momma wants you back, sweet thing," she said. "Hang in there."

He came back in with a plastic bag and tube that looked a little like an IV bag from a hospital, except it was filled with a liquid that looked like eggnog. He lifted the calf's rear end and took its temperature. "She's borderline," he said gruffly. "Stupid. I knew today was going to be the day. I knew the pressure change would bring it on. I thought they looked okay before I left, but obviously I was wrong. I don't even know how long she's been this way."

He reached his hand into the water. "You'll have to turn up the heat. She's so cold she's cooling off the bath water." He got an aluminum heat lamp out of the closet and hung it from the curtain rod. The calf weakly moved its head, and Poppy was startled. She had been certain the calf was dying.

Colton arranged the calf so she was lying on her chest with her front legs folded. "Party time," he said, and turned off the water. He took off his boots and socks and rolled up his jeans. Then he climbed in, putting one foot on either side of the calf. He handed Poppy the eggnog bag and took over supporting the calf's head. Then he took the end of the tube, measured it alongside the calf, and started inserting it into the calf's mouth and down its throat.

The calf chewed halfheartedly. "Come on, baby," he said. Rather than being about strength, getting the tube in seemed like a delicate waiting game. He rubbed the calf's throat, checked the spot he'd marked on the tube, and kept going swallow by swallow until the mark was at the calf's mouth. Then he undid a clip near the bag, and the warm liquid started pouring down into the calf's stomach.

The calf fussed a little, then settled down again. Then, as the contents of the bag were nearly gone, she fussed some more. Colton clipped off the tube and pulled it out of the calf, handing support of her head to Poppy once more.

The calf couldn't keep her head up, but she was moving now. Her big black eyes were open, and Poppy was awestruck by the long lashes, the silky fur, and the change in the calf. "What was that stuff?"

"Colostrum. The real stuff. Don't know if I got it to her in time, but I had to try."

"She looks so much better."

"She does. The bath warms her up from the outside, and the colostrum warms her up from the inside. But she's not out of the woods. If we can get her temperature up, then it's a race to get her dry and back to momma."

She stroked the calf's arched forehead. "That was amazing work, Colton," she said.

"Amazingly stupid of me," he said, and he stood up to take the tube and bag away.

But she thought it was almost miraculous. He had been so sure, so determined and calm. And Poppy had the sweet face in her hands that proved it.

While Colton cleaned the bag and tube in the kitchen, she watched the calf change minute by minute and added hot water as needed. She was a beauty, jet black and as big-eyed as a cartoon character.

The little calf finally found her feet, and after he had taken her temperature, he told Poppy she could drain the water and picked the calf up. In the living room, he placed her in what looked like a very big dog crate. He'd hung another heat lamp over the top of the crate, and he repositioned the lamp from the bathroom onto the tile floor at the calf's feet. There was also a small fan blowing into the crate, and Poppy assumed that was there to help her dry faster.

"She'll probably be okay for a bit, so I can take you home now," he said. "I'll help you get past her momma. Normally I'd keep her in the barn, but—"

"But I messed that up by opening the gate."

She pulled on her coat because Colton was donning his. Outside the cow moaned, the sound moving from one end of the deck to the other as if she were pacing.

"It's okay, Poppy. As soon as that calf is dry enough to move, I'll get her set up in the barn and then try her with her mother and hope she isn't rejected. And as soon as that's done, I start the calf watch. And I have to get you back to the homestead somehow."

Disappointment flooded her, making her feel tired for the first time that night. He was busy, and worried, and she got that. But at the same time she felt so lucky to be helping, he seemed to be in a hurry to be rid of her.

Was it the kiss? Did he regret it? He said he was sorry. "I don't want to go."

"To Arizona?"

"No." Where had that come from?

He looked as if he was going to say something, but she couldn't read his expression. He bowed his head and closed his lips into a thin line. Whatever it was, he wasn't going to say it now.

"I don't want to go to the homestead, Colton. I want to see what happens. I don't want to be in your way, either, I just want to help. I know that sounds stupid since I don't know anything—"

He met her eye again, and instead of the annoyance she expected to see, she saw...relief? "Okay. But it's going to be a weird night."

"Like it hasn't been already?"

He smiled, the first time since before they'd kissed, and some unnamed worry was soothed in her heart.

CHAPTER 35

$\mathcal{C}$olton turned on the light in one of the bedrooms, Poppy heard a closet door slide, and he returned with an armful of gear. "We should get your clothes in the wash. None of this is pretty, but it'll do," he said, handing it to her. "Hold on. I have a sweatshirt you can wear." She checked the tag on the jeans. They were nearly her size, just a little shorter. "These are definitely not yours," she said.

He nodded. "The thing about ranch hands is they usually travel light. The bunkhouse has gotten quite a collection of castoffs over the years." He gave her a hoodie that read PRCA in big blue letters. "You can use my room to change. The floor is pretty wet in the bathroom."

She took him up on that, mostly because she wanted to see what the room looked like. But it didn't look like anything. There was wood paneling on the wall and two twin-sized beds. There was a framed print that looked ancient and was covered in dust. On one bed, the one that was made, sat a stack of boxes and a handwritten tally on a tablet. The other bed looked slept in, and the only thing on it was a well-worn leather-bound book.

The room's tiny closet was open, revealing several full duffel bags and some dirty laundry on the floor, and on the rack, about a dozen long-sleeved shirts. At the foot of the bed, she found his dresser, an old hard-sided suitcase halfway full of folded clothes.

She looked around again and noticed the tiny picture on the shared bedside table. It was a faded color photograph of two young people, a tall, thin man with unruly hair and a tall, thin woman with long blond hair. She was cute, but sort of plain. The man had Colton's smile and one dimple. His parents?

"How's everything working out?" he called.

She hurried to take her clothes off. The jeans felt soft and warm, despite a big tear across one thigh. She pulled off her blouse—it was wet but not stained like the skirt—and put on the hoodie in its place. It was enormous. She couldn't remember the last time she'd worn something that was too long for her. It had frayed edges on the cuffs, and it was warm, soft, and smelled like Colton.

When she came back out, Colton was beside the calf, and he stood and looked at her, then looked nervously down at his boots. She felt the color rising on her neck. "You look cute," he said, glancing up at her again.

The cow was indeed pacing, and as she passed by the porch light, Poppy gasped. "It's Sparkle." The ear tag reading 222 came into view next, confirming it was the cow they'd rescued in the first big snowstorm and one of the cows that regularly came up to Poppy for treats. "And I thought she liked me."

"Don't take it personally. A lot of cows act that way right after their calves are born. Being mean is a good thing if it keeps her calf safe." He came up behind her and moved the curtain aside to get a better look. All Poppy could think about was how close he was and what it felt like to kiss him. She should have gone back to the homestead.

"The calf's almost dry enough for the barn. This should be an adventure. Laundry room's through the kitchen, and there's a sink in there if you want to soak that stuff. I already got your coat going." He threw his hands up when he saw the frown on her face. "Gentle cycle, powder detergent, cold wash, and I closed all the fasteners."

"You are a man of many talents."

"I even rescued two horseshoe nails, a rock, and a couple of dead plant parts from your pocket. For a girl who travels light, you sure collect some strange stuff."

She poured water into the sink along with a little detergent and came through the kitchen again. It wasn't dirty, but it wasn't exactly organized, either. "What are all the boxes for?"

"Just some old stuff I'm getting rid of." He opened a closet near the front door and rummaged through some coats.

She hadn't seen a box big enough to fit the third saddle, which was now missing. She was pretty certain she knew where the things in Emmaline's room were disappearing to.

"I have just the thing for you, Poppy." He held up something that looked like a cross between a barn coat and a one-piece ski suit, and it was the worst of both worlds. It was dirty yellow canvas, big and bulky, padded and lined with flannel.

"It's a onesie."

He chuckled. "It's warm."

"I don't wear onesies. I haven't since I was... one, probably."

"Girls with wet coats don't get to be choosy. Someone left a pair of muck boots here, too. I'll just get you a couple more pairs of socks, and they should do."

She climbed into the suit and found the pants were short and the top part was too long, which made it feel as if she was wearing a diaper. She pushed up the sleeves and started buttoning. When Colton emerged from his room and started chuckling, she shot him a withering look.

"Maa!" the calf cried.

"I know," Colton said, "she's scary. I'll protect you, little one."

"Spark," Poppy said. "Her name is Spark. As in a little Sparkle." Her gloves and her beautiful new hat were sitting by the front door along with the nails, rock, and pieces of a plant she wanted to identify. Putting the hat on made her think about Colton's hands in her hair. "Ready to go?" Her voice sounded shaky.

Colton finished disconnecting the fan and lamps and opened the gate, wrangling the speedy little thing as she tried to escape. He picked her up, and she kicked and called with all her might, sounding like a cross between a goat and a cow. "Maa!"

"I'll go first and distract Sparkle," he said.

She smiled at the name. She was certain it chafed his cowboy sensibilities.

As soon as Colton went out the front door, Sparkle stopped her pacing and stood still, puffing and wide-eyed. She didn't seem angry anymore. She seemed scared. Poppy carefully got into the truck, where the key was waiting in the ignition, and started it up. She felt the truck shift as Colton got on the tailgate, his feet hanging off.

"Maa!"

Poppy started out slowly. It had almost stopped snowing, but there must have been another inch of flakes on the tire tracks. She opened the window to listen for instructions from Colton, but all she heard was the crunching snow and the calf's cries. She looked for Sparkle in the glow of the red taillights. She hadn't moved.

"Come on, Sparkle, it's okay," Colton said softly. Just when Poppy was about to stop and ask Colton what they should do about the cow, Sparkle started after them. Poppy exhaled for what felt like the first time in a long time.

As she crept down the driveway, she could hear Colton's soothing voice, the calf's cries, and then, at last, one angry moo from the cow. Poppy could have cheered.

Colton took the calf through the gate, and after Sparkle followed, Poppy closed it behind her and opened the next gate for him. The calf squirmed in his arms. He disappeared into the barn, and she saw the red glow of a heat lamp go on inside.

Sparkle stared at Poppy, stared at the gate, and snorted. She held her hand out as if she had the morning cow treats. The cow came closer, blew a steamy puff of air over her outstretched hand, then trotted through the gate and into the barn. Clearly, she knew where the bag of treats was kept. Poppy followed as a brighter light turned on inside the barn.

The barn had been transformed. Four of the stalls had fresh straw bedding. There were bales of greenish hay down the center corridor. It had only been a couple of days since she'd last visited the hayloft—had she just missed the changes? She was pretty sure the gate Colton was holding open was new, or at least newly hung.

Sparkle had caught sight of the calf, and she stood halfway in, staring and sniffing. When the calf wobbled over toward her momma, Poppy froze. "Please," she whispered. Colton threw a glance at her, then kept his eyes on the cow. He looked ready to intervene if he needed to.

But there was no need. The cow finally joined the calf, sniffing her so curiously that the calf lost her footing. But she got up again. Colton closed the gate and rested his arms on top of it. "Looking good," he says. "Now we'll see if the calf is strong enough to nurse."

"She looks strong," Poppy said as she came up beside him.

"It's the new hairstyle."

Poppy laughed and looked into his eyes. "She is fluffy. And you are amazing."

He shook off the compliment. "Just ranching. Same old, same old."

They watched the pair for a while as the calf tried out the wrong side of Sparkle, then the wrong end, and finally the right end for milk. "Touchdown," Colton said softly. Poppy made quiet crowd-cheering noises.

"Now what?" she asked.

"Now I take you home. After that, I'm going to take a stroll through the pasture and have a good look at the problem girls' rear ends."

"Sounds charming when you put it like that. Can I go with you?"

He raised one eyebrow. "Sure." He reached out

to button the top button of her winter suit, stepping closer as he did. "Let me know if you get cold," he said softly. In the barn light, his eyes were a stormy clash of grays.

Cold? Not likely with him standing so close, Poppy thought wryly.

They toured the pasture as the skies thinned and stars came out. He gave her a crash course in the changing anatomy of pregnant cattle, which was both weird and fascinating. He singled out three cows that looked near their time, and one of them, he said, should be moved to the barn tomorrow. As she listened to him, she realized he was talking about checking on the cattle every two hours.

Every two hours, for up to two months. And then the main herd would start to calve. There was no way one person could manage that. Hadn't he said lack of sleep aggravated his head injury? It certainly made him strange.

"I could take a couple of watches," she said. Since he didn't look at her or comment, she clarified. "Once you think I know what to look for. Then if something looks wrong, I could come get you."

Her words hung in the air as they walked up into the shelter of the barn. "You don't need to do that," he said finally. She felt disappointed. Maybe she should have asked more questions about the heifers. Maybe there was something she just didn't get.

He turned off the overhead light, and the only remaining light was the red heat lamp over Spark and Sparkle's stall. She went over one last time to see the calf and momma. The baby was sleeping curled up in the straw, and momma was next to her. She looked at Poppy, looked at her calf, and burped. And chewed. "Excuse you," Poppy said. There were few things that looked more full of contentment than a cow chewing her cud.

"It's after your curfew. Good thing your mom's not here or I'd be in trouble." Colton came up beside her.

"I never had a curfew. My parents were into free-range parenting before it was a thing."

"Free range? Really?" He shook his head. "You haven't told me much about your parents, but I have to admit I'm surprised that you came from them."

"I rebelled."

He turned to face her. His hat blocked much of his face from the dim red light, but she could see the grin on his face, and she saw his dark eyes shift to gaze at her lips, and she knew he was going to kiss her again. Half of her wanted to run.

Something was bubbling up inside her. Something dark and fearful, something bad she didn't want to remember.

Colton put two hands on her arms and pushed himself away from her. "I want you to know something, but I don't know how to say it."

Her mind rifled through the possibilities. She was certain he was going to tell her the kiss had been a mistake, that he wasn't interested in her that way.

"You know the world I used to live in. And if you haven't heard some bad things about me, you will. Sometimes it's like old habits just take hold ..." He trailed off, his eyes focused on the sleeping calf in the stall. "But they don't take over anymore, God willing. So I want you to know that I'm not looking for...company. I'm looking for something more. You know what I mean?"

Poppy shook her head.

He laughed at himself. "Okay, let me try this again. I need to know if you're serious about me. Because I've been getting serious about you. And I'm pretty sure you haven't noticed that at all."

Serious? Was he *serious* about her? She tried to find another way to make sense of what he was saying, but she couldn't. What if he did care about her, what would that mean? And at the same time her heart swelled at the thought of him caring for her, that dark feeling roared inside of her again. It was making her feel something she didn't want to feel, didn't want to think about at all, especially now.

"I know you're leaving soon, and I don't know what's going to happen then. The next move is for you to make. And if you want just to go on being friends, that'll be okay. If not ..." He gave her an awkward grin. "That'd be a lot better."

He reached for her hand and pulled her toward the barn door and out into the night. It felt colder than it had a little while ago. "Want a ride to the homestead, or can I walk you home?"

She chose to walk, and they climbed the slope toward the homestead together, crunching through the snow, the Milky Way glistening above them. Then he stood on the porch facing her as if they were in some old-time movie and he wouldn't presume to come in.

"Sleep well," Colton said, and he let go of her hand and walked away. No kiss, not even a hug, just that one-dimpled smile by the porch light. *The next move is for you to decide*, he'd said.

As she walked inside, the dark feeling rose

again. This time, there was no way to push it back down. She was no princess. In fact, she had nothing to offer someone like Colton. She didn't fit in his world. If she didn't contribute anything to Geoff's life, the man whose world dovetailed so neatly with hers, what did she have to offer someone like Colton?

Colton's life had always been big. From the rodeo to the ranch, nothing was small in his existence. Even he seemed outsized, a little too loud, a little too lanky. She thought of his hands, calloused from work she knew nothing about. She had nothing to give someone like him. At least nothing that a hundred girls in Moose Hollow couldn't do better.

And there was his faith. Church every Sunday. And that thing Mara had talked about, the three-strand braid. Unequally yoked. All of it sounded like threats from God to take away His blessing if Colton married someone like her. Someone used up, with nothing left to give.

She was no princess. No virgin bride. No Christian to whom he could be equally yoked.

"I'm just broken," she said out loud. She didn't whine, didn't say it expecting an answer; it was just a statement of fact. Colton was a man on the cusp of something big. And she was just broken.

CHAPTER 36

*D*ouble digits. The morning hour was in the double digits, later than she'd slept in years. She dragged herself off the comfortable mattress and down to the fire. It was nearly out, and it took her awhile to get it going.

A horrible sound had intertwined with her dreams until finally it woke her. She recognized the sound; it was the same one Sparkle had made over her nearly frozen calf, only worse. She tucked her sleeping bag around her shoulders and went into the other bedroom to look out the window. Lights were on in the barn, and it looked as if Colton's truck was parked there.

She texted Colton. *Can I help?*

The answer came back after a few minutes. *No.*

She waited for more, but it didn't come. The low moaning of the cow broke the windless silence. No, it wasn't the same as the sound Sparkle had made. It lacked her urgency.

Visions of stroking the domed forehead of another baby calf vanished. Colton wasn't driving anyone up to the bunkhouse for a hot bath and warm milk. This momma cow was grieving. Whatever had happened, it was done.

Poppy padded back upstairs to the bedroom and turned on her computer. Her advisor had written. If she didn't finish her thesis on time she could be expected to pay another semester of tuition. Her thesis had to be turned in to the committee by the Monday before Christmas.

She needed coffee.

As she went down the stairs, she ticked off all the things she still had to do. The list got so long she turned around when she was only halfway down and jogged back up to get her tablet and a pencil from her bedroom. And she still didn't understand the calculation variations in the Jones and Culbertson article. When had her thesis turned into a dissertation on computer modeling instead of lily propagation?

She went down the stairs again, balancing her thoughts like juggling balls. Formatting issues, seed samples, photos; did she need more information about the hawkmoths? She wrote it all down. She would have to be in Arizona before the first Monday in January, ready to go. She needed to be steeped in the research so that the names of other scientists and other details rolled off her tongue like the alphabet.

Then what? They had been pushing her to get applications in. She'd dragged her feet, saying that it didn't make sense to get a job interview if she was in Montana. What had she been thinking? The master's degree had been her goal since seventh-grade science. Why was her plan for what came after it such a blur? She pictured herself as an accomplished, educated, respected ...

Wife. And mother. It had always been there in the back of her mind. Get all the diplomas, get married, have the family she had always wanted to have. Have it all. But that wasn't what was going to happen. She was about to be alone and homeless. And the best she had to hope for was a decent paying job that stuck her in a lab or in front of a computer most of the time. A life of little sunshine. And no snow.

Was that why she had jumped so wholeheartedly into the relationship with Geoff? Because he was her last-minute ticket to a family? She thought of what Julie had said at the first meeting.

"I thought I was Cinderella," she said out loud. She used to say a master's was a great excuse to wander around alone in the mountains, just like she wanted. But in the back of her mind, she had always pictured coming home to someone. A real home. That's not what most botany-related jobs were really like. Maybe if she got on with the Forest Service she had a chance to split indoor and outdoor time. But the only way to move up in a government job was to transfer from place to place, job to job.

She couldn't do that and be a mom. Not after the way she was raised. She just couldn't.

She got the coffeemaker ready to brew. There was so much pressure on her chest she found it hard to breathe. *I'm leaving.* She looked at the cabinets she had painted so carefully. And another thought started vying for her attention. If it had been a real thing, she would have turned around and smacked it in the face, but it was nothing more than a thought, a vapor teasing at her mind and popping up just when she thought she was free of it.

Colton.

No, she thought firmly. She wasn't going to jump from one hopeless relationship to another. She was leaving in weeks. No, days.

I could stay in Montana.

Stupid, stupid girl. With a master's degree on a rare Arizona plant under her belt, just how marketable was she for a job up north?

She was in love with the house, that's all. And the big family all seated at one table, the sunrises, and the doe-eyed calf. They had all colored her opinion of Colton. She was smitten with the ranch. She couldn't possibly know Colton well enough to be certain how she felt about him.

The coffee couldn't brew fast enough.

She looked at her cell phone. She wished someone would call, someone with good advice and words of reassurance. But there were no messages. She stared at the icon for the Bible app instead. She had never looked at the Bible app in Emmaline's house. Most of the time she read it in the hayloft. She'd heard enough from Colton and Mara, and seen enough in Emmaline's room, to understand that Emmaline had been devout. To sit in her house and treat the Bible like the plain old book it was, and nothing more, seemed disrespectful.

If she'd learned anything from the Saturday night group, it was that Christians like Emmaline tried to put God's will above their own. How on earth they expected to understand the will of an omniscient, absent overlord escaped her.

But they claimed to. Perfectly normal women had discussions in which they said things like "I knew God was telling me ..." and "The Holy Spirit was convicting me ..." Outside of the context, they might have sounded freakish and even pathological. The women also claimed to sometimes not know God's will, and they talked about waiting for Him to speak to them.

Her parents once spent a night in a sweat lodge waiting for the Great Spirit to speak to them. When her father had called near sunrise, he was an incoherent mess. She'd had to borrow a car from one of their many transient lodgers to retrieve them and take her mother to the emergency room. She'd been treated for severe dehydration.

The house phone rang, and she picked it up hoping for her sister's voice on the other end of the line. "Hello?"

"Emmaline?" It was the voice of an older man.

"I'm sorry, this is Poppy. Emmaline passed on

last summer, and I'm staying in her house right now."

"Oh." A long silence. "I knew that." Another silence. "I miss her."

Poppy was taken in by the sorrow in the man's voice. "I'm sorry."

"I'm sorry to have bothered you."

"You didn't bother me at all," Poppy said.

"You're very kind. So was Emmaline. She must like you very much if she let you live in her house, dear."

She knew the man was disoriented, but the words brought tears to her eyes. It seemed ridiculous, but just the thought of approval from that woman, someone she'd never met, meant the world to her. She wasn't sure what to say, so she simply said, "Thank you."

"Have a good day, dear, and God bless," he said before hanging up. She wished she knew who it was. Not that it mattered. But if he ever called again, she would ask. She sighed. If he ever called again, she wouldn't be here anymore.

CHAPTER 37

*P*oppy was already awake, so she knew no vehicle had driven to the homestead. It was four thirty in the morning when someone started pounding on her door. She pulled on sweats and a hoodie. She stopped at the top of the stairs and wondered what to do.

Then she heard Colton's voice. "I need to come in!"

Then why didn't he just come in? He had a key, didn't he? She hurried down the steps and flipped on the porch light as she opened the door.

Colton was wearing a barn coat, open to the freezing cold. No hat. His face was shadowed from the porch light, but she could make out the expression on his face and her heart lurched. "They're all dying."

"What? Who?" she asked.

He opened and closed his hands and looked around on the porch as if he had just dropped something. "I can find it. I have to save them."

She looked down, where he was looking, and noticed the untied boots and laces caked in mud. He looked up and through her as if she wasn't even there. His eyes were like black holes, and it sent a shiver down her spine.

"I have to find Grandma. They're all dying."

"Who is dying, Colton?" she asked evenly.

"The cattle. All of them. I have to save them." His hands lifted, clenched and unclenched.

She shivered. It was frightening, yes, but she knew what was going on. She'd done a little research after Colton's last bout with creepy weirdness, and she knew what to do. At least she knew how to handle night terrors in children, but that would have to be good enough.

She took hold of his sleeve and pulled him inside. He resisted. "I have to save them," he repeated.

"I can help you." She got the door closed behind him. She thought about turning on the living room lights, mostly for her own reassurance, but she'd read that unlike nightmares, the best cure for a night terror was to get the person back to a deep sleep.

"I have to find Grandma."

Emmaline. She wondered if Emmaline would have known what to do with a large, scary man at four in the morning.

"Sit down here," she said, motioning him to the couch.

"I can't do this. I have to find her."

"She's on her way," Poppy said in her most soothing voice. It occurred to her that this would be a great setup for a ghost movie. And she didn't like scary movies at all. She reminded herself that although Colton's completely dilated eyes made him look possessed, he was just having a night terror, something she learned was far less rare than she would have guessed.

Talking to him seemed to calm him down. He sat down, but he stared at his shaking hands and then searched the floor around his feet again.

"All you have to do now is sit here and wait for her," Poppy reassured him.

He didn't seem to understand. When he started to stand up again, she pulled him down by the coat sleeve. The way he looked at her gave her a fright. "I can't be here," he said.

He was scaring her. She had a choice—leave him to his own devices or get him to lie down. She tried to sound more convincing than she felt. "Colton, you are supposed to lie down. Right now. It's what you have to do."

A flicker of confusion crossed his face.

"Lie down. Right now."

He looked at the couch. "On the bed?"

Close enough. "Right here." She reached down and pulled off his boots. They felt damp on the inside, as if he'd gone through water. When she lifted his feet to the couch, they felt damp and cold. Even his legs felt cold underneath the jeans. How long had he been wandering around outside? She grabbed the throw blanket and pulled it over his body.

He pawed at it with one hand. "I can't do this." At the same time, his head hit the new throw pillow and his eyes closed. "I can't figure it out."

"I can help," she repeated. Please let that be true, she thought. As quietly as she could, she opened the door to the wood-burning stove and placed three more logs. When he didn't move, she crept up the stairs to get her sleeping bag and brought it back down. He looked as if he was sleeping, but a worried frown still pulled at his face. As gently and quietly as she could, she put the sleeping bag over Colton, careful to tuck it in around his feet. Now and then he shuddered.

Could he be hypothermic? She crouched lower and pressed her hand to his temple as if feeling for a fever. He felt warm enough, although she knew that was hardly a medical diagnosis. As she tried to pull her hand away, he reached up and grabbed it. He frowned deeper and said something she couldn't understand. Then his other hand grasped her hand as well. She held on, and his expression started to ease.

Poppy sat on the wooden floor, her hand in both of his, and watched him fade into sleep by the dim porch light that filtered through the living room window. Her mind went so many different places at once. Where had he been? How many night terrors had he been having that she didn't know about? Was this aggravating his head injury or was it the other way around?

And other, more selfish questions. Why hadn't he called the last few days? Why had he let a texted "No" be the last thing he'd said to her? Most of all, she wanted to know why he wouldn't let her help. She felt as if he'd decided she was more trouble than she was worth.

She studied his face, slowly relaxing, smoothing, seeming to grow younger. He didn't treat her like she was trouble when he was with her. Even when she said things that were too brusque. When she'd said blunt things around Geoff, his eyes had narrowed and his speech had slowed to quiet, clearly enunciated words, as if she was mentally impaired. He'd responded the same way if she didn't know something he thought was important to know.

But she made Colton laugh. And he liked to push her into doing things herself. Instead of feeling as if Colton was giving her remedial cultural-literacy lesson, when Colton taught her about the ranch, he looked as if he was having fun. And happy to share the things he loved.

She loved that. All of it.

She watched Colton sleep and felt his hands grow warm, then loosen, but she did not pull her hand away. Not just yet. Her trip back to Arizona hovered in the back of her mind. It was always present. Holding his hands now felt like a good-bye she wasn't ready to say.

But there was work to be done. She couldn't be certain when he'd last checked on the girls, or the main herd, and the feeding would still have to be done. She went upstairs to put on her warmest clothes. She wanted to write him a note, and debated about what it should say, but finally she decided to write something direct.

I've got this. Eat something. Go back to sleep. Back soon, P.

Then she sneaked out the front door of the homestead and left him to sleep in peace.

CHAPTER 38

*a*fter checking the herd, Poppy went back to where Sparkle was standing. She could make out the small shape of Spark in the moonlight. The light on the barn glinted off her big, dark eyes.

"Hello, baby," she said. She looked strong, and already very different from the newborn she had held in the bathtub. Sparkle moved forward to block her view of the calf, and Poppy smiled. "You're a good momma," she said.

She'd used Colton's spotlight to sweep the herd, spending much more time than Colton at the same task because she wanted to make sure she didn't miss anything. By the time she was done, it was time to feed. She threw alfalfa flakes to Colton's horse, patted him on the shoulder, and started up the diesel. It was time to load the baler, but there was still no sign of Colton. She hoped he either trusted her to do the work or he was sleeping. Either one was good.

When she closed everything up, she found Sparkle waiting at the gate for her cow treat. She ducked back inside and got a handful, and she apologized for forgetting. In return, Sparkle let her calf come closer to the gate and get a look at Poppy.

Poppy bent low and reached her hand through the metal rail, talking softly. The calf came close, her nose working and eyes wide, then she bolted away and bucked so hard she nearly knocked herself off her own knobby legs. Poppy pressed her lips shut. She didn't want to laugh out loud and scare her.

She checked her watch. She'd checked the girls, fed the cattle, and in twenty minutes it would be time to check the girls again. How on earth did Colton get any rest?

She climbed the steps to the hayloft. She scanned it with the spotlight to chase away any mice and look for bats, but as usual, there were none. She just felt better checking. There were no angry text messages from Colton on her phone.

That was good too. Her finger hovered over the Bible app. Why not? She had a little time to blow.

She'd heard on a radio program that everyone recommended reading the Gospel of John first. They were crazy. The first few verses alone made her head spin. All she could make of it was that spoken words had real power. The kind of power that defied the arrow of time. And that was about as woo-woo as she was ready to get. Luckily, the narrative made more sense after that.

The sky was brighter when she went out to check the girls on the four-wheeler again. Over-all, they were happy and ridiculously wide. At least two were showing some of the birth signs Colton had said to look for.

When she returned to the homestead, Colton was still reclined on the couch, but the sleeping bag was on the floor, his feet were stretched over the arm of the sofa, and his arms were flung over his head. She took off her boots and coat as quietly as she could and sneaked into the kitchen to start the coffee.

She heard rustling in the next room. "You sure are bossy," Colton growled. "Do this. Do that. Stay here."

She grinned to herself. "Did you eat something?"

"No, the bus that ran me over took my appetite, too."

She switched gears and took out her blender. She packed most of it with a mix of greens from a bag, added water, then dumped in part of a bag of frozen berries from her freezer and hit the "smoothie" button. The shrill sound of the machine brought a groan from the other room and she stifled a laugh. When the greens were cut up into pieces too small to recognize, she stopped it and poured two big glasses.

Colton was sitting on the couch with his head in his hands. She held one glass under his nose, and he reacted as if she was holding a dangerous animal. "What is that?"

"Smoothie," she said, and took a drink of her own. "See? Not poisonous."

He took the glass from her and rotated it. "It's black and brown and green—good grief, woman. Did you get this out of the pasture this morning?"

"You're afraid of a smoothie."

He glared at her, took a sip, and his face slowly twisted up. "Really, what is this stuff?"

"Blackberries. Strawberries. Blueberries too, I think."

He took another sip and cut her a sideways glance. "And?"

"Kale. Spinach. Chard."

"You're sick."

"I am not. But you'll be sick if you keep eating frozen pizza for every meal and never sleep."

He stilled. That was how she knew when his irritation switched from dramatic effect to the real thing. Before he could shut her down yet again, she said, "Do you have any idea how you got here last night?"

He swirled the smoothie in his glass and said nothing.

"Drink more and I'll tell you."

"I'll take that coffee I smell."

"No coffee until you finish the smoothie, Colton," she said, and he scowled. When he started drinking, she went on. "You had another night terror."

"Another?"

"Yup. You had one before, and that's how I knew how to handle you this time. You came to my door looking for Emmaline. You said all the cattle were dying."

He drew in his breath and winced.

"Are you embarrassed?" she asked.

"Of course I'm—"

"Well, that's stupid. There's nothing you can do about it. But what really would be embarrassing is to realize you've pushed your body too far and then just keep on doing it. I'd be very embarrassed if I did that." She drank half her glass and got up to rinse out the blender. By the time she'd poured two cups of coffee, she found him with an empty glass, staring out the window and wearing a fierce expression.

He looked as though he was carrying the weight of the world alone. It made her heart hurt. She wanted to help more than anything, but he wouldn't let her—unless he was passed out on her couch. "I like mornings. Have I ever mentioned that?"

It took him a while to respond. "You like sunrises. I never understood why they're any different from sunsets."

His compassion is new every morning, she thought. It was something Wendy had said. It resonated with how she felt. She'd have to look it up. "I like new beginnings." She looked at her coffee cup. "I think you should let me check the girls at three and five, and you do the morning feedings. I did it today without any trouble."

His expression darkened again.

"I didn't break anything. Not that I know of. I was careful."

He shook his head. "Poppy, I know you did a

great job. I trust you better than most of the hands I've worked with because most of them don't give—they don't care."

"Then let me help. Get a few hours of uninterrupted sleep and I bet—"

He turned to her with such a pained look that the words died on her lips. His eyes searched her face, then his lips pressed into a thin line, and he looked away again. "Until you leave."

She was leaving, and sooner than he knew. But the same thoughts whirled in her mind as they always did when she considered her future. You could come back to Montana, part of her whispered. Then there was the cascade of memories, of being shocked and scared as Geoff had destroyed her world and settled in to watch a hockey game on TV. Of everything that Julie had talked about in the Saturday night group about feeling used up.

"I have to go back to defend my thesis," she said. And she wanted to say more, that she wanted to come back. That she wanted him to trust her to look after the problem girls, and laugh at her lame jokes, and kiss her again a thousand times. But she was too scared. What if she was wrong? What if what he felt for her was just a passing phase, and once again she'd staked her future on the wrong man? Ending things with Geoff had broken her—and she hadn't even loved him.

I love Colton, she thought.

Just thinking the words brought a kind of aching calm to her mind. Like getting a good grade on an exam she feared she'd failed. Of course she loved Colton. But that didn't make it okay.

"I appreciate your offer." He took a deep breath. "I might even take you up on it, at least until you go. I guess I need to find something to sell because I'm going to have to hire someone."

"You could hire Zane."

"Zane's doing property management for Cash in exchange for cheap rent."

"And I bet Cash made up that job just to help Zane out. But Zane loves it here. And he's young; he probably stays up all hours of the night anyway. He could still help Cash out on the weekends."

"The last thing I want to do is stay in the bunkhouse with a couple of newlyweds, Poppy."

There was only one other person that her heart felt belonged in this house. "Then you move in. Give them the bunkhouse. And for heaven's sake, let them renovate the bunkhouse if they want, it's pathetic."

He gave her another sideways look.

"If you aren't going to sell the homestead, I don't know why you wouldn't live here. Sometimes I think you don't believe you deserve to live here."

"I didn't fix it up for me." His voice was barely higher than a grumble. "But after that last meeting with Travis and that lawyer, I'm pretty sure selling the girls is a better financial decision."

She looked out the window, toward the cattle she couldn't see. She knew it was ridiculous to feel so much loss at the thought, but she did.

"I'm sorry," Colton said. The regret in his voice nearly brought tears to her eyes.

"I think you're making the right choice. I just wish there was a way to hold on to them."

"I have to be smart. A lot smarter than I have been." He took his empty glass into the kitchen, boots thumping slowly. "I think you might be onto something with Zane," he said.

She couldn't even answer. The morning's little triumphs were disappearing into a feeling of loss she couldn't escape. "There's a cow that didn't want to feed this morning. She was hiding up in the brush above the ditch, just a little south of the wooden bridge. You said to watch for cows who want to go off on their own."

She heard him approach. "Thank you."

"And two of the problem girls look like their milk is coming in."

"Thanks again."

"Can I make you some breakfast?" It was an effort to get him to stay, but she knew it wouldn't work.

He shook his head. He found his boots by the door and looked around the room. "No hat or gloves?"

"No." She didn't mention how cold he'd been.

His shoulders slumped. "I hope I didn't scare you. A few of the guys on the circuit refused to room with me. And one thought it was a great chance for a practical joke, but that backfired. Thanks. For everything."

He said it like he was saying good-bye. Poppy got the feeling that if she didn't intervene, they would never really talk again.

She jumped to her feet. "I was thinking about the business proposal. I know you wanted to get it to everyone, but the timing is off. What if we had a big potluck dinner here? Get the whole family together so you can talk together?"

"That could go wrong in so many ways."

Poppy thought about the wedding and Thanksgiving dinner at the hotel restaurant, how sweet and warm it was sitting at that family table. "It might be nice, too."

"It's been a long time since everyone was here. Julia hasn't set foot in the homestead since Emmaline died." He shoved his hands in his jean pockets. "But it's a good idea. Let me find out when everyone is free. Are you leaving soon?"

"I have to leave the day after Christmas." That sounded as if she was inviting herself to the Gunnersons' Christmas celebrations. "Or earlier, so that I can get settled before the defense."

"Oh." He looked down. "Thanks, Poppy. I think the dinner is a great idea. I don't think I've said enough how much I appreciate all the work you did on that proposal. And thanks for having my back this morning." He hesitated on the way out as if he might say more, but he didn't.

When he was gone, Poppy leaned back against the couch. Her brain felt as if she'd had an electric shock. *I love him, and that doesn't change a thing.* It just made leaving harder.

CHAPTER 39

Sawhorses and long stretches of old fence boards covered by cast-off linens from the hotel did the trick. Poppy used cheap white flowers from the grocery and put them in the three old blue jars from the cellar. She wrapped the necks of the jars with gold ribbons in an attempt to fancy things up, and to her, they looked pretty. She wanted it to be just like the old table Colton had described, the one that had disappeared who knows where but was long enough to hold all the Gunnersons at once.

Colton put the old kitchen table out on the back porch just to get it out of the way, but they set all six of the chairs at the table. Emmaline's old milk-white glass dishes were at every place setting, and there were just enough glasses and fruit jars to go around.

Just as she was about to declare the table a success, Colton said, "It stinks in here."

She sighed. "I'm boiling eggs."

"Again? You did that yesterday. And the day before."

"It didn't work. I tried the ice bath. I tried bringing them to a boil slowly and placing them in already boiling water. I've tried salt, and vinegar, and nothing I try will give me eggs that peel without falling apart."

He shrugged. "Doesn't change the taste."

She looked at him in utter frustration. "You can't make deviled eggs with messed up egg whites."

Colton stopped rearranging chairs to stare at her. "I thought you didn't know how to make deviled eggs."

"I'm trying to learn," she said. Her voice sounded so whiny she bit back the rest of her words. Colton closed the gap between the two of them in a couple of steps and put his arms around her, pulling her reluctantly into a hug.

"You made that jalapeno spread, a bean salad, and a regular salad, which doesn't look regular because of all that extra stuff you put in it. And you helped me make those little toast pizzas."

"Bruschetta."

"Gesundheit. The point is, Julia and Anson are bringing a couple of chickens or something, Zane and Mara are bringing rolls—and they'll probably forget the butter—and take my word for it, Cash will forget his date and the dessert. That makes you the star of the show." He leaned back to get a better look at her, but she kept her face down. She didn't want him to know how good it felt to have his arms around her, or that she hardly cared at all about the deviled eggs just then. He hadn't tried to kiss her since the night Spark was born. He'd given her a few hugs, but this was different. It was like chocolate and a warm fire and a shot of espresso all at the same time.

"I don't have dessert," she said into his shoulder.

"I have ice cream."

"Good. Thank you."

"You can't force my uncles into liking the idea of holding on to the ranch."

"I could serve a lot of wine."

He laughed, and she just had to look up. He must have read her thoughts, because his expression grew more serious.

"You haven't kissed me since Mara's wedding," she said. Saying it made her blush.

"No." His gaze focused on her lips. His voice lowered to near a whisper. "I was hoping if I didn't kiss you, I wouldn't like you as much."

Her face was blazing. But her mouth had a mind of its own. "How's that working for you?"

"It's not."

He lowered his lips to hers. Sparks shot down her spine. She breathed in Colton's own scent, leather and pine trees, dust and hard work, and tasted coffee. His lips were warm. His arms, his hand sliding up her back to slip into her hair, his chest pressed against her own, it was all warm. She could feel the heat pouring through her veins.

Then he deepened the kiss, and she lost track of everything. There was only softness and fiery sparks, the sensation of him pulling her, and her pulling him into one tangle of something dangerous and intoxicating.

He ended the kiss. He leaned his head back. "Whoa."

She smiled and took a deep breath, keeping her eyes closed. She wasn't ready to let go of this feeling yet. *I love you.* She said it again and again in her mind. *I love you, please ask me to stay.*

But already reality was creeping back in. *He doesn't know me,* she thought. If he did, he wouldn't want her. Geoff had known her better than any man, and he didn't want her. Broken. She closed her eyes tighter.

"I'm sorry," Colton said. "I told you I'd let you make the next move. And the next move is back to Tucson, right?"

She felt as though she was sinking. The sensation was so real her stomach roiled. "I don't ..."

I don't want to go. The words stuck in her throat along with that sick sensation.

"I know," Colton said. But he didn't know at all. He pulled away from her with a wry smile. "One thing at a time, right? Let's see if I get to keep the ranch. Then I think you and I should talk."

She nodded. The buzzer went off, and she turned away to face yet another dozen hard-boiled eggs. She let cold water run over them, then pulled one out to test. As she peeled the shell away, the flesh beneath tore up along with it until the yellow heart of it showed. Colton looked over her shoulder. "Maybe the other eggs will be better," he said. "I'm going to go check the girls before everyone gets here."

She nodded, but she couldn't meet his gaze.

The door opened and closed, and she tried three more eggs. They were all impossible to peel. She tossed those and put the rest in a plastic bag. They would be good on salads next week.

Except there was no next week. Tomorrow was Christmas Eve, then she had seven days to make a three-day drive, meet with her advisor, prepare for the thesis, and find a place to stay. The sooner she left, the better. The open invitation from Geoff hovered over her. What if he took her back and wanted to marry her? Would these wounds feel healed then? She couldn't think about it now, not with the heat from Colton's kiss still flowing through her veins.

Although things had been smooth the last few days between her and Colton, they hadn't talked about Christmas. She was certain he had plans with his family. But she didn't want to miss her last day with him.

There was a knock at the door. She felt a sickly wave of dread. She wasn't ready to face Julia and Anson, not with her lackluster, eggless dinner and terrible hostess skills. She was relieved to see Zane's well-worn baseball cap through the window, and she hurried to open the door. She didn't care what Mara thought. She was so happy to see her again that she gave the girl a big hug. "I missed you," she said.

Mara laughed at her. "I guess you did!" But she hugged back just as tightly. "Do I look different married?" She spread her arms wide and struck a pose. Her coat wasn't buttoned, and the first thing Poppy noticed was her belly.

"Yes. You're huge."

"Poppy, if you were an ambassador we'd be at war," Mara said.

"Let me clarify. Your stomach is huge. The rest of you looks the same. And I guess that's pretty awesome, right? Hi, Zane. It's good to see you."

Zane was taking in the updates. He hadn't seen the floor completely trimmed and cleaned. "Wow, you did a great job. How's Emmaline's room coming along?"

Poppy closed the door behind him. "The renovations pretty much stopped when ..." When he started talking to Travis about leasing part of the ranch. "I can't say when. But Colton will a little later on."

"I bet I know," Mara said, dumping her coat on the bottom steps as she always had. "Colton talked to Zane about working on the ranch."

Poppy didn't know he'd done that. It made her feel a little left out. "Really?"

"Yeah. Zane's pretty excited."

Poppy cut Zane a glance. He kept his face cast downward, but a big grin was spreading across it. "It'd be sick."

Poppy assumed that was a good thing. "What about you, Mara?" She noticed Mara had a little less makeup on than usual, and her hair fell in pretty, natural waves over her shoulders. She knew better than to comment on it.

She shrugged. "I think it'd be good. The apartment is loud. But it's nice to be in walking distance of everything since we only have one car. I guess it depends."

"On what?"

"Depends on if you're staying." Mara put her fists on her hips. "I'm not going to live in the middle of nowhere alone."

"You're married."

"That's not the same, and you know it. And you have to get me through one more semester of school. Besides, I heard you and Colton were spotted noshing on the street the night we got married. At least I assumed it was you. It was you, wasn't it?"

"One kiss."

"I knew it! So Colton's moving in with you, right?"

"No," Poppy said firmly. The last minute of conversation had been all kinds of wrong, and from Zane's expression, he was as misinformed as Mara. "And since when is one kiss worth beating the Moose Hollow jungle drum?"

"Since it involved Colton, Moose Hollow's most eligible bachelor, who hasn't dated anyone in ages. Well, maybe second most eligible, since he had that DUI. Travis is hot."

"He never had a DUI."

"Really?"

The door opened behind her, and she didn't know whether to feel relieved or embarrassed.

"We were just talking about you," Mara said with a smile.

"That's never good," Colton said. He walked up to Poppy and put a hand on her arm. Not wanting to fuel any more gossip, she turned to him and slipped her arm away at the same time. "I think we're just about an hour away from a new calf," he said to her. "You'll have to go down to the barn with me and name it."

"Name it?" Zane made a face.

"Why not?" Mara said.

"Do you name your hamburgers too?"

Colton shook his head at Zane. "Funny. But it's a balance, Zane, you know that. The moment you start seeing them as walking dollar bills, you stop being a good shepherd."

Zane looked dubious. "You never named them before."

"And I still don't. But I know someone who does." Colton smiled at Poppy like she hung the moon, and for a moment Poppy couldn't even breathe.

Then came another knock.

"Cash was right behind me," Colton said. "No date. Don't ask." He walked back to the door.

Mara and Zane nodded knowingly. Whatever they knew, Poppy didn't.

Cash came in with his customary smile, the kind that involved his whole face and put Poppy at ease even though she didn't know him well. "Hey, Colton! Thanks for setting up this little get-together. Wow." He looked around. "Gosh, this is amazing. The place looks brand new." He stepped inside. "I saw a lot of new fencing on the way in. And you straightened out that mess on the east side of the barn. And I'm guessing you got that bale hauler running, too." He slowly shook his head. "I didn't realize everything you've got going on."

"Maybe you should drop by once in a while," Colton said. "I could put you to work."

"Yup. Because that's just what I need," Cash said. "Hey, I've been here for a whole minute and you haven't offered me a beer, Colton."

"I'll get it," Poppy offered. "Light? Dark? Hoppy?"

"Beer's beer to me, thank you. Colton, did you contract out much work?"

"None. But Poppy, Zane, and Mara all had something to do with it."

"Really?"

Poppy searched a drawer for a bottle opener. She couldn't see Cash's face, but she could hear the doubt in his voice. She wondered again how Cash, Anson, and Julia had become so distant from Colton and the ranch.

As she turned the corner to the living room, she saw Colton opening the front door again. Anson came in first. He was a mountain of a man, she thought, as tall as Colton, but with more bulk. He was carrying something covered in aluminum foil. It had to be the ham. Julia was right behind him with two large casserole dishes. Poppy felt her heart sink a little. It was clear who the real hostess was.

Then she noticed that Julia looked as nervous

as Poppy felt. Poppy stepped forward to help. Julia looked up, and her eyes settled on the beer in Poppy's hand. Cash was busy greeting Anson, so Poppy waited to pass him the drink. By the time she did, Julia and Anson were on their way into the kitchen.

"Oh, my word!" Julia exclaimed. "Are these new cabinets?"

Colton flashed her a grin as he passed by her. "Nope. Poppy talked me into letting her refinish them."

Poppy peeked around the corner. Anson was taking the casseroles from his wife's hands. Julia was looking at the upper cabinets. "They aren't off kilter anymore," she said wistfully.

Colton laughed. "You noticed that too? Hanging these things was an exercise in patience, let me tell you. Hers, mostly, I think." He turned to wink at Poppy. Behind him, Anson and Julia exchanged a look and went back to unwrapping the food. Poppy backed out of the kitchen.

Poppy remembered it was almost the shortest day of the year. The *Almanac* officially placed sunset at about four thirty, but the sun was down behind the mountains long before that. Twilight stretched out across the sky, and the pastures, with their dusting of new snow, were shades of blue in the remaining light. She looked and found one star, then another, as if they were taking turns blinking on.

Mara stepped up behind her. "You okay?"

"I think so. You?"

She gave Poppy a sideways glance. "I don't know yet."

"Yeah."

"What are we waiting for?" Colton called from the kitchen. "Let's eat!"

Chaos broke out. There was barely enough room for all the food on the makeshift table. "Where would you like us to sit?" Julia asked Colton.

Colton looked at Poppy, and Poppy's mind instantly grasped the variables. She could repeat where people had sat at the wedding, but they didn't have Drew's family or Liam there. She glanced at Mara, who saw the look in her eyes and instantly took charge. When Mara was done, Colton was seated at the head of the table with Poppy on one side and Cash on the other. Mara seated herself next to Poppy, across from Julia. Poppy couldn't have been more relieved to have Mara next to her again, although it felt silly to rely upon an eighteen-year-old girl for comfort.

An eighteen-year-old mom, she reminded

herself. One who knew how to seat people at a table. Poppy had to stop underestimating Mara.

Passing the food around the table wasn't any easier. The casseroles and the ham were too big to hand around, so there was a flurry of plates and serving spoons, but everyone chipped in and Poppy noticed the mood lightening. Poppy remembered the wine and passed two bottles around, red and white. She had no idea which was supposed to go with ham. They came back untouched, although Anson did accept the beer Colton offered, and Cash chimed in, his first bottle finished.

Of course, Mara and Zane were too young for wine, and Poppy hadn't thought of an alternative for them. "Coffee?" she whispered to Mara.

Mara shook her head. Then she reached under the table and gave Poppy's hand a squeeze. Poppy wondered if her discomfort was that obvious.

She tried to keep her eyes off Julia. But she couldn't help but notice the woman taking in all the changes—and the mixed emotions on her face. Of course, Emmaline's house had been her family home too. It must have been hard to see it changed.

"We haven't changed anything in Emmaline's room," Poppy said.

Silence fell over the table. Of course her words were completely out of context. Realizing they had been aimed toward her, Julia blinked and said, "Oh?"

Poppy nodded. She didn't know whether to keep her mouth shut and cut her losses or explain. She explained. "I was just thinking that we've made a lot of changes, and it might be a bit of a shock since you haven't come by since Emmaline passed."

That went over worse than her first statement. It sounded like an accusation. And she hadn't just brought up a dead relative, she'd called her Emmaline as if she knew her. She was treading on someone else's sacred ground.

But the woman was Emmaline to her. Emmaline of the yellow roses, the astute cattle trader who slept in a neatly arranged bedroom with the Bible beside the bed. The woman who chose her lost grandson to carry on for her. They didn't know the affection Poppy held for that woman. How could they? They didn't know the affection she held for Colton.

Mara saved her again. "Wait until you see the upstairs," she said enthusiastically. "All the lath is gone, all the old wires and pipes, everything. It's pretty amazing."

Julia was frozen. Her husband glanced at her and said, "Sounds good. After we eat, we'll do that."

They went on in silence for a while after that, although Cash added his appreciation for the bean salad and the ham. Poppy appreciated his diplomacy.

Colton set his fork down. "I wanted you guys to see the house, but the truth is I wanted you here together to talk about something else. I have some important news." He reached over and gave Poppy's hand a squeeze. "We have a proposal for you guys."

Across the table, Poppy saw Cash's eyes grow wide. She glanced toward the other end of the table. Mara had an expression of happy surprise on her face, and Anson wore a look of serious concern. Julia looked white as a sheet, and as her eyes met Poppy's own, she saw an anger simmering there.

They thought Colton meant to propose to her.

And this was their reaction. Worry, concern, anger. "I'll go get the proposals," she said, pushing her chair back. Her knees were shaking so badly she could hardly stand. Colton's warm hand pressed her shoulder. "I've got it," he said. He was happily oblivious.

All Poppy could think was, this is what they think of me. This was what the people who knew Colton best thought she had to contribute to his life.

Colton handed out the proposals. He gave one to Zane and Mara, as she'd asked him to, because if Zane was going to work at the ranch, he should know what was going on. One went to Anson and Julia, another to Cash. The last one he set down beside her.

"I have to leave just for a few minutes. There's a cow in the barn I need to check on, but I don't want that to interrupt us, so I'm going to check her now while you guys read. Then when I come back, I can answer any questions."

"What is this?" Zane asked, flipping through the pages.

"Why don't you come with me? I'll give you the executive summary," Colton said. Zane stood to leave, and as Colton headed for the door, he said, "If you have any questions, just ask Poppy. She wrote the proposal." Thinking he was sharing the credit with her, not throwing her under the bus, he looked excited. "I'll be right back. If I get held up, I'll text you."

The door closed and all eyes turned her way. Anson, Julia, and even Cash looked at her with expressions of betrayal on their faces. "I just put the proposal together," she said. She was going to go on to say she hadn't actually proposed any of it, but everyone had gone back to reading the booklets.

"He's selling part of the ranch?" Mara asked. She was looking at the map where Travis's horse rehabilitation lands were outlined.

"No, it's a lease," Poppy replied.

"A hundred-year lease," Anson said. "That is not substantially different from a sale."

Poppy bit her lip. Zane had said Anson played the part of the serious and intimidating hotel owner when they had a disgruntled guest. Now she understood why. "Travis was looking for some reassurance that the ranch wouldn't be sold after he put in the infrastructure."

"Travis?" Mara turned to her. "He wants to put a barn up on the ranch? He's a great guy. And he's Moose Hollow's number one most eligible—"

"Yes," Poppy said as she gave Mara a gentle kick under the table. Mara let the man's eligible bachelorhood remain unspoken.

"He doesn't have sufficient funds for operating expenses." Anson was not asking a question, he was making a statement.

Poppy wished Colton would hurry. "He's aware of that."

"I thought he was going to sell the house," Cash said. "Isn't that why he did all these renovations?"

"That was the plan, but to make it viable and have good access, he'd have to give up so much land that—"

"There are too many capital improvements outstanding," Anson said.

Poppy felt more flustered by the minute. "You should ask Colton. He has a plan."

"It's just plain stupid to sell land and put money into the barn when you haven't got the equipment to grow your own hay."

"Comparably sized ranches do well outsourcing the hay. It cuts overhead."

Anson set down the proposal and fixed a stare on her. "And I suppose you are an expert on hay shortages in the Northwest?"

It wasn't just that Anson was big, or smart. It was the look of disapproval on a face that was undeniably handsome. Poppy wondered if this was what it would feel like to have Colton disappointed in her. It made her want to run. But

Colton had worked so hard to find a solution, and they weren't even giving it a chance.

"The barn is at a critical point. Without improvements, preferably before spring, the damage could be so great that the cost of fixing it would be prohibitive. That takes precedence."

"Which is exactly why he should let someone else do it."

"He'll have the money. He's going to sell the first calf heifers."

"The rest of the herd is old," Cash said.

Anson nodded. "Economics of scale. A herd that small can't support the expenses of maintaining this much land. Selling the heifers is foolish."

She knew her face was livid, and she felt her shoulders shaking. Before she had time to think, before she had time to make sense of it all, the ragged edges of an idea occurred to her. "If he were to sell the heifers to someone looking for an investment, someone who would then turn around and lease the land—"

"Another hundred-year lease?" Anson said. His narrowed eyes made it clear what he thought of that.

"No. Just leave the heifers here until they

calve. A normal ranching lease." She kept herself from adding a sarcastic *You've heard of that, right?*

"Who would do that? Colton has no standing in the ranching community."

Poppy could see Anson as clearly as if his thoughts and feelings had been written out in black and white, right in front of her. People didn't feel that sort of anger toward someone without a reason. Colton's failures had hurt Anson, disappointed him in a deep way. Then Emmaline had given controlling interest of his family land to Colton, not Anson, who had built a good life. A solid life. Anson was like the prodigal son's brother, the one who worked hard and never got the fattened calf.

"Someone who knows him and how hard he works would," she said. She glanced at Julia. She knew Julia cared for Colton. Why didn't she step in to defend him? "Someone who had money to invest." She swallowed. She never, never spoke of it. Her trust fund was more like a scarlet letter than something to brag about. "Someone who had money on hand. From an inheritance."

Julia gasped. "And how would you know about that?"

"My family." Not her family, her grandmother.

She alone had provided for her granddaughters. "They worked in the hotel industry and—"

"How dare you?" Julia said.

Shocked, Poppy shut her mouth. She knew she had misstepped again, but she didn't understand how. She felt a vibration from the phone in her back pocket. It had to be a message from Colton. Her hopes that he would walk in the door any moment faded.

Julia threw her paper napkin onto the table. "You've never had a problem getting involved in things that are none of your business. Not with Zane and Mara, not with me, and certainly not with Colton."

Mara shot Poppy a perplexed look. It helped Poppy a little to know she wasn't alone in her confusion.

In fact, Anson looked confused too.

"What makes you think you have the right? He's renovated the house for you, using money that would have been better spent on the barn. Or hay. Or anything other than your whims. And that's not even enough. You think I should put my money into your upkeep as well? And Zane, who hasn't even got a financial stake in this ranch? Did you even think of that?"

Julia hardly took a breath before continuing.

"If Colton had sold it, we'd have money to help them start out. And so would Colton, to start fresh in whatever life he wants, not to be stuck here with ghosts and"—she looked down her nose at Poppy—"another vampire sucking him dry for whatever it is you want from him. Money? Fame?"

"Julia." Anson seemed as surprised by his wife's outburst as everyone else.

Julia's eyes were brimming with tears now, but her voice was steady. "And you think you can guilt me into neglecting my own family once more just so you can play house with Colton? Oh yes, I know about him asking Zane to move into the bunkhouse. And it's pretty obvious where he'll be. Where he's already been, probably. But that's how you do business, isn't it?"

"Julia," Anson said more firmly.

She turned to him. "I'm sorry. I should have told you. I got the check almost three months ago. I haven't even cashed it. I had no idea my grandmother had named me as a beneficiary for a life insurance policy. I didn't even know she had died. I thought all the ties were cut after...after ..."

"After you married me," Anson said.

Julia let out a bitter laugh. "Apparently they forgot one."

"Why would you keep this from me?" Anson's words were gentle.

Julia bit her lips. "The lawsuit. I thought if I didn't cash it yet no one could take it."

Poppy didn't give Julia a chance to respond to her husband. "What do you mean 'how I do business'?" As she said it, another word registered. Lawsuit.

Julia's gaze went back to her. "Information travels both ways, Poppy. You show up in Moose Hollow looking strung out, no job, no home, nothing but one-dollar bills, and then suddenly you have enough money to rent the homestead? You're not the first problem girl Colton has taken in."

"She's in school," Mara said weakly.

Problem girl. Any other time she might have laughed at the irony of being called that, just like one of the heifers. One-dollar bills. The Moose Hollow gossip mill had been working, and Poppy knew what assumptions had been made about that. Of all things, her silly attempt to save money had led to this.

"That's not all, of course," Julia said. She glanced at the red-ribboned bracelet on Poppy's wrist.

Mara sucked in a breath. "Julia?"

Poppy stilled. Did they think she was a prostitute? Or just a gold digger? Maybe she just knew Poppy had a past and that whatever it was, it couldn't be good for Colton. She wasn't good enough. She was broken.

"Are you looking at Poppy's bracelet?" Mara said. Poppy heard the tone in her voice and felt an explosion coming. She put a hand on Mara's arm and tried to get her attention, but Mara jerked her hand away. "You mean like this one?" She held out her wrist.

Julia looked unsure, then shocked. The bracelets were so different she must not have made the connection.

"I get it," Mara said. "Once a tramp, always a tramp."

Julia covered her mouth with both hands.

Mara glanced back at Poppy. "Thank you for dinner, Poppy. I need to go now."

Poppy had to race to catch up with Mara, but she couldn't get the girl's attention until they were outside. When Mara turned around, Poppy saw the tears in her eyes. She stopped the words she had planned to say to bring Mara back inside. Instead, she said, "Get in my truck. The keys are in it. Just start it up and I'll be right back out. Don't go anywhere without me, okay?"

She marched back inside to a silent house. Anson looked as troubled as she'd ever seen, and Cash had disappeared somewhere.

"You should be ashamed of yourself," Poppy said. She faced them both. "Everything you think about Mara is wrong. And if you ever find out—if you ever become the kind of people worthy of her story, you're going to regret every thought you've ever had about her."

Julia looked awful. She shook her head a little from side to side. "Poppy, I don't know what got into me."

"Don't," Poppy said. She wasn't ready for an apology because she didn't want to have to respond to it the way she should. "This night meant a lot to Colton. He put a lot into it. The very least you owe him is to consider what he's proposing."

Anson spoke up. "Poppy, this isn't what—"

"Don't," she said to him too. "He's been working himself into the dust for this. And why? Wouldn't it have been easier for him to cash out and buy a place of his own? Haven't you for even one second tried to figure out why he wants this ranch whole again? Why he wanted to renovate this house? It wasn't for him. It was for Emmaline. And for you. To try to feel like he earned"—she waved her hands through the air—"all of this. To stop feeling guilty."

She was met with silence. But her words kept coming.

"I envied you, your tight-knit family and fancy dinner. I even envied your faith. But you don't know the most basic thing about Jesus. That none of us deserves whatever goodness we have. Not me, not Mara, and not you, either."

Poppy took a breath. She had to leave. But there was one more thing to say.

"Colton didn't pay for the renovations with money from the ranch. He sold his truck, his saddles, his buckles, every single little thing he ever got from the rodeo to pay for it. He burned those bridges. And if you can't respect that, you don't deserve to have any part of this ranch."

She stormed out, grabbing her coat and slamming the door behind her. She got in the driver's side, pushing Mara over as she did, and pulled out of the drive. "Put on your seat belt."

Mara sniffled beside her, but she didn't say anything. Then as Poppy blasted past the well-lit barn, Mara said, "Wait! Where are you going?"

"You'll find out. I'm on a roll tonight."

Mara figured out their destination soon enough. "What kind of friend are you?"

"Not a very good one. But I do know a few things about being a big sister."

"I'm not going to talk to him."

"That's your choice. He's home now, right? And probably drunk. You don't have to say a word to him. I'll do all the talking."

Curiosity must have won out in Mara's mind because she settled back into the seat. When she saw Poppy slow down in front of a house, she pointed to the next one. Poppy recognized the circular driveway. She pulled up to the front and got out, leaving the truck running.

She rang the bell twice and got no response. That was when she started pounding on the door with her fist. That felt so good she got both fists going and was taken aback when the door opened.

Seeing Mara's father was like a flashback to the night of Zane and Mara's accident. *You and your whole lowlife clan. I'm going to sue you for every cent you ever touched.* "You're suing Anson and Julia."

Mara's father looked like he had that night, his anger barely contained. He didn't say anything, which she took as an answer.

"You're suing them even though you know Mara was driving that night."

"I know no such thing," he said. "And neither do you."

"You won't win. Their injuries, their history, everything points to the fact that Mara was driving the Escalade."

"Zane confessed."

"Zane was trying to protect her. Which is more than you ever did."

He flicked his hand at her. "Get off my property," he said lazily.

Poppy put one boot in front of the door. He looked at it, looked at her, and his lip curled. "You're giving me permission to defend myself."

"Mara told me what kind of dad you were. After your wife left. Before you started drinking so much."

The sneer grew more menacing. "I'll count to five."

"She's going to have a baby. And if you don't talk to her, that baby's never going to know your name."

There was a flicker, almost a wince, in his eyes.

"Are you willing to throw that all away?"

"Mara threw it all away," he said. But he didn't

count. And he didn't push her out of the doorway.

"You'd better find out why. I have her in my car. But she didn't want to come here. And if you keep acting like this, she'll probably never come again. So if you want to know what happened, you're going to have to invite her in and then shut up and listen."

"Who do you think you are?"

"That's not shutting up." She turned and pointed to her truck. "She's right there. You're supposed to be smart. Ask yourself, do you think you're going to get another chance with her or her baby?"

Mara's father stood still, breathing hard, his hand so tight on the door that his knuckles turned white. Poppy realized she was shaking. She wanted to make a run for the car. *Wait*, came the thought, and she did.

The change in Maxwell was slow. He didn't speak a word. The warm, stale air from his house came out in puffs, blowing the hair back from Poppy's face. She waited. And just when waiting longer seemed unbearable and foolish, his eyes met hers. There was nothing friendly in them, but she saw surrender.

She walked over to her truck and pulled the

passenger door open. Mara had cracked the window and heard every word. Tears soaked her face. "You need to tell him," Poppy said.

"He's a jerk."

"Then you never have to speak to him again after this. But you need to tell him." Mara didn't move. "He deserves to know. And you need to tell him what kind of man Zane is."

"Zane's better than all of them." She sniffed. "I need to call Zane."

"I'll tell him where you are. Just text him when you're ready to have him come pick you up."

Mara nodded. She stood up but didn't move. "I'm scared."

"I can stay here if you want me to," Poppy offered, but Mara shook her head.

"It's not like that. You know, he hates me, but he loves me too."

Poppy watched Mara approach her father, and she watched Maxwell's eyes. She saw the hurt there. But he didn't say a word. He reached out his hand, and she took it. Then with a glance over her shoulder, Mara went inside and Maxwell closed the door.

Poppy waited a little while, but only because she couldn't bear to go back to the homestead. She texted Zane that Mara was fine. She added that she'd explain when she got back to the homestead.

She hoped Julia and Anson were gone by now. Poppy could try to explain to Julia that she had been talking about using her own trust fund to invest in Colton's herd. But it wouldn't change anything. With or without money, they had made up their minds about her, and she wasn't welcome.

She knew what had to happen next. She had a life to create and a goal to meet, and there was nothing for her here. She would do a video conference with Mara every Friday and help her through her last semester. She would tell Zane the importance of leaving a solid six hours for Colton to sleep, and he would understand. And Colton. She'd find a gift to thank him for everything. And that was the end of it.

There were only two vehicles in front of the homestead when she returned, Zane's and Colton's. She was relieved the others were gone, but she still didn't want to go inside. When she opened the door, she saw the table looking just as she'd left it. Colton was pacing, running his hands through his hair, and Zane was looking at his phone. "She still hasn't—"

They both stopped when they saw her walk

in. "Where is Mara?" Zane said. There was a desperate tone to his voice, and Poppy regretted making him worry.

"She's at her father's."

"Her father's? Why would she go there?"

"He's suing your parents."

"He's what?" Colton turned to Zane. "Did you know about this?"

Zane's jaw dropped. "No. I have to go get her."

"Leave her alone," Poppy said softly. "They need to talk. She promised to text you the minute she's ready to go."

"I have to go now."

"She wants to talk to him alone," Poppy said.

"Fine, but no one said I have to be more than few feet away from her when she does." Zane hurried out the door, leaving it ajar. Poppy went over to close it behind him.

"That explains why everyone was so upset," Colton said. "Cash ran out of here saying there was an emergency at the apartment complex, and I couldn't get Julia to tell me what happened. I don't think I've ever seen her cry before."

Poppy felt the first wave of regret. She was certain there was an ocean's worth waiting for her, but she would have time to deal with that on the drive to Arizona. "Colton, I'm leaving tonight."

His face fell. His green eyes stared without blinking. "What happened? I couldn't get Julia or Anson to talk to me. Julia said to ask you first."

Poppy shook her head. "It's not about tonight. I just need to go." Excuses bubbled up in her mind, but they all sounded like the half-lies they were. "Thank you, Colton. This whole time with you has been—"

"Don't," he said.

She winced at the harsh tone in his voice. She knew she'd sounded that harsh, and worse, talking to Julia and Anson. She had it coming.

"Just go." He walked toward the door. "Don't worry about dinner. I'll clean up tomorrow." He grabbed his coat and left without looking back.

CHAPTER 40

Colton sat in the dirt and hay next to the gate and watched the newest Gunnerson Ranch baby. Another heifer. Another chance to build the herd, soon to be sold.

He felt drained and confused, but there was a feeling of calm in this space. He sat still, afraid that moving would chase it away. It was as if all the responsibility for the ranch had, for a moment, been taken off his shoulders. And it was in good hands. He could breathe again.

All because his family was at odds. All the disapproval and discord he'd feared had come to pass. And he was still okay.

He could see more clearly now, too. He owned 51 percent of the ranch, and he was going to make a go of it. He couldn't convince his family, and he couldn't win their agreement, but no matter what, he would do what he thought was best. He hadn't felt certainty like this for a long time. God wasn't promising him a happy ending, he knew that. That's not how the world worked. But he was promising him a path to walk, and he was going to walk it.

After all, he'd been certain about the rodeo, and if he hadn't walked that path, he wouldn't be here now. He might lose the ranch. But he'd lose it in one piece.

God had a way of making things right. Not the way you wished, necessarily, but right. The older he got, the more he saw it. No wonder Emmaline's faith had been so strong. If he kept his eyes open, he might feel the same way at her age.

After Christmas he would contact a cattle buyer and see if anyone was in the market for the heifers. They would bring a good price with such good-looking calves by their side. In the end, Beau had done a good thing buying them. Maybe sometime he'd say that to his father's face.

He waited for the sound of Poppy's truck. He thought about praying she'd stay. He even thought about running all the way up to the homestead and blocking her way, forcing her to see what he knew, that she belonged to the ranch. She belonged to him. But just when his frustration threatened to rise again, the peace settled down.

No, Poppy wasn't his, not unless she chose to be. She was amazing, and she'd be amazing wherever she landed. She learned fast, and she kept that calm cheerfulness about her that soothed his soul. If she was quick and kind and good for him here on the ranch, he could imagine how good she would be at the work she had chosen to do. They were lucky to have her—the boss, the friends, and even the boyfriend she would choose.

He wouldn't try to talk her out of it. He wouldn't even pray for her to stay, because she'd made her choice. All he could do was pray that she did what God meant for her to do. After all, she had a path too, and it didn't involve him anymore. Just like the rodeo, he'd get over losing her. In time.

A long time, but he would.

CHAPTER 41

*P*oppy woke at seven in the morning at a rest area in Colorado Springs, worried that Colton wouldn't remember to add wood to the fire or to turn the baseboard heat on again. But she couldn't tell him how to run his house. Not now. And a few hours of dreamless sleep was all she was going to get.

The mountains and plains rolled by. She drove at the speed her old truck preferred and let the cars pass her. She wasn't in a hurry. The trip south from Montana wasn't much different from the trip north, although it was colder and she was thinking about Colton instead of Geoff. And she wasn't crying this time. Maybe that proved she had learned something valuable in her time there.

As the sun moved from her left side to her right, she began to think about the blowup at the homestead. She thought about Julia, Anson, and Maxwell's lawsuit. She was pretty sure they'd kept it from Mara and Zane, probably because they were trying to protect them.

From what she knew, Maxwell had the money and the determination to do real damage to their finances. It wasn't about winning the suit, of course. It was about punishing Zane for getting his daughter pregnant. The irony of that was rich. And sickening. What mattered now was that Anson and Julia had been carrying that burden alone. No wonder Julia was on the edge.

When Poppy had talked about her trust fund money, Julia thought she'd heard about the insurance check from her grandmother. It was a weird coincidence that they were both children of "hotel people," as her mother said. Maybe they had more in common than she had realized. Julia didn't know Poppy, and what she did know hadn't been good. Julia thought she wasn't any better than the girl Colton had lived with in Cody. And if Colton ended up in jail now, she doubted Julia and Anson could save him again.

There were wounds in that family she hadn't understood. And wounds in Colton. She'd been so wrapped up in her own that she hadn't noticed, and hadn't helped. That beautiful Thanksgiving dinner wasn't a sign of family perfection; it was a choice. Every person at that table had made a choice to put their love for each other first.

Poppy hadn't made any such choice. She'd chosen the immediate satisfaction of nasty, biting words. If she'd stayed calm, could she have gotten Julia and Anson to understand?

She sighed. Maybe Mara could get her father to stop the lawsuit. And Zane could help Colton just enough to get them through. Maybe he could hold on to the ranch and his uncles would forgive him for that someday. Without her around, things were bound to go more smoothly.

She was outside Santa Fe, New Mexico, when she realized it was Christmas Eve. She'd heard it was a beautiful place this time of year. On a whim, she pulled into town and headed for the plaza she'd heard so much about. Maybe she could find a room and stretch her legs for a while, too.

But the plaza was inaccessible. There were too many narrow one-way streets crowded with traffic, and other streets were blocked off. The parking lots of nearby hotels were overflowing, but she caught glimpses of the beautiful Spanish colonial buildings, their adobe skins looking as smooth as human skin in the sunset. She found herself on the wrong road headed away from the plaza, but then suddenly another beautiful adobe hotel was before her. She pulled into the parking lot and found a single empty parking place.

When she walked up to the hotel's front desk, a dark-skinned woman with beautiful ebony hair greeted her. She pointed to her headset and continued her conversation. "Yes, your credit card has been refunded."

Poppy looked around the lobby. It looked more like a spacious living room, lovely and intimate, full of honey-colored wood and warm Native American textiles.

"No, don't worry. I'm sorry you've had such trouble. We've heard about the storm in Chicago. Your room will be here when you arrive, and hopefully we can help make up for your troubles." She touched something on the headset and turned to Poppy. "Welcome to Santa Fe. May I help you?"

"I was wondering if you had any rooms," Poppy said. "I'm sure you don't, but—"

"As a matter of fact, we just had a cancellation for tonight. The guest isn't expected to arrive until the day after tomorrow, so you could have it for two nights."

Poppy only needed one night, but she found herself nodding in agreement. She answered the woman's questions and read the little placard that explained the hotel was owned by a local tribe, describing its history and mission.

Her room was just as warm and comfortable as the rest of the hotel. She retrieved her bag and settled in to watch the last of the sunset. It ended with a thin red line that glowed like embers on the western horizon. On Colton's ranch, the mountains hid the last light of sunset.

Poppy wasn't very far from the plaza. She put on her Montana winter-warm coat and the hat Colton had given her and went out into the cold, which didn't have the same bite as a Montana blizzard. She walked all the way to the heart of Santa Fe, its ancient plaza. She walked along side-walks lined with luminarias, admired the Palace of the Governors, and listened to carolers. She saw a group of men huddled together, some sitting on a bench and others kneeling, heads bowed and speaking in low tones.

With time to spare, she wandered farther from the square. She found a famous church and was curious to go inside, but there was a service

going on, and it was packed with people who belonged there. She headed back toward the hotel,
the long way around.

When she saw a cross above a doorway, she
stopped. The building it belonged to looked
like a renovated home. It had a few South-
western touches, but it wasn't anything special,
and it was hemmed in on both sides by ware-
houses. As she stood there, wondering what
made a church a church, a woman appeared on
the other side of the building's double glass
doors.

She smiled at Poppy. "Did you forget something?" she said through the glass.

Startled, Poppy couldn't answer.

The woman tried to open a door, which took
some wrestling and even a good kick at the metal
frame. Finally, it gave way with a terrible metallic
scrape. The woman laughed. "Someday we're
going to replace these awful things. Did you
forget something inside?"

"No," Poppy said.

"Oh." The woman's eyes narrowed. "You didn't
look familiar, but we get a lot of guests for the
Christmas Eve service. I forgot my hat inside. I
thought maybe you'd done the same."

"No." Poppy knew she sounded like an idiot,

but she couldn't think of anything else to say. "I didn't go."

"Then how can I help you?"

Poppy really looked at the woman for the first time. She had long, slightly wild hair streaked with gray. Her face was tan and marked by a few fine lines, many of them trending toward a smile. "I'm sorry. I was just walking by. I just thought this didn't look like a church."

Rather than being offended, the woman laughed. "I know, right? It's not a lot better on the inside. Although the Christmas decorations are very nice. Would you like to see?"

Poppy shook her head.

The woman stepped outside and started wrestling with the door again, and it loudly scraped back into place. She took a key ring from her pocket, sorted through the dozens of keys, and locked the doors. "I guess I should have asked Santa for new doors for Christmas." She pocketed the keys and held out her hand for Poppy to shake. "My name is Eloise. I'm the pastor's wife."

"Poppy." The woman had a firm grasp.

"Which way are you headed?"

"Back to the hotel." She realized that she was pointing ninety degrees away from the direction she'd been walking. "I was just looking around. I'm not from Santa Fe."

"Me either. I'm from Washington. I miss the trees, but that's about it. If you're headed this way, I can walk a few blocks with you, if you don't mind."

The woman, Poppy discovered, was on her way to a little cafe. She said her husband was at the plaza with other church leaders who liked to get together every Christmas Eve to pray for the children of the city. She was going to meet him there. The owner, she said, liked to open it up for any members of the church who didn't have family around on Christmas Eve.

Poppy knew an invitation was coming, and she planned to decline it, but instead of asking her, the woman simply ushered her to the door. The cafe owner then ushered her in, and she found herself seated before she had a chance to refuse. She was at a table with strangers, some of whom looked about as unhappy to be there as she was. But there was a fair amount of teasing going on in the cafe, some heartfelt welcomes, and the conversation started to flow.

Poppy didn't know what she expected Eloise's husband to look like, but it wasn't the scraggly, blue-jeaned mountain man she saw. He was friendly, too, and easy to talk to. Everyone was. It reminded her of Mara's Saturday night group. No matter how different they were, there was always something they had in common.

The pastor stood to say grace. Dinner tasted and looked a little like a school lunch, but it hit all the right notes. Turkey and gravy, mashed potatoes, cranberries. Santa Fe's famous cuisine hadn't touched this diner. Pumpkin pie was dessert, and that was when the pastor suggested they each say something they were grateful for this Christmas Eve.

Poppy dreaded her turn. All around her people were thankful for family members, healing, and their church. She tried to think of the right thing to say. Her blessings and troubles were so tangled together that she couldn't pull one out. When everyone's gaze turned to her, she said, "My time in Moose Hollow." Her throat closed. She couldn't have said more even if she'd known what to say.

"One more thing," Eloise's husband said. "Christmas is about the day our Savior arrived. The one person who could set us right with God. He took on our sins and by his grace, we start brand new. So I like to take this time to share one thing we're ready to hand over to Him."

Now she was on the spot. Hand it over to Jesus? As if she could. Of course, she'd read enough to understand the concept. She'd even listened to a few Christian radio programs, mostly of dubious quality. A person was supposed to admit they were a sinner, hand over those sins, and ask Jesus to take the driver's seat. It was like a mantra. She didn't like mantras.

But all the aphorisms, mantras, and "life messages" her parents had spoken over their lives were about how great they were. How much money they would have. How peaceful they would feel. As far as self-help went, this was unusual. Rather than "The godhead in me is beautiful," one of her least favorite mantras—and one that conjured up nightmarish images—the Christian view was something like "I messed it up. All of it. Please clean up this mess, and the next one I'll make, and the next. I want to try life your way." Who would pay a thousand dollars for a retreat that left you with that?

That was when she felt it. The clear sensation that this was different. Like a tap on her shoulder, a cleared throat. *Pay attention.* This wasn't about feeling better. This was about getting things worked out with the Creator. The one who had made her, faults and all. The one who promised he had a plan for her.

Her own plan for her life ended the moment she earned her master's degree. And suddenly she wanted to know what her Creator would have planned for her after that, if he existed. If she decided to follow him.

They were all looking at her, of course. Because this is how a Creator would do things. He would put her on the spot at the exact moment she would usually run, feel distracted, or reason him away. What would she put on the cross for Jesus to bear?

"Everything," she said out loud.

No one laughed. In fact, more than a few people nodded as if they understood. Maybe they did.

CHAPTER 42

It was an odd group of people, Poppy decided. The bar had a wraparound balcony that would have suited New Orleans as well as Old Town Tucson. They sat down in the shade and looked out over the busy street and the even busier shops. The college students were back in town. And only a week after Christmas everyone seemed ready to spend money again.

It was good to see her advisor looking relaxed. Beside him, Dr. Madonson was already on his second beer, which even for his larger-than-normal size was probably a bad idea. They paid her a few compliments. She realized they probably felt as relieved as she did at having passed.

They were held accountable for her success—or failure.

Dr. Simeon arrived on the balcony with a bouquet of daisies, which she said was from the whole thesis committee. The surprised look on the faces of the other two professors belied that. Then she ducked back inside and handed her a potted lily. "This was sent to the office," she said. "And this."

It was a letter from Moose Hollow. Poppy tucked it inside her other papers. Whatever it was, she'd rather read it alone.

"Beautiful day," Dr. Simeon said, sitting down beside her. The lily on the table between them hid her face from view. The weather was beautiful, sunny and still, and her jean jacket was more than enough to keep her warm. "Have you sent in any more applications?"

"I have," Poppy said. "It's a shotgun approach. I've had a few responses."

"Good girl," the woman said. "It's a big life. Don't let yourself get pigeonholed. I suspect botany is only one of your talents." After a moment she stood up again and reached out to shake Poppy's hand. "You did well. Now make sure to have some fun." She waved at the others, and over their protests, she left.

Her advisor and Dr. Madonson were soon deep in an argument about the "repatriation" of rare species, and the letter was calling. It pushed at the comfort she'd found since her two days in Santa Fe. Eloise had told her she needed to contact Colton. Judging by the handwriting on the envelope, he'd made the first move. Maybe he'd left room open for friendship; maybe he'd closed the door. She wasn't ready to find out. "No matter what, you need to tell him how you feel," Eloise had said. "You'll regret it if you don't."

She took four sips of her beer, which despite being a raspberry ale was bland and bitter. She'd done the three things she'd felt most driven to do. She'd sent an anonymous donation to a church in Santa Fe, three thousand dollars only to be used to replace the front doors. That made her feel like Santa Claus, and she'd giggled about it for days in her sterile Tucson hotel room.

Then she'd bought some cattle. That had been a little trickier. The markets were sluggish between the holidays, and she'd had to find a trader who would keep her anonymous. But she'd come away with a good deal, for both her and the rancher. She put up the cash, he would do the work, and in the end, the new generation of steers would belong to her, and the heifers would be his to keep in return for his care. Her banker was pleased she had decided to start investing, although he considered the investment a little unorthodox.

She called her new cattle company New Beginnings. And sometimes she thought the best part of it was the thought that Sparkle and all the other momma cows would be together at home, not run through the ring and scattered to the four winds. They would have a life in Moose Hollow.

And finally, she'd earned her master's degree. Everyone had signed off on her thesis, and her advisor had walked across the hall from the conference room to the office and filed the paperwork. It was done. She was free.

Realizing that, she picked up her lily and the bouquet of flowers, said her thank-yous and good-byes, and walked down the stairs and out onto the street. The air felt lighter. Was it just her imagination? Her shoulders felt lighter too. Even walking felt strange, like getting off a boat onto dry land. She was overtaken by the feeling of it. She moved, and miles passed. She could go anywhere. *Thank you, Jesus.*

Once she climbed into her truck, she checked her phone. Messages from Mara were waiting for her. She wanted to know how the defense went. And she said there was a mouse in the bunkhouse. She'd made Colton, Zane, and somehow even Travis clean and set traps, then check for holes because she was sure pregnant women shouldn't be exposed to mouse poo.

The ranch would never be the same with her there.

Sierra had called, but she hadn't left a message. She'd sent a text message with nothing but a heart in it.

Poppy opened her truck window a bit and pulled the letter out of her pocket. It was from Colton. She lingered over the way he'd written her name, a blur of cursive and printing, bold and leaning forward as if he was anxious to get to the next word.

I hope it's okay I'm writing you. I wanted to let you know I sold the problem girls. But I heard the cattle company that bought them is having water-rights issues, so they're leasing my land for a year. Maybe even longer.

. . .

Poppy smiled. For once, Moose Hollow gossip had broken her way.

I know you don't like the thought of breaking up the herd. But the heifers will be mine, so Spark will be living here for the rest of her life. I thought you'd want to know.

I'm sorry about everything that happened. I'm still piecing it all together. I wish I'd never left you alone that night. A few days later, Julia got me, Anson, and Cash in a room, and we talked. I think it's going to work out. Not quite sure how, but I haven't put up a for-sale sign, and that's a good thing.

I guess Mara told you her dad dropped the lawsuit. That girl's a force of nature. She told me you made it to Tucson and you'll graduate in a few days. I hope you find everything you want there, Poppy, and more.

I sent you a flower too. Julia helped me find it. I wanted to send you a lemon lily, but I guess it's illegal or endangered, something like that. But the one I sent is a hybrid, so it's half lemon lily and half something else. Maybe a flower from Montana.

I'm not good at writing. Not so hot at phone calls either. There are things I wish I could say to you, but you probably don't want to hear them. If you ever end up this far north again, drop in. You'll always have a place here.

With love,
  Colton

She hoped he meant what he wrote. If he didn't, things were about to get awkward.

CHAPTER 43

*H*er truck skidded a little as she slowed down at the intersection, but she had plenty of room to stop. Her new apartment was right up the road, three blocks to the left, second floor, first door on the right. She hadn't seen it in person, but she knew the landlord. It would be fine. She'd only need a few trips to the truck to move in, so there was no rush. She turned right, away from town.

She climbed carefully out of the river valley and up onto the prairie, where she could see the snowy, moonlit mountains rise straight out of the earth and touch the sky. Stars glittered above her, and the sweep of her headlight made the fresh snow glitter as well. She liked the crunching sound the snow made as she drove slowly down the county road.

She tried to calm her racing heart. Her arriving would be a shock for Colton, to be sure. She shouldn't expect anything good to come of it. She also tried not to imagine all the ways it could go wrong. What if he had someone there with him? What if it was a woman? She shook her head. No matter what, she was certain Moose Hollow was the place for her, at least until summer. She could avoid him if she had to.

But still, she hoped he wanted to see her.

The last thing she expected to see when she pulled up the drive was every Christmas light on and a light in every window of the homestead. She remembered the first time she'd seen the house, how she'd imagined it dressed for Christmas. It took her breath away. But Christmas was weeks ago.

Only Colton's truck was in front of the drive, parked neatly in the circle she'd marked out. She turned off her truck, listened to it make ticking and hissing noises, and then got out. Her jean jacket would be good enough to get her to the front door, so she left her coat in the truck. The cold felt good—it chased away some of her anxiety, somehow. She breathed in the slightly smoky air and pushed herself toward the door.

Her boots crunched on the snow. At the door, she resisted the urge to rise onto her toes and look in the window. She knocked three times and waited.

The door opened, and there was Colton, taller than she remembered, wearing his black hat and a nice plaid shirt. He even had it tucked in. The thought that she might be interrupting something struck her dumb.

He tilted his head sideways. "Fancy seeing you here," he said, and he stepped back, inviting her in.

She stepped onto the floor she had helped install. The purple couch was still in its place. And there was a coffee table where her trunk had sat, a quirky thing that would have been as comfortable in the Santa Fe hotel as anyplace else. He closed the door and she turned to face him. "I have a job," she said. "At least I'm pretty sure I do. They wanted an interview, but it sounds good. The wildlife sanctuary just outside of town is hiring. They're moving into a new facility, and they wanted someone to plan out a native plant exhibit. I guess they were looking at using landscaping companies and they were pricey, and they didn't know much about rare plants. One of my committee members heard about it."

She stopped. There was no trace of surprise on Colton's face. No censure, either. Just a vaguely cheerful expression. His green eyes were pure emerald, too brilliant to be believed.

"You already knew I was moving here, didn't you?"

"Julia's on the board of the sanctuary."

Poppy's jaw dropped. "Oh." She thought about all that meant. She hated nepotism. But that didn't change the fact that she would be excellent at the job. Then she realized something. If Julia had gotten her the job, she must have wanted her to come back to Moose Hollow. "Oh," she repeated. Her heart was beating so hard she wondered how she managed to stay on her feet.

"Mara had me move your mattresses into their old apartment," he said, walking away and into the kitchen.

Mara. The girl couldn't keep a secret. But the thought of sleeping on her old two-mattress "bed" tonight made her grin.

So Colton had known she was coming. He didn't seem upset. Neither was it the romantic welcome she had wished for, but it would do.

"After all, you can't live here anymore," he said

from the kitchen. "Until I convince you to marry me, of course."

She froze. Maybe it was a cruel joke.

"Come in here. I have something for you."

She turned the corner cautiously. The kitchen was a smelly mess. There were dirty bowls and dishes, something orange was smeared on the countertop, and there were eggshells on the floor. "I found out the secret, by the way. Wash the eggs and leave them out of the fridge overnight. Wait until you see how simple Emmaline's recipe is. I found it in the bathroom closet, of all places, when I was cleaning it out. I started renovating her room and the master bath, by the way. I don't like sleeping upstairs. If I sleepwalk down those stairs, I'll break something."

He was mixing something mushy and yellow in a bowl, and he scooped it out with a spoon and held it out to her. "Close your eyes. Then tell me what you think."

She did as he asked, opened her mouth, and he gently slipped the tip of the spoon in. It tasted like summer picnics, sunshine, swings, and running through the grass. And laughter, lots of laughter. She swallowed, but she kept her eyes shut, savoring the taste, the memories, and the moment, until the last taste was gone. "You made me deviled eggs."

He stepped so close she could feel the heat from his body through the thin denim of her jacket. One hand held her arm, pulling her closer. "I did," he said softly, and his lips pressed against hers. "I'll do it again too." He kissed her again, and every nerve in her body fired. "And again."

Poppy wrapped her arms around him and raised up onto her toes to kiss him back the way she'd been wanting to, and she heard the spoon clatter to the floor.

The doubt was gone, all of it washed clean away in a moment. She'd found her way home.

The End

Made in the USA
Middletown, DE
15 February 2023

24963121R00308